CHASING THE SUN

CHASING THE SUN

KAKI WARNER

THORNDIKE PRESS

A part of Gale, Cengage Learning

GALE
CENGAGE Learning®

Detroit • New York • San Francisco • New Haven, Conn • Waterville, Maine • London

GALE
CENGAGE Learning

LIBRARY OF CONGRESS CATALOGING-IN-PUBLICATION DATA

Warner, Kaki.
    Chasing the sun / by Kaki Warner.
        pages ; cm. — (Thorndike Press large print romance)
    ISBN-13: 978-1-4104-4889-7 (hardcover)
    ISBN-10: 1-4104-4889-4 (hardcover)
    1. Unmarried mothers—Fiction. 2. Birthfathers—Fiction. 3. Ranchers—Fiction. 4. Ranch life—Fiction. 5. Large type books.
    I. Title.
    PS3623.A8633C47 2012
    813'.6—dc23   2012008805

Published in 2012 by arrangement with The Berkley Publishing Group, a member of Penguin Group (USA) Inc.

Printed in the United States of America
1 2 3 4 5 6 7 16 15 14 13 12

To Jason — brave, brilliant, bodacious.
And to Carlee, the beautiful lady
who loves him anyway.

ACKNOWLEDGMENTS

This trilogy wouldn't have been possible without a vision, a lot of luck, and many hours of hard work by people too numerous to list. And it wouldn't have become a success without people who were willing to take a chance on a new author. So I thank you, dear readers — for your support, for your lovely e-mails and kind words, and for welcoming the Wilkins family and me to your bookshelves.

Bless you all.

ONE

"Desire Etheridge." Mr. Markham frowned at the paper atop his desk in the tiny manager's office behind the stage. "That's an odd name. Desire."

"Desiree," Daisy corrected, pronouncing it *Dez-a-ray.* She pointed to the paper. "If you'll notice, there are two *e*'s on the end."

He squinted up at her, rolling an unlit, well-chewed cigar stub from one corner of his mouth to the other. "You French or something?"

"I try not to be," she quipped.

His teeth clamped down, snapping the cigar stub to attention. "What's that supposed to mean?"

"N-Nothing," she stammered, taken aback by his challenging tone.

"My mama was French."

That explained a great deal. "I didn't know that."

"If you got something against the French,

9

missy, then you can just march your skinny ass out of here right now."

Mortified by the reprimand, yet pleased that he thought her backside skinny, she forced a smile. "It was a poor joke, Mr. Markham. I like the French. Truly."

The stub relaxed, rolled to the left side of his mouth and settled between his gum and cheek like a damp little rodent sliding back into its burrow. He returned to his perusal of her application. "Says here you been singing at the Silver Spur. That in the red light district?"

"No." But it was near enough to open the eyes of a farm girl from Quebec who had to walk past those busy doorways every night after work.

"Still, it's a saloon," Markham went on without looking up.

Since it wasn't a question, Daisy didn't respond. Besides, it seemed every time she opened her mouth lately it got her into trouble. How was she to know that the drunken lout who had tried to stick his hand down her dress during last night's chorus of "Bridget's Lament" was the mayor's wife's second cousin's son? *The nitwit.*

She studied the man before her, wondering if he was any better.

He was old, at least double her twenty-one years, judging by the gray in his whiskers and in the curly sideburns showing beneath his bowler hat. He seemed fit enough, but there was a weary slump to his shoulders. He reminded her of a sour old draft horse that kept plugging along, no longer caring where it was headed or where it had been, just getting through the day.

When she didn't respond, his head came up, a challenging thrust to his chin, the cigar stub battle-ready. She watched his gaze slide over her, coming to rest on the bosom that always seemed to draw attention no matter how tightly she corseted. "You're not a whore, are you?"

"Of course not," Daisy sputtered, addled that he would say such a thing. Nervously she pressed a hand to her chest, wondering if a button had come undone and a breast had escaped, but both dress and breast were securely corralled.

"This is a legitimate theater company, missy. We don't take on whores."

"I am not a whore," she said with stringent emphasis. An unwed mother, perhaps, but not a whore. There was a big difference.

An oddly disappointed look came into his dark eyes. "You sure?"

"That I'm not a whore? Of course I'm sure." *The very idea.*

The stub drooped. With a sigh, he turned back to her application.

As Daisy waited, she tried to regain her composure by studying the old playbills

11

pinned to the wall behind the desk. Some of the names she recognized from earlier times when her mother, a frustrated singer herself, would declare a holiday from farm chores and take her to nearby Quebec City to see the latest theatrical productions passing through.

"Someday it will be you up on that stage, *ma petite cherie*," her mother would say. "It will be the name 'Desiree Etheridge' on the posters out front."

Daisy smiled, filling her mind with the lovely images her mother had painted so many years ago — the flickering light and oily smoke from the lamps along the front of the stage, the rapt faces of the audience staring up at her, the musicians poised, instruments ready, that hush of expectancy as she opened her mouth and the first glorious notes —

"Says here you got a kid."

Daisy blinked. The images dissolved. Reality pressed like a weight against her throat. "Yes, a daughter."

"Where's her pa?"

"Gone."

"Gone where?"

"West."

That narrow-eyed look again. "We *are* west, missy. It don't get any more west than San Francisco."

Reminding herself how much she wanted

— *needed* — this chance, especially since that scene last night with the mayor's wife's second cousin's son had gotten her fired from the Spur, Daisy hid her irritation behind a smile. "Australia." At least that was where the bounder had been headed when he'd left over two-and-a-half years ago. Afraid her patience would stretch to the point of snapping if these useless questions didn't end soon, she said forcefully, "I am a vocalist, Mr. Markham. A good one. I can read music, I play the piano fairly well, and I also have a four-octave range and a —"

He cut her off with a wave of his hand. "Never mind all that. Can you *sing,* girl, and loud enough to reach the back row of the balcony?"

Daisy let out a deep breath. "Yes, Mr. Markham. I can sing." And she showed him — right there in his tiny office, without music, accompaniment, or proper acoustics — just how powerful her voice was.

She got the role.

A role anyway. She wouldn't know which until she returned the next day to audition for the director and the owner of the theater. But it was a start. Hopefully it would pay well enough to support her and her daughter and cover the raise in pay Edna Tidwell demanded to watch Kate while Daisy was working. If she needed more, Mr. Markham said she could help with the sewing chores in wardrobe.

A few minutes later she left the Elysium Theater, a bounce in her step. Mr. Markham turned out to be a nice man after all, in a middle-aged, cranky sort of way. And he seemed to like her voice. Daisy smiled, remembering the astonished look on his face when she hit her high notes. That nasty stub had almost fallen from his mouth. And he had been most insistent that she return the next day, making her promise twice before he let her leave. It would feel good to be singing real music again. Saloon songs had been no challenge at all.

It's really happening, she thought as she turned off Broadway onto Powell Street, taking the long way back to the boardinghouse to avoid the dangerous waterfront area. *I'll be singing on a real stage!*

She giggled then laughed out loud, startling a drunk dozing behind a refuse bin outside a garment maker's shop. "I'm going to be a star," she called gaily to him as she hurried by.

She had dreamed of it, prayed for it every day since she had seen her first musical puppet show at a traveling fair fifteen years ago. To be able to sing arias rather than lewd ditties or maudlin ballads, to fill a hall with her own voice, singing music composed by the masters . . . she still couldn't believe it.

At Commercial Street, she turned left, hop-

14

ing it was still too early in the day to bring out the worst of the criminals that prowled the shadowed alleys like rats hunting fresh meat. A few blocks farther, she turned onto her street and breathed easier. Here on the fringes of the red light district, the saloons and gambling dens catered to a richer, cleaner clientele and the brothels were a little more discreet. Dirt and mud gave way to cobblestones, and the row houses were less shabby, although each year more of them boasted the red-painted doors and lamps that identified them as houses of ill repute. Perhaps if she did well in the theater company, she could land a bigger role that would bring in enough money to move Kate to a safer neighborhood, maybe one with parks and other children to play with.

"Daisy," a woman's voice called.

Looking over, she saw Lucy Frisk waving from the front stoop of a narrow four-story building that rented rooms by the hour — a bordello, although a clean one, run by a nattily dressed Southern gentleman named Stump Heffington, who had lost everything in the Rebellion, including the greater portion of his left leg. As procurers went, he was benign. Having learned the value of contented workers during his slave-owning years, he treated his girls passably well. They considered themselves lucky to be in his employ and, by and large, were a clean, friendly lot. Lucy, in her early twenties and nearest in age to Daisy, always had a kind word for Baby Kate whenever they passed by.

"Hello, Lucy," Daisy called back, angling across the street, delighted to have someone with whom to share her wonderful news.

Five years ago, when she had first arrived in San Francisco with her parents, she would have been shocked to find herself on such friendly terms with a harlot. But since then, she had lost both parents to a mudslide, fallen in love, had her heart broken, and borne a child. In other words, she had grown up. And although she might still be a farm girl from Quebec, she had learned to value friends whenever and wherever she found them.

"You hear about Red Amy?" Lucy asked as Daisy neared the steps.

Daisy could see she had been crying. "No. What?"

"The Indian got her. Took all that pretty red hair clean off her head then stabbed her twice through the neck. Damn bastard scalp-snatching sonofabitch."

Daisy pressed a hand to her throat. "She . . . she's . . . ?"

Lucy nodded and swiped at a tear. "Deader 'n a carp. Third this month."

Daisy stood in stunned silence. Red Amy was the youngest in the house and one of her favorites, mainly because Daisy often saw a shadow of herself in the trusting, hopeful look behind the girl's lovely brown eyes.

"I'm thinking of dyeing mine." Lucy fingered the flowing, straw-colored tresses that were her best feature. "He don't seem to like dark hair as much as blond or red. The Indian in him, I guess. Yours ain't as light as mine, but I'd keep an eye out anyway, since he seems partial to young, pretty ones like you. Watch out for Kate, too, with those blond curls of hers."

"But she's just a baby," Daisy protested, fear coiling in her chest. "Why would he go after a baby?"

"Probably wouldn't," Lucy said quickly, giving Daisy's shoulder a reassuring pat. "I'm just saying keep her close, is all. And keep an eye on that Widow Tidwell while you're at it. There's something about that woman . . . something that ain't right."

Daisy needed no warning on that score. When she had first taken a room in Edna Tidwell's boardinghouse, the woman had seemed kindly enough. Having lost her own daughter to smallpox, she had been almost heartbreakingly grateful to have an infant to take care of again. But over the last months as Kate neared her second birthday, which was the same age as Edna's daughter when she'd died, the woman had started acting strange . . . almost angry that Kate had survived while her own child hadn't. She'd upped her price several times, even though her care of Kate had grown sloppier and sloppier. Daisy suspected she might be drinking. Plus, Edna had started keeping company with a man Daisy didn't altogether trust. Bill Johnson seemed friendly enough, but there was a coldness about him . . .

Daisy shook off that worrisome thought. "Don't worry." She patted her coat pocket. "I've got my Remington Double Derringer, remember." Kate's father had won the palm-sized, double-barreled .41-caliber rim fire pistol in a poker game. Considering it more of a toy than a weapon, he'd given it to Daisy. Now she carried it everywhere she went — as much for protection as sentimentality. It was the only thing he'd given her, except for Kate.

"Thing's useless unless you're up close," Lucy said. "Does Edna know you're looking for someone else to watch Baby Kate?"

"I'm afraid to tell her until I find someone. If she learns of it beforehand, she's liable to toss us into the street. Then what would I do?"

Like most big cities, San Francisco was overrun with war widows and lost children trying to escape the terrible excesses of the Reconstruction. Some were able to hire on as servants in rich neighborhoods like Pacific Heights and Nob Hill. The unlucky ones sank to new levels of depravity in the brothels and

18

opium dens along the Barbary Coast. Many died of despair or disease.

Daisy was more fortunate. She had a talent. After her parents died, rather than squander what money they had left her, she had used that talent to support herself as a saloon singer. But then she had gotten pregnant, and when she could no longer work in the Silver Spur, that money had supported her until Kate was born. But within a week of her birth, Daisy was back at the Spur, begging for her job back. Considering the other options open to a young woman with a child and no husband, Daisy considered herself lucky to find work, even if it was singing in a smoky saloon.

And after today, luckier still.

"You can always work here, if you get tired of the Silver Spur," Lucy offered. "You'd make more money. And Stump likes big titties."

Daisy snorted. "I wish I could give him mine. They're a lot more trouble than they're worth." Hopefully after tomorrow's audition, she would be valued for more than the size of her bosom. "Besides, I don't work at the Spur anymore."

"You don't?"

Grinning at Lucy's look of surprise, Daisy told her about the audition. "I am now working at the Elysium Theater on Broadway."

"Doing what?"

19

"I'll know tomorrow." Glancing up at the gray sky, Daisy realized it was growing dark. "I better go. You know how cranky Edna gets when I'm late."

"Be careful," Lucy warned, that sad look returning to her tear-reddened eyes. "Fog's coming in and that always brings out the crazies."

Daisy slept badly that night, partly due to excitement, but mostly worry.

Kate was teething, Edna Tidwell was acting even more nervous and furtive than usual, and her gentleman friend, Bill Johnson, had never taken his eyes off Kate throughout the meager supper Edna had provided. Daisy awoke tired but resolved that as soon as the audition ended and she knew what her salary would be, she would find another place for her and Kate to live.

She adored her daughter. But there were times when the weight of responsibility for another life — even one she treasured — almost overwhelmed her. After her daughter's birth, the realities of survival had forced Daisy to set aside her naive hopes of singing on the legitimate stage. Such dreams were not for a woman on her own with a daughter to raise.

So with grim determination she had put those girlish dreams away, pushing them so far to the back of her mind they hardly ever resurfaced to pester her with lingering "what-ifs" and half-formed yearnings. In the months since, she had spent every night at the Silver Spur Saloon, pretending she loved being surrounded by drunken fools and shifty-eyed gamblers. And if the smoke often burned in her throat and eyes, and the bawdy remarks and lewd stares made her skin crawl and her temper flare, she reminded herself at least she was singing, and contented herself with that.

Until now. Now all those hopes and dreams had surged to the surface again, and despite almost two years of hard-won experience, she was daring to believe again.

It was a heady feeling.

Moving quietly so she wouldn't wake Kate, Daisy brushed her long light brown hair into a smooth twist, and wiped every speck of dust off her best dress — a yellow gingham that she'd once been told brought out the fire in her hazel eyes. After leaving her daughter with Edna, she set off for the Elysium, praying this would be the last time she would have to relinquish Kate to her landlady's erratic care.

Mr. Markham met her at the back door with a fresh stub in his teeth — "fresh" being defined by the length and dryness of the un-chewed portion of the cigar. Since the ends were never lit, she figured he must break the cigars in half so he would have twice as many butts to chew. A disgusting habit, but less irritating to her throat than smoking would have been.

"About time," he said, locking the door behind her then towing her by the arm down the unlit hallway behind the stage.

"I'm early," Daisy protested, almost trotting to keep up. He was quite a bit taller than she and solidly built, and the hand gripping her wrist was broad and strong. Suddenly uneasy, she realized the building seemed ominously quiet, the hall narrow and dim. Was anyone else around? Would anyone hear her if she screamed? "What's the rush?" she demanded, digging in her heels so forcefully she almost pulled him off balance as she yanked her arm free.

He turned to blink down at her, his expression one of surprise. "They're waiting."

"Who's waiting?"

"The director and owner." His eyes narrowed. The stub came up. "You better not be thinking to back out on me, missy. I went to a lot of trouble setting up this audition and I won't be made a fool of." He reached for her arm again.

She stepped back. "I have no intention of backing out, Mr. Markham. But I don't like being dragged down a dark hallway like a sack of potatoes either."

He almost smiled.

Daisy made a shooing motion. "Lead on. I'll follow."

Muttering under his breath, he continued down the hall. Stepping over ropes and cables coiled on the floor beside the stage curtain, he stopped and motioned her forward. "It's all yours. Go out there and sing like you did for me."

Daisy peered past him at the brightly lit stage and the endless expanse of empty seats stretching into the darkness beyond the light. "Is there any accompaniment?" she asked, surprised by the tremor in her voice.

"You don't need any. Just sing." He turned.

She caught his arm. "In case — if I don't — if this doesn't work out, Mr. Markham," she finally managed in a rush, "I just wanted to thank you for giving me this chance."

That almost-smile again, quickly covered with a stern look. "Don't disappoint me, missy. That's all the thanks I need." He nudged her past the curtain. "Now go break a leg."

On wobbly knees she walked into the light, her footfalls echoing loudly in the stillness. The stage seemed huge, as broad as a city block, the planked floor covered with odd markings and scuffed by hundreds of feet that had trod across it through the years. A sense of unreality swept her, and for a moment she feared she was dreaming and would soon wake up to find herself back in the Silver Spur.

Halfway across, she stopped and stood

uncertainly, nearly blinded by the light from the lamps along the front edge of the stage.

Then a figure emerged from the darkened rows. "Miss Etheridge, is it?" A short, round man with muttonchop sideburns bustled down the left center aisle toward the orchestra pit.

Daisy answered with a nod, afraid her voice would betray her nervousness if she spoke.

"I'm Bernard Bridgeport, the musical director here at the Elysium. You've heard of me, no doubt."

"Ah . . . yes, sir," Daisy lied, figuring a little flattery wouldn't hurt.

"Excellent. Myself and the owner, Mr. Langdon" — he motioned over his shoulder to a man Daisy could barely see, who was seated in the shadows twenty rows back — "will be listening to your audition. What will you be singing?"

"What would you like?" She clasped her hands tightly behind her back so he wouldn't notice they were shaking.

"Your choice. Perhaps a medley of your best pieces?"

"Yes, sir."

"Excellent. Whenever you're ready, my dear." Turning, he walked back to his seat beside the owner.

Daisy took a deep breath and slowly let it out. Then another. She closed her eyes as a calmness stole over her. With it came a heightened awareness of the openness all around her, the musty odor of the heavy curtains, the sharp scent of burning kerosene, the beat of her own heart. And out in the darkness beyond the two men in the center row, far in the shadows at the back . . . she sensed a presence. Someone watching. Someone waiting for her to sing.

So she sang.

She sang as if her daughter's future depended on it, as if this might be her only chance to perform on a real stage, as if every hope and dream she carried within her heart rested on this one moment in time.

Which it did.

The acoustics of the hall were extraordinary, magnifying the scope and intensity of each sound, sending the notes out and back again, louder and fuller than when they left, until her voice filled all the empty spaces and she stood surrounded by glorious music.

She sang the songs Mama had taught her — romantic sonatas, bel canto arias by Rossini and Verdi, lilting Irish melodies, and sad ballads of lost love. Then when her throat grew tired and her lungs began to burn, she brought the sound back down with the haunting French lullaby her mother had sung to her every night of her childhood.

When the last notes faded away into silence, she opened her eyes and waited. For what seemed like a long time, there was no sound or movement. Then far in the rear of the theater, she saw a shadow move. A moment later, a figure stepped out of the back row and slowly made its way down the aisle toward the stage. A bent figure. A woman.

As she passed the row where the director and owner sat, Mr. Bridgeport rose. When he started to speak, she waved him to silence, and continued her halting steps toward the front, her attention fixed on the stage.

Daisy watched her approach, her nervousness returning as the woman drew near.

She was quite old, her white hair pulled severely up in a tight knot perched on top of her head. Her back curved at the shoulders and she used a cane, her wrinkled hand clutching it so tightly every tendon showed.

But her eyes were fiercely alive. Black as pitch, they seemed to take in the lamplight and reflect it back, making it appear they were lit from within. Probing, ancient eyes that left Daisy feeling vaguely exposed.

The woman stopped at the front of the stage and for several moments stared up at Daisy with unblinking intensity. Then she nodded as if she had seen something in Daisy's face that pleased her. "You have the gift," she said in a rusty voice with a thick Italian accent. "Now you must learn how to use it."

Before Daisy could ask what that meant, the woman turned and walked slowly back up the aisle. When she came to the row where the men sat, she paused only long enough to say, "I will take her," then continued her slow progress. A few moments later sunlight flashed as the front door opened then closed.

As if abruptly released from a frozen state, the owner and director leaped to their feet. After conferring excitedly for a moment, the owner followed the old lady out while Mr. Bridgeport hurried toward Daisy.

"Excellent, excellent," he cried, clapping exuberantly. "She loved it. Just loved it. You're one lucky girl."

"She, who?" Daisy asked.

"You didn't recognize her? No, no, of course not. You're just a child. Markham, where are you?"

Mr. Markham stepped out of the wings on the left.

"Tell her who that was," Mr. Bridgeport ordered with a flutter of his fingers.

"Sophia Scarlatti."

"*Madame* Sophia Scarlatti," the director corrected archly. When Daisy still offered no reaction, since she had no recollection of the woman or the name, Bridgeport sighed dramatically. "She doesn't know. Lord help us, she doesn't know. Tell her, Markham."

Mr. Markham might have rolled his eyes, but in the smoky light Daisy wasn't sure. "The Sicilian Songbird."

Realization finally struck. "Oh my gracious.

The Sicilian Songbird? You're jesting. That was really her?" Daisy had thought the woman long dead.

The Sicilian Songbird was only the most famous soprano who had ever lived. Daisy had never heard her sing, but her mother had been fortunate enough to do so. She had declared the woman had the voice of an angel, a voice so beautiful, grown men had wept to hear it. "I sang for the Sicilian Songbird?"

"And impressed her," Bridgeport added smugly. "She has graciously consented to train you."

"Train me?"

"As she is no longer able to sing, she helps others learn the craft. Under her tutelage, you can become the greatest soprano of your time."

"Me?" Daisy was too stunned to do more than stutter. "But — But —"

"You will join a handful of chosen apprentices," the director went on as if she hadn't spoken, his gestures growing more flamboyant with each word. "Together you will travel to the famous opera houses of the world as her special theatrical company. Meanwhile, she will teach you how to read music, how to project your voice, how to breathe properly, and how to perform before an audience. Then once you are trained, she will present you to the crowned princes of

Europe. Just think of it, little one. The world will be your stage!"

"B-But I have no money," Daisy said, afraid she might burst into tears. "How would I pay for all that?"

Bridgeport gave a tittering laugh. "You silly little thing. She pays *you!* Tell her, Markham."

Crossing his arms over his barrel chest, Mr. Markham recited in a bored voice, "She pays for everything until you're presented. Then for three years after, she gets fifty percent of whatever you earn. And she also gets seventy-five percent of whatever the tour brings in while you're being trained. After expenses. The other twenty-five percent is split between the members of the troop. It's not much, but since everything else is paid for, it's free money."

Daisy stared at him, still not daring to believe. "This isn't a joke, is it, Mr. Markham? Tell me this isn't a joke."

This time his smile was real. "It isn't a joke."

"Sweet heaven." For a moment Daisy felt dizzy, her mind soaring with all the possibilities. Then reality brought it crashing back down. "What about Kate?"

"Who's Kate?" Bridgeport asked.

"My daughter."

The director glared at his stage manager. "You didn't say she was married."

"I'm not. Not really."

"He's in Australia," Mr. Markham told Bridgeport, neatly covering for Daisy's omission. Then to Daisy he added, "He won't be a problem, will he, missy?"

She read the warning in his narrowed eyes. "No, he won't be a problem. But I can bring Kate, can't I?"

"Don't be tiresome." Bridgeport made an offhand gesture. "Leave her here. Surely there's a relative or someone you can leave her with. It'll only be for a year or two, after all."

A year or two? Neither of them would survive it.

"There's no one," Daisy said in a strained voice. And even if there were, she didn't think she could leave Kate behind. An idea came to her. What if she found a way to bring Kate with her? "How much would my salary be during training?" Maybe it would be enough to hire a nanny to come too.

Markham must have read her thoughts. A sad look crossed his face. He shook his head. "Not enough."

"You either stay behind with your daughter like a good little mommy," Bridgeport said with impatient sarcasm, "or come with us and be a star. It's your choice. But you'd best decide soon. The company meets in New Orleans in two months' time, then we sail for Rome."

Two

New Mexico Territory

Sister Maria Elena Ramirez shifted on the buggy seat, trying to ease the ache in her damaged hip. She had been traveling for the last five days, by train, then coach, and now hired buggy out of Val Rosa, and she was beginning to wonder if the pain was God's way of suggesting she shouldn't have made the trip.

But what choice had she? She was nearing the end of her years as a novice, and next month she would go into retreat to prepare for her final vows. If she was ever to explain her decision to the Wilkins family, or forgive her brother for the heartache he had brought them all, this was her last chance.

The buggy bounced over a rock. She bit back a gasp of pain and glanced at the driver beside her, wondering if he was asleep. Or blind. Or simply in league with *El Diablo*.

An unworthy thought. She would have to say five *Pater Nosters* to cleanse her soul.

Perhaps ten. Trying to focus away from the pain, she studied the landscape rolling past as they began the long descent into RosaRoja Valley.

Spring had come early this year. Already the native plants were starting to green, and under a lingering coat of morning dew, the broad valley glistened like an emerald in the sun. Twice they slowed to pick their way through shallow, fast-moving water that cut across the road. Fed by the last of the snow melting on the high peaks, it rushed down the slopes to overflow the creek that bisected the valley floor. Birds darted through the trees that crowded the canyons. Newly budded aspens shivered in the gentle breeze. Cattle littered the flats, greedily munching the green shoots pushing through the dirt and growing heavy with the calves they would drop soon.

She smiled, breathing in the sweet scents of damp earth and new grass, lulled by the music of birdsong and trickling water, and enjoying the clean, cool breeze after three years of foggy, sooty air in San Francisco.

Nowhere else did spring bring such a dramatic rebirth of life and hope and energy as it did in this starkly beautiful place. She reveled in it, committing each glorious scent and sound to memory to sustain her through the long years ahead. The cycles of RosaRoja Rancho had been born and bred into her, and she loved them almost as much as she loved God.

The road began to level off. She saw they were approaching the southwest boundary line, and being so close to the place where she had lived for most of her life made her heartbeat quicken with both anticipation and dread.

Should she have told them she was coming? Would Jack be there? Would the Wilkins family understand her decision, or had the brothers left all the destruction behind and moved on?

When she had left three years ago hoping to have her crippled hip repaired, everything had been in chaos. The feud between the Ramirez and Wilkins families had finally ended, but at a terrible cost — the rancho nearly destroyed by fire, her brother dead, Jessica and her son sent back to England by Brady Wilkins, while he and his brother, Hank, struggled to start over again. Throughout the long months of her recovery after surgery, she had prayed for each of them every night, these generous people who had been dearer to her than her own blood kin. Would they welcome her now, after the anguish she had caused the youngest brother, Jack?

"What the hell?" the driver muttered, yanking back on the brake so hard the buggy lurched.

Clutching the arm rail for balance, Sister

Maria Elena saw a man standing in the road ahead, a rifle cradled in his arms. Another man, also armed, stood behind him, leaning against the cairn of stones that marked the ranch boundary, while a third man, little more than a boy, sat on a boulder, watching them. The only horses she saw were in a small rope-strung corral set far back from the road.

"Howdy," the man on foot said as he strode toward the stopped buggy.

Muttering under his breath, the driver reached under the seat for his rifle.

"*Está bien,*" Sister Maria Elena said, smiling to reassure him. "*Conozco a este hombre.* I know this man. He is a friend." Lifting a hand in greeting, she called, "*Señor* Langley, *cómo está usted?* How are you?"

The man in the road hesitated then lowered the rifle to his side. "Miss Elena? That you?"

"*Sí.* It is good to see you after so long."

"Well, I'll be." Grinning, Langley continued toward the buggy. He had been with the rancho for many years and was one of RosaRoja's most trusted hands. If he was still here, then hopefully the brothers would be as well.

He stopped beside the buggy, looked at the driver, then peered down the road they had just traveled. "Jack with you?"

Hiding her disappointment behind a smile, she shook her head. "No. I hoped he would be at the rancho."

"Haven't seen him since the two of you

34

left." As Langley's faded blue eyes looked her over, a frown drew his gray brows together. "Are those nun clothes?"

"Novitiate."

"Well, I'll be." He scratched at the whiskers on his jaw. "The folks at the house know about this?"

"Not yet."

"Well, I'll be." Apparently having run out of words, he stood blinking and scratching until the man seated beside her shifted impatiently.

"You mind?" the driver said. "I got to get back to Val Rosa by dark."

"Right." Leaning his rifle against the buggy wheel, Langley lifted his hands to Sister Maria Elena. "Let me help you down, miss — ma'am, I mean Sister — heck, I don't know what to call you."

"Sister is fine. Or Elena. Do we walk the rest of the way?" she asked once he'd lowered her carefully to the ground. She hoped not. They were still at least fifteen miles from the ranch house.

"No, ma'am — er, Sister. We can ride, or I can send for a wagon."

Knowing her hip wouldn't tolerate a jaunt on horseback, she chose to wait for the wagon.

After sending the boy, a blond, gangly young man Sister Maria Elena didn't recognize, back to the house to fetch it, Langley pulled her small carpetbag from behind the seat.

"I was paid to take her to the house," the driver argued. "And I ain't giving no refunds."

Langley set down the bag, picked up his rifle, and looked at him. "No?"

The other ranch hand moved up behind him, his rifle held loose but ready in his hands.

The driver cleared his throat. "Well, maybe this one time, seeing as she's a holy person and all." Digging through his vest pocket, he separated several coins from a sticky wad of tobacco and handed them over. "And I was told to give you this." Bending, he retrieved a string-tied bundle of mail from under the seat.

Langley took it and passed it on to the other ranch hand. "Any sick horses in Val Rosa?" he asked, turning back to the driver.

"Some."

"How 'bout this one?" Langley nodded at the roan hitched to the buggy.

"Nothing so far."

"Stable him with any sick ones?"

"Hell no."

Langley stepped back. "Move on, then. And tell folks in Val Rosa that RosaRoja is under quarantine. No horses in, no horses out, and any that come through without our brand, we'll shoot."

The driver looked surprised. "You posting

guards around the whole ranch? Must be a hundred square miles."

"Hundred and thirty-five, give or take."

"Jesus. How many men does this outfit have?"

Langley allowed a tight smile. "Enough. Have a nice trip."

Brady Wilkins and his three-year-old adopted son, Ben, were standing outside the foaling pen watching Brady's brother, Hank, coax a shy foal into the world when Amos Logan rode in with news that there was a visitor at the boundary line and he needed a wagon to go get her.

"Hellfire," Ben said, earning a halfhearted warning look from his father. Brady didn't mind a little cussing now and again. But his wife wasn't so tolerant.

"Her?" Brady kept his voice low so it wouldn't disturb the laboring mare.

Amos nodded vigorously. "Didn't catch her name, but Langley seemed to know her. Came in a hired buggy. From Val Rosa, I think."

"Did the horse look sound?"

"No runny nose and it wasn't coughing or nothing."

Brady tugged at his mustache as he thought it over. "Go get her then. And since it's a woman, take Jessica's big carriage."

After Amos headed into the barn, Ben trailing after him, Brady turned back to see the foal's front hooves protruding from the birth canal. Hank continued to murmur reassurance to the mare as she shuddered and heaved with birth cramps.

"Your wife should be out here helping," Brady said.

Hank didn't respond. But then, he rarely did.

"She's a nurse, after all," Brady added.

"A human nurse."

"I know she's human."

The mare lay panting, her distended belly bunching and rolling as her body worked to expel the foal. The air smelled of hay and manure and sweating horse.

"I'm just saying if she can bring my twins into the world, she ought to be able to help this mare. I mean, how hard can it be?"

Hank sent him a smirk. "Why don't you ask your wife that?"

"Still."

The mare tried to sit up. Hank stroked her neck until she relaxed again.

Brady admired his brother's way with animals. Children too. Being as big as he was, Hank cultivated a gentle touch with anything small and helpless, probably knowing he could do real damage if he wasn't careful. But that soothing touch could turn deadly in a heartbeat, as he'd proven last year when he'd crushed a man's throat with his bare

38

hands after the fool had threatened his wife and stepchildren.

Definitely not a man to cross — his brothers could attest to that.

In addition, Hank also had an analytical mind, an inventive nature, and an astounding way with women, which Brady never understood, since he considered himself to be the pick of the litter. Nonetheless, he was proud of his little brother.

With a final push from its dam, the foal, a leggy bay colt, slipped into the straw. Hank broke the sac over its nose, then stepped back so the mare could clean him up and imprint her scent on his awakening mind.

It was a wondrous thing to behold.

Moving over to stand across the fence rail from Brady, Hank wiped his hands on a rag and sighed wearily. "Four down, twenty-two to go. A good year so far."

"We'll need it." In fact, the ranch's very survival might rest on something as fragile as this foal's life. A harrowing thought.

They stood in silence for a while, watching the colt try out his wobbly legs until he finally got himself upright and stayed there long enough to nurse. Then Brady said, "We got company. A woman."

"I heard."

"Wonder who it is."

Hank shrugged.

With a sigh, Brady pushed away from the

rail. "I better go warn Jessica. She'll probably want to repaint the house or add another wing or something. You know how she is."

"Yeah. I do."

Brady didn't have to repaint or add on a wing, which was a good thing, since the house was mostly stone and log construction. But he did have to change shirts and slick back his unruly mostly black hair, then corral his four kids and Hank's two stepchildren and carry them upstairs to be tidied up by the Ortega sisters. The Garcia sisters used to have the job, but they'd begged off, saying they'd rather go to Santa Fe and work in their uncle's house. Kids.

"Brady!" Jessica called from the entry. "They're coming! Hank! Molly!"

Motioning the Ortega girls to get the twin babies, Sam and TJ, Brady scooped up two-year-old Abigail with one hand and steered Ben down the hall with the other. Hank met him at the top of the staircase with his wife, Molly. Penny, who was seven, and Charlie, who was ten and almost as talkative as Hank, trailed behind their stepparents.

"Hurry along now," Jessica prodded, the clipped tones of her English accent making them all step lively.

"Who is it?" Molly asked Brady as Jessica herded them out onto the sprawling front porch.

Brady could tell Molly was nervous, as she always was around strangers. Eighteen months ago she and her orphaned niece and nephew had been on the run when their train had derailed, leaving two men dead and another — a stranger who happened to be Hank — mortally injured. Being a resourceful and intelligent woman, she had immediately seen a way to get the money she desperately needed to keep running. All she had to do was present herself as the injured stranger's intended, marry him, then collect the railroad settlement when he died.

But Hank, being stronger than a mule and hardheaded besides, didn't die, although he did lose his memory for a time, which complicated matters between the newlyweds somewhat. But he and Molly had gotten past that and had been happily married for almost a year. Odd, how things work out.

"It's not Jack, is it?" Molly persisted.

"No, it's a woman."

"Do you know who?"

"I don't."

Molly had never met Jack, the youngest Wilkins brother. He and Elena had left for San Francisco almost three years ago to have Elena's crippled hip fixed, and they'd been missing ever since. Then last spring a letter had come from Jack. "Be home in a year," was all it said. More of a talker than a writer, Jack was.

"Here they come." With brisk efficiency, Jessica assembled them across the porch like a troop of soldiers lined up for inspection.

Brady smiled, watching her. Her face was flushed. Her eyes sparkled. By her proud smile, it was obvious how pleased she was with her family, which greatly pleased him.

Satisfied all was in order, she took her place at his side. "Do I look all right?" she whispered, smoothing back her coppery curls and brushing wrinkles from her skirts.

Brady leaned down to kiss her temple. "You always look all right."

She flashed a smile. "As do you. Except perhaps for the whiskers."

"I didn't have time to shave."

"Do you ever?"

"I thought you liked it."

"It makes you look rakish."

He waggled his eyebrows. "Which you like. Especially when I —"

"Hush." Biting back a smile, she hiked her forceful little chin and watched her large, four-wheeled closed carriage roll through the arched gate and up the long drive to the house.

"Can you see her?" Jessica shaded her eyes against the afternoon glare. "I can't see her."

"That's because she's inside." Brady studied her, wondering why she was so worked up. Was she that lonely out here so far from town that the prospect of a visitor would put her in such a dither? Had he been wrong to take her away from England and the genteel life she'd known there? The thought settled like a stone in his chest. He loved this woman more than he'd ever thought possible. He would kill for her, die for her, do anything. Except live without her. "Regrets, Jessica?"

She glanced up, a tiny frown between her whiskey brown eyes. "About what?"

"This. Us. Being stuck out here on the ranch."

His beautiful, proper, highly decorous wife punched him in the arm. "Dolt."

Reassured, Brady allowed himself to relax, enjoying the way her eyes followed the movement of his lips as he grinned. It was gratifying that even at thirty-seven he could still prime her pump with a smile. "She's here."

"What? Oh!"

The carriage rolled to a stop beside the wide steps leading down from the porch. No face showed in the curtained window. No hand threw open the door.

Langley hopped down, lifted the mounting step from the driver's box, and walked briskly to the side of the carriage. After setting the step on the ground, he opened the door.

A woman's booted foot showed, then a black-clad figure stepped out of the doorway. Black from head to toe, except for the white wimple around her face. "Hello, Brady, Jessica, Hank," the woman said in a Spanish-accented voice.

"Holy . . ." Brady began before his wife elbowed him to silence.

"Elena?" Jessica spoke hesitantly, her eyes round in her freckled face as she stared at the figure smiling up at them from the foot of the steps.

"Is that a nun outfit?" Brady muttered.

Jessica didn't answer because she was already halfway down the steps. "Elena!" she cried, arms wide, laughing and crying as she rushed toward the woman.

Brady turned to Hank. "Is that a nun outfit?"

Hank shrugged.

"It appears so," Molly ventured.

"What's a nun outfit, Aunt Molly?" Penny asked.

"Later, dear. I'll explain it all to you later."

"Then you can explain it to me," Brady said.

"A nun," Hank mused, still rooted to his spot on the porch. "When did she get to be a nun?"

"She can't be a nun," Brady decided, watching the two women hugging and laughing and crying by the carriage. "Married women can't be nuns." He frowned at Hank. "Can they?"

Hank frowned back.

They both frowned at the coach. "Where's Jack?"

The women finally separated. Elena moved to the bottom step then stopped, hands clasped at her waist. She looked up at Brady. *"Hola, querido,"* she said with a tremulous smile.

"You're a nun."

"A novitiate. Next month I will be a true nun."

"How? I don't understand. And where's Jack?"

Her smile slipped a bit. She spread her hands in welcome, revealing the heavy silver cross hanging on her belt. "Have you no welcome for me, *querido?*"

Brady went slowly down the steps toward her. "Am I allowed to hug a nun?"

"You are always allowed to hug me, *mi hermano.*"

Brady felt an odd stinging behind his eyes as they embraced. He shared so much past with this delicate, damaged woman. So much pain. And now this new twist in the history that bound them together. Wondering if there was more sadness ahead, he stared over her head at the distant ice-capped peaks of the mountains. Despite the clear skies, he sensed a storm brewing.

When he released her and stepped back, he could see fresh tears in Elena's dark almond-shaped eyes.

"Is he alive?" he asked, dreading the answer.

"I pray so. But I have not seen or spoken to

him in almost three years." Blinking hard, she put on a brave smile. "Come." Taking Jessica's arm on her right and Brady's on her left, she gently steered them up the stairs. "First you will introduce me to these beautiful children and that lovely woman standing with Hank. Then you will tell me all about the rancho and how you came to build such a fine sturdy home. And later, when the house is quiet and the children are in bed, we will speak of your brother and what happened in San Francisco."

San Francisco

After leaving the theater, Daisy walked aimlessly until afternoon, trying to calm her turbulent thoughts. She had no family to leave Kate with, even if she could bring herself to do such a thing. Her closest acquaintance was a harlot who lived in a brothel. She had no money to hire anyone, nor would the small salary she would earn while training be enough to cover the extra expenses of bringing Kate along, much less a nanny.

Either stay behind with her or come with us.

Pain pressed against her heart. To be so close. To have the dream almost within her grasp only to have it snatched away. It was too much.

Fighting back tears of bitter disappointment, she walked woodenly toward the board-

46

inghouse. She would have to find another position. Maybe go back to the Silver Spur and beg for her old job back. The thought made her stomach cramp. She would also have to find another place to live, another person to watch over Kate while she worked.

Come with us and be a star.

The unfairness tore at her, left her trembling with resentment and despair.

If only she hadn't fallen in love.

If only she hadn't allowed him to talk her into his bed.

If only she had known she was pregnant before she had let him sail away.

If only . . . if only . . . if only.

But then there would be no Kate. It was late by the time she turned onto her street. As she neared the bordello, Lucy came down the steps of the brothel, dressed for errands, rather than work. When she saw Daisy, she stopped and waited for Daisy to reach her. "How was the audition?"

"It's not going to work out." As they fell into step together, Daisy told her about Madame Scarlatti and the offer to join her traveling theater company. "But they won't pay for Kate and I won't earn enough to meet her costs and those of a nanny. And since I have no family to take her in and I won't leave her with strangers, I won't be able to go with them to Rome." Daisy blinked back tears. "And now I don't even have a job at the Spur, either. Lord, what a mess."

"Stump says she can stay at the house. But only if you stay, too. He is running a business, after all."

Raise Kate in a brothel? Never. Besides, Daisy didn't have it in her to be a whore. It was one thing to give yourself to a man you loved, and quite another to lie with a stranger. "I'll think on it," she hedged, hoping to God it would never come to that. Forcing a change in subject, she asked, "Where are you headed?"

"Apothecary. Hazel's got the itch."

But Daisy hardly heard her. They had neared the boardinghouse, and she could hear cries coming through the open upstairs window of the room she shared with Kate. "That doesn't sound right." Alarm exploded in her chest. "Something's wrong!"

Charging up the steps, she threw open the front door to the boardinghouse, banging it into Edna, who lay sprawled on the entry floor, her neck twisted at an odd angle. The reek of whiskey filled the narrow space. Without stopping to check on her, Daisy ran up the stairs. When she rushed through the open door into their bedroom, she saw Bill Johnson bent over Kate's cot. "Get away from her!" she screamed as she slammed into him.

He staggered, caught his balance, then with a snarl, drew back his arm. "Bitch!"

Daisy kicked, aiming for his groin but getting his hip instead.

He stumbled back, his fist missing her jaw, but striking a glancing blow high on the side of her head. She fell against the iron foot rail of her cot, her ears ringing.

Then he was on her, his hands around her throat. "You stupid bitch!" he shouted, his voice rising above Kate's terrified shrieks.

Daisy clawed at his fingers, fighting for air. Her vision narrowed. A buzzing began in her head. In flailing desperation, she grappled for her coat pocket, found the pistol. Without pulling it from her pocket, she jerked the hammer back, thrust the barrel into Johnson's gut and squeezed the trigger.

A muffled "pop," then his grip on her neck loosened. As he lurched back, she smelled spent powder and scorched cloth and the hot, rank scent of blood.

Johnson stood swaying, a look of stunned disbelief on his face. He looked down at the blood blossoming across the front of his vest then up at her. Surprise gave way to fury. Roaring like an animal, he charged toward her.

Pulling back the other hammer, Daisy yanked the pistol from her pocket and fired her last shot up into his open mouth.

THREE

Lucy burst into the room then stumbled to a stop. She gaped at Johnson's bloody face, then at Daisy, who stood frozen, the pistol wobbling in her hand. "Holy Christ!"

"Is he . . . is he . . ." Daisy shook so hard she could hardly form the words.

White-faced, Lucy peered down at Johnson. "Dead as a dog in a ditch." She kicked him to make sure. "What happened?"

"He was a-after K-Kate." Daisy threw the pistol onto her cot and grabbed Kate. "Shh, baby," she crooned over and over, holding her wailing twenty-two-month-old daughter's face to her chest so she wouldn't see the dead man. "It's all right. Mama's here."

Lucy leaped into action. Yanking open drawers on the small bureau, she threw the contents on Daisy's bed. "We gotta get out of here quick. You got a valise?"

Daisy blinked at her, still so frozen by what she'd done she couldn't think, couldn't move. "Under the b-bed."

50

Lucy pulled it out, opened it, and began stuffing it with their clothing. She moved with such savage determination that within a few minutes the room was stripped bare of all of their belongings. After buckling the straps on the valise, she straightened and looked around. "Anything else?"

Daisy looked at her, feeling detached and adrift, her shocked mind still unable to come to grips with the dead man on the floor. *God. What had she done?*

"Titty," Kate cried, reaching for her stuffed cat, which had fallen to the floor.

Lucy picked it up and put it in her pudgy hand. "Where's the pistol?"

"I-I'm not s-sure. My coat — no, there." She pointed to the bed. "Under the valise."

Lucy snatched it up and slipped it into her pocket. "Take off your coat."

"My c-coat?"

"Hurry! Before someone comes! And wipe that blood off your face."

Daisy lifted a hand, felt splatters of sticky wetness on her forehead and cheeks, and felt her stomach lurch. Setting Kate on her cot, she yanked off her coat, desperate to be rid of it when she saw the bloodstains on the front. She scrubbed at her face with a sleeve, then handed the coat to Lucy before picking up Kate again.

Throwing the bloody coat over her arm, Lucy grabbed the valise. "Come on."

On wobbly legs, Daisy followed her down the stairs. When they reached the entry, Lucy set down the valise and bent over Edna's prone body. "Help me get your coat on her," she ordered. "We need to make it look like she killed Johnson in a drunken rage then fell down the stairs."

Reluctantly, Daisy set Kate down on the steps and turned to help Lucy. It took only a few moments. But when they lifted Edna to slip the coat around her shoulders and Daisy saw the way her head rolled on her shattered neck, she almost gagged. After Lucy put the pistol in the dead woman's hand, she straightened, took a last look around then picked up the valise. "Come on."

As soon as they were back on the street, fear almost sent Daisy into flight, but Lucy made her walk slowly, as if nothing was wrong. Luckily Kate had settled down, although there was still a hitch in her breath. The click of their heels sounded unnaturally loud to Daisy.

"Keep your head down and quit crying," Lucy ordered.

Daisy wasn't aware she was.

"If anyone asks, tell them your husband just died."

"W-Where are we going?"

"There's a church on Morton Street. I know the pastor. He'll let you stay there until you can get out of town."

"Out of town?" Daisy looked over at her friend, the numbness of terror fading enough that she could think again. "Where would I go?"

Lucy didn't answer. At the end of the block, they turned left then cut into the alley that ran behind the brothel. At the back stoop, Lucy let the valise drop and sank onto the bottom step. "I gotta rest a minute." She gave a shaky laugh. "I don't know when I been so glad to see this old whorehouse."

Daisy slumped down beside her. Even now her heart drummed with fear and relief at how terrifyingly close she had come to losing her daughter. She looked down into Kate's sleeping face, tears burning behind her eyes.

"What was he doing in there?' Lucy asked after she caught her breath.

Swiping the back of her hand over her eyes, Daisy said, "When I came into the room, he was standing over her bed." She shuddered, the image of Johnson's hands on Kate burned forever into her mind. "I don't know why."

"To sell her."

Daisy blinked at Lucy in surprise. "Sell her? To who? And why?"

Lucy looked down at her clasped hands with their bitten nails and nicked knuckles. They looked like they'd seen their fair share of fights. "I heard the girls talking. Said a man named Wild Bill was going around to all the whorehouses talking about a blond girl baby he had for sale. I didn't think of Kate until I heard him yelling upstairs. Baby-stealing bastard!"

"I don't understand," Daisy said. "Why would anyone want to buy a baby?"

Lucy turned her head and looked at her. She didn't speak, but the hard knowledge behind her sad brown eyes said it all.

Daisy drew back in horror, her arms tightening around Kate so much the exhausted child whimpered in her sleep. "No, Lucy. Surely not. She's just a baby."

"There's a lot of crazies out there."

It was obscene. Beyond evil. Monstrous. Daisy felt like vomiting.

"We got to get you away from here," Lucy said after a moment. "Someplace far away. Where the law won't find you. Or Johnson's friends."

"But he was attacking my baby," Daisy argued.

"Don't matter. You're a woman, he's a man. That's the way it works."

"But, Lucy —"

Her friend rounded on her, her eyes hard as flints. "Do I have to explain it? I'm a whore and you're my friend. I may already be in trouble. Somebody may have seen us — seen me. Stump won't pay bribe money, so we got no protection."

"But how could they blame you?" Without thinking, Daisy reached out and put her hand on Lucy's shoulder.

Lucy shied away then tried to cover it with an embarrassed smile. "I'll be okay. If he has to, Stump will hide me until it all blows over. He'll even cover for us, maybe pass the story around that drunk old Widow Tidwell shot Johnson then fell down the stairs and broke her neck." Lucy gave a crooked smile. "Who knows? Maybe the old lady really did try to stop him and he killed her for it."

Daisy felt tears well up again. A drunk, a harlot, and a jaded procurer. What an odd assortment of guardian angels. She wanted to hug Lucy in gratitude, but knew her friend wouldn't like it. Lucy might earn her living allowing strangers to use her body, but she didn't like to be touched. "Oh, Lucy. You've done so much to help me. Even put yourself in danger. How do I thank you for that?"

Lucy looked away, a flush further staining her rouged cheeks. "You take that sweet baby out of this hellhole. That's how you thank me."

"Take her where?" Daisy slumped wearily, the false energy of fear draining away, leaving her trembly and dispirited. "I've got hardly any savings, no job —"

"What about her Pa?" Lucy cut in. "Would he keep her while you trained?"

"Jack?" Daisy gave a strangled laugh. "I don't even know where he is."

"How about his family then?"

"I don't know them. And even if I did, I couldn't leave Kate for two years."

"You don't have to *leave* her," Lucy argued with strained patience. "Just get enough money from them to take her with you."

Get enough money *how?* Just waltz in there and ask for it? Ridiculous. That would never work. Would it?

Foghorns on the bay signaled the mist was rising. The sky hung low, clouds draped like frothy gray blankets over the peaked roofs of the row houses. Already the air was so wet Kate's blond curls had started to frizz. *We should get to the church before the fog comes in,* she told herself. But she couldn't seem to move.

Lucy's voice cut into her thoughts. "If you stay, they might throw you in jail. What would happen to Kate then? You got no choice but to go to his family."

Daisy stared at her, hearing the words but not daring to believe she had no other option. Leave? Travel all the way to New Mexico Territory? Throw herself on the mercy of people she didn't even know? How could she do that?

She tried to remember what Jack had told her about his family. It wasn't much. Two older brothers. A ranch somewhere in New Mexico Territory not far from a town named after a flower — a rose. Val Rosa. Yes, that was it. Ranchers had money, didn't they? And even if Jack was still off somewhere trying to get over his lost love, wouldn't his brothers want to help his daughter?

"Kate is their kin, too, you know," Lucy reminded her.

Daisy nodded, thoughts racing through her head. "Yes. She is."

RosaRoja Rancho

"As you can see," Elena motioned to her hip, "the operation was not a success."

They were gathered in the main room. Dinner was long past, and the children had gone upstairs an hour ago with the Ortega sisters — their keepers, as Brady thought of them. Other than Elena, only the two brothers and their wives sat before the fire crackling in the huge stone fireplace.

"Dr. Sheedy did the surgery?" Molly asked.

Elena smiled her surprise. "How did you know? Have you met him?"

"Brady asked about him. I'd heard he was a fine surgeon." Molly explained that in her travels as nurse to her surgeon-father, even though most of her training during the War of the Rebellion had been below the Mason-Dixon, she had heard of Dr. Sheedy, a gifted medical officer in the Irish Brigade of the Union Army.

As Molly spoke, Brady studied her, noting the lines of strain around her mouth and the sadness in her hazel eyes. He knew she was fretting. The other day when he'd gone into Hank's wing of the sprawling house he'd heard her crying. He wondered why.

"I read some of his early articles in my father's old medical journals," Molly went on. "Papa thought highly of his innovative ideas about antiseptic procedures in the surgical room."

Elena laughed. "I am not sure what that means, but he was the cleanest man I ever saw. He made the nurses *loco* with his demands that they wash their hands."

"What went wrong with the operation?" Molly had a deep interest in the mechanics of surgery even if the practice of it often made her sick.

After the derailment that had almost cost Hank his life, Brady had witnessed her affliction when she'd worked so hard to save Hank's crushed arm, then vomited like a muleskinner on a three-day drunk as soon as it was over. A woman of extremes, Molly was, and not above killing to protect those she loved. A good match for Hank. But lately, Brady had sensed something had started to unravel between them. He didn't know the cause, but he recognized discontent in a woman's eyes and figured it was something Hank had done — or not done. He resolved to talk to him about it later.

"Dr. Sheedy did his best," Elena said. "But even though he removed most of the scar tissue, the bones broken where my brother kicked me had healed crookedly and could not be straightened. The infection it had caused also did damage to other organs." A blush crept over her olive cheeks. She lowered her eyes to the cross she gripped tightly in her fisted hands. "Such damage would have prevented me from being a true wife or bearing children."

Brady frowned, trying to piece together what Elena wasn't saying. Was she barren? Was that why she chose God over his brother, to spare them both the disappointment of a childless marriage? If so, considering the way she had felt about Jack when she'd left, she should be heartbroken. Yet she seemed content. Happy, even.

Jessica must have wondered the same thing. "Is that why you and Jack didn't marry?"

Elena looked up. Her eyes shimmered like dark, glistening pools in her pale heart-shaped face, so black they seemed to swallow the faint light from the kerosene lamps scattered throughout the room. "It is the reason I opened my heart to such a possibility. When I did, I saw another way of life waiting for me."

"A reclusive life," Brady said, still not convinced it was a true vocation.

"A life devoted to God," she corrected gently. "Which I would have chosen whether the church accepted me or not. In the end, it had nothing to do with Jack."

They sat in silence except for the snap of burning wood and the soft whisper of wind around the balcony supports off the back of the house. Brady looked beyond the glass doors flanking the fireplace to the hilltop where the rising moon highlighted the angular shapes of the tombstones under the mesquite tree. Most of his family was buried up there. With Jack still missing and Elena lost to them forever, it would be like burying two more.

Hank rose, added more logs to the fire, then returned to his seat beside Molly.

Brady wondered what he was thinking. His brother was such a closemouthed sonofabitch, Brady never really knew what went on in that prodigious brain of his. Did he feel it too? That sense of change coming?

Brady didn't like change. Being head of the family since he was twenty-one, he had spent most of his adult life struggling to protect the ranch and the two brothers he had left. Change was a threat to the precarious balance he worked so hard to maintain. Jessica was teaching him to ease up a bit — to be less controlling, she called it. But even now, with new perils rising against them, his first impulse was to gather his family close and bar the doors.

"So you don't know where Jack is now?" Jessica asked. "We're quite worried about him." She was almost as protective of the family as Brady was, but somehow that didn't count as controlling. He didn't even try to make sense of it.

Elena shook her head. "He was *muy enojado* — very angry — when I told him of my decision. He said many things, tried many times to talk me out of it. But once I entered the abbey as a postulant and was no longer able to speak to him, he stopped trying to see me. That was close to three years ago. I have heard nothing from him since. I pray he is still alive. I pray that God will help him understand and forgive me." She turned her head and looked directly at Brady. "I pray the same for you."

Brady forced a smile. "It's not you I have to forgive, Elena. Never was."

A sad look came into her eyes. "My brother. Sancho."

"And myself." Brady felt Jessica's hand slip into his. As always, her touch calmed him, anchored him until the flood of terrible memories receded.

Elena sank back into the upholstered leather cushions of her chair. "My brother was an evil man who did terrible things. He broke every law of God and died because of it." Her gaze shifted to Jessica, whose grip on Brady's hand tightened until her nails bit into his fingers. "Do not blame yourself, *hermana de mi corazón* — sister of my heart," Elena said to her. "You were God's instrument. Nothing more."

Before Jessica could respond, Elena turned back to Brady. "And you, *querido,* what you did for your little brother was an act of love, not evil intent. How can you blame yourself for that?"

Brady didn't answer. He didn't want to talk about Sam's death, or the agony his little brother had suffered at Sancho's hands, or the soul-shattering act of mercy Brady had been compelled to perform to release him from the pain. All of that was thirteen years in the past. Today he had another brother to worry about.

"Could Jack still be in San Francisco?" he asked, changing the subject.

Elena gave a weary shrug. "He spoke of Australia. Perhaps he went there."

"I can see you're tired, Elena." Jessica stood, pulling Brady up with her and glaring Hank to his feet as well. She was a stickler for proper behavior. Probably her English upbringing. "We've kept you up too late after such a long journey. Perhaps we can talk more tomorrow after you're rested."

"Gracias, amiga."

Molly stood, offering assistance as Elena pushed awkwardly to her feet, trying to keep her weight off her damaged hip. Once upright, she paused to pass around a wide smile.

"I am so happy to see all of you again. Thank you for your kind welcome." After giving her goodnights to the brothers, she went with Jessica and Molly upstairs.

When their footfalls faded, Brady turned to Hank. "My office or yours?"

"Mine. Bob stinks too much."

The house had a rectangular design with a three-story center and two-story wings on either side. The entry, which also held the stairwell, was bisected by open hallways leading to the east and west wings. Across from the double-entry doors was the huge main room, the back wall of which held a twenty-foot-tall rock fireplace and bank of windows overlooking the hilltop cemetery and mountains beyond. At one end of the room was a reading area — Jessica called it a library — and at the other end was a dining area that led into a large kitchen in the west wing. Brady had stocked the kitchen well with the biggest cookstove he could buy and an abundance of cabinets and countertops. There was also a long family dining table in the middle of the room and access to a coolroom that held the boiler Hank had built to pipe hot water throughout the house. So far, it hadn't exploded.

Above the entry was a U-shaped mezzanine that overlooked the main room, with hallways leading off the arms of the U into his brothers' bedroom wings. Brady's section was over

63

the entry in the center of the U. Hank had the east wing over the library and offices, while Jack's rooms were over the dining room and kitchen — if he ever got his ass home to use them. After Abigail was born, Jessica converted the third-floor attic into a nursery for the kids and their keepers. The rambling house might seem a bit crowded sometimes, with six children and double that number of adults moving in and out of it, but Brady liked having his family close by so he could watch over them.

Spanning the front of the house was a covered porch with a steep roof. The back porch was uncovered, with hanging balconies off his brothers' bedrooms. Twelve bedrooms and six water closets, not counting the nursery. A strong, masculine house made of two-foot-diameter logs and weathered rock taken from their own land. Brady was proud of it.

Of course, Jessica had tried to soften it by removing most of the taxidermy and adding ruffled pillows and lace doilies and tiny claw-footed tables that could barely hold a coffee mug. That English upbringing again. But it was still a fine house, and Brady figured if Hank didn't blow it up with one of his innovations, it would last a century at least.

His and Hank's offices were on the main floor behind the library, which was where Brady was headed now. After gathering up the cut-glass decanter of Scotch whiskey and two crystal tumblers, he went next door to Hank's office.

The offices were mirror images of one another, each with its own fireplace flanked by bookcases, windows, and a door onto the back porch, and each furnished with two oversized leather chairs set before a broad desk. But Brady's had the added touches of crystal and cut glass, Spanish leather desk accessories, and oil paintings depicting that ridiculous English sport of chasing after foxes — a waste of time if there ever was one. Jessica again, bless her heart.

He had subtly countered those feminine touches by installing Bob, a ten-foot-tall stuffed grizzly with a ferocious demeanor that Jessica had banished from the main room for various reasons. Mostly the smell. Admittedly it was rank, reminding Brady of a Mexican saddle that had been cured with manure and piss then left in the rain too long. But he put up with it because in addition to serving as a fine coatrack, Bob was an excellent kid repellant.

In contrast, Hank's office was a disordered mess of parts, tools, projects-in-progress, and the dismantled remains of items his brother had liberated from other rooms in the house when Jessica wasn't looking. A tinkerer's idea of heaven.

When Brady entered, he was hard at work

on something that looked a lot like a smaller version of the boiler in the basement, God help them.

"What's that?" Brady asked as he searched out a clear space on the cluttered desk for the decanter and glasses.

Hank didn't look up. "A pop valve for a steam-powered windmill."

"I thought windmills were powered by wind. Hence, the name."

"They are, except when there's no wind."

"So why isn't it called a steam mill?"

Hank muttered something under his breath.

Undaunted, Brady pressed on. "And if the purpose of a wind — or steam — mill is to pump water out of the ground, where does the water come from to make the steam in the first place?"

"Just shut up and pour the whiskey."

Brady poured, picked up his crystal tumbler, and settled into one of the chairs across from the desk. "It's a righteous question."

Hank continued working on his whatever. Brady stared idly out the window and wondered how to ask about Molly. He didn't like it when his family was suffering, since as head of the family, it was his job to see that they didn't.

He decided to jump right in. "Glad to see Molly's feeling better."

That brought Hank's head up. "What're you talking about? Molly's fine."

Brady shrugged. "Seemed upset a few days ago. Heard her crying."

"It happens." Hank bent to his task again.

"It does," Brady agreed. "Fairly frequently, it seems." When his brother didn't respond, he pressed harder. "Is she mad at you?"

"You're nosier than a preacher's wife, aren't you?"

"Jessica's worried," Brady defended. "We both are. We care about her."

With a sigh, Hank put down his tools and reached for his glass. He took a deep swallow, coughed a bit, then said, "She's upset there's no baby. That's all. Now tend your own knitting and leave us alone."

Brady was taken aback. It wasn't the answer he had expected. He'd thought it might be something he could fix. Like money or . . . something. But this, well, this was personal. "Oh," he said lamely. "Keep at it, then. It'll all work out."

"Keep at it." Hank shot him a look of disgust. "Hell, why didn't I think of that?" Leaning back in his chair, he propped his heels on a clean corner of his desk. "You go through the mail?"

"I did."

"And?"

"Like we thought, Grant signed the Coinage Bill a month ago. All gold, no silver. As of February twelfth, our silver mines are virtually worthless."

67

"Hell."

"I know. It's got the banks scared too. They're shutting down loan money, which means farmers and cattlemen who operate on credit will go down first."

"Not us."

"Not us. Not yet anyway. We still have the Army beef contract."

They drank in silence for a time. Brady comforted himself with the fact that the mines were about played out anyway, although they still produced enough to keep the workers paid and the machinery running. Now he'd have to shut them both down and let the miners go. *Damn that Grant.*

"Anything new on the horse flu?" Hank asked.

Brady snorted. "They're calling it 'The Great Epizootic.' Sounds like a damn carnival act." Leaning forward, he picked up the decanter, topped off his glass, and returned the decanter to the desk.

"They say it started in Toronto," he went on after he took a sip. "And from there headed south, then west. A real mess. Even the Army is on foot. Without horses, Indians don't get fought, locomotives don't get coal, ships don't get unloaded, and fire wagons don't get pulled. Boston near burned to the ground."

"What about the horses?"

As usual, Hank was more worried about

the animals than the humans. Not that Brady blamed him. With the mines no longer supplying income and the cattle market in jeopardy, the ranch's future might rest solely on their slow-growing but highly regarded breeding program of mustang-and-Thoroughbred-crossbred horses. Which was why RosaRoja was under quarantine; they could ill afford an outbreak of horse flu, especially now.

"It's bad," Brady said. "At least twenty-five percent dead overall. Close to eighty percent in some places."

"Hell."

"I know. But the *Chronicle* said it had spread as far west as Prescott as of last week, so maybe it's passed us by. We'll give it another week then see."

Outside, the wind picked up, rattling the windowpanes and moaning through the gap under the porch door like some poor lost soul begging to come in.

Hank took a deep swallow then sucked air against his teeth. "And Blake?"

Brady didn't want to think about Franklin Blake right then. Or how the bastard had convinced the bank to sell him the loan papers they'd been holding on the smelter Brady and several other mine owners had built as a cooperative enterprise.

Blake had been after RosaRoja's highly profitable mines for a while now. They had never considered selling to him, mainly because they didn't need the money, but also because Blake had a reputation for dodgy deals. But now Brady wished they had sold, especially since the mines were now damn near worthless. He had to wonder if Blake would try to come after the ranch next.

"How you figure to pay him?" Hank asked.

"I'm thinking on it."

"Better think fast. He'll be calling in the note soon."

"I know."

Silence again. The fire had died down to embers, but neither of them bothered to add wood. The moon started a slow slide down the western sky, and coyotes added their voices to the wind serenade.

"I guess we could use Jack's share of the mine profits," Brady said after a while.

"We could," his brother allowed. "If it was ours to use."

"Don't go moral on me."

Hank looked at him over the rim of his glass.

"It's not like he did anything to earn it," Brady persisted. "Hell, he doesn't even know it's there."

Hank continued to watch him.

Brady hated that. Hated how Hank played him like a trout with those watchful silences. "Jesus. You're one hardheaded sonofabitch, you know that?"

Still no response.

It wore Brady down. With a sigh of defeat, he thunked his empty glass onto the desktop and rose. "Okay. We'll wait until Jack comes. He said he'd be home in a year and it's been almost that long. Then we'll ask him. Meanwhile, I'll try to come up with another plan to raise the money."

"Whatever you think best, Ma," Hank said.

"Go to hell."

His brother just smiled.

If he wasn't so damn big, Brady would have hit him.

San Francisco

"How long do I have?" Daisy asked from the doorway of the stage office the next morning.

Markham looked up from a stack of papers. "For what?"

"To make a decision about the tour."

"The troupe leaves New Orleans the end of May. Two months. Why?"

Daisy stepped inside and shut the door behind her. "I've got an idea, a way to come up with enough money for Kate." She had lain awake most of the night on her narrow cot in the storage room at Saint Michael's, reliving Johnson's death and thinking about Lucy's suggestion. And the more she thought about it, the more she liked it. It wasn't really coercion. Just a friendly request for a little money. She truly had no choice. Now that

71

Johnson was dead — she shuddered, remembering that ghastly scene — they had to leave. And since she had no family of her own to run to, where else could she go but to Jack's?

Markham took the stub from his mouth, removed a piece of tobacco from his tongue, flicked it away, then replaced the stub. "And do what, missy? Leave her in the wings while you're on stage? What kind of life is that for a kid?"

"I'm thinking to bring someone along to watch her," Daisy said, refusing to be discouraged by his lack of enthusiasm. "A nanny."

"A nanny. And how you going to pay for all that?"

"Her pa."

The stub dipped. His eyes widened. "I thought he was in Australia."

"Maybe. Maybe not. But his family is in New Mexico."

"New Mexico." His chair creaked as he tilted it back on two legs, hand planted on the armrest, elbow pointing out at a sharp angle. With his other hand, he took the stub out of his mouth, rolled it between his thumb and forefinger, then studied the unlit end as if he saw something there of great importance.

He had an entire routine going with that cigar butt, Daisy thought, watching him in amusement. He ought to take it on tour with them.

"Do you even know where New Mexico is, missy?"

The pastor had shown her a map. "It's between here and New Orleans. And since I'm headed that way anyway, I thought I'd stop off and say hello." *And beg for help.* The idea was distasteful, but again, what choice did she have? "I take a train to Santa Fe, then a coach to Val Rosa, and a buggy from there. It'll take about a week." And almost every penny of her meager savings. Still, she had to try.

"That's Indian country, you know."

"I heard."

"Dangerous place for a woman on her own. Especially one with a kid."

Daisy felt a tug in her heart. Mr. Markham really was a kind man, despite his touchy ways. Mentally she added his name to her list of guardian angels. "You worried about me, Mr. Markham?" she asked with a smile.

His gaze slid away. He leaned forward and the chair thumped back to the floor. "I quit worrying about fools a long time ago," he muttered, the cigar back in place as he riffled through the papers on his desk. "Go on if you're leaving. I got work to do."

Daisy studied the dusty bowler hat that hid his face from her. A sad, regretful feeling moved through her, and she realized this good-bye would be almost as painful as the one to Lucy. This man had been kind to her.

He had given her a chance when no one else would, and for a few moments had made her believe in the impossible. In herself. Even if she never made it onto the stage again, she owed him for his kindness.

"You've been real good to me, Mr. Markham," she told the crown of his hat. "I thank you for that. And for letting me audition."

Without looking up, he shrugged. "It was my job. Nothing more."

"Of course it was."

South of San Francisco
"Gone? What do you mean she's gone?"

Jack Wilkins glared at the ancient nun guarding the gate of the Catholic Abbey perched like a boil on a hilltop above the shimmering Pacific. He was tired, his foot hurt, his stomach still hadn't found its land legs, and after months at sea the last thing he wanted to hear was that he'd come back too late. "Gone where?"

The nun blinked up at him like a startled bird. "New Mexico Territory."

He almost fell off his crutch. "New Mexico?" Had she given up this crazy nun-thing? Was she back at the ranch, waiting for him to come home? "She's not a nun anymore?" he asked, daring to hope.

"Novitiate," the old woman corrected. "Sister Maria Elena hasn't yet taken her final vows."

74

If she hadn't taken final vows, he still had a chance. "What's she doing in New Mexico?"

"She has gone to say good-bye to her temporal family before beginning her ministry in . . . hmm, now where was it?" She frowned, tapping a gnarly forefinger against her wrinkled cheek as if to roust a memory loose. "It's an island, I believe. Yes!" She showed toothless gums in a pink smile. "An island in the Kingdom of Hawaii."

Hope faded. Jack had been to the islands of Hawaii. In his desperation to put meaning back into his life after Elena had deserted him for the convent, he had spent months — years — traveling all over the South Pacific, from Samoa to Tahiti to New Zealand and Australia and back again. He knew of only one reason a nun would travel such a distance to take a ministry.

"The Island of Molokai?" he asked, his voice so strained he could hardly get the words out.

"That's it! Yes, Molokai. There's a small town . . . on the coast, I think."

The muscles in his chest clenched. "Kalawao?" *Please, not Kalawao.*

"Yes! The settlement of Kalawao." The nun crossed herself. "May God bless her."

For a moment Jack couldn't catch his breath. He felt shaky and light-headed. Not his beautiful Elena in Kalawao. It was obscene. Unacceptable. Wrong.

Perhaps sensing his turmoil, the little nun reached through the ironwork of the closed gate to touch his shoulder. "Are you all right, my son?"

Jack stared bleakly at her, silently willing her to say she was mistaken, that she had the wrong nun, the wrong settlement, on the wrong island.

But her face remained serene and her faded eyes showed nothing but pity.

It made him want to yell at her, hit something, bellow his rage at God for this new insult. "How long?" he ground out.

The old woman patted his shoulder and smiled. "Why, forever, my son."

"No, before she leaves! How long before she leaves?"

He must have shouted it. With a skittish look, the nun snatched her hand back and scuttled out of reach. Eyeing him from a safe distance, she spoke so quickly all the words ran together. "May, but she must prepare for her vows, so she will return in mid-April."

A month. He had a month to convince her.

Resolved, Jack turned, his crutch banging on the stone steps as he limped to his horse.

"Go with God, my son," the old nun called.

Not likely, Jack thought. He and God had parted company three years ago. Now they were bitter enemies. And Jack would fight Him, the Devil, and all the hounds of hell before he'd let Elena live the rest of her life in a leper colony.

FOUR

Intent on getting to the ranch and Elena as fast as he could, Jack arranged with his ship's captain to have his trunk sent to the ranch as soon as the harbor agent cleared the cargo, picked up some cash from his San Francisco bank, then hurried to the train depot. Figuring it would be better for his broken foot to sit rather than ride over twelve hundred miles by horseback, he sold his horse and tack to a disembarking passenger, then went inside to buy a ticket.

He wasn't sure how close to the ranch he could get before having to either take a coach or buy another horse. When he'd left New Mexico three years ago, the southern route of the transcontinental wasn't even finished. Now, as he studied the giant railroad map painted across the back wall of the depot, he could see that dozens of intersecting lines and spurs and branches had sprung up in his absence. Even more surprising was the notation above a twenty-mile stretch of track that snaked down from the main line southeast of Santa Fe to a small town named Redemption. The notation read, "Wilkins Cattle and Mining."

Mining? When had they gotten into mining? And mining what?

His second shock came a moment later when upon closer examination of the map he saw that Redemption was located well within the northwest corner of Wilkins land.

Mines, a rail spur, and their own town too?

We must be rich, Jack thought with a grin. Apparently his brothers had been busy in his absence.

After purchasing a ticket on the eastbound departing that afternoon — which actually followed the coast south for four hundred miles before turning east — he hobbled over to a small cantina behind the depot, where he ordered a celebratory drink and a plate of frijoles.

Wilkins Cattle and Mining. He liked the sound of that. The previous name — Rosa-Roja Rancho — was past history, too reminiscent of the feud between his family and Elena's and all the lives that had been lost because of it. Besides, the roses it had been named for were gone. After Elena's brother, Sancho, set the ranch afire, most of the roses their mother had planted around the foundation of the house in honor of his birth had been charred to cinders along with everything else.

He wondered if his brothers had rebuilt the house yet. He hoped they hadn't just copied the original. He hated the sprawling *hacienda* the Ramirez family had built so many years ago. All adobe and tile and dark carved wood, it had been a constant reminder of Elena's lost heritage and the bloodshed that had followed. He'd always felt like an intruder in someone else's home.

The train arrived only five hours late, and by the time he'd hobbled on board and settled in a window seat on the shady side of the passenger car, they were heading out of the depot.

The miles clickety-clacked by at an astounding pace. Jack had never moved so fast on land or sea, and if the train hadn't lost a half hour out of every two hours stopping to fill the water tank on the tender, they could have made over three hundred miles in a day. A stupefying achievement.

But boring.

Luckily he was able to relieve the tedium for the first couple of days by joining a rolling low-stakes poker game in the mail and baggage car. But at Yuma, after losing two players when the Deputy United States Marshal and his prisoner disembarked, the other fellows called it quits.

After that he mostly slept or took bets on

80

how many jackrabbits he could shoot with his Sharps .50 as the train sped by. Having seen the damage rabbits had done in both Tasmania and parts of Australia, he had no great fondness for the little pests. But shooting them was harder than it looked — trying to hit a moving target from a bouncing platform while balanced on a crutch — and it wasn't long before he'd lost almost everything he'd won in the poker game and had run out of bullets. He'd never been that good a shot.

By the morning of the fifth day he was ready to get out and crawl the rest of the way to the ranch when they finally chugged into Redemption. Wilkins land at last. With a deep sigh of relief, he limped off the rear step onto the depot platform and looked around.

Redemption was a typical bustling mining town. Newly built, it boasted unpainted wooden structures bordering a single street, with scattered canvas tents clustered along the creek south of town. Main Street housed the usual shops, saloons, and emporiums down one side; on the other, a hotel, an assay office, a bank, and a restaurant. Behind that, a back alley served the livery, a blacksmith, a Chinese laundry and bathhouse, and several outhouses. A small but busy town.

Oddly busy, in fact.

As he clumped down the boardwalk, Jack noticed that many of the wagons and carts moving past were loaded high with all manner of furniture and household belongings. Several men leading similarly loaded pack-horses rode by as well. And they all seemed to be headed in the same direction: away from town.

As Jack pondered the meaning of that on his way to the livery to see about a horse, he heard a voice call his name.

Pausing to look around, he saw a youngish, well-rounded woman waving from the doorway of a little shop on the other side of the street.

"Jack Wilkins! Is that you?"

He recognized the body, but not the face. She looked somewhat like Martha Burnett, his favorite Val Rosa whore, but her hair was darker and she wasn't wearing face paint, and with her dress buttoned all the way to her chin and hiding the part of her he most vividly remembered, he couldn't be sure.

Stepping off the boardwalk, he dodged around a cart stuck in the road, and crossed toward her, his crutch making sucking noises in the four inches of mud churned up by the constant traffic.

It was Martha Burnett, he realized as he drew near. Up close, she was surprisingly handsome. Or maybe she always had been but he'd been too distracted by her two best features to take much notice of her face. "Hello, Martha," he said with a grin. "What are you doing here?"

She grinned back. "I was about to ask you the same thing. Here to stay?"

"For a while at least. You?"

She glanced past him at the cart still stuck fast in the mud. "Until there's no one left, I suppose."

He turned to follow her gaze. Several men had gathered to push against the rear of the cart, rocking it to free the mired wheels. "What's going on? Where's everybody going?"

"California. Wyoming. Wherever there's something worth digging out of the ground."

With triumphant shouts from the mud-spattered pushers, the wheels rolled forward. Jack returned his attention to Martha. "These mines are played out?"

"Not yet, but with the government switching to the gold standard, the market for silver has gone flat as a toad in a road. Hank shut them down a couple of days ago. Lucky you made it in when you did. They're sending the last of the ore to the smelter this week, then they're shutting down the rail line too."

So much for being rich.

Putting on a bright smile, Martha gestured to the storefront behind her. On the door was painted, MARTHA'S MISCELLANY AND MIL-LINERY SUPPLIES. "This here's my shop. What do you think?"

Jack studied the front window, which was

crammed with hats, ribbons, bits of lace, and various female-type doodads. He didn't know what to think. How did a woman go from being a whore to a shop owner? And why? He bet men from here to Val Rosa were crying into their whiskey glasses. "Catchy name."

She chuckled. "That was Miz Jessica's doing. You know how she is with big words. The rest was Molly's idea."

So Jessica was back. Jack was glad to hear it. He wondered if Brady had gone after her or if she and Ben had returned on their own. "Who's Molly?"

Martha's grin bubbled into that hearty laugh he remembered from lazy afternoons he'd enjoyed in her brass-railed bed. "Hell, you *have* been gone a long time. Molly is Hank's wife. Never met a smarter woman or a harder worker. She saved Hank's life after the derailment."

Jack could only stare. Hank was married? To a woman named Molly? What happened to Melanie Kinderly from the fort? And what derailment?

"What happened to your foot?" Martha asked, breaking into his confused thoughts.

Jack glanced down at the dirty wrappings around his right foot. "Busted."

"Won't heal if you keep walking on it."

"So I've been told." He needed to get home quick. His questions for his brothers were piling up fast.

84

"Ask Molly to tend it," Martha suggested. "Finest healer I ever saw."

A healer too? Jack was starting to get dizzy trying to sort through such an onslaught of information. "Best get going, I guess." If he left now, he could be home late that afternoon. "The livery still operating?"

Martha nodded. "It is, but you can't get a horse there. And even if you could, your brothers wouldn't let you ride it up to the house. Brady's got the ranch buttoned tight because of the epizootic."

Jack had heard about the devastation the horse flu had visited on various parts of the country but he hadn't realized it had spread this far west. "Is it that bad?" A cattle ranch couldn't operate without horses.

"Here? So, so. At the ranch, nothing so far. That's why the quarantine. So the ranch *wouldn't* be infected. 'No horses in, no horses out.' And they're backing that up with guns."

"Then how am I supposed to get to the ranch?" *And to Elena?*

After a quick look around, Martha stepped closer. Dropping her voice to a whisper, she said, "If you can make it on foot, about three miles south of town is a small box canyon. Your brothers keep a few horses there to ride to and from the ranch. Curly and Bishop are nursemaiding them. You remember those two, don't you?"

"I do." After thanking her for her help, he

headed out. It was hard going on a crutch with his saddlebags over one shoulder and his rifle scabbard over the other. The added weight wore his arm down, and by the time he reached the canyon, his armpit was almost as raw as his temper.

Curly and Bishop acted glad to see him. But after the initial effusive, backslapping, arm-pounding greetings, they seemed to run out of things to say. They didn't appear to have changed much. But then maybe Jack's own travels had matured him more than he'd thought.

"Stay on the road," Curly advised as he tightened the cinch on the lively chestnut gelding he was saddling for Jack. "We've got patrols out. If they catch you cutting across country, they'll shoot your horse out from under you and ask questions later."

Bishop nodded in agreement. "B-B-Boss's or-or-orders."

Some things hadn't changed, Jack thought dryly. Such as Bishop's stutter and Brady's fondness for issuing orders . . . the latter being one of the things he had missed the least over the last three years. "Seems a bit harsh," he muttered, vaulting into the saddle rather than using the stirrup out of concern for his throbbing foot. "But I'll stay on the road."

"Boss is just worried about his new cross-breeds," Curly said, stepping back as the energetic gelding came around.

"B-B-Boy, you sh-sh-should s-s-see 'em," Bishop added with a grin. "Pur-Pur-Purtiest horses you ever s-saw."

As if Brady would settle for anything less.

With a backward wave, Jack pointed the gelding south.

After spending over four days in a swaying, jostling train car, he was glad to settle into the easy rhythm of a smooth-gaited horse. RosaRoja had always produced fine horses. In addition to being a hardheaded, interfering, bossy sonofabitch, his oldest brother was also an excellent judge of horseflesh.

It was a beautiful day — everything green with the flush of early spring, trees stretching over a hundred feet high, puffy lint ball clouds hanging in a bright sky almost the same clear blue as the shallow waters off Australia. Jack had learned a lot about stars and clouds and wind from his months at sea, and today promised to be dry and calm. He enjoyed the quiet solitude of it, knowing as soon as he got home his peaceful moments would be over for a while.

He had a lot of questions to ask.

And a confrontation with Elena to get through.

But first he would have to answer to his brothers for his long silence.

In the beginning, after Elena's operation and the long months of recovery, he had put off writing in the hopes that she would improve and he'd have better news. Then she caught religion. Not wanting to accept that, or admit to his brothers that he had been cast aside by the woman he'd chased all the way to California, he hadn't written then either. He was the brother, after all, with the golden touch where women were concerned. Instead he'd unsuccessfully tried to sear away his bitter disappointment with red rye whiskey. After a month-long binge, he had sobered up enough to find himself out of money and almost married to a pretty woman he hardly knew. Not wanting to admit that either, he had hired onto the nearest clipper headed west and had spent the next two years trying to figure out what to do next.

He was still trying to figure that out, which was why he was out on this lonely road right now, still chasing after a woman who didn't want him, and riding back to the ranch he'd tried so hard to leave behind. *Hell.*

Time passed with the steady clop of the horse's hooves on the rocky path. Timber gave way to bare ridges. The ground grew damper, and here and there, tiny flowers pushed up through the last patches of snow clinging to shady crevices. This was the roughest section of the ranch, but also one of the most beautiful. Steep bald cliffs, deep canyons, tumbled boulders as big as houses. Formidable country. Country even Brady didn't try to tame.

Once he cleared the pass and headed down the long slope that led to the home valley, he began to feel impatient and excited. He loved this place, loved the wildness of it, the starkness of upthrust rock and eroded spires. He loved the clean smell of juniper, sweet cactus blooms, and sharp-scented creosote. He loved the sound of wind through pine needles, the taste of cool alkaline water after a long hot day, the sense of smallness that overcame him when he looked at the mountains. He loved it all. He just couldn't live here. He needed something . . . else.

Maybe this time his brothers would accept that.

It was late afternoon when he rode out of the trees and onto the rolling flats that were the heart of the ranch. Twice as long as it was wide, the dished basin stretched for miles from one rising slope to the other. Yet as he rode slowly across it, the valley seemed smaller than he remembered.

Maybe it was because he'd spent so many months at sea, where the horizon hung at the far edge of the world, flat and undisturbed. Unconfining. Here, the mountains brought it closer, creating a looming barrier that reduced vision to a few miles and blotted out almost half of the sky. Yet, strangely, that old feeling of entrapment wasn't as strong as it had been when he'd left. Probably because he'd escaped this country once, and he knew if he had to, he could do it again. Smiling, he kicked the horse into a lope. Or maybe he was just homesick and glad to be back.

He could see the house from two miles away. It was a monster and looked more like a grand hotel than a home. Rising a full three stories, it was all log and stone, with a broad covered porch sweeping across the front. He figured Brady must have designed it. Having a deep aversion to confined spaces, his brother had always been partial to big open structures.

Carl Langley came to meet him as he rode up, a wide grin splitting his grizzled features. "Well, I'll be. You finally came home." His grin folded into a frown when he saw the crutch. "What happened?" he asked, holding the restive gelding as Jack slid down onto his good foot.

"Long story. Where is everybody?"

"Eating. Your brothers expecting you?"

"Thought I'd surprise them."

"Lots of surprises this week."

Jack gave the older man a sharp look. "Oh?"

"Miss — *Sister* — Elena's here too."

"Is she?" Jack tried to sound unconcerned, but knowing she was so close set his heart pounding.

"You know she's a nun?" Langley asked.

"I do." So she hadn't changed her mind. He hadn't really expected her to, but had still nurtured a spark of hope. Hiding his disappointment, he headed up the porch steps on his crutch. "Tell the boys I'll stop by the bunkhouse later to give my hellos."

"They'll be glad to see you."

He entered quietly then followed the sound of voices across a huge open room, past a long, empty dining table, and through a deep archway that opened into a kitchen as large as a clipper's forecastle.

And there they were, all the faces he remembered. And a lot he didn't.

And Elena.

A warm, tight feeling surged through him.

Unnoticed, he paused for a moment in the shadows of the arched doorway, struggling to bring his emotions under control. Then he took a deep breath and stepped into the room. "Anything left for me?"

Stunned silence. Then the room erupted into a tumultuous uproar as people rushed toward him — Jessica crying and laughing and hugging him, Brady pounding him on the back, Hank grinning and shoving a pretty woman in his face, Consuelo jabbering, a stern-faced old Scottish fellow speaking with such a strong accent Jack didn't know if he was being greeted or cursed, kids everywhere, and Elena . . . observing quietly from her chair, a joyful yet sad smile on her face.

He was home.

"You should have written," Brady said.

The kids were long in bed, and the women had retired after a rowdy evening catching up on all the news. Now Jack and Brady sat in stuffed leather chairs in Hank's office sipping aged Scotch whiskey from tiny crystal glasses, while Hank hunched over his desk, tinkering with something that looked like two hoops with a wheel spinning in the middle. Jack still hadn't had a chance to talk to Elena.

Slumping back against the cushions, Jack propped his sore foot on the corner of Hank's desk and enjoyed the smooth slide of fine whiskey down his throat.

No jug of Buck's home brew now. No coarse laughter or plinking guitar music drifting out of the nearby bunkhouse. No whiffling snore from a rank-smelling hound dog dozing at their feet.

Now they were rich. Now they were living in this overbuilt, sprawling, doily-laden home that his brothers had built on the ashes of destruction. Now it was all fine bone china and silver teapots and women's soft laughter.

And kids. Kids everywhere.

Not that Jack was complaining. He liked living rich. He had a knack for it. He liked to hear women laugh and he liked kids, even when they weren't laughing. And he especially liked this smooth, smoky whiskey a whole lot better than Buck's throat-burning, gut-churning brew . . . but he'd have to have a few more glasses of it just to be sure.

"So why didn't you?" Brady prodded.

Pulled from his musings, Jack looked over at him. "Why didn't I what?"

"Write. I did teach you to write, didn't I?"

Jack sighed, wishing he could have gotten at least one night's sleep before butting heads with his oldest brother. "Because I didn't want to."

"That's a piss-poor excuse."

"It wasn't meant as an excuse. You asked why I didn't write. I answered. That's all."

Hank chuckled as he tightened a screw on the outside hoop.

Brady glared at him, then aimed his ire at Jack. "You should have written. That's all I'm saying. We were concerned."

"About what?"

Brady let out a huff of exasperation. "About Elena. How her operation went. Whether you made it to San Francisco or got scalped on the way. Christ."

Jack blinked, genuinely surprised at the vehemence behind his brother's reaction. "I didn't think it mattered." Then realizing how cold that sounded, he hastily added, "And anyway, someone would have told you if we'd died."

"Who? Some sage rat who saw your pretty blond hair on a lodge pole somewhere? Jesus, Jack. Of course it matters. You're our damn brother."

Hank backed that up with a stern look and a nod.

Jack was touched. He'd always felt like an afterthought around his forceful older brothers. He'd assumed they'd been glad to see the end of him. Apparently he'd been wrong.

"You're right," he conceded. "I should have written."

Brady looked taken aback for a moment. Then he nodded and sat back. "All right, then."

Confused that the expected lecture had ended so quickly, Jack studied his brother, surprised anew at the changes he saw.

Brady seemed as strong and fit as ever. Tall and lean without being gangly, he still moved in that authoritative way that made other men step back when he entered a room. But now there were deep grooves carved into his leathery cheeks, and new lines fanning out toward his temples, and almost as much gray as black in his hair and beard stubble, even though his brows and drooping mustache remained as dark as ever. Their pa had had the same odd coloring, the same sharp turquoise gaze, and a similar unyielding line to his jaw and chin.

Time had definitely left its mark on his older brother. Hell, it would, with three kids, not counting Ben, and Her Ladyship for a wife — a hot-blooded redhead who could filet meat with that sharp tongue of hers. But

Brady seemed content. More than content. Happy. So much so that the signs of aging made him look almost dignified . . . more relaxed and mellow.

Which was a load of horse manure if there ever was one. Brady was about as mellow as a stepped-on rattler.

Hank, on the other hand, looked younger, although it was hard to be certain, since at the time Jack had left, ninety percent of Hank's head and face had been covered with dark brown hair. Marriage must agree with him, too, if it influenced his overgrown brother to take up the civilized habit of shaving. He still looked fitter than fit, but then Hank always had. He was the mule of the family — smart and strong and stubborn as all hell. Jack guessed he'd have to be, to live in the same house with Brady. But despite that, and despite taking on two kids to raise that weren't his, he seemed happy too.

Jack wondered if he would ever find that same level of contentment in his own life. Without Elena beside him, he doubted it.

"Who's the Scotsman?" he asked, remembering him from supper.

"Dougal," Brady said, sourly. "He came from England with Jessica and is apparently too dim-witted to find his way back."

Jack recalled how the old man waggled his bushy eyebrows at their old housekeeper whenever she entered the room. "What's go-

95

ing on between him and Consuelo?"

Brady gave a faint shudder. "Don't ask."

"Buck and Iantha still around?" They were runaway slaves who had been with them since the Wilkins family had taken over RosaRoja. When Jack had left, they'd been showing their years. He hoped all was well.

"Buck's rheumatism keeps him close to home. Iantha comes up now and then to check on the kitchen girls, but she won't stay gone from Buck for long." Buck had been Brady's right hand after Pa died and Brady had taken on the running of the ranch. He and Iantha were as much a part of the family as Elena was. "You should go see them."

"I will."

They drank without speaking for a while. It was a calm, comfortable silence. The kind that comes when you know your companions so well words aren't needed and thoughts seemed to flow from one mind to another without barriers or misunderstanding.

Jack had missed it.

He watched Hank search through a pile of parts strewn across the desk. "What are you working on there?" he asked.

"God knows," Brady muttered.

"A gyroscope." Having found the part he sought, Hank carefully fitted it to the rotating center wheel.

"What's it for?"

"It goes on an auger to keep it straight

while it's drilling."

"Drilling for what?"

"Water, ore, postholes, whatever."

"A posthole driller." Grinning, Brady reached for the cut-crystal decanter he'd set on the floor beside his chair. "Finally an idea that makes sense."

Hank muttered something Jack didn't catch.

After refilling his glass, Brady passed the decanter to Jack then settled back with a sigh of contentment. "So what do you think of the house?" he asked, looking around the room as if seeing it for the first time.

Jack did likewise. "It's big," he allowed after a careful inspection.

"I wanted something sturdy."

"It's definitely sturdy."

"Something that would last."

As Jack tipped his head back to empty his glass so he could refill it, his eye was drawn to the intricate beams across the ceiling. Planed and polished, with fancy supports where they met the wall. All sparkly clean and new. It was nice, but he missed the cobwebs. Cobwebs gave a room such a sense of history. "There's a buffalo in my bedroom," he said.

Brady nodded.

"And a grizzly in your office."

"Bob," Brady said with another nod.

"Why?"

Brady took a sip then smoothed the corners of his mustache. "Jessica wouldn't let me keep them anywhere else. The kids kept climbing on them, and she was afraid they'd tip one of them on top of themselves and get squashed."

"No, I mean why do you have dead animals in the house at all? And how in the hell did you get a buffalo up those stairs and through the door into my room?"

"We took it over the balcony and through the double French doors. And what's wrong with having them in the house?"

"They stink," Hank muttered.

"They're animals," Brady defended. "They stink even when they're alive. And since when do you mind a little stink?"

"I don't stink. At least your wife doesn't seem to think so," he added with an evil grin.

Brady's blue eyes narrowed. "What's my wife got to do with it?"

The grin widened.

"You better stay away from my wife."

"Or what?"

"Now, girls," Jack chided with a laugh.

It was good to be home.

FIVE

Jack awoke the next morning to a ring of curious eyes staring at him, topped by colorful halos — blond, red, and something that looked like an Indian headdress with jelly smeared all over it.

"Hi." The face with blond hair grinned down at him. She had no front teeth.

"Hellfire," said the redheaded boy next to her.

Sputtering, Jack bolted upright, which sent the redhead and Indian chief into shrieking flight from the room. "What are you doing?"

"You're Uncle Jack," the blond said.

He sagged back against the headboard, blinking hard to clear the fuzziness of too much whiskey from his mind.

"I'm Penny." She thrust a battered doll three inches from his nose. "This is Miss Apple. She got her hands cut off by a monster, but Aunt Jessica sewed them back on."

"Oh. Well. That's nice." Gently he shoved the doll aside. "What are you doing in here?"

Instead of answering, she danced away, the skinny arm not clasped around Miss Apple raised in an arc over her head. "I'll turn eight next month," she said, hopping a lopsided circle. "How old are you?"

"Twenty-nine. You're Hank's kid, aren't you? The wanderer."

"What's your buffalo's name? I think you should call him Stinky. Can I ride him?"

Jack shrugged and yawned. "I don't know. Can you?"

"You're funny." She stopped hopping and spinning and came back to lean her elbows on the mattress beside his shoulder. She studied him hard, and by her expression didn't seem impressed with what she saw. Probably too young yet.

"What did you used to be?"

He blinked at her, thoroughly confused.

"Papa-Hank said you changed. What did you used to be?"

Before he could come up with an answer, Hank appeared in the doorway. "Penny, I thought we talked about this," he said in a warning tone.

"But I didn't do anything, Papa-Hank," the girl protested in a high voice. "He woke up all by himself. Didn't you?" This last was directed at Jack with a hopeful smile that promised beauty once her teeth grew back.

Jack was prepared to back her up when Hank cut him off. "You're not supposed to be in here, Penny. You know that."

"It was Ben and Abigail's idea. They just wanted to see him."

Hank looked at her.

The kid drooped like a wilted flower. "Yes, Papa-Hank."

Hank drooped a bit himself, Jack noticed. Ever the softhearted giant.

"Go on then. Leave the man alone."

"Yes, Papa-Hank."

Once the kid left, Hank seemed to find his backbone again. "Get dressed," he ordered. "Molly wants to see you."

"About what?" Jack asked around another yawn.

"Your foot. And you better not upset her by fainting."

Jack grimaced. He'd fainted only one single time in his life . . . when he was ten years old and his ax had bounced off a knot and cut into his leg. His brothers never let him forget it. With a sigh, he swung his legs over the side of the bed, one hand pressed to his pounding temple.

Hank retrieved the saddlebags from the floor and tossed them against Jack's chest. "What's wrong with it?"

"Broke." Jack dug through the pouches, finally coming up with a pile of mostly clean clothes, the brush he used to clean his teeth, and his shaving mug.

"Broke how?"

After giving it some thought, Jack returned the mug to the saddlebag. He needed to wake up more before he went at his throat with a blade. "In a fight."

"With who?"

"Damn, you're a nag. With a better fighter. Okay?"

"So you lost."

Jack scraped his tongue over the back of his teeth, trying to rid himself of the cottony aftertaste of too much whiskey. "The last thing I remember is flying through the air. What do you mean, I've changed? Changed how?"

Hank studied him for a moment. "You're older."

"It has been three years."

"And you're not as argumentative."

"Without Brady around, I haven't needed to be."

"And you're . . . well, smarter than I remember."

"Or maybe you're just dumber."

Hank smirked. "Yeah. That must be it."

Gathering up the clean clothes, Jack nodded toward the door leading into the water closet. "You said all I had to do was turn the left knob and hot water would come out?"

"Eventually. If the boiler doesn't blow. And be watchful that the knocking of the pipes doesn't jar the fittings loose and scald you."

When he limped back into the bedroom a

half hour later, unscalded, dressed, and clean — except for his foot, which was too tender to wash — he found Hank's wife waiting for him in one of the chairs beside the unlit fireplace.

She was an average-looking woman, with a trim figure, a mass of glossy chestnut hair, and intense hazel eyes. Until she smiled. Then she was downright pretty. At her elbow stood a small table draped with clean toweling. On it sat two cups, a brown jar with a white label, and a wad of cotton batting — the kind used to sop up stuff. Like blood.

"How's the foot today?" she asked with a pleasant smile.

"Better," he lied, trying to ignore the odd quiver in his stomach. He hated doctoring.

"May I look at it? I might be able to help."

With a shrug, he hobbled over to the chair across from hers. As he eased down, he noticed a jug of Buck's potent brew on the floor beside an ominous-looking black leather satchel.

The quiver became a rolling cramp.

"How did you injure it?"

"In a fight."

Her expression of disdain gave a clear indication of what she thought about fighting.

With some trepidation, Jack watched her dig through the satchel until she came up with a pair of scissors. She held them out.

"Will you cut off that filthy bandage or shall I?"

Not trusting that glinty look in her eye, he took the scissors and carefully cut off the wrappings to expose his enlarged foot.

She had him lift it up so she could look it over top to bottom, then began rummaging in the black bag again. "Has it always been that swollen?"

"At first. Then it got better. Then a week or so ago it started hurting again." He watched her extract a short-bladed knife and set it on the towel. "What's that for?" he asked, trying to hide his alarm.

"Pass me the jug, please."

He passed her the jug.

After pouring a goodly measure into one of the cups, she dropped the cutting tool into the liquid. "Best antiseptic I've ever seen," she explained.

Jack didn't doubt it.

After pouring a smaller amount into the other cup, she held it out with a smile Jack didn't altogether trust. "Bottoms up."

Reluctantly, he drank.

The reaction was immediate. Choking, coughing, fire in his throat. And while he fought to catch his breath and stem the shudders that wracked his body, the evil woman plunged the knife into the sole of his foot.

If he hadn't been rendered immobile and mute by Buck's brew, he might have offered more of a reaction than a pitiful mewl.

"Interesting," she said, examining something bloody she had plucked from his foot.

"Jesus," he gasped, swiping tears from his eyes, expecting to see the floor awash in blood. Oddly, other than a red stain and some yellow stuff on a corner of the batting, there was nothing.

"The hard part is over." Dropping the object onto the towel, she picked up the cup in which she'd soaked the knife. "Except for this." And she poured the remaining brew over the wound she had made.

Jack refrained from screaming like a girl. Barely. Luckily Buck's concoction soon numbed him — both inside and out — to the point that he hardly felt her do God-knows-what-else to his poor foot before smearing it with a slimy salve, slapping on a fat bandage, and wrapping it tight.

"All done," she said, returning the items on the table to her satchel. "It should heal nicely now."

Wondering why his brother would marry such a sadistic woman, Jack glared at her. It seemed to have no effect. Disgruntled, he peered at the bloody thing she had hacked from his foot. It was smaller than he'd expected. "What the hell is it?"

"A chip of bone that must have broken off when your injury occurred. It was working its way out the sole of your foot. That's what was causing the swelling and pain. It had almost pushed through —"

Jack raised a hand. "I don't want to know."

Tipping her head to one side, she studied him through eyes so fiercely intelligent they were unnerving. "What were you fighting about?"

"Nothing. It was an arranged fight. For money."

"You took money to fight?" Her voice held a tinge of disgust.

"No. I *paid* money to fight." Some of the numbness in his foot was wearing off, he noticed, yet there was much less pain than before. Maybe her stabbing and gouging had done some good after all.

"Whom did you *pay* to fight?" No tinge this time. Full-blown disgust with a touch of disbelief.

Women. They just didn't get it.

"Not *whom.* What." At her look of confusion, Jack shrugged. "If I told you, you'd go blabbing to my brothers."

"I would never do that."

"You'll laugh then."

"No, I won't."

Jack looked at her.

She gave a reassuring smile. "I promise."

He sighed. "It was a kangaroo."

A moment of shock, then she burst into laughter.

"You said you wouldn't laugh."

Which made her laugh harder. And hearing the throaty sound of it and seeing the way her eyes danced with amusement and her stern features softened into a full smile, Jack understood exactly why his brother had married her.

He spent the rest of the morning and most of the afternoon trying to figure out how to get Elena away from his family so he could talk to her.

It seemed every time he turned around, there were kids underfoot or nosy sisters-in-law watching him or that talkative old Scotsman pestering him with questions. Then Brady insisted he come to the barn to see his new Thoroughbred-cross foals, and Hank needed help with a contraption he was building for a windmill, and the fellows in the bunkhouse wanted to hear more about the bare-chested native women on the islands he'd visited. Then he stopped off for a visit with Buck and Iantha, and tried to keep his dismay from showing when he saw how frail they had become. It wouldn't be long, he realized sadly, and doubted the ranch would be the same without them. So it wasn't until late afternoon when he saw Elena up by the mesquite tree, sitting on a bench in the little hilltop cemetery behind the house, that he finally got his chance to talk to her.

It was a difficult climb on a crutch — probably more so on a crippled hip — but he was determined to talk to her. He needed her to look him in the eye and explain in a way he could understand why she preferred death in a leper colony to life with him.

A reasonable question, he thought.

It was another beautiful day with just enough breeze to rattle last year's few remaining mesquite pods that hung too high for the cattle to reach. Time had rendered them dry and leathery and the hollow sound they made when they bounced against each other made Jack think of skeletons dancing a fandango. A depressing image, but fitting for a graveyard, he supposed, and one that matched his dark mood.

He had a sense of time slipping away from him. Of chances missed and changes to come. Of loss. It was almost like a part of him was dying and he didn't know how to stop it. And that discouraged him more than anything ever had. Time had always seemed endless to him, the unknown future stretching far into the distance, barely imagined but rife with potential and possibility. What if . . .

What if he left the ranch.

What if he went to Australia.

What if he married Elena and took her with him.

It had all sounded so possible when he'd left three years ago.

Then had come the failed operation and

Elena's growing fixation with the church, and suddenly the bright future of his imaginings had seemed unattainable and empty. Endless time had dwindled into purposeless days — how long before his next drink, his next woman, his next sailing. And as the months had passed, all the hopeful "what-ifs" had gradually become regretful "if-onlys" until even they had begun to fade away. Now all he had left was "why."

If he was ever to get on with his life, he had to hear Elena's answer to that.

The rusty iron gate squealed in protest when he swung it open. As he limped between the stone markers, lush green grass tangled with his crutch and the ground felt soft and damp beneath his boots. In another few months the grass would wither and the earth would bake dry and the breeze would taste like warm dust. That was a cycle that would never change no matter how much time passed. He took some comfort in that.

He could see she had been crying. Tears still clung to her long, spiky lashes, and her lips had puffed up the way a woman's did when she wept. It touched something deep inside him and made him want to put his arms around her and comfort her. But he knew he shouldn't. Instead, he stood there until she got herself in hand and finally looked up at him. "Been avoiding me, Elena?"

Not what he meant to say. He could tell the

brusqueness of it hurt her, so he tried to cover his mistake by quickly adding, "You look well."

The hurt look died in a smile. "As do you."

He motioned to the empty space on the bench beside her. "Mind if I sit?"

"*Por favor.* Please."

He sat.

For a long time they didn't speak. Like awkward strangers, they sat side by side staring out into the valley, trying to pretend the weight of three years of unspoken words didn't hang between them.

"I went to the abbey," he said after a while.

"Oh?"

"The nun at the gate told me you'd come here."

She nodded and looked down at her hands. "Sister Mary Margaret."

He watched her fingers move up and down the string of beads that tied a heavy silver cross to her belt and wondered if she was praying or if it was just a nervous habit. "She said you'd be taking your final vows next month."

"*Sí.* After retreat."

Movement caught his eye, and he looked up to see a red-tailed hawk rise from the ground halfway down the hill. A snake dangled from its talons. The bird carried its prize to an outcrop thirty yards away, where it worked at the twisting body with sharp quick pecks.

"So you're still going through with it," he said. "Taking your vows."

"Yes."

He glanced at her downcast face, wishing she would take that headdress thing off so he could see her hair. She had beautiful hair. The kind a man liked to feel in his hands.

Silence again. Thunderheads crowded the far peaks, promising evening showers along the high slopes. On the outcrop, the hawk pecked and tore.

Had it always been this difficult for them to talk to each other? By nature, Elena was quiet. He was a talker. But had they ever actually *talked* to each other? It bothered him that he couldn't remember. It bothered him that despite his desperation to reach out to her, he didn't know how to do it.

Such indecisiveness irritated him. He thought he'd grown past the stupid, bumbling kid his brothers had always accused him of being. He had traveled halfway around the world, for Crissakes. He had fought in the Maori wars and had watched friends die. He had outrun fire and outswum sharks and he'd looked down into a bubbling caldron of lava and seen the beating heart of the earth. Surely he could think of something interesting to say.

Apparently not.

It was laughable. Jack Wilkins — a man who

could spin a line that women on two continents had gladly hung their clothes on — and he couldn't think of a thing to say to the only woman that mattered.

He ought to shoot himself.

Having finished its meal, the hawk lifted off the outcrop. Jack watched it soar higher and higher on the updrafts until he lost it in the lowering sun.

"Why Kalawao?" he asked.

She turned her head to look at him.

"Why a leper colony?"

"I may not even be allowed inside the settlement. The church has not yet decided."

"And when they do?"

She spread her hands and smiled. "I will do God's will."

He couldn't let her get away with such an easy, pat answer. "It was God's *will* to give the poor bastards leprosy in the first place. Are you thinking to undo His work?" He tried not to sneer when he said it.

"Not undo, Jack. There is no cure for leprosy. But perhaps I can ease the suffering of those afflicted."

"By becoming a leper yourself?"

She shrugged.

Fury burned through him. "And how will that help? Is that what your *God* wants?"

"He is your God, too, Jack."

A bitter taste rose in his throat. "I don't want Him. Not if this is His doing."

Reaching out, she rested her fingertips on his arm. "Please. Do not hate God or blame Him for my decisions. He simply opened the door to me. It is my choice to walk through it."

He saw that his hands had curled into fists. Forcing them open, he wiped his palms on his thighs. "Was the idea of being with me so bad, Elena, that you'd choose to live with lepers to avoid it?" He hated the way that sounded, hated the self-pitying tone. But he needed to ask the question as much as he needed to hear her answer it.

She sighed and took her hand off his arm, sadness etched on her beautiful face. "I do not know how to explain this to you, *mi amigo.*"

Friend. Was that what he'd been reduced to after all they'd shared? "Try, Elena. Please. Just try."

For a time she stared out into the valley, her fingers dancing over the beads. Then, in a hesitant voice, she said, "In the hospital, when Dr. Sheedy told me of the damage Sancho had done, and how I could never live as a normal woman —"

"That doesn't matter."

She held up a hand before he could say more. "Shh, *querido.* You must let me say this."

When he reluctantly nodded, she continued.

"I cannot share a marriage bed without pain. I cannot bear children. You heard him say that."

"It doesn't matter," he said again.

"It does to me."

"I swear I don't care about that, Elena. I just want you safe. And with me."

But in truth, he did want more than that. He wanted all the things a man shared with the woman he loved. He wanted more than prayers and pious looks and a cold bed. He wanted everything he'd dreamed his life could be.

And he wanted her in it.

Elena's pale hand brushed along his cheek, sending a warm pulse all the way to his heart. "I am unsuited to be a wife, *querido.* But I can still do other things. Good things. Things that will bring meaning to my life and perhaps help others. Would you deny me that?"

Unable to answer, he looked away from her searching gaze. He could feel them coming — the final words — the words that would kill his last remaining hope and change everything forever.

Dread perched like a demon on his chest.

"Dear one," she said softly. "My love for you will dwell inside me forever. I will never forget that no one on this earth has ever cared for me as you have. But all of my life I have sensed that I did not belong in this place. Over the years, every tie that has bound me to it has been broken — my parents, my brother, your kind and generous family. You are the last thread and the hardest to break. You are wrapped so tightly around my heart that parting from you will tear a hole in it that can never be filled."

He watched tears well up and course down her cheeks. Yet she smiled. How could she smile when he was dying inside?

"You are the very best of all that I leave behind, *mi hermano. Te quiero para siempre.* I will love you forever."

"Then why —"

"But I love God more," she cut in gently.

Jack's throat ached. His chest burned. Every fiber in his being rebelled against her words.

"I can't accept that," he said hoarsely.

"You must."

"I won't."

Then because he didn't know what else to say or do, he picked up his crutch and left the cemetery.

It wasn't until he was near the bottom of the hill that an odd thought came to him. He'd wanted to shake some sense into her. He'd wanted to hold her and comfort her when she wept. He'd wanted to stroke her fine, silky hair and take her pale hand in his. But he'd never had the urge to kiss her. Or taste the tears on her cheeks, or feel her body

pressed against his.
And he didn't know why.

Six

"Heard you were looking for a ride to the Wilkins place?"

Hitching Kate higher on her hip, Daisy turned to see a well-dressed gentleman picking his teeth and watching her from the doorway of the Val Rosa Hotel situated next door to the Overland Stage Office.

"Maybe I can help." Flicking the toothpick into the street, he moved toward her. "As it happens, I've got business out that way. You and the little one are welcome to ride along."

Daisy frowned, so exhausted after a week of travel with a restive toddler she could hardly think, much less make coherent decisions. "Well, I . . ."

"Franklin Blake," he said, tipping his broad-brimmed hat. His eyes flicked over her, small eyes, set a bit too close together, but sharply intelligent. "You a friend of the family?"

"Not exactly." Kate twisted in her arms to study Mr. Blake. She didn't usually take well to strangers. Especially men, and especially after that horrid scene when Bill Johnson had tried to take her away. But the child was as weary as Daisy and offered no reaction other than to stare at him with solemn smoky blue eyes.

Ignoring her, Blake smiled at Daisy, showing an abundance of small crooked teeth the color of aged ivory. "Ask around. Anyone can vouch for me."

Daisy tried to think. He seemed kindly enough — a smooth-shaven, middle-aged man with the hands of a banker and the sound of authority in his voice. He was mannerly and clean and seemed to pose no threat.

She had little choice in the matter anyway. The trip from San Francisco had taken longer than she had anticipated, and the extra two days had severely depleted the last of her savings. Without enough money left to cover the cost of a hotel room, she couldn't wait around on the hopes that someone from the ranch would come to town. Nor could she hire anyone to ride to the ranch with a request to send a wagon back to get her. Not that she had any assurance they would honor such a request from a complete stranger.

Well, not a complete stranger — to Jack anyway. Although he'd been so drunk the last time she'd seen him, and for most of the time before that, in fact, he might not even remember her name.

Ridiculous. Of course he would remember her name.

If he was even at the ranch.

"When would you be leaving?" she asked, hoping she was doing the right thing. At least she was younger than Mr. Blake, and fit, and Lucy had shown her a few tricks on managing a rowdy male, so she wasn't completely helpless. Although she did wish she still had her little derringer, just in case.

"I was on my way to the livery to get a buggy." He motioned to the small valise at Daisy's feet. "Can I carry that for you?"

Reluctant, but not sure how else she could get to the ranch, Daisy nodded. Picking up a pouch of baby items with one hand, she resituated Kate on her hip, checked to be sure her daughter still held her stuffed cat, then set out after Mr. Blake.

"Do you know how far it is to the ranch?" she asked, hurrying to keep up with his longer strides. The day was warm enough, but if they had to travel far, it might turn cool later, and she wanted to have ample clothing on hand for Kate.

"A good twenty-five miles," he said over his shoulder.

That far? Daisy was already bone-sore from spending two days in a bouncing stagecoach. The thought of hours more in a jostling buggy almost made her weep. And what if they wouldn't see her and she was forced to suffer another twenty-five-mile trip back to Val Rosa? *No, by God.* They would see her. She would insist.

Blake slowed so they walked side by side. "Are they expecting you?"

"No."

For some reason that made him smile. "Not to worry. The Wilkins brothers will always welcome a pretty little thing like you."

That comment almost stopped Daisy in her tracks. "I thought they were married." The older two anyway.

"That they are. The two I've met, anyway. Kids and all. Quite a clan they've got going out there."

Well, that sounded ominous. "What do you mean, clan?"

If Blake sensed Daisy's growing doubts, his smile didn't show it. "Why, not a thing. Not a single thing."

They spoke no more until they reached the livery. Once there, he told Daisy to wait beside a four-wheeled buggy with a fold-down top, then went inside the barn to speak to the hostler.

Kate was becoming fidgety again, so Daisy let her climb around in the buggy to wear off her restlessness while they waited for Blake's return. He seemed to be taking a long time. At one point, she thought she heard raised male voices coming from inside, but when Blake emerged a few minutes later, he was smiling. However, the livery owner, a muttering, sour-faced elderly man leading a spiritless horse with a runny nose and drooping head, didn't seem as pleased.

"Clem will have us ready to go in no time," Blake assured her.

Daisy eyed the listless animal the hostler was backing between the shafts of the buggy. "You sure the horse is up to the trip?" She'd heard about the horse flu sweeping the country. As it hadn't yet reached San Francisco, she hadn't witnessed it firsthand, but she recognized a sick horse when she saw one. "That horse looks ill."

Blake laughed. "He'll be fine. Just a little dust in his lungs. Right, Clem?"

Clem continued to mutter under his breath as he buckled the horse into the harness then attached the harness to the buggy. A few minutes later, after Daisy made a spot for Kate behind the front bench where she could move around without risk of falling out, Blake reined the horse back down Main Street.

As they passed the Post Office, a man came out and waved them down. "Heard you were heading out to RosaRoja," he said, approaching the buggy after Blake reined in. "Mind delivering this?" He held out a string-tied bundle of mail.

At first Blake seemed reluctant, but finally he took the parcel and threw it under the seat. Ignoring the other man's thanks, he slapped the reins on the horse's rump, and they were off again.

For the first two hours they made good time. Then they started up into rolling foothills, and from that point on, the road climbed steadily and the horse began to struggle. Several times it stumbled, coughing and wheezing, and Blake had to use the whip to get it moving smartly again.

Daisy felt bad for it. The horse was obviously quite ill, and it angered her that Blake would abuse an animal that was already suffering. "Please don't do that," she said as Blake drew back the whip again.

"You want to get there or not?" The whip popped. The horse crouched away from the sting on its rump and picked up its speed.

"I can't believe the livery didn't have a sounder horse," she complained, aggravated with both the hostler and Blake for their callous disregard of the animal, and with herself for coming along even after she had seen the condition of the poor creature.

"Oh, he's just the horse I wanted," Blake said, then laughed as if he knew something she didn't.

Barely able to hide her growing disgust and irritation, she gave up trying to talk to the man and stared stonily ahead. She wished she had never come.

She wished she had never left San Francisco.

She wished a lot of things.

Disheartened and weary, she tried to ignore the horse's struggles and focused instead on entertaining Kate until finally the exhausted child fell asleep on her blanket behind the bench seat. Daisy was about to doze off as well when Blake's voice roused her.

"How do you know the Wilkins brothers?"

Blinking groggily, she looked around. It felt like they had been traveling forever, but if she read the position of the sun correctly, they still had miles to go. Keeping her voice low so she wouldn't wake Kate, she told Blake the only one of the family she knew was Jack.

"The youngest?"

Daisy nodded.

"Haven't met him. They say he's the wild one."

Wild? The Jack she knew had been brooding. Lost. Almost desperate for something that seemed just beyond his reach. It wasn't until that last bitter argument that she had found out the "something" was another woman.

"Heard he was back," Blake went on, pulling her from her dark memories.

"Back?" Her stomach seemed to drop to her feet. "Jack's at the ranch?"

Something in her voice caused him to look

over at her, his close-set eyes narrowed in speculation. "You didn't know that?"

"Well, I . . ."

"So it's not him you're going to see." With a sly smile, Blake faced forward again. "Interesting."

Jack was at the ranch. Daisy didn't know what to think or how Jack's return would impact her reasons for coming here. She didn't know what name to put to the tumultuous emotions pounding through her. But suddenly the journey that had felt interminable a moment ago now seemed to be moving along too rapidly.

"How much farther is it?' she asked.

"The boundary line? Not far. Things will start happening real soon."

"What do you mean?"

Instead of answering, he leaned forward and started popping the tasseled snapper on the end of the whip against the horse's rump. "Get on! Get on, you!"

The buggy lurched forward as the horse broke into a labored gallop.

Alarmed, Daisy grabbed the roof support for balance. "What are you doing? Why are we going so fast?"

The buggy rocked wildly as they picked up speed. Behind the seat, Kate awoke with a cry. Clinging to the support with her right hand, Daisy reached back with her left to pin the child to the floor as the buggy careened along the rocky road.

"Slow down!" she shouted at Blake. "You'll tip us over!"

He swung faster, the whip whistling through the air, making sharp snapping sounds as it struck the horse.

Up ahead, a man ran out of the brush and into the road. He waved a rifle over his head and shouted something she couldn't hear. She looked at Blake, waiting for him to slow down.

Instead, he laughed and struck the wheezing horse harder.

Daisy tried to grab the whip.

He blocked her with his shoulder, almost knocking her from the buggy.

Two more men ran into the road, shouting, their rifles raised to their shoulders and aimed at the buggy bearing down on them.

Terrified they would start shooting, Daisy made a desperate grab for the reins.

Cursing, Blake jerked his hands aside, causing the horse to stumble. As he sawed on the reins, the horse whipped its head side to side, slinging streamers of bloody foam from its mouth.

"Stop!" Daisy grabbed Blake's arm.

He shook her off, slamming his elbow into her cheek, driving her hard into the roof supports. Behind them, Kate clutched at the backrest, shrieking.

They were almost on the men now. Blake

was laughing, too lost in his own insanity to heed the danger. Panting with terror, her head reeling from the blow, Daisy balled her hand into a fist and drove it as hard as she could into Blake's eye.

He rocked back, arms coming up. The leathers slipped from his grip. The horse stumbled on the loose reins tangled in its legs as one of the men in the road ran alongside and grabbed for the halter.

The buggy shuddered to a stop.

"What'd you do that for?" Blake whipped toward her, teeth bared. "They wouldn't have shot at us, you stupid woman!" Snarling, he drew back his hand.

With a cry, Daisy ducked over Kate.

But instead of the expected blow, she felt the buggy rock. Shouts. Then she looked up to see Blake flying through the air. He landed in a sprawl at the feet of three men who loomed over him with rifles pointed at his face.

The next moments passed in a blur of confusion. The men in the road seemed to know Blake. Soon all four men were shouting.

Daisy just wanted out of the buggy. Grabbing Kate and her valise, she climbed down onto wobbly legs as an older fellow walked around to her side. She drew back, one hand clutching Kate, the other ready to swing her valise at his face.

"Are you all right, ma'am?"

"Yes." Daisy eyed him warily, still shaking from the ordeal. "No thanks to that madman." She glared over to where Blake argued with the other two ranch hands. "I don't know what came over him — he's — he almost got us killed."

The man must have seen her agitation. "It's over now, ma'am. You're safe. The little one okay?"

"Yes." Daisy took a deep breath and let it out. It helped. Feeling calmer, she lowered the valise and asked the man if he was from the ranch.

He was. And after hearing that she was on her way there to see Jack, he introduced himself as Carl Langley and offered to escort her to the house himself.

Daisy hesitated, wondering if this man was any more trustworthy than Blake. He looked kindly. But she'd thought the same about Blake. "And him?"

Langley glanced over at the disheveled man arguing with the others. "No, ma'am. He'll be heading back to Val Rosa." The way he said it told Daisy he didn't care whether Blake made it back in one piece or not. She just hoped the horse would.

"Can you ride?" Langley asked. "It's only about ten more miles."

Only? "Yes." Although it would be difficult holding Kate, Daisy would manage. At this

127

point she would do anything to get away from Blake and get this ghastly journey over with. After she retrieved the pouch and Kate's blanket from the buggy — as well as the bundle of mail, which she slipped into her pouch — she followed Langley toward the rope-strung corral situated quite a distance from the road.

As they walked away, Blake yelled after them, "You tell that bastard he'd better pay up or I'll have his smelter, his mines, and his ranch. You tell him that, Langley!"

Langley continued on, giving no indication that he'd heard.

At the corral, Kate was delighted to be able to totter around while they waited for the horses to be readied. Once he'd secured Daisy's belongings behind his saddle, Langley helped Daisy to mount, handed up a squirming Kate, and they were off, leaving Blake behind to work his own way out of the mess he'd made.

Ten more miles. This had to be one of the worst days of her life.

It was almost dark when they finally rode up the rutted road toward an imposing house built of log and stone. Daisy was so exhausted her legs almost buckled beneath her when she slid off the horse. With the pouch over one shoulder and her sleeping daughter resting against the other, she followed Langley up the steps. As they crossed the porch, the front door opened.

A tall, redheaded woman with a baby on each hip stepped out. One glance at Daisy's bruised face, and her look of curiosity became one of concern.

"Oh, you poor thing," she said in a cultured voice with an English accent. "Langley, bring her things inside, please. Come along, dear." And before Daisy's sluggish mind registered what was happening, the woman was herding her through the entry, past a staircase, and down into a large room dominated by a huge rock fireplace. "Someone get Molly and the Ortegas. Where's Brady?"

Almost before the words were out, a tall, lean man appeared, trailed by a redheaded boy of three or four years. Close on their heels came two young Mexican women, who took the babies from their mother and left the room.

"Step aside, Jessica," the man ordered, moving to face Daisy.

The woman blinked at his back, her expression one of surprise. "Brady . . . ?"

Brady. The oldest brother. The one Jack had called bossy and hardheaded. Daisy could see why. The boy must be his son, Ben, and the redhead, Jessica, his wife, Her Ladyship. She was every bit as striking as Jack had said she was.

The man loomed over Daisy. "Who are you?"

129

She frowned up at him, taken aback by his angry tone. But before she could respond, the redhead grabbed his arm. "Brady, what is wrong with you? Can't you see she —"

He whipped around, cutting her off mid-sentence. "She was with Blake. They tried to run through the quarantine with a sick horse. I need to know why. Now step aside, Jessica." Without waiting for a response, he turned back to Daisy. "Who are you and why are you here?"

The boy planted himself at his father's side, hands on his hips. "Yeah, why?"

"Ben, hush," his mother scolded.

Fighting to calm her own rising temper, Daisy retrieved the packet of mail from her pouch. "We were asked to give you this." She thrust it toward him, mildly surprised to see her hand was shaking. It would, she supposed, after almost a week without sleep, hardly any food, being knocked in the head by a madman, and now having to deal with this bully. Still, she hated the sign of weakness.

He tossed the packet onto a nearby table. "Why were you with Blake?"

"Why," the boy echoed.

"Ben!"

"He offered me a ride."

Kate must have sensed her distress. She gave a soft whimper and moved restlessly against Daisy's neck. Daisy patted her back in reassurance, hoping to forestall a frightful outcry should Kate awaken to find herself surrounded by a roomful of strangers. "But the real reason I'm here," she went on, "is to see your brother Jack."

His eyes narrowed — odd-colored eyes, almost turquoise in color, and as sharp and cold as two chips of ice.

Jack's were warmer, Daisy recalled. More of a smoky hue with sooty rings around the irises, and framed by dark brown lashes and brows. A striking contrast against his sun-browned skin and wheat-colored hair.

"Why do you want to see Jack?" his brother demanded.

Before she could answer, Kate straightened in Daisy's arms. Twisting around, she looked at Brady Wilkins.

His face went slack with astonishment. "Holy Christ."

"Actually, her name is Kate," Daisy snapped.

"Hellfire," the little boy said, then seeing the menace in his mother's eyes, quickly fled the room.

His father continued to stare in shock at Kate.

Jessica moved closer. She looked at Kate, then at Daisy. "Oh my." A smile spread across her freckled face. "She is absolutely beautiful. Kate, you say?"

Daisy smiled tentatively back, warmed by

this first show of welcome since she had entered the house. "Katherine is her full name. But I call her Kate."

"Kate. It suits her." The woman brushed a lock of blond hair off Kate's brow. "Welcome, little Kate. I'm Jessica."

Kate held out her stuffed cat. "Titty."

Jessica marveled over the ragged toy. "I have a kitty too. Would you like to see?" When Kate nodded, Jessica glanced at Daisy. "May I hold her?"

Hesitant to relinquish her child to a stranger, yet not wanting to offend the only person who had shown her kindness, Daisy reluctantly passed Kate over into Jessica's arms. "She's tired. She may act up. It's been a long, stressful day."

"Poor dear," Jessica crooned. "I'll wager you're hungry as well." Elbowing the befuddled Brady Wilkins out of the way, she carried Kate over to the tall bank of windows beside the fireplace. "See the kitty?" She pointed to a cat perched on the porch rail, licking its paw. "We can't let him inside because he makes Penny sneeze. But perhaps tomorrow you might want to go out and pet him?"

Kate grinned. Lifting a pudgy arm, she waved her toy. "See Titty."

Brady Wilkins seemed to come out of his trance. Turning back from his shocked perusal of Kate, he stared hard at Daisy. "You're sure she's —"

"Jack's daughter?" Daisy glared at him, liking this man less by the moment. "Yes, I'm sure. Aren't you?"

"Does he know about . . ."

"Kate?" Couldn't he even say her name? "No, he doesn't."

"Holy Christamighty hell."

"Brady," came a singsong reprimand from the window. "Not in front of the children."

"Well . . . hell."

The front door slammed. Footsteps crossed the entry, then two men stepped into the room — a huge dark-haired man who must have been the middle brother, Hank, and beside him, the man she had come to see. Jack.

Her heart thudding in her chest and her stomach knotted so tight it hurt to breathe, Daisy watched him walk toward her. His hair was lighter. His skin darker. His easy rolling gait had given way to a limp. But those eyes . . .

"Heard we have company," he said.

His brother rounded on him. "Not we. *You.*"

"Me?"

Daisy studied him, searching those well-remembered features for a spark of recognition.

It never came.

The bounder doesn't know me. He doesn't

133

have any notion of who I am.

The humiliation of it almost choked her. She had given herself to a man who had no memory of it. She had borne his child, and he didn't even remember her name. God, what a fool she was.

For a moment she thought her knees might fold beneath her.

"Well, hello," Jack said, flashing the smile that had been the ruination of her heart, her will, the last shreds of her common sense.

"Hello, Jack," she managed to say.

He looked a little more worn, but the puffiness of too much drink and too little rest had been replaced by honed muscle, and that angry, frantic look in his eyes had mellowed into something that looked more like weary resignation. He had matured. Yet he was even more beautiful to her now than he had ever been.

And he didn't even know who she was.

Humiliation turned to fury as those eyes she could never forget — the same smoky blue, dark-ringed eyes that looked at her out of her daughter's face — swept over her in total confusion.

"Have we met?" he asked, a frown forming between the dark brows.

"You don't remember me, do you?" Daisy's lips were so tight with anger she could hardly form the words. "Two and a half years ago. In San Francisco."

His frown deepened. His gaze moved over her again, then jerked back to pause on her breasts. "Wait. San Francisco. Daisy!" He looked up with a wide grin. "You changed your hair. Or something."

Her breasts? He remembered her breasts but not her?

Fury exploded. And that was when, for the second time that day and only the second time in her life, Daisy struck a man in the face with her fist.

Jack staggered back.

The room erupted in chaos — Brady and Jack arguing, Hank pulling both toward the hall, Jessica issuing orders, and Kate shrieking.

It was too much.

Defeated, Daisy sank onto the edge of a chair, dropped her head into her hands, and wept.

SEVEN

Jack sprawled in one of the chairs in front of Brady's desk. Hank took the other while Brady paced before the unlit fireplace, muttering.

"I don't understand why she hit me," Jack mumbled through the kerchief pressed to his bleeding lip.

Brady sneered at him. "You can't be that dumb."

"Why? What did I do?"

"Lost your touch with women, for one thing." Chuckling, Hank propped his boots on the corner of Brady's desk. "An amazing thing."

"It's not funny," Jack muttered.

"Rampaging women rarely are."

Brady stopped pacing to loom over him. "You really don't know, do you? You have no idea why a woman would drag her baby all the way from San Francisco to see you."

Jack blinked up at him. He vaguely remembered Jessica by the porch door, holding a kid. He'd thought it was one of the twins. "That was Daisy's baby?"

"No, you stupid bastard! It was yours!"

The rag slipped from Jack's hand. "Mine?"

"And hers," Hank reminded them. "It takes two —"

"Shut up," Brady snapped.

"I'm just saying —"

"Well, don't."

"Wait a minute." Jack raised a hand like that might stem the confused thoughts flooding into his mind. "Who said it was my kid? 'Cause they'd be lying. I don't have any kids. If I did, I'd know. Right?" He looked from one brother to the other, expecting confirmation.

One stared furiously back. The other grinned. Neither spoke.

"Jesus." Jack slumped back into the chair. "It can't be my kid."

He replayed the scene in his mind. The woman — Daisy — glaring at him, even after he gave her his best smile. Brady looking thunderous, which wasn't that unusual, and Jessica over at the window with a baby in her arms. His baby?

How could that be?

Feeling a trickle, he lifted the kerchief to his split lip. "Why didn't she just tell me, instead of hitting me?"

"Hell, you're lucky I don't hit you too," Brady said.

"Why? What did I do, for Crissakes?"

"Other than getting her pregnant then leaving her?" Hank asked, that smile still tugging at his lips.

Ignoring him, Brady said, "You didn't know her, that's what you did. She shows up with a kid — *your* kid — all the way from San Francisco, and you didn't even know who she was."

"Only at first."

"After you looked at her . . . you know . . ." Brady waved a hand in the direction of Jack's chest. "When Jessica saw you do that, she almost hit you herself."

"They are nice," Hank mused. "I've always appreciated a fine bosom."

Brady rounded on him. "Would you shut the hell up! You're not helping."

"What's to help?" Hank asked mildly. "The deed's done. Our little brother is well and truly caught. And by a woman who might actually keep him in line."

"Is that what this is about?" Jack was stunned. "She's upset just because I looked at her tits?"

"Best not let Jessica hear you say that," Hank advised. "She's got a whole list of words we can't use, and I'm pretty sure 'tits' is on it."

"Christ, Jack!" Brady stomped across the room and back, hands planted low on his hips, chin jutting. "How could you go off and leave a woman after you got her pregnant? I raised you to be a better man than that."

Jack recognized the stance and the tone, but he was no longer as susceptible to it as he'd been when he'd left three years ago, so he managed to hold his temper in check. "In the first place, you didn't raise me. In the second, I didn't know she was pregnant when I left. And third, how do we even know the kid is mine?"

Brady threw his hands up in disbelief. "Did you even look at her?"

"The kid's name is Kate," Hank reminded them. "A nice name, I think."

"I was too busy trying not to bleed on your wife's fancy rug," Jack retorted, his control slipping. *The kid. A daughter. Kate.* The name felt odd in his head. The whole idea of her — of Daisy — of being a father — felt odd.

"When did you leave San Francisco?" Hank, serious now, spoke in that calm, logical tone he used when Jack and Brady started in on each other.

Despite his quips, Jack was glad Hank was there. He had worked too hard to pull himself out of the role of being Brady's little brother, the wild one, the irresponsible hothead. He'd cleared that chip off his shoulder years ago and didn't want to be goaded into putting it back on. Tasting blood again, he dabbed at his lip. "It was after Elena went to the abbey."

139

"How long after?"

Jack shrugged. That time was a dark spot in his memory, the days running together in an alcoholic haze. Thinking back on it, he realized the only good thing about that bleak period was Daisy. The little fool had hoped to save him. But even she hadn't been strong enough to pull him out of the hole he'd dug for himself, and if he hadn't come out of his stupor long enough to sign on to that clipper bound for Australia, he would probably be buried in it right now.

"A month," he finally said. "Maybe two. I was drinking a lot."

"Apparently not enough," Brady muttered.

Jack checked the rag and saw that the bleeding had slowed. He tossed the cloth onto Brady's desk and looked up with a cold smile that stung his lip. "There was never enough."

"Exactly when," Hank persisted.

Jack gave it some thought, but still couldn't come up with a specific date. "In late fall. The grays hadn't migrated south yet, but the whalers were already rigging up."

Hank glanced at Brady. "It fits."

Jack sighed and rubbed his temple where a headache was beginning to form. None of this made sense to him. Daisy showing up, Elena still insisting on the church, and now a daughter he didn't know he had. He would

140

have been better off following the China trade.

"You'll do the right thing."

Dropping his hand, Jack looked up at his oldest brother, a little irritated but not really shocked that Brady was still trying to run his life. Maybe he couldn't help himself. Maybe all those years managing the ranch and his brothers had warped him somehow, made him think nothing could get along without his supervision.

"You're right, Brady. I will do the right thing. But it'll be what's right for me and Daisy and . . . and the little one. Not you."

Something flashed in his brother's icy eyes. Something angry and sad at the same time. "I'm not your enemy, Jack. I never have been."

Jack continued to look at him, letting his doubt show.

"Does make you wonder, though," Hank said, cutting into the staring contest. "How it is we attract such violent women."

Brady turned to glare at him. "Jessica's not violent."

"She set Sancho on fire. Seems pretty violent to me."

"She had reason. And what about Molly killing Hennessey?"

Hank waved the comment aside. "I'm just saying our wives are not females to cross and Jack's woman seems no different. So far they

141

haven't killed us, but the way Jack is going, he could be the first. He should take note, is all."

"She's not my woman," Jack muttered.

"She must have been at one time," Brady said.

"What I want to know," Hank cut in before Jack could rise to the bait, "is if she didn't know you were at the ranch, why is she here?"

"She didn't know I was back?"

"Langley says not."

Jack decided he needed to talk to Langley. He needed to find out more about what happened and about that man she came with — that Blake fellow. One of the hands said he'd tried to run the quarantine and threatened to hit Daisy before the boys dragged him from the buggy. No matter what Daisy might have done — even socking a man in the mouth just for looking at her, ah, chest — there was never a reason for a man to use his fists on a woman.

"So if it wasn't to see you," Hank went on, "why did she come?"

"Maybe she expects Jack to marry her," Brady said.

"Or she's hoping to leave the kid here," Hank added. "But why now, after all this time?"

Good question. Jack rose. "I guess I'd better find out."

"You want my gun?" Hank called as Jack

stepped into the hall.

"Keep it. Or better yet, use it on Brady."

He tracked Daisy to the bedroom across from his. She sat in a rocker by the window while Molly worked on her bruised cheek and Jessica stood over her, twisting her hands together like she did when she was worried or upset. Luckily Elena was still at her evening prayers and didn't yet know about this fiasco.

The women were deep in whispered conversation and didn't hear his approach, so he paused in the doorway to look around.

The room had already been set up as a nursery with a crib, a trunk loaded with baby clothes, a basket of books, and more toys than any one kid could play with. The baby — his daughter, supposedly — was asleep in the crib, snuffling softly under a blanket with puffy pink bunnies sewn all over it.

"Money?" Jessica whispered in a tone that drew his attention. "You came here to extort money from us?"

Jack frowned. This was about money, not the kid?

"Not extort." Daisy winced as Molly spread yellow ointment on a tender spot. "Borrow. I would have paid back every cent."

"Would have." Jessica stopped working her hands and crossed her arms at her waist. Jack remembered that pose too. Any second she would start tapping a toe. "Does that mean you no longer need the money?"

"Oh, I still need it. But now that Jack is here, I'll get it from him. You can be sure of it."

A threat? She was threatening him?

Molly began returning the jars and ointments to her black satchel. "Why do you need money?"

"For Kate. For me." Daisy slumped back into the rocker, her shoulders drooping with weariness. Brushing her fingertips over the swollen knuckles on her right hand, she added, "To help us get a new start."

She looked defeated. Hopeless. A sharp contrast to the pretty woman he vaguely remembered as being so full of spirit and laughter. And passion. He recalled that most of all. That, and her chest.

He didn't like the change. And he didn't like the way Jessica was badgering her with questions when it was obvious Daisy was so tired she could hardly hold up her head. He needed to end this.

"It's a long story," Daisy said in a flat voice as Jack limped into the room.

"And an interesting one, I'll warrant," he cut in, smiling all around.

Her gaze flew to his.

The anger in it gave him pause, but he pushed ahead anyway. "And a story I'd like to hear. Maybe later. Evening, ladies." He nodded to his sisters-in-law. "If you're fin-

144

ished here, I'd like to talk to Daisy."

In a flutter of skirts, Jessica rushed over to plant herself between him and Daisy. Pinning him with that steely stare he had once found a bit unsettling, she said, "Perhaps later, Jack. She's quite tired. I think it would be best if we let her rest awhile, don't you?"

"No, Jessica, I don't," he said, still smiling. "Be sure to close the door on your way out."

Another staring contest. Jack won this one handily.

As his brothers' wives reluctantly departed, Daisy remained seated, watching him with a wary, tense expression, her face pale except for red-rimmed eyes and the bruise marring her cheek. He wondered if Blake had hit her after all, but didn't ask, not wanting the added distraction until he said what he came to say. A little unnerved by her stillness and the anger that seemed to radiate from her like heat from a stove, he wandered around the room, trying to gather his thoughts.

Despite the time they had spent together, he and Daisy were almost strangers. He wasn't sure how to act, or what to say, or what she wanted from him. An unusual circumstance for him, especially around women.

And then there was the kid. Kate. His daughter.

And Elena.

Jesus, what a mess.

145

Looking down, he was surprised to find himself standing over the crib. Curiosity getting the better of him, he gently lifted the corner of the blanket.

She was sprawled on her stomach, a well-worn stuffed animal tucked under her arm. She snored. He sometimes did, too, but that didn't mean anything.

He studied her sleeping face, but saw nothing in it to mark her as his. It was just a face. Small and round with dark lashes that looked odd with her blond curls.

A lot of people had that coloring. It didn't automatically mean she was his.

Carefully lowering the blanket back over the tiny form, he turned to find Daisy glaring at him with those strange yellow-hazel eyes.

He'd forgotten her eyes, and how they seemed to cut right through him when she was mad, and pull him in when she wasn't. They were the kind of eyes that hinted at things, that promised to warm up at the right time and place.

Which this wasn't.

Moving closer so they could talk without waking the baby, he folded his arms over his chest and spoke in the same calm, unthreatening tone he used with sailors aboard ship. "First, you'll tell me why you're convinced this baby is mine. Then you'll explain why you're here and why you need money. All right?" He finished with a smile to show her

146

how reasonable he was being.

"Go to hell, Jack."

Taken aback and a bit chilled by the frost in her voice, he tried to calm her ire by giving her his best smile again, even though it stung his lip. "Now, Daisy."

It seemed to have as little effect as it had before.

"I'm tired, Jack. I don't want to fight with you right now. Please leave."

Damn hardheaded woman.

Jack studied her, wondering how to reach past that wall of anger. He didn't want to fight either. He just wanted answers. But he could see how brittle and shaky she was, so venting his frustration with a sigh, he nodded. "All right, Daisy. I'll go. After you answer one question for me." He glanced at the crib. "You're sure . . . ?" He let the sentence hang.

"That Kate's your daughter?"

He could see he'd upset her again, and was sorry for it. But he had to hear the answer from her and he had to look into her eyes when she gave it.

Tears threatened but she blinked them away. "I was a saloon singer, Jack. Not a whore."

"I never said —"

"No, you didn't. But you're not sure, are you? Even now you're sifting through that whiskey-soaked memory of yours, wondering about it and thinking if I was a whore, that

147

might let you off the hook."

When he didn't respond — was too ashamed to, in fact, because to do so might reveal how close to the truth her accusation had come — she continued in a voice as cold and hard as ice.

"You were the only man I ever took to my bed, Jack. Whether you believe that or not, be assured Kate is your daughter. I hope you will take responsibility for her. If not, after meeting some of your family, I feel confident they will."

Anger shot through him. He definitely didn't want his family involved in this. "Daisy —"

"No more." She held up a hand to stop him. "That's all I'm going to say for now, Jack. It's been a horrid day and I'm tired. If you still have questions, we can talk more tomorrow before I leave. Good night."

Whirling, Jack limped from the room. *Damn hardheaded woman.*

He spent a dismal evening with his family.

Supper wasn't so bad, although it was uncharacteristically quiet — or as quiet as a meal could be with six kids and a talkative old Scotsman yammering nonstop. The food was tasty, though, and a welcome change from months of sea rations, so Jack ate heartily, knowing he had a long night ahead.

As soon as the kids headed upstairs and the

Scotsman went scampering after Consuelo — something Jack was afraid to think about too much — the rest of the family and Elena retired for the inquisition in front of the fire in the main room.

It was awkward with Elena there, insomuch as the whole time he'd been pining over her, he'd apparently been busily impregnating Daisy. An embarrassing thing to have to admit to. Luckily, since everyone already knew about it, he didn't have to do so aloud. In fact, he didn't say much of anything, since there wasn't much he remembered.

Overdrinking was a poor excuse, but it was all he had. Once his family realized they'd wrung out of him all the information they could, they moved on to a heated discussion of how best to rectify "Jack's unfortunate situation" — Jessica's words. Brady's were less kindly.

Everyone had an opinion on what he should do and how he should live his life, ranging from the escape to Africa, to marriage, to suicide. Although the suggestion that he eat a bullet might have come from within his own mind. But as the evening wore on and on, it began to sound like one of the better options.

The only people who didn't offer advice were Hank, who wasn't much of a talker anyway; Daisy, who had taken an early supper in her room then retired for the night; and Elena, who let her varying expressions of

149

shock, dismay, and disappointment speak for her.

Jack could hardly look at her. Not just because of the hurt, bewildered looks she sent him, but because of his own rising anger and his intense desire to say, "This is partly your fault too. You drove me to it."

Of course, that wasn't true. None of this was her fault. Jack knew that. But when a man is faced with the dire results of his own baseness and stupidity, it always helped to mentally point a finger at someone else.

But mostly throughout his family's discussions of his future, he remained silent, and after a while their chatter faded to a distant buzz in his head as he sat holding his untouched glass of whiskey and staring into the fire.

He was a father.

A difficult concept to get his mind around. It redefined him and created a whole new way of looking at things. It altered his entire future.

He was a father. A man with responsibilities. A man who was no longer answerable only to himself.

It scared the hell out of him.

At midnight a reprieve was granted when his family decided it was time to retire. With sad looks and murmured promises to resume discussions the next day — oh, joy — they filed solemnly past like mourners at a wake, leaving Jack still sprawled in his chair, still nursing his full glass of whiskey.

Only Hank stayed behind. Sending his wife on without him, he began digging at the dying fire with a metal poker.

Jack waited. Hank didn't normally talk much. But when he did have something to say, it was usually worth listening to.

After he'd gotten the fire going again, Hank hung the poker back on its peg, rested his elbow on the mantel, and looked down at Jack. "Remember Melanie Kinderly from the fort?"

"I do." And not fondly. Melanie and her mother had been on the stagecoach with Jessica when it had crashed over a bluff. She had stayed at the ranch while her mother recovered, and during that time she and Hank had developed a strong liking for each other. In fact, when Jack left three years ago, Hank had been planning to follow Melanie to the fort that her father commanded. Jack had wondered what had happened, but since Hank seemed so happy with Molly, he hadn't asked.

"I went up there to court her," Hank went on. "I figured it was time I settled down, and she was pretty and accommodating, so why not? She seemed taken with the idea at first, then all of a sudden she's marrying a soldier there at the fort."

"She always seemed a little stupid."

"Not stupid. Just ignorant. And easily led. I saw that as an advantage, thinking it would make her a biddable wife."

Jack preferred a little more fire himself. Someone capable enough to carry her own bullets, as it were.

"After I married Molly, I came across Melanie in Val Rosa. We talked for a minute, and I realized then how close I had come to making a costly mistake."

Jack nodded in understanding. He preferred Molly too.

"Well." With a sigh, Hank pushed away from the mantel. "Good night then."

"What? Wait."

Hank turned to look at him.

"That's it?" Jack made a vague gesture, sloshing whiskey over the rim of his glass. "The end of the story? No sage advice on avoiding costly mistakes or marrying women who aren't biddable?"

Hank shrugged.

"Then why the hell did you tell me all that? What's the point?"

"There is no point. I just thought you might be curious about what happened between me and Melanie but didn't want to ask in front of Molly."

"Jesus, Hank. There has to be a point."

"Oh." Hank scratched at the dark stubble under his chin for a moment then said, "If you've got feelings for a woman, you ought

152

to know why. How's that?"

Now Jack was even more confused. Why couldn't his brother ever talk in a straight line? "Are you talking about Daisy? Because I don't have feelings for Daisy. I mean, I have feelings, but not the kind that —"

Hank sighed.

"Not Daisy?"

"You going to drink that?" He nodded toward the glass in Jack's hand. "Hate to waste such good whiskey."

"Elena then. You're talking about Elena, right?"

Leaning over, Hank plucked the glass from Jack's unresisting grip, tossed back the contents, and set the empty glass on the mantel. He belched then yawned. "I give Jessica credit. This Scotch whiskey is one change I really like. 'Night."

After Hank left, Jack sat for a time staring into the fire and trying to figure out what his brother had been trying to tell him. Daisy was definitely not biddable. His swollen lip was proof of that. And he'd already made a costly mistake, which was why he was in the situation he was in now. But in not accepting Kate as his daughter, was he committing another?

Or maybe Hank was talking about Elena after all.

She was definitely biddable. And kind and generous. And she would never swing a fist at him, even if he did look at her chest. Which he almost never had. Which, now that he thought about it, seemed a little odd.

So why did he have such strong feelings for her? Why couldn't he let her go like she wanted? And why couldn't he remember a thing about her chest?

Hell if he knew.

With a sigh, he rose and headed up the stairs.

Outside the door to his bedroom he paused, thinking he might have heard a noise coming from the kid's room across from his, some unknown and unidentifiable sound that he should probably investigate.

Moving quietly, he stepped across the hall and eased open the door.

The room was dark except for the faint moonlight coming through the thin curtain. The kid was snoring again. Jack went over to make sure she wasn't suffocating, and found her sprawled on her back, arms thrown wide, palms up. She had the tiniest hands, yet every finger seemed perfect. Her skin looked like pale marble, and he wanted to touch her cheek but was afraid it would wake her. Instead, he tucked her toy cat against her side in case she woke up and looked for it.

She. The kid. His daughter. Kate.

An odd feeling, like a small whirlwind, moved through his chest. For a moment he experienced that same jolt of exhilaration and heart-pounding panic he'd felt last year just before he'd dived off the bow of the clipper into the cool, crystal waters off Tasmania. He was spiraling again toward unknown waters. But this was his most terrifying plunge yet.

What in God's name was he going to do with a daughter?

EIGHT

Kate's cries awoke her.

Even though Daisy was still groggy with sleep, the part of her mind that never rested — the mother part — came instantly alert, taking only a fraction of a heartbeat to register that the cry was not one of distress, but impatience.

I want up. I'm hungry. Come get me. Now.

Staring dully at the patterns of light and shadow across the beamed ceiling, Daisy waited for her body to wake up. She felt horrid, aching in all kinds of places from that wretched buggy ride and her first jaunt on horseback in several years. Her head throbbed, her bruised cheek hurt, her throat burned from all the tears she had shed into her pillow, and the last thing she wanted to do was go out and face the Wilkins family.

The dream that had brought her here now seemed like a cruel hoax, another harsh reminder — *it's not going to happen, Daisy. Give it up. Go back.*

But back where? San Francisco? To another saloon? A brothel? Not with the death of Bill Johnson hanging over her head. She couldn't return to Quebec either. The farm had been sold long ago. There was nothing left there for her.

No, she couldn't go back. She'd come too far to give up now. But she hadn't thought it would be so hard.

Kate's wails grew louder.

Probably couldn't find Kitty. With a sigh, Daisy threw back the covers and sat up. She sat for a moment, scanning the luxuries surrounding her. Stone fireplace, upholstered chairs, thick rugs, a balcony, and an indoor water closet with a hot water bath. She had never been in a room so grand. These people were rich. Surely they would help her if Jack wouldn't.

Jack.

Even now, despite the anger that still smoldered within her, the pull was so strong that just knowing he was near made her thoughts scatter. He was part of her now, in her bones and marrow, forever in her memory as the first man she had ever loved.

And he didn't even remember her. How sad was that?

Abruptly Kate's crying stopped.

Daisy tensed, listening.

Silence.

Concerned but not yet alarmed, she rose.

The room was cold, making her shiver beneath the thin cotton of her gown. Since she had no robe, she pulled on her worn gabardine coat and padded across to the door that led into Kate's adjoining room. Quietly she eased it open, hoping to find that her daughter had fallen back to sleep and she had a few more moments to herself.

Instead, she saw Jack, wearing nothing but trousers and a bemused look, hunkered on his heels beside the crib, engaged in a silent staring match with Kate through the slats.

Surprised and wondering what he was up to, Daisy paused in the doorway, watching him slowly walk two fingers up the side of the mattress and through the slats to poke Kate's toe.

Kate looked at her toe, then at him.

He withdrew his fingers just as slowly, walking them back down the side of the mattress and out of sight.

For a moment, nothing. Then Kate inched her foot forward in silent invitation, her gaze pinned to the spot where his hand had disappeared.

The fingers came up again to poke her toe.

Kate jerked her foot back.

The fingers went away.

Hesitantly, Kate slid her foot forward again. This time when the fingers came up to poke her toe, she giggled.

Daisy was utterly amazed. Not only that

Jack would engage in such fanciful play, but that Kate would allow it.

But then, Jack instinctively knew how to charm.

Bracing herself, she stepped into the room.

Kate saw her and grinned. "Ma-ma-ma-ma."

Rising in one fluid motion, Jack turned to face her. There was such a mix of expressions on his face Daisy couldn't tell what he was thinking, which was rare with Jack.

"What are you doing in here?" she asked more harshly than she'd intended.

"I heard her crying and came in to see if she was okay." A smile started, spreading from one corner of his mouth to the other until his entire face was involved, his eyes crinkling at the corners and his dark brows slanting upward over the bridge of his nose and his fine teeth showing white against the dark stubble on his sun-darkened face. "I believe it now," he said in a wondering voice. "I wasn't sure but when I came in and she looked at me, I knew. It was like looking into my own eyes, Daisy. She truly is my daughter."

She let out a breath, not aware that she'd been holding it until her lungs demanded air. "I told you she was." Shutting her mind to the lure of that smile, Daisy pushed past him to lift her daughter from the crib. "Thank you for your concern, but she's fine. You needn't stay."

When he didn't move, she had to step around him to carry Kate over to the trunk of clothes. As she passed by, the scent of him wafted over her — that tangy, musky, morning scent she remembered from those crisp fall dawns when the fog pressed against the windowpanes, narrowing the world to just the two of them waking up in each other's arms.

The memory of it brought an almost physical pain.

She felt him watching as she knelt beside the trunk to sift through the baby items Jessica had generously left for Kate's use. At first Daisy had wanted to refuse, but the enticement of seeing her daughter clothed in dresses as lovely as she deserved proved too much.

Pulling a peach dimity with a satin sash from the pile, she held it up to Kate. It looked beautiful with her rosy cheeks and blond curls and appeared to be the right size. Setting Kate on the floor, she began stripping off the baby's nightclothes.

"You can't leave," Jack said.

She tilted her head to look at him, prepared to argue the point. But he wasn't even looking at her. He was totally focused on Kate, and his expression stilled her words. She'd seen anger, grief, desire, laughter, even drunken befuddlement on his face. But never this raw, open vulnerability.

Jack was incapable of dissembling. He might not always be wise or deliberate in his thinking, or was sometimes too ready to take chances or follow his whims, but he was always honest in his emotions. The face he presented to the world was a true reflection of what he felt. And what he was showing now as he looked at his daughter almost made Daisy weep.

Had he ever looked at her with such joy and wonder and yearning?

Ignoring Kate's squirms and giggles, she hurriedly dressed her in fresh pantalettes. "I can't stay, Jack." Not with a man who didn't love her, who didn't even remember her, who only wanted her here now because of her daughter.

"Why not?"

He walked toward her, his limp less noticeable than the day before. But even with that small imperfection, he moved with all the strength and grace she remembered. Seeing him without his shirt, she realized he was more muscular now and leaner. But she would have known those wide sloping shoulders, the long curve of that back, those strong hands even in her sleep. Especially in her sleep.

Hunkering down beside her, he reached out to twine his finger in one of Kate's curls.

Grinning, Kate tipped her head back to

watch his hand.

"Stay. Just for a while." Turning his head, he looked directly into Daisy's eyes and smiled. "Please."

That was one of his greatest allures. When Jack looked at a woman, his attention was total, as if she were the only person in the room, the only person of importance. It was flattering and intimate and addictive. Even knowing it was the way he treated every woman, it sent a thrill through her. And that smile . . .

Daisy forced her attention back to dressing Kate.

"You can't take her from me, Daisy. Not yet."

It's not you he wants, she reminded herself. *Once he wins over Kate's wary heart, he'll probably walk away from her too.*

A feeling of desperation seized Daisy. She wanted to run. She wanted to stay. She wanted him to move back and give her space to breathe.

"I have to go," she said.

"Give me a little more time. That's all."

"I have plans, Jack." When he didn't respond, she looked up to see his expression wasn't so kindly now. And she knew that within the last few seconds something valuable had been lost.

"I'll pay you. I know you need money. How much will it take to keep you here for a month?"

"Jack —"

"How much? I'll pay whatever you ask."

Kate, sensing the rising tension, began to fuss again, her smoky blue eyes darting from her mother to her father. Daisy tried to reassure her with a smile, even though she felt like crying herself.

"Just a few weeks," he argued. "That's all."

"Yes. All right. Two weeks." At that moment she would have agreed to anything to put some space between them. "Then I have to go."

With a curt nod, he rose and left the room.

As the door closed behind him, she took in a shaky breath, telling herself she had done the right thing. She had over six weeks before the opera company left for Rome. Surely she could allow Kate a little of that time with her father.

And maybe by then she could finally put the man out of her life.

After she got herself and Kate washed and dressed, they headed downstairs. It was slow going because Kate insisted on walking without help, inching toward the edge of each tread before hopping down to the next.

Daisy didn't mind. She dreaded the day to come — the curious stares, the probing questions, the speculative glances. She was happy to put it off as long as possible.

The main room was empty, the house quiet

except for the low murmur of voices coming through an open arched doorway on the far side of the dining area. Daisy assumed it led into the kitchen. After Molly had tended her bruises last night, she hadn't gone back downstairs for supper, but had taken her meal in her room. Mentally preparing herself, she took Kate's hand and walked through the archway.

It was the grandest kitchen Daisy had ever seen, big enough to handle a dozen workers and equipped lavishly with a huge cookstove, two sinks, and enough cabinets to store the belongings of three families. In the center of the room stood a well-used dining table, and seated at the far end were Jessica and Molly, speaking quietly over a plate of muffins and two steaming teacups.

Daisy had no doubt they were discussing her and Kate. Pasting on a smile, she said, "Good morning."

Their heads came up. But instead of guilty looks, they gave Daisy welcoming smiles. At least Jessica did. Molly was more reserved, not from a lack of friendliness, Daisy suspected, but more as part of her nature. Less a talker than an observer, Molly had eyes that missed nothing, much like those of her husband, the towering and intense second brother, Hank. Even though Daisy hadn't spent much time with that couple the previous day, she sensed they were both highly intelligent. Molly certainly seemed more logical in her thinking than Jessica, who appeared a bit high-strung and emotional in comparison.

Daisy liked them. With the exception of Brady, the overly protective, rather intimidating oldest brother, she liked all of the family she had met. Her unannounced arrival with Kate had been a shock, but they had handled it surprisingly well, and she was grateful.

"How did you sleep?" Jessica rose to add another plate and mug to the table. "We sent the children out to the barn to see the new foals so they wouldn't wake you. They can create quite a stir running through the house."

"Children?" Daisy glanced inquiringly from one woman to the other. She vaguely remembered Jessica answering the door with two babies on her hips, but didn't remember if Molly had any.

"Four." Jessica sent a quick look at Molly, who was staring fixedly at Kate. "A son, a daughter, and twin boys. Four years, two, and one. In that order."

"How wonderful." Smiling, Daisy waited for Molly to respond.

Molly's return smile seemed a bit forced. "Only my niece and nephew. So far."

Sensing she'd blundered onto a sore subject, Daisy busied herself pulling out a chair. After settling Kate on her lap, she said, "I want to thank you again, Jessica, for the lovely dresses." She beamed proudly at her daughter. "Kate has never looked so pretty."

"Oh, I think that child would look beautiful no matter what she wore." Bustling about, Jessica soon had a chair with an elevated seat for Kate and the ever-present kitty, a wide bib tied around Kate's neck, and a bowl of oatmeal set before her. "Now what would you like, Daisy? Coffee or tea?"

She took coffee and a muffin. While Kate gobbled her breakfast, Daisy answered Jessica's and Molly's questions as best she could, or at least the ones she felt comfortable answering.

She was hesitant to reveal her opportunity to train with Madame Scarlatti. Part of it was pride — she didn't feel she had to justify her reasons for needing help from her child's father. Jack had a responsibility to Kate too.

But she also didn't want to open herself to ridicule. Few people understood her passion for music. Most viewed her singing abilities as a nice entertaining talent but hardly the kind of thing one should devote one's life to. Other than her mother and Mr. Markham, no one had ever taken her music that seriously. Not even her father. Jack knew her only as a saloon singer. He might not be willing to give her money if he knew it was to be used to hire a nursemaid for his daughter while her mother traveled through Europe performing on stage. She couldn't risk it.

And she certainly couldn't tell them that she was fleeing San Francisco because she'd killed a man.

So she evaded any pointed questions about why she needed the money by explaining she had lost her position and her place of residence and needed funds to hold her and Kate over until she reestablished herself. Mostly that was true. And mostly Jessica accepted it. Daisy wasn't so sure about Molly.

As they were cleaning up the dishes, an accented voice said, *"Buenas días, niñita."*

Daisy turned from the sink to see a woman she hadn't met standing beside Kate's chair. She was dressed as a nun and was one of the most beautiful women Daisy had ever seen. Her presence immediately changed the atmosphere in the room. Jessica seemed flustered, Molly even more reserved.

Daisy noted the newcomer seemed less interested in the ladies than in Kate, her face reflecting an odd expression of wistfulness as she studied the child drawing circles in the last of the oatmeal in her bowl.

"Good morning." Jessica sounded almost too jovial. "Morning prayers are over?"

"Sí." Despite the smile, the dark, almond-shaped eyes glittered as if she were fighting tears. "So this is little Kate," she said, her gaze still pinned to the child. "She is very beautiful." She glanced at Daisy. "You are a

lucky woman."

"Yes, I am." Daisy felt a shiver of unease. The woman seemed kindly enough, although there was something . . .

"She is much like her father." The nun brushed a fingertip over Kate's blond curls. "And more than just the eyes, I think."

And suddenly Daisy knew. In an instant, doubt became certainty, hitting her so hard it almost drove the air from her lungs.

It was her. The woman Jack loved.

Oh, God.

The ground seemed to shift beneath Daisy's feet. Pressing a palm against the countertop for balance, she struggled to quiet the terrible thundering in her chest.

A nun. He's in love with a nun.

It was unbelievable. Ridiculous. So ironic she would have laughed out loud if she hadn't been so close to tears.

Perhaps sensing Daisy's turmoil, Jessica stepped forward to hurriedly usher the nun around to an empty chair. "Would you like some tea? A muffin?"

Daisy could see the woman was crippled, but took no comfort in that. None of this wretched situation was the nun's fault. Daisy had orchestrated her own humiliation by becoming involved with Jack in the first place, then by showing up here uninvited, expecting . . . what?

"Elena is an old friend of the family," Jessica explained. "She —"

"I know who Elena is," Daisy cut in. "I just didn't know she was a nun."

"A novitiate." The nun settled awkwardly into a chair. "I take final vows next month."

"So you might still change your mind?" No wonder Jack was here. What had she stumbled into? A family reunion? A last attempt to win her over?

It was sick. The whole thing made Daisy's stomach turn.

"No." Elena's gaze bored into Daisy. "I will not change my mind. I have neither the desire, nor the reason, to do so."

"I see." Not that it mattered. None of it mattered. The man she loved had given his heart to a nun — that most perfect, pure, unattainable woman of all. How could Daisy compete with that?

Compete?

At that moment a terrible realization burst into her mind, one that had been in her heart all along even though she had refused to acknowledge it. She hadn't come here just because of the money, or Kate, or because of the dream.

She had also come because of Jack.

You stupid, stupid fool.

Elena's brow creased in a frown. "He spoke of me?"

Fury burned in Daisy's throat, arousing something cruel and dark within her. She tried to quell it with a smile, but the way the other women stared at her, she wondered if instead of forming into a pleasant expression, the muscles beneath her skin had contorted into a hideous grimace. Then before she could stop them, words poured out. "Once. He said your name only once. I believe he was on top of me at the time. Perhaps at the exact moment this beautiful child was conceived." She tried to laugh, but it came out garbled and ugly and bitter as bile. "I'm not sure which of us should be more insulted."

As Daisy's rage had built, it seemed Sister Elena's sadness had increased until her beautiful eyes clouded with tears. She held out a trembling hand. "I have upset you. Forgive me. Let me explain why I have come."

"No need." Realizing her nails were digging into the wood of the counter, Daisy loosened her grip. Rather than touch the woman's proffered hand, she picked up a towel and walked to where Kate sat staring at her with round, troubled eyes. Fighting to calm the chaos in her mind, she attended the simple task of cleaning up her daughter while reminding herself over and over that this gentle woman was not her enemy.

"I know why you're here, Sister." She was grateful her voice didn't wobble and her hands no longer shook. Hurt and anger had hardened into unshakable resolve, burying whatever foolish expectations she might have harbored. It was almost a relief.

"God sent you here as surely as He sent me," she went on, carefully wiping oatmeal from Kate's tiny hands. "To free me. To rid me of the curse that is Jack Wilkins. And I am grateful for it." Tossing the towel aside, she lifted Kate from her chair and set her on her hip. Looking from one woman to the other, she gave a strained smile. "Now if you will excuse us, Kate and I have a kitty to pet."

As soon as Daisy and Kate left, Jessica sank into a chair at the table. "Lord, what a ghastly tangle."

Elena dabbed at her eyes. "I should not have come. But I thought —"

"No." Reaching across the table, Jessica laid her hand over Elena's. "This is not your fault. It's Jack's. He's an even bigger dolt than Brady, I fear."

"I have caused her pain."

"Jack caused her pain. Not you."

But Elena seemed unconvinced, no matter what Jessica and Molly said.

"I do not know what to do," she said, pushing herself up from her chair. "But I will pray on it and ask for guidance. Perhaps God will show me a way to mend this wrong I have done."

Jack spent most of the morning holed up with his brothers in Hank's office, going over the mail and discussing ranch business. It amazed him how quickly he slipped back under the yoke of the endless chores, worries, hopes, and strategies that kept RosaRoja plodding along. In many ways it was stifling. In others, it reawakened a long-dormant sense of connection to his brothers and the land that had been the driving concern of the Wilkins family for almost twenty-five years.

Apparently he had returned at the beginning of a downward spiral. Ranching had always been a risky business with more lean years than good. But with the discovery of silver four years ago, things had been really good. In addition to building this monster house, his brothers had also started crossbreeding range cattle with imported Herefordshire and Angus, as well as developing a fine herd of mustang-Thoroughbred horses. Both results were impressive. Already Wilkins beef was in high demand and took top dollar every fall when they invariably won the Army bid for beef distribution to the Indian reservations. And although Brady wouldn't sell off any of his horses yet, they were generating a lot of interest as well. The first batch of colts would be ready for market after spring roundup, and he expected double that number to be ready next year. So far the epizootic hadn't impacted the ranch, and with no more cases of equine flu reported since the one in Prescott almost three weeks ago, it seemed

RosaRoja might have weathered the crisis untouched, although Brady intended to retain the quarantine for another week, just to be sure.

That was the good news.

The bad news was that with the government no longer buying silver to mint into coin, the mines weren't producing the income needed to offset the cost of the spur line and the smelter his brothers had built in partnership with three other local mine owners. Hank had already closed the mines. Now he was looking to shut down the spur line and sell off what machinery they could.

"I've gotten an offer on the locomotive and ore gondolas." Hank shuffled through a stack of papers weighted down by a rusted gear the size of a small plate. Finding the note he sought, he shoved it across his desk to Brady. "It's not a good one, but with the way the railroads are wobbling right now, I think we better take what we can get before the market crashes completely."

Brady studied the paper for a moment then tossed it back across the desk. "What about the concentrator?"

"A fellow is coming to look it over, but with so many mines closing down, there'll be too many on the market to get a good price."

"Maybe we could dismantle it and sell it piecemeal."

While his brothers discussed the possibility

of selling off various other pieces of mining machinery, Jack stared absently out the window and thought about his confrontation with Daisy in Kate's room earlier that morning.

She had seemed wary of him. He wondered why, or what he might have done to put such a guarded expression on her face. He knew he had used whiskey to blunt his disappointment over Elena. Apparently he had used Daisy too, and their time together had meant something different to her than it had to him. He regretted that. He liked Daisy, at least what he remembered of her. Mostly all he recalled was a terrible emptiness that seemed to ease a bit whenever he was with her. Like he was drowning, and whenever he sank too deep, Daisy was there, reaching down to pull him back to the surface.

Then something had changed. But what? Had he told her about Elena? Had he harmed her during one of his drinking bouts?

The idea of hurting a woman was so alien and repugnant to him he wouldn't even consider it. He liked women. He liked the way they smelled, the sound of their laughter, the softness of their bodies. He didn't always understand them, but he never tired of trying to figure out how their minds worked. And he would never knowingly hurt one.

But it was obvious he had hurt Daisy. He'd done something to put her defenses up, and if he were ever to find his way to Kate, he would have to get past those walls of anger. Normally, he would have relished the challenge, but this time the stakes were too high. If he failed to win, he would lose his daughter forever.

Win what? Daisy? Kate? And what would he do with them if he did win?

But Kate was a fascination to him. He couldn't seem to get her out of his mind, and he wasn't ready to let her go just yet.

"Then all we've got to worry about is the debt on the smelter."

An odd note in Hank's voice grabbed Jack's notice. Shifting his gaze from one brother to the other, he sensed tension between them but didn't know the cause.

Hank scratched at his chin, then sighed. "I guess now would be the best time to ask —"

"I've changed my mind." Brady's voice was abrupt, curt.

Hank stopped scratching. "Then how do you plan to pay Blake?"

"I'll think of something."

"Like what?"

"I'll let you know. Just drop it for now, okay?"

Jack knew his brothers. He knew all their tricks and evasions and what every eye roll and smirk meant. And he especially knew when they were keeping something from him. Like now. "Are you talking about the same

175

Blake that Daisy and Kate rode out with?" he asked, watching their faces.

Neither answered.

"Why do you owe him money?"

Hank sat back, his expression shuttered, his gaze on Brady, as if waiting for him to speak first.

Which Brady did. "He bought the paper on the smelter loan from the bank."

"Why would he do that?"

"To get a hold over us. He thinks if he squeezes hard enough, we'll cough up the ranch."

Jack was astounded. They had been through rough patches in the past, years when cattle froze by the hundreds, or when grass fires or drought or tick fever decimated the herds. But the ranch had never been in real jeopardy. "Is that a possibility? We could lose the ranch?"

"No," Brady said sharply, his chiseled face as hard and unyielding as their father's had ever been. "That'll never happen. It's just a temporary cash problem. Something every rancher deals with."

In other words, *Butt out. I'll take care of it.*

Jack knew Brady was still holding back, but he also knew the harder he pushed, the more his brother would dig in. It was a pattern Jack knew well. Brady hoarded his troubles like a miser with his gold, as if to admit to them would show an inability to handle any crisis

176

that came along. Jack's brain knew that.

But his heart heard a different refrain — *don't tell Jack. He's too young, too dumb, too useless to help.*

He was weary of it. And long past the age of allowing himself to be protected — or intimidated — by his big brother. "How much do you owe?" He had some money set aside. Maybe he could help. If Brady would let him.

When Brady didn't answer, Hank did.

Jack was stunned. He didn't know much about smelters or mining, but it seemed like a huge amount. "Is that the total, or just what we owe?"

"Both," Hank said.

Jack frowned, confused. "What does that mean, exactly? I thought you had partners."

"We did." Brady sent Hank a warning look, which Hank ignored. "Blake was pressuring them to sell, so rather than risk him getting controlling interest, we borrowed from the bank to buy them out. Apparently Blake bought the loan from the bank, so now we owe him. But with no more silver being coined, the smelter is worth less than we owe."

"No it isn't," Brady insisted. "It can be used for other kinds of ore, not just silver. Iron, gold, copper. We'll find a buyer."

Hank snorted. "In what? A month? Five weeks?"

Brady looked out the window, his mouth a thin, hard seam beneath his black mustache.

Jack thought he saw fear in his brother's eyes, but wasn't sure. He'd never seen that expression on Brady's face before.

"And if not?" Hank persisted.

"There's always the horses."

Hank waved that idea aside. "We only have a dozen ready and that won't cover it."

Brady continued to stare out the window, his jaw set.

"Hell." Hank shook his head. "You're not just talking about the colts, are you? You're talking about all the horses. Brood mares and studs included. You're talking about everything."

Brady finally turned from the window. Jack recognized the unyielding jut of his chin. "We'll do what we have to do."

"It'll kill the whole breeding program, Brady. Four years of work."

"Then we'll start again."

"Hell."

NINE

As Jack rounded the corner of the upstairs hallway, he saw Daisy walking ahead of him toward her bedroom door. *Finally.* "You been avoiding my family?" he called, continuing toward her.

With a start, she turned, one hand on the doorknob. He saw surprise give way to wariness and hoped she wouldn't bolt before he had a chance to talk to her.

He'd had a time tracking her down. After leaving his brothers, he'd checked the bedrooms, the porches, the barn, and the paddocks. No luck. Then it was noon, and figuring he'd corral her at the house, he went to the kitchen, which was loaded with women clearing away dirty dishes. Apparently he'd missed lunch too. Jessica — who seemed unusually irritated with him — said Daisy had just taken Kate up for a nap and shouldn't be disturbed.

Ignoring the hard looks sent his way by both Molly and Jessica, Jack snagged what food he could from the serving dishes and quickly ate. It wasn't until he was into his second helping of roast beef that he realized Elena wasn't in the kitchen. When he asked about her absence, Jessica's scowl deepened until her eyes were two brown slits in her freckled face. Definitely mad at him for some reason.

"She's praying," was her terse reply, as if that had some hidden meaning he should understand, which of course, he didn't. He understood regular women fairly well. Religious ones, not at all. He always had the feeling they were praying for him, or about him, or against him. And anyway, it was Daisy he needed to see, not Elena.

As soon as he'd finished eating, he had headed upstairs to his wing, hoping he would figure out what to say to her once he got there. But now, as he walked down the hall toward her, he decided that maybe accusing her of avoiding his family hadn't been a good start.

"Not your family," she replied, her chin coming up. "You."

His smile faltered. Why was every woman in the house so mad at him? He stopped before her, so close he could smell flowery soap, and near enough to realize again how small she was. Not short. She came up to his chin, after all. But small and fine boned, with delicate wrists and long-fingered, graceful hands, and a rib cage so narrow it was a wonder it could support such a robust chest. It took monumental effort not to look down and check that it still did.

"Avoiding me why?" he asked.

She lifted one of those graceful hands, showing swollen, scraped knuckles. "My hand is still sore and I was afraid I might hit you again." With a dismissive glance, she swung open the door.

Before she could shut it in his face, he stepped through behind her. "Why do you want to hit me?"

"Do you need the entire list?" She crossed to the windows, putting most of the room between them before turning to face him. "Or just the latest reason?"

Closing the door behind him, Jack stood in front of it, arms crossed, feet braced. He smiled. "Let's start with the latest and go from there."

"I met your other lover this morning."

Jack blinked. "Other lover?"

"You really do have a poor memory, don't you? I'm referring to Elena."

Oh, hell. "Elena and I aren't lovers. We never were."

For some reason that made her laugh. It wasn't a happy sound. "This just gets better and better."

"How so?"

"Never mind." Moving to one of the wingback chairs before the unlit fireplace, she sat and folded her hands in her lap. "What do you want, Jack?"

He'd forgotten. She had an uncanny ability to make him forget things. And rattle him. Being unaccustomed to it, he retreated to safer ground. "I'm sorry."

Women, he'd learned, loved for men to apologize, whether there was reason for it or not. Apparently they saw it as a victory of some sort. And he'd further learned that triumphant women became forgiving women, which in turn made them generous women. It was in their nature. They might fight like wolverines over some inconsequential matter, but once assured of victory, they became as docile as lambs. He thought it was one of their finer traits.

"Sorry for what?" she asked.

Damn. She wanted a reason. There were so many — forgetting her, looking at her chest, doubting Kate was his, Elena. As the list grew, his confidence waned. He really had treated her badly. And he really was sorry for it. *Damn.* Suddenly he didn't want to fight with her anymore, or try to sweet-talk her. She deserved better.

He walked to the chair across the hearth from hers. "Can I sit?" he asked.

She studied him for a moment as if trying to read motive in his eyes. He'd seen friendlier expressions on feral cats. Then she

182

shrugged. "If you like."

He sat. Leaning back, elbows on the arm-rests, fingers twined over his belt buckle, he studied her, trying to spark a memory of their time together. He found few and that troubled him. "Why didn't you tell me you were pregnant, Daisy?"

She took her time answering, as if debating what to say. Then finally, in a weary tone, she said, "I didn't know until you'd been gone two months." Tilting her head, she studied him. "Had you known, what would you have done?"

"I'm not sure."

"At least you're honest."

Silence. He watched her pluck at a loose thread on her skirt and had a sudden image of those same fingers twining in the hair on his chest. They had just made love and he was sinking into a sated, whiskey-warm sleep when her voice had jolted him awake. "I love you, Jack." He had heard a similar sentiment from other women and had always managed to dismiss it, or laugh it off, or talk them out of it. But hearing that declaration from this woman had sent his befuddled mind reeling. Unable to come up with a response, he had pretended to be asleep. As far as he knew, she had never said it again.

But now, thinking back on it, he felt an odd regret. The loss of that moment, of those words and of her, saddened him and he wasn't sure why.

"I'm sorry," he said again.

Anger flashed in her yellow-green eyes. "About Kate?"

He shook his head. "I could never be sorry about Kate. But I am sorry I left you to go through that alone. That I wasn't there to help." *That I couldn't love you back. That I used you.* He'd never felt those regrets before. It made him wonder how many other angry, resentful women he'd left in his wake. And how many children he didn't know he had.

Leaning forward, he braced his elbows on his knees and looked directly into her eyes. "What can I do now, Daisy? Tell me what you need and you've got it."

"Money. That's all I need." Her gaze didn't waver, but the flush on her cheeks told him it had bothered her to ask.

It wasn't the answer he had expected. Women had been trying to drop a rope on him since he'd groped his first breast. But Daisy, the only woman with a sure chance of success, didn't even try. It was disconcerting. "Money for what?"

"For Kate." She made an offhand gesture. "And for me. I want to get out of the saloon. Find a better way to support us. A better place to live. But I'll need money to do that."

He'd forgotten she was a saloon singer. In his mind he saw her standing by the piano, staring at the back wall, singing over the noise of the gamblers and drinkers and lechers, as if the filth and degradation couldn't reach her. And somehow it didn't. Even in that skimpy dress the saloon owner made her wear, and despite the paint on her face and the smoke and whistles and leering grins, she stood unblemished and untarnished. Proud. He didn't recall much about her voice, but he did remember the look on her face when she sang. She loved it.

"Do you still sing?" he asked.

Her gaze slid away. "At the moment, no. But I hope to again."

That evasive look confused him. Why would she lie about singing? Pushing that thought aside, he said, "Maybe I can help. Whatever you need." He had money in San Francisco, earned over the years by investing in the cargoes of the various ships on which he'd sailed. He had thought to offer it to his brothers to pay off the smelter loan, but now realized it should go to Daisy and Kate first. What they didn't need, he could always add to the ranch coffers.

"Thank you." Her flush deepened. Her lips pressed into a tight line.

He could tell this was as awkward for her as it was for him. She didn't like asking for his help. Or even being around him. Yet the pull was there. It pulsed in the air like a lightning charge. He wondered if it was just because of Kate, or their past history, or

185

something else. Daisy was a beautiful woman, not as beautiful as Elena, but there was something in her face, a liveliness that was absent from Elena's serene expression. It drew him.

He remembered they had laughed a lot. And fought — mostly about his drinking. And had made love with an eagerness that had left his body drained and his head spinning. Or maybe that was the whiskey.

"Why are you smiling?" she asked.

Jack blinked the memories away, a bit addled to be caught trying to conjure up an image of Daisy's naked body. He sat back. "When does Kate wake up?"

She checked the clock on the mantel. "Soon. She's been down an hour and a half already."

"Has she ever ridden a horse?"

"She's twenty-two months old," she reminded him with a roll of her eyes.

"Then it's time."

"Why didn't you ask him for the money?" Hank said over Brady's shoulder as they stood at a window in the hallway across from his office, watching Jack and Daisy and Kate in one of the paddocks off the barn.

Instead of answering, Brady nodded toward Jack, who was leading their ancient kid pony with the improbable name of Greased Lightning in a slow circle while Kate clung to the saddle, kicking her stubby legs and laughing like a loon. Daisy, standing outside the fence, seemed to be clinging just as hard to the top rail, but she wasn't laughing. "They look like a family, don't they?"

Hank sighed. "You're interfering again."

"Interfering how? I'm just standing here."

Shaking his head, Hank went down the hall to his own office.

A moment later, Brady appeared in the doorway. "They deserve a chance."

Ignoring him, Hank settled in his chair behind the desk and began rummaging through a box of parts, hoping his brother would take the hint.

"If we take his money," Brady went on, "it'll tie him to the ranch and you know he doesn't want that."

Finding the spring he wanted, Hank checked it carefully for cracks, set it aside, and started rummaging again.

Crossing to the chair in front of the desk, Brady plopped down with a long exhale. "Besides, Jessica says Daisy needs money. For Kate."

Hank gave up his search and sat back. "Speaking of money, any chance you would go to Jessica for the money to pay Blake?"

"None whatsoever. She knows nothing about it. Didn't want to worry her."

Hank expected no other answer. Jessica had a small but profitable estate in England. Her sister, Annie, and her family lived there and kept an eye on the coal companies that were mining a rich deposit that ran under her land. The estate, Bickersham Hall, had been in Jessica's family for hundreds of years, passing down through the eldest daughter of each generation. Someday it would belong to Brady's daughter, Abigail. Hank didn't know what the financial situation was, but guessed Brady would rather cut off a foot than go to his wife for money or tell her anything that might cause her distress. Shortsighted, but understandable.

"If the horses aren't enough, we'll sell off some cattle," Brady said. "The mines, if necessary."

Hank didn't point out that the price of cattle was down and the mines were near played out, even if the silver market rallied. He knew it wasn't just the money that bothered Brady. Part of it was as he said — concern for Jack and Daisy. But another part was his reluctance to ask for help, mostly out of pride. Brady had an abundance of that. And since he had always been more of a father than a brother to Jack, having to turn to his little brother for money would be intolerable to him.

And Jack, well, with his volatile nature, restless spirit, and seeming lack of commitment to the ranch, he was the exact opposite of Brady. As the eldest, Brady had been born and bred to run RosaRoja, and because of it felt more than he should the weight of all the lives that had been lost to hold it. And part of the burden of that responsibility had been to keep Jack on the straight and narrow, which was no small chore.

It brought out the worst in both of them so that over the years, what had once been a normal brotherly relationship had become a fierce rivalry, at least on Jack's part. Hank suspected Elena was at the heart of it, since at one time Jack had thought Brady wanted Elena. Maybe Jack still had doubts. And maybe Brady suspected he did, which was another reason he wanted to keep the way clear for Jack and Daisy. It was a mess, sure enough.

Pushing the box of parts aside, Hank sat forward, folded his hands on the desktop, and looked hard at his brother. "You're risking the ranch, you know."

"I'd risk it for you. Does Jack deserve less?"

"It's not about that, and you know it. I could make it without the ranch. Jack too. But not you. It would kill you to lose it."

"It's just dirt."

Hank snorted. "You sound like Jessica."

"She has a point." Brady's gaze swung toward the window and the graveyard hilltop beyond, and Hank knew by the sadness etched on his brother's face that Brady was thinking about Sam — the lost brother. Sam's death haunted Brady still, and made him so fearful of losing another brother or of letting any of them down, he watched over the family with a stifling vigilance, holding the reins of their futures in an iron grip.

"Maybe I'm tired of it, Hank. Maybe I'd like to go chasing after bare-chested women on some coconut island like Jack."

"I'll tell Jessica."

"I mean it. Jack won't stay. And I know you and Molly have been hinting that you might go up to Santa Fe. What's it all for if there's no one left?"

"You're not going to cry, are you?"

"Bastard." Brady made a crude gesture, then let his hand drop back to the armrest. "The point is I can't do it alone. Maybe it's time to let it all go."

"To Blake. Just hand it over." Hank sat back with a sigh. "Helluva plan."

Brady thought about it for a moment then shook his head. "You're right. I'd have to burn it first and I wouldn't like that. Let's sell off some horses and cattle instead."

Hank knew selling his herd of crossbreeds would be hard on Brady, but if he wouldn't ask Jack or Jessica for the money, they had little choice. "I'll send a rider to the fort. Heard they lost a lot of horses to the epizootic and were desperate for remounts."

"Send riders to all the nearby forts. And see if they need any beef to tide them over."

Brady rose. He looked down at Hank, the momentary sadness over Sam replaced by a look of fierce determination. "We'll weather this, Hank. We won't lose the ranch to Franklin Blake."

"I know." Hank tried to sound convinced.

Abruptly Brady flashed that startling grin that was part devilment, part humor. The one that always made Hank wary. "And hell, if all else fails, little brother, we'll just shoot the sonofabitch."

Franklin Blake was running out of time. Stanley Ashford, the advance man for the El Paso & Pacific Railroad, was due today and expecting results that weren't there. Now Blake would have to tell him every plan to take over RosaRoja had failed.

He'd tried to pressure the other smelter owners into selling. They'd sold their shares to Wilkins instead. He'd tried to infect Wilkins livestock by driving a sick horse through their quarantine. And had ended up walking halfway back to Val Rosa on foot. And now they'd found a buyer for their locomotive and ore gondolas, and were angling to sell their herd of fancy crossbred horses to the Army. Hell, he'd never get a hold on them.

Christ. Trying to manage the Wilkins brothers was like pissing into the wind. Every time he tried, it all came back at him tenfold.

Overwhelmed by the unfairness of it, Blake kicked the woman lying next to him. "Get up, you stupid sow. You're bleeding on the sheets."

With a whimper, the whore rolled out and hobbled toward the door, her thighs smeared with blood, the dozen bruises and lacerations on her nude body making it look like she'd been splattered with purple and red paint.

"And don't come back," he yelled after her, "until you learn how to satisfy a man. Stinking pig."

After the door closed behind her, he sat up, wrinkling his nose in disgust. The room stank of sweat and whiskey and vomit. The goddamn woman couldn't even clean up after herself. He'd have to ask the hotel to give him a different room in case Ashford came up here. For all his cold-bloodedness, the little dandy was as fastidious as a maiden aunt.

When Blake went downstairs a half hour later, Stanley Ashford was already sitting in the hotel lobby in his fine suit, one leg crossed over the other, a thin cheroot clamped between his teeth. Oily pomade that smelled like a whore's perfume plastered every sparse golden hair against his bony skull. Pockmarks cratered his cheeks, and his dark brown eyes held all the warmth and welcome of a skunk hole.

"Evening, Ashford," Blake said, striving for

a robust tone. "Didn't know you'd arrived. Been waiting long?"

Ashford didn't answer. Taking the cheroot from his mouth, he stubbed it out in a potted plant beside his chair, then looked at Blake. And continued looking until Blake felt sweat begin to bead on his top lip. "Do you have it?" he finally asked in his cultured voice.

"The deed? Not yet." Nervously pushing back the lapels of his jacket, Blake hooked his thumbs into the armholes of his vest. "But soon."

"How soon?"

"Hard to say." Rocking on his heels, Blake frowned at the far wall in the pose of a man making mental calculations.

In truth, he had no idea how much longer it would take to bring the Wilkins brothers to heel. He'd tried everything he could think of to push them off their land, short of an out-and-out range war. The railroad already had enough trouble wresting water rights from other landowners along their route, and he doubted they'd want to take on such formidable foes as the Wilkins clan. Besides, that would take men and money, neither of which he had.

"With the end of the silver standard," he said, "banks are failing, and the silver and cattle markets are falling fast. It shouldn't be long. The note on the smelter is due in a few weeks, and they've got no way to pay it."

"A few weeks." Ashford pursed his thin lips and tapped a long, manicured finger on the armrest. "We can't wait that long. We need their water now." He sighed. "Since it's obvious you're incompetent, I guess I'll have to try."

Blake bit back a sharp retort, wondering how this prissy man intended to convince the hardheaded Wilkins brothers to do something they didn't want to do. Reaching into his coat pocket, he pulled out the notice he'd pulled off the board outside the sheriff's office when he'd returned from RosaRoja last week. "Maybe this'll help." He handed it to Ashford.

The railroader took it in two long, slender fingers as if afraid it might dirty his fine hands. "What's this?"

"A wanted poster for a woman with a kid I took out to the Wilkins ranch a while back. Far as I know, she's still out there."

Ashford studied the drawing. "Desiree Etheridge. You're sure it's the same woman?"

"Don't remember the name. But if it's not her, it's her twin."

Ashford continued reading. "Says she's wanted for questioning in the murder of Bill Johnson of San Francisco. Interesting." He looked up. "Did you tell the sheriff about her?"

Blake shook his head. "What are you going to do?"

Ashford slipped the paper into his pocket. "Perhaps I'll go for a visit."

"To the ranch?" Blake laughed. "I doubt they'd see you."

"Oh, I think they will." Ashford's varmint-hole eyes narrowed. "We're old friends, you see. I know where all the skeletons are buried. And now, from where — and for whom — the arrest warrants have been issued."

Blake had no idea what he was talking about. Nor did he care. Stifling a yawn, he watched Ashford pick a speck of lint from his sleeve and awaited further orders. When none came, impatience finally got the better of him. "So what do you want me to do?" he asked.

Ashford looked up with an expression of mild surprise, as if he'd forgotten Blake was still there. He appeared to think for a moment, then shrugged the overly padded shoulders of his fine custom-tailored suit. "I suppose you could kill yourself and save me the expense of a bullet. But even that might be beyond your meager talents. So continue to pressure them about the loan. You can handle that little chore, can't you, Blake?"

Blake almost choked on a rush of angry words. He wanted to hit the bastard. Grind him under his heel. Cut off his balls and stuff them down his throat.

Instead, he smiled. "Sure, Ashford. I'll take care of it." *And then I'll come for you, you little pissant.* Nobody talked to Franklin Blake that way.

TEN

"Now was that so bad?"

Jack stopped the pony next to the paddock rail that Daisy held in a white-knuckled grip.

"Are you asking me or Kate?" Daisy said in a strained voice.

"Go again!" Kate bounced in the saddle so vigorously her stuffed cat almost fell to the ground. "Go again. Now!"

Jack tossed the stuffed toy to Daisy, then proudly patted his daughter's chubby knee. "A born Wilkins, aren't you, Katie-girl?" Glancing back at Daisy, he made a subtle shift in his smile. "We're all good riders, you know. And not just horses."

Instead of the anticipated blush, she smirked. "I wonder if Jessica and Molly would agree."

Undeterred, Jack leaned against the rail beside her. "Probably not as enthusiastically as their husbands might wish, but then they are older. Their husbands, I mean."

"Get her down before she falls."

"The ground's soft. Besides, kids bounce."

"Jack!"

"Okay. But don't blame me if she starts crying." Lifting Kate from the saddle, he settled her astride his shoulders, a hand locked around each ankle.

Kate immediately began to cry and lean toward the pony, arms outstretched.

"Uh-oh, Katie-girl." Jack sent an I-told-you-so look to Daisy. "You're scaring Lightning. I think he actually blinked." Moving closer to the dozing pony, Jack turned so Kate could reach the animal's neck. "Why don't you pet the poor horse, Katie-girl, and make him feel better."

Kate did as instructed, crooning, "Nice horsy," as she wound her little fingers in the coarse black mane.

Jack smiled, enjoying his daughter and admiring the day. The sky was that sharp clear blue that came only in the early spring before dust hazed the air and the horizon disappeared behind dancing heat shimmers. And even though the mountains still wore their caps of snow and the slopes were just starting to bud, the valley floor was already such a vibrant green it reminded him of some of the tropical islands he'd visited. Standing silhouetted against it, Daisy looked as pretty as a museum painting.

"It's a beautiful place," Daisy said, echoing his thoughts.

"It is. Brady always says living in this valley is like going to heaven without having to die first."

She chuckled, the sound friendly and relaxed. "And what do you think?"

With the sun bringing out the gold in her hair and eyes, and a smile tugging at her lips, she was a striking woman. He could see why he'd been attracted to her, even though he'd been in love with another woman at the time. And still was, he quickly reminded himself. "I think he needs to travel more."

"You're not as taken with the ranch?"

"Don't get me wrong, Daisy. I love this country. I'm proud to be a part of it. But behind every mountain out there is another mountain, another lake or river, another city or island or ocean. And I want to see them all."

She studied him for a moment, then nodded. "I can understand that. I'd like to travel too."

He felt as if a connection was forming between them, something so tenuous and fragile just to acknowledge it would snap the bond. So he remained silent under her scrutiny, hoping she saw nothing that would alarm her or cause her to pull back. He told himself because of Kate it was important that Daisy accept him. But he sensed there might be more to it than that.

Kate's high voice shattered the moment.

"Go again! Go again!" She started bouncing on Jack's shoulders so hard he had to tighten his grip on her ankles. "Ouch," he muttered when she grabbed a handful of his hair and tugged.

Daisy raised her brows. "You started this."

Gently lifting Kate from his shoulders, he leaned over the fence and set her on the ground beside her mother. Immediately the scamp tried to crawl through the rails to get to the horse. Laughing, he reached over and swept her up again. "How about we put Lightning away and go on a picnic?"

"It's the middle of the afternoon," Daisy reminded him.

"Then we'll go on a snack. It's a pretty day and the walk will do you good." Sensing hesitation, Jack gave her a lopsided grin. "Come on, Daisy. Do it for Kate. You know she'd love it."

"She can't walk very far. She's still a baby, after all."

"Not a baby!" Kate protested, squirming in Jack's arms. "Go again."

Shifting smoothly into his most disarming smile, Jack gave Daisy a wink. "You know you want to. I know I sure do. We'll go to the creek."

Daisy burst out laughing. "Does that really work?"

His grin faded. "Does what work?"

"Never mind." Still chuckling, she pushed

away from the rail. "A walk sounds nice. Watch Kate. I'll get a few things and be back in ten minutes."

Thirty minutes later, Daisy stood beside Jack, who had Kate and Kitty on his shoulders, and studied the flooded creek. The cottonwoods and aspens along the bank were just beginning to bud and the warm afternoon sunlight shone brightly through the web of bare branches high overhead. The sound of rushing water created a musical background to the chirp of birds darting through the brush.

The water was running high and fast, churning with sticks and tinted brown with silt from the spring runoff. Daisy suspected it would be a beautiful spot in summer, but now, with the slippery banks and swirling currents, it was too hazardous for a toddler. "I don't think this is a safe place for a picnic," she ventured, watching a six-foot branch bob by.

"It isn't. Especially in spring or after a rain. It's really dangerous then. Hank said they built a bridge farther up. We'll cross there."

The bridge was constructed in the same overbuilt style as the house, with two-foot-diameter logs spanning the water, anchored on either bank to huge rock and log abutments. The spanners were topped by thick, rough planks held in place by railroad spikes, and were bordered on each side by sturdy rails. The bridge was wide enough to accommodate a buckboard wagon, but Daisy still felt uneasy, knowing the rushing water had risen to within a couple of feet of the planks beneath her feet. Once on the other side, they followed a trail that wound past toppled boulders, up through a stand of spicy-scented junipers, finally ending in a large clearing atop a low ridge.

"Is this better?" Jack asked, swinging Kate off his shoulders and setting her on her feet.

Daisy would have said yes even if it weren't. Her arms felt like they'd been stretched on a rack from carrying a pouch packed with blankets, jackets, and toys for Kate. "On the way back, I'll carry Kate," she said, letting it thud to the dirt.

Jack grinned over at her. "I told you we didn't need all that."

"You would have had us sit on the bare ground?"

His grin widened. "If you're worried about getting our clothes dirty, we could have taken them off."

"And gotten our . . . selves . . . dirty instead?" She looked askance at the sparse grass pushing up through the sandy soil. "There could be bugs and things. Lizards. Spiders even."

"I thought you were a farm girl."

"Living on a farm doesn't automatically mean you like crawling things. Kate, come away from there."

"She's fine." Jack moved to where his daughter clambered over a pile of rocks. "I'll check it for snakes."

"Snakes!" She must have shrieked it, judging by the way Kate startled and Jack flinched. "You never said there might be snakes."

Laughing, Jack scooped his daughter up in his arms. "Your ma is such a sissy-girl. Not brave like you." He made slurping noises against Kate's neck, which sent the child into thrashing giggles.

"There's brave and there's foolish," Daisy muttered. Bending to pull the blanket from the pouch, she felt again that prickle of uneasiness at the sudden closeness that was developing between Jack and Kate. How was she to shield Kate from the heartache that was sure to come? Resentment eddied through her. Jack was a fine playmate but more likely to chase the sun across the sky than stay in one spot. And this time it would be a confused child he would leave behind.

As she spread out the blanket, she watched Jack dig through the rocks while Kate, who still had difficulty with the *sn* combination, called, "Come out, nake," every time he turned over a stone. With their blond heads together and their grinning faces only inches apart, they made such a beautiful picture it brought a catch to Daisy's throat.

I could have loved this man. I did love this man.

But it wasn't enough.

She wasn't enough.

Lifting her face to the warm sunshine, she willed the pain away. She'd wept enough tears over Jack Wilkins. She would never let him get past her defenses and cause her that pain again.

But how was she to protect her child?

Pushing that dreary thought aside, Daisy concentrated on enjoying the lovely day and watching Jack introduce his daughter to the wondrous treasures all around them — a bird's nest in a low bush, mouse holes beneath the rocks, shiny bits of quartz and mica in the weeds. The man could make dirt sound grand.

Daisy smiled as pleasant memories washed over her.

Jack's greatest gift was his passion for life. The simplest things brought him delight, and every new experience was a joyful challenge. His enthusiasm was so compelling it pulled one along like a dinghy sucked into the wake of a giant barge.

The experience was all — the moment, everything — now overshadowed past and future. It had been like a lifesaver for Daisy, newly orphaned and feeling so lost and alone when he had come into her life. He had been the light at the end of a long tunnel of loneliness. He had been the cure for her despair.

At first.

She had seen him in the Silver Spur. How could one not notice a man like Jack? Looks and stature aside, his ready smile and laughing eyes were a lure no woman could resist, although Daisy had tried.

She didn't think much of him at first. He was just another gambler, another anonymous face. Then she heard the other women talking about Jack Wilkins and curiosity made her take a second look. What she saw was a big, laughing, cheerful man who was such a charmer even the men who gambled against him seemed to take their losses with good humor. Most of them anyway. Those who quibbled often found themselves resting on the floor for a while.

He didn't notice her at first either, although she did find him staring at her breasts a time or two. Not surprising, since she was required to wear a low-cut gown when she sang. A whore dress really. Daisy had a time of it convincing the men ogling her that she was a singer and not a prostitute. But Jack didn't seem to see her that way. In fact, he rarely looked at her at all. Above the neck anyway. Which left her free to look at him.

He was handsome, for sure. Clean-shaven, with dark brows and lashes in contrast to sandy, sun-bleached hair. Eyes the color of storm clouds, as changeable as smoke, the irises edged with dark bands that made them even more distinctive. Despite his size, he moved with the controlled assurance of a man comfortable in his own skin. He didn't gloat over his wins or pout over his losses, and laughed with the same good-natured enthusiasm when he brawled, whether he was giving damage or receiving it. He wasn't a smoker and despite his high spirits, he wasn't that much of a drinker either.

At first.

Then something changed.

For over two months she had watched him every night as she sang. He had become the one joyful aspect of her dreary evenings, one of the few faces that didn't reflect back her own despair and helplessness. She needed his easy smile and deep laughter to counterbalance the empty days, the bleakness of harsh reality.

Then suddenly it was gone. The laughter, the joy, the easy banter with the other gamblers. It was as if Jack Wilkins had died. Or someone close to him had.

He began to drink more and more. He gambled foolishly, lost more often than not, and erupted in violence at the slightest provocation. Soon no one would sit at the table with him, so he sat in a shadowed corner and drank alone.

She missed him. Even though they had never spoken, she felt the loss of the man she had come to think of as almost a friend. Until one evening, when she had felt more depressed than usual, and she had sung a sad Irish ballad about a briar and a rose that told of heartbreak and lost love.

Halfway through the second chorus, he lurched to his feet so abruptly his chair toppled to the floor. Teeth bared, his face twisted in fury, he stumbled toward her.

Daisy stood frozen, words caught in her throat, not sure what to do, or why he was so angry. She tried to continue the song, but suddenly he was looming over her.

"Don't," he said hoarsely.

She shrank back as he reached out and clamped his big hand around her jaw in a firm, but not hurtful grip.

"Don't sing that. Don't say it. Just . . . don't."

She stared into bleak, empty eyes and felt something long smothered stir within her. Empathy. Pity. A reflection of her own pain perhaps. It sang through her veins in a refrain no woman could ignore.

He needed her.

He was broken and she could fix him.

And God help her, she had tried, only to get her own heart broken in the process.

But that was years ago. She had stitched herself back together and was whole now. Stronger and wiser. And as she watched Jack weave his magic around Kate, she used more hurtful memories to beat down any softening toward him, to remind herself of the heartache after he had left her, and the terrible loneliness that had nearly driven her off a bridge one foggy night. Never again would she let Jack Wilkins into her heart. She couldn't survive it a second time.

"It's getting late," she called to them. "I think we should head back."

Jack started to argue with her, but Kate yawned. "Titty come too?"

"Yes, bring Kitty and I'll pack him in the pouch. Come along, or we'll miss supper."

This time, instead of riding on Jack's shoulders, Kate nestled against his chest, her head tucked beneath his chin. Before they'd gone fifty yards, she was asleep. When the path widened, Jack slowed to let Daisy catch up. They walked in silence for a bit, then he said, "I would have done the right thing, you know."

She squinted up at him through the lowering sun. "About what?"

His gaze dipped down at Kate. "If I'd known, I would have stayed."

"And done what?"

"Married you."

She stumbled, then caught herself. Lifting a hand, she brushed a loose strand of hair behind her ear. "How noble you are."

If he heard her sarcasm, he ignored it. "I still will. Marry you."

She stopped and stared up at him. "Is that a proposal?"

"Well . . . sure." And why not? Jack thought. If he couldn't have Elena, why not Daisy? They'd been compatible once, maybe they could be again. Besides, Kate needed a father. "Marry me, Daisy." He watched her brows rise until they arced over her eyes in obvious surprise. Her lips parted. But no sound came out. "Rendered you speechless, have I?" He tried to hide his sudden nervousness behind a grin.

She burst into laughter. Not the nervous titter of someone unsure if she was the butt of a joke she didn't quite understand. Or the shy breathless giggle of a woman receiving her first marriage proposal. Or even a half-smothered chuckle of delighted surprise. It was a full-out, head-tossed-back belly laugh that went on and on until she was gasping for breath.

Not the reaction he'd expected.

"You're jesting, right?" she managed once she had herself back in hand.

"No."

"You want me to marry you."

He nodded, mentally cursing himself for not thinking this through. He should have used a softer approach. Something romantic. Women loved that.

"Why?"

Why? He studied her, sensing a trap. But

she seemed sincerely curious, so he responded with equal sincerity. "Because it's the right thing to do."

"For Kate?"

"Exactly."

"No." Turning, she walked quickly up the path.

He caught up in two strides. "Not for Kate?"

"No, I won't marry you."

He blinked, shocked by her answer. It had never occurred to him that she might say no. He'd been dodging women for half his life, but now when he'd finally coughed up a proposal, he was refused? It was inconceivable.

He should have been relieved.

He should have taken it as a reprieve and let it go at that.

"Why not?" he asked, instead.

"Don't be silly." She softened the words with a pat on his arm. "Why would I want a gambling, womanizing drunk in my life?"

He reared back in offense. "That's not fair. I'm not a drunk. Not anymore." He shot her one of his best smiles, a boyish grin guaranteed to disarm. "And we do have a daughter, so you must have wanted me in your life at one time."

"In my bed, perhaps." It took all of Daisy's strength to keep up this nonchalant charade when her heart was screaming, *Do it! Say yes!*

But if she couldn't be first in Jack's heart, she didn't want to be there at all. "Oh, don't look so offended," she said with a brittle laugh. "You were, as I recall, in love with another woman. And still are, it would seem."

She watched his face. Saw surprise and maybe a flash of guilt. Surely he hadn't forgotten about his true love?

"Elena will leave in a few days. I'll never see her again."

"But that won't change the way you feel about her, will it?"

Daisy waited for his answer, dreading it but needing to hear it, as if it might cut through the hope and anger and hurt to finally sever the emotional tie that still bound her to this man.

"I don't know," he finally said.

Ever honest, Jack was. He would kill her yet. She continued walking down the trail, mildly surprised that she still could. The sun was sliding behind the peaks, staining the high snowfields a soft pastel pink. The cloudless dome overhead was a wash of color ranging from a dusky blue in the east, growing brighter and more vibrant as it bled into oranges and fiery reds in the west. On distant ridges, trees rose in stark silhouette and the breeze sweeping down the slopes was fragrant and cool.

Too beautiful a day for hope to die.

Jack caught up and matched his pace to

hers. From time to time, she felt him watching her over Kate's head, but she didn't look his way.

"So it's just the money, then," he said after a long silence. "That's all you want from me."

Daisy nodded, not trusting her voice.

"Then you'll go back to San Francisco?"

"Perhaps."

"And do what? Sing in another saloon?"

She turned her head and looked at him. Frustration tightened his mouth, and his beautiful eyes showed bewilderment and maybe a touch of anger. Saddened, she looked away again.

Poor Jack. Usually he could so easily bend a woman to his whims. This must be a shock, and as difficult for him as it was for her, although for wholly different reasons.

"And what about Kate?" he persisted. "Who'll watch over her while you're flaunting yourself in some filthy saloon?"

His accusation ignited her own anger. "Was I flaunting myself? I thought I was singing. Or trying to, over the catcalls and whistles and vulgar remarks from your friends."

"Christ." Savagely, he kicked a pinecone from the path. "They weren't my friends."

"No? But you fit in with them so well."

Stopping abruptly, he grabbed her arm to pull her around to face him. "I don't want you going back to that kind of life, Daisy. You deserve better. Kate too. Marry me and you

212

won't have to spend your nights in such places."

"And where will I spend them, Jack?"

He seemed taken aback by the question. "With me."

She felt like laughing. Or weeping. She didn't know which. "With you. You'll stay and be the father Kate needs and the husband I need. Is that what you're saying, Jack? You'll give up your wandering and stay with us?"

"Well, I . . ."

His hesitation said it all. And one more time, her hopes lay in shambles at her feet. *Silly woman.* "You needn't worry, Jack. Go see the world. I can take care of myself." Bill Johnson was proof of that.

She resumed walking. He fell into step beside her. For a moment, neither spoke, then Jack asked in a challenging voice, "What is it you want, Daisy? A white-fenced cottage? Church socials and singing in the choir? Neither of us could tolerate that. I know you. I've seen the look in your eyes when you sing. You've got too much spirit to bury yourself in a life like that. So what is it you really want?"

You, she almost said. *All of you. For you to say just once that you love me.*

But that could never be, and since she wouldn't allow herself to settle for anything less, she threw out the bald truth, harsh as it was. "Money, Jack. That's all I want and all you can give me. Can't we just leave it at that?"

"You want money? Fine." Grabbing her arm with his free hand, he swung her around. Gone was the laughing Jack she remembered. In its place was a big, bristling male with fury in his eyes. "I'll give you however much you want. Just name your price. Then I get Kate."

ELEVEN

With savage efficiency, Jack saddled the lively chestnut gelding he'd ridden in from Redemption back in what seemed like a lifetime ago.

"Hell and damnation," he muttered, pulling the cinch strap snug against the horse's belly. "Sonofabitch." How could things go so wrong so fast? It seemed every time he opened his damned mouth, he found himself choking on his own foot — or her fist. The woman had a helluva swing.

"Running off?"

He glanced up to see Hank peering over the stall door.

Lifting the bridle from a hook, Jack slipped the bit between the chestnut's teeth. "I'm thinking about it."

"Thinking? Then maybe I should come along so you don't hurt yourself."

"Go to hell."

Chuckling, Hank pushed away from the door. "Let me saddle up first."

They rode without speaking, Jack setting a hard pace in a westerly direction toward Blue Mesa and the steep trails that wound up the southeast face. He needed to get out of this valley, to find a high place so he could see past the peaks that felt like they were closing in on him a little more every day. He needed to reassure himself that the world was still out there, beyond these sloped canyons and looming mountains. He needed to breathe.

He might have ridden straight on to the ocean if his horse could have held up to the pace. Reluctantly, he reined back to a walk so the winded animal could catch its breath.

Hank pulled in beside him. They rode for another couple of miles before his brother finally broke the long silence. "What happened to your eye?"

Lifting a hand, Jack touched the ridge of his cheekbone, wincing as his fingertips found the puffy tenderness of a rising bruise. *Damn hardheaded woman.* "Ran into something."

"Daisy, I'm guessing."

Jack looked over.

Hank shrugged. "I recognize the knuckle marks. What'd you do this time?"

Jack ignored the question. He didn't want to talk about Daisy. Or Kate. Or the fact that all his carefully constructed strategies and rationalizations had been driven back down his throat by one small, well-aimed fist.

Hank dropped back to stay clear of the dust

216

as Jack's horse started up the long switch-back trail to the ledge that overlooked the valley. Every step felt like a move backward in time until Jack found himself reliving that fateful morning almost a quarter century ago, just before his seventh birthday, when he saw RosaRoja for the first time. Was that when everything had started to go wrong?

He remembered it had been cold. He and his older brothers slept in bedrolls on the ground under the wagon their parents and baby brother, Sam, shared and he had been trying to stay close to Hank to stay warm. Hank was like an oven, and he didn't mind Jack sharing his heat the way Brady did.

At thirteen, Brady had been as gangly and rawboned as a new colt. He'd always needed a lot of space around him and didn't like being crowded. Maybe he'd sensed, even then, the burdens that would be placed upon him someday, and was just trying to find room to stretch while he still could.

It had been just before dawn when Pa had nudged each of them awake. "Dress," he'd said, tossing a bundle of clothing onto the ground beside their bedrolls. "And don't wake your ma and Sam."

Shivering as the night air sliced through his worn unions, Jack opened the bundle.

Hell and damnation. New clothes!

He glanced at his brothers and saw they had new clothes too. Grinning in the darkness, he quickly put them on — a blue shirt, dungarees so stiff they scratched going on, a new red kerchief, and a black, flat-crowned, wide-brimmed hat exactly like the one he had admired in the window of Hargrove's Emporium when they'd driven through El Paso three days before. There was even a pair of shiny new boots too.

Jack almost hopped a circle, he was so happy. He hadn't had new store-bought clothes in almost forever. He liked the way the new cloth felt, and the way it smelled, and the rustling sound the stiff dungarees made when he walked.

He was strutting for his brothers when Pa walked up leading Pat and Moe and Little Joe, the saddle horses he and his brothers rode. Jack noticed his father had on new clothes too. None of them had ever looked so grand.

Pa handed over their horses, then leaving Buck and Iantha to watch over Ma and baby Sam, Pa led Jack and his brothers on foot away from the campsite.

Except for the crunch of their footfalls on loose pebbles and a coyote's yodel bouncing along the ridges, it was so quiet Jack could hear Little Joe breathing at his shoulder. The stars had begun to fade, and as the faint purple tint behind the eastern ridges grew brighter, shadows emerged from the darkness — spindly-armed cactus, lacy mesquite, his father's broad form. Just above their heads, wispy bands of smoke from last night's fire hung in the still air, while underfoot, tendrils of morning mist clung to their new boots like lost clouds. To Jack, it was like moving through a dream.

They walked until the sky lightened enough that they could see the ground from horseback, then they mounted and rode at a brisk walk toward the flat-topped shadow of a mesa looming in the dawning sky.

Jack wasn't sure where his father was taking them, or why he'd given all of them these fine new clothes, but he didn't ask. Pa didn't welcome questions. If he wanted you to know something, he told you.

Jack didn't mind. He was just glad to be away from the crowded wagon they'd called home for the last three months, glad to be out and doing something, rather than waiting for Pa to finish his business so they could move on to the new ranch he said he'd gotten them. Jack liked traveling. And even though they'd already covered over a thousand miles since Missouri, he would gladly have gone a thousand more, just to see what was over the next hill.

He glanced at his father's profile. It was a sharp face, almost mean, with pale, far-seeing eyes that could cut right through a person's skull. The short beard was new. Brady said Pa had grown it to cover the scar he'd gotten fighting in the Mexican War, and Jack thought it added greatly to the fierceness of his expression. He couldn't wait to grow one. People might think Pa was as hard as one of those rocky spires pointing straight up to God, but Jack was proud to be his son.

After an hour of riding, they started up a long switchback trail. Riding drag, as usual, Jack caught most of the dust churned up by the horses' hooves, so he tied his new neckerchief up over his nose and mouth in the *bandito* way. It made him feel sneaky and dangerous. He just hoped his new hat wasn't getting too dusty.

The trail was long and steep, and every now and then, his father would stop to let the horses blow, and each time, Jack would take advantage of the brief rest to study the land around him.

There was a lot to see. Mountains all around. Fat lizards, great, dark-winged buzzards, prickly cactus, and snakes that left odd, twisting tracks in the dust. This place was as different from Missouri as anything he could imagine, but Jack liked it just the same. There was a wildness about it that appealed to him, an openness that made him want to shout as loud as he could, just to hear the echo of his own voice bouncing back at him. It was a grand place.

Pa must have felt the same. "It's formidable country," he said during one of their stops to rest the horses. He was leaning forward in the saddle, his crossed forearms resting on the saddle horn, his pale eyes slitted against the early morning sun.

"Yes sir, it is," Brady agreed.

When Pa spoke, it was mostly to Brady, so it was usually Brady who answered. Hank wasn't much of a talker, and Jack always worried that if he spoke up and brought attention to himself, Pa might be reminded of how young he was and send him away from whatever it was they were doing. So usually he just listened and watched.

"Country worth fighting for, I'd think," Pa went on.

"Yes sir." Brady hesitated, then dared to ask, "Is this where you fought the Mexicans?"

"Not yet."

Jack wasn't sure what that meant. From the puzzled expressions on his brothers' faces, they didn't either. But rather than ask questions that might sound stupid, Jack took off the new hat and brushed away dust that had caked along the tooled leather band. Aware that his father watched him, he looked over and grinned. "I sure like this new hat. And the new clothes too."

"A man needs to look his best on the important days."

"Is this an important day?"

"It is. Mark it well." Then with one of his almost-smiles, his father straightened and nudged his horse up the trail.

The higher they climbed, the more excited Jack became. He sensed something waiting just over the ridge ahead, something so monumental and perfect and important, it would change his life forever.

At the top, the track flattened out to weave through a stand of pinyon and juniper. When they came to a small rise where the trees were thin, Pa reined in and waited for them to catch up. There was an odd light in his eyes, and when they stopped beside him, he gave one of his rare grins. "Go on, boys," he said, motioning them ahead. "Take a look at your new home."

New home! Heart thudding, Jack raced his brothers to the top of the rise. As he hauled Little Joe to a stop, the first thing he noticed was the tree. Huge and droopy, it stood guard on a hilltop at the head of the valley, almost as big as the little graveyard beside it. It was the biggest mesquite Jack had ever seen, but it was nothing compared to the land spreading below it.

Shaped like a huge bowl, the valley stretched for miles, ringed by tall trees and high, rocky peaks. Even with summer full on them, it was as green as the finest Missouri bottomland. A creek lined with cottonwoods ran down the middle of the valley, and beside it, perched on a rocky shelf above flood line, rose a big, two-story house with red flowers blooming all around the foundation. It looked like a picture book painting and was the most beautiful place Jack had ever seen.

"Hell and damnation," he said in delight.

Brady reached over and thumped the top of his head. "Watch your mouth."

Jack shied away, afraid Brady would hurt his hat. "You say worse."

"I'm older."

"I don't give a damn."

"Shut up," Hank muttered as Pa rode up. He hated when they fought.

Falling in behind Pa, they headed down toward the house, with Jack, as usual, bringing up the rear. But he didn't mind. He set his own pace, his head swiveling as he studied his new home.

Home. How was that possible? They were poor. Where had his father gotten the money to buy a place like this?

Straddling the lane leading to the house was a high arched gate. At the top, in fancy iron filigree, were back-to-back *R*'s. "Rosa-Roja Rancho," his father told them as they rode under it. "That's Mexican for Red Rose Ranch."

Kind of a girlish name, Jack thought. Hard to say too.

As they drew closer, he saw that the house was even bigger than he had thought: two levels at the center, with one-story wings pointing out back and joined together by a high wall with an open courtyard in the middle. Everything was made of whitewashed adobe — which Pa said was Mexican for mud and straw — and the walls were so thick the windows and doors looked like they were set back at least two feet. They'd make grand places to hide from his brothers, Jack thought, grinning at the prospect. Ma was going to love this place, he decided. Red roses blooming everywhere, nothing like her skimpy flower patch back in Missouri.

A man in white clothes, wearing sandals and a big round Mexican hat, met them as they rode up. At Pa's nod, Jack and his brothers dismounted, handed their reins to the man, then followed Pa through the courtyard gate.

Once inside, Jack stopped in amazement.

The smell of flowers was so strong it almost made him dizzy. Bright color exploded on every side. Birdsong filled his ears. In the middle of a round raised pool stood the stone figure of a monk with a deer at one side, a lamb at the other. From his outstretched hand hung a wooden cage filled with chirping birds. Their song was unfamiliar to Jack and sounded almost sad.

"They are beautiful, no?"

Turning, Jack saw a small gray-haired man crossing the courtyard. He was old and skinny and over a foot shorter than either Pa or Brady, but he held himself proud, like he had a board strapped to his back. His eyes were as round and black as wet agates and he had a sharp, pointy nose, a thin gray mustache, and even thinner lips. Jack thought he looked mean. But remembering his manners, he forced a smile.

"They come from the deep forests of Mexico." As he spoke, the old man thumped the birdcage several times with his knuckle, scaring the little birds so bad they threw themselves in panic against the woven bars of the cage. "The *mestizos* bring them to me."

"It's a big song for such a helpless little bird," Brady said.

Jack recognized the disapproving tone, since Brady directed it at him a lot. But this time, Jack agreed, and wished the man would stop thumping the cage.

"A song of pain," the old man said with a lizard smile. "My wife tends them but they bring her no joy." He pinned Pa with his bright unblinking gaze. "They sing best when they have no distractions, so I have them blinded."

His father's face showed nothing, but Jack was too shocked to remain quiet. "You put out their eyes? On purpose?"

Pa sent him a shut-up look. His oldest brother's hand clamped down on his shoulder.

Jack tried to pull away, but Brady's grip tightened as he bent to whisper in Jack's ear.

"Not now. We'll take care of them later."

How? Jack wanted to ask. *They're already blind and hurt.* But he said nothing, knowing better than to speak up against either Pa or Brady, and instead, elbowed his brother hard in the ribs to make him let go.

"I see you survived the war," the bird-blinder said to Pa.

"As did you."

The old man shrugged. "I am Spanish, not Mexican. It was not my war."

"Maybe so. But now you're an American." Pa reached into his vest pocket, pulled out a folded piece of paper, and passed it over. "And as an American, you abide by its laws or pay the consequences."

Frowning, the man took the paper. "What laws?"

"Those in the Hidalgo Treaty. The territorial government sent out notices telling you what you had to do to register your grant. You should have done it."

"*No es importante.* I do not recognize this territorial government."

"Then you've got a problem."

While Pa explained about the treaty and the back taxes he'd paid and how that meant the ranch was now Wilkins land, Jack glared at the bird-blinder, wishing he had a stick to poke out his black eyes. He didn't want his ranch. He didn't want anything to do with this place and this bastard sonofabitch bird-blinder. He wished they could just leave. This wasn't a good place.

He glanced at his brothers, wondering if they felt it too. If they did, they weren't doing anything about it. *Lily-livers.*

"You should have heeded the notices, Ramirez," Pa said. "You were warned this day would come. This ranch is ours now."

The old man looked about to choke. His face turned red. His eyes bulged.

Jack wished they would pop all the way out so he could stomp them.

"You are wrong," Ramirez argued in a loud voice. "This land has been in my family for almost one hundred years. It was granted to my great-grandfather by King Charles III himself." Wadding up the paper, he threw it at Pa's feet. "I did not fight this war and I am not bound by its treaties."

"You may not be, but your land is." His father bent and picked up the paper. After smoothing it out, he shoved it back into his vest pocket and gave the old man that flat, icy stare that always put fear in Jack's bones. "It's all legal, Ramirez. You've got a month. Use one of the line shacks if you want, but be out of the house when I come back."

The old man's face turned the color of freshly skinned meat. He stepped toward Pa, fists clenched.

Jack perked up, knowing no one could take down his pa in a fair fight. But then the heavy carved door to the house crashed open and everyone whirled as a little girl no older than Jack ran into the courtyard, her face wild with terror.

Elena.

And that was when, for Jack, everything had changed forever.

Even now, almost twenty-five years later, he remembered how perfect she had seemed to him — like a little china doll — even with her bloody legs and skinny arms, and those dark, slanted eyes that seemed too big for her pale, pointed face.

She had run toward him, crying. Chasing after her and swinging a short whip was a boy about Hank's age but a lot smaller. He had laughed each time the braided leather had cut into her legs.

Jack hadn't known who she was or why she was being whipped or what he could do to help her, but he hadn't been about to just stand there and let it happen.

But before he could move, Brady had stepped forward to yank the whip from the boy's hand. And when Elena had turned those terrified eyes on his big brother, that had been the end of the hunt for Jack.

From then on, it had been Brady.

Always Brady.

But for some reason, on this fine spring day, with the wind rustling through the pines and his cheek throbbing from a blow dealt him by another woman, Elena's defection didn't seem to bother Jack as much as it once had. She had made her choices — then and now. And there was nothing he could do about either.

Still, it hurt. And probably always would.

As he and Hank continued up the trail, another thought came, one that shouldn't have surprised him, but did. Of all the memories of that day that kept circling in his head, the one that haunted Jack most was the warbling song of those poor blind little birds trapped forever in the dark in their wooden cage. Even with all he'd seen and done in his travels, that was still the saddest sound he had ever heard.

The track ended at a jumble of boulders. Without waiting for Hank, Jack dismounted, dropped the reins, and walked out onto the ledge.

The valley opened below him. As it had always been. As it always would be. The cruel and savagely beautiful place that he could never completely escape.

A sad feeling came over him. A feeling of loss and regret. He loved this land that had been so much a part of his life for the last quarter-century. But he couldn't spend the next twenty-five years here, because no matter how beautiful it might be, to Jack, it was still and always a cage.

Which was why he was here now, as he had

been so many times in the past, poised on this narrow ledge overlooking the valley. Because this was the highest place he could reach, and standing here, with the sun in his face and the windy silence all around him, was as close to flying as an earthbound human could get.

Lifting his face to the sky, Jack took in several deep breaths, then closing his eyes, he tried to imagine what it would feel like to fly. He needed that feeling as much as he needed air in his lungs. It calmed him and cleared his mind of the taint of the past. It sent his soul soaring.

To fly. To be that free.

A high-pitched "skree" sounded, and he opened his eyes to see an eagle floating high overhead, its great wings spread to capture the rising currents. He watched it, filled with longing and wishing he could be up there with it — drifting above the treetops and mountains — so far up in the sky the earth would look like a giant map spread below him, showing where each river began, and every road led, and where the ocean met the shore and turned mountains into sand.

To see all that. To be up there so high. To be that free.

"You're not going to jump, are you?"

The spell broke. With a sigh, Jack turned and gave his brother a weary smile. "Not today."

"Well, good. That's good."

They stood in silence for a moment, enjoying the view. Then Hank said, "Because if you are considering it, there's something I probably ought to tell you before you do."

Seeing the seriousness of his brother's expression, Jack mentally braced himself. "What?"

"I always liked you better than Brady."

Jack blinked at him, the words so unexpected they were slow to sink in. When they finally did, he started laughing so hard he almost lost his balance and fell off the cliff.

TWELVE

"Damn things drive me crazy," Jack muttered, swatting a fly from his face.

He and Hank were on their way back down from the ledge, and had stopped at a small spring to let the horses drink. With the days growing warmer, the flies were on the hunt, plaguing anything with a pulse. Another thing Jack didn't miss when he was at sea. "Ever think of leaving?"

"Leaving where?"

"The ranch."

"Because of the flies?"

"Because of anything. I figured you'd have moved on by now." Hank had always gone his own way, and he'd never seemed that attached to the ranch.

"Molly likes it here. We're all the family she has left."

"What about you? Don't you have a need to know what's out there behind those mountains?"

"Not particularly. I got what I need right

here." Hank tapped his index finger against his temple. "Seeing new things doesn't interest me as much as thinking up new things. And I can do that wherever."

"So you never plan to leave?" The idea of staying in this valley for an entire lifetime left Jack feeling a little short of breath.

Hank gave it some thought then shrugged. "Without the mines to oversee, I might. There's a man in Santa Fe who's working on a pressurized drilling apparatus. I'd like to talk to him. And maybe take a look at some of the mining techniques they're using up in Colorado."

"Sounds exciting," Jack lied. Once their horses had taken their fill of water, he and Hank reined them back onto the trail. They rode without speaking for a time, then Jack said, "I don't think Daisy would like staying here on a permanent basis." At least, he hoped not.

"You ask her? That why she hit you?"

Jack grinned and shook his head, his temper having cooled enough that he could see the stupidity of what he'd done. "She hit me because I asked her to sell me Kate."

Hank gave such a bark of laughter it startled the horses into a sidestep.

"It must wear you out," he said, once the animals had settled back down, "to carry such a big brain around all day."

"Go to hell."

"I do believe you're even dumber about women than Brady is."

"Surely not that dumb." If so, Jack might have to shoot himself. "But I will admit I've never been confronted with a more hard-headed woman. No matter what I say or do, Daisy seems set against me, and I have no idea why."

Hank looked at him.

"I know," Jack agreed, even though Hank hadn't yet spoken. "You're thinking it's because of Elena. But I already told her that Elena will be gone soon and I'll never see her again, so I don't know why she's still upset."

"Hmm."

Jack nodded. "You're right about that. Women are abso-damn-lutely nothing but trouble. Be helpful if they made sense once in a while so a fellow could figure out what to do."

Leaning forward, Hank flicked a horsefly off his gelding's neck.

"Still." Jack scratched his neck and sighed. "You probably think I should keep at her."

"Looks to be an itchy year," Hank observed, eyeing the mosquito orgies in the puddles of water left by the melting snow.

"Maybe I should use humor," Jack mused. "Daisy always enjoyed a bit of a laugh. I could wear her down with humor and make myself so goddamn charming she'll fall quivering at my feet." He smiled, liking the

234

idea of that.

Hank said nothing.

The horses picked up the pace when they smelled home, and by the time they came to the arched gate, they were feeling perky again and Jack's confidence was restored.

He'd figured out what to do. He'd be charming and persistent. He'd apologize when necessary and grovel when he had to. But mostly he would make her laugh. As far as women were concerned, that was the second best thing he did.

He reined in. "I'm going to Val Rosa."

"Now?"

"I'll be back tomorrow afternoon. Don't let Daisy leave. No matter what she says, just don't let her leave until I get back." Jack grinned at his brother's skeptical expression. "Relax. I'm not running off."

"I hope not. I'd hate to have to come after you. Brady's still got the quarantine up so remember to change horses at the check-point."

"I will." With a nod, Jack turned west and kicked the chestnut into a lope.

It was full dark when Jack rode into Val Rosa. He hadn't seen the town since he'd gone after Elena three years ago, but even in the dim light shining through a window here and there, he could tell it hadn't changed much. Same saloons and whorehouses, Val Rosa Hotel on the right side of Main Street,

Milford's Emporium and General Store on the left. In the middle, The People's Bank, and up by the sheriff's office, the jail and one-room courthouse. Except for the hotel and the drinking and whoring establishments, all were closed for the night.

As he rode down Main Street, he studied the horses tied to the hitching rails outside the various businesses that catered to vice. All seemed healthy enough, so maybe the reports that the horse flu was over were right.

Cutting through an alley, he rode on to the livery, which was situated at the end of town, across from the laundry and bathhouse and next to the smithy. The barn was dark, but he knew the owner, Clem — assuming he was still alive — and rather than wake the old man, Jack dismounted and led his horse through the open double doors. There was enough moonlight to show him the way to an empty stall in the back. After stripping off the saddle, he began rubbing down his substitute horse with a scrap of burlap, then froze when he felt the unmistakable hard edge of a gun barrel between his shoulder blades.

Keeping his hands in sight, he straightened slowly and in a friendly voice said, "I'm hoping that's you, Clem."

"State yer name." The speaker punctuated the question with a hard jab of the gun barrel. "And you better have a ding-dang good reason for skulking around in my livery."

"Jack Wilkins. And I'm just looking to bed my horse down for the night."

"Jack Wilkins? The one who ran off after that Mexican woman?" The pressure between Jack's shoulder blades eased. "Heard you were back."

Letting his hands fall to his sides, Jack turned. Pasting on a smile, he nodded to Clem, then glanced down at the rifle the old man still held in a ready grip, although thankfully, it was now pointed at the dirt floor, rather than at Jack's spine. "Expecting trouble?" he asked.

"Goddamn epizootic." The hostler let out a huff of breath and relaxed his arm so that the gun dangled from one hand by his side. "Folks are so desperate for horses they'll steal anything with four hooves. I've already had two good mules stolen from my own goddamn barn. Hell, they're probably in Mexico by now. Goddamn horse thieves." The old man leaned over and spit into the straw. "You want grain or hay?"

"Both."

After leaning the rifle against an upright post, Clem ducked into his feed room. A moment later, he came out with a lit lantern, which he hung on a hook outside the stall, and a gallon can of sweet feed, which he dumped into a wooden box attached to the inside wall. "What happened to your eye?"

"Ran into something."

Clem gave a cackling laugh that ended in a cough. "A fist, by the looks of it. Got any sick horses out your way?"

"Not yet. Hopefully the worst of it is over."

"Probably is." Clem crossed to the feed room, tossed the empty can inside, secured the door, then went on to the mound of hay piled in the back of the barn, speaking over his shoulder as he went. "But that don't bring the dead horses back. Whole damned country's on foot." Returning with an armful of hay, he dumped it into the corner of the gelding's stall. After closing the door, he slid the bolt home and dusted his hands. He gave Jack a considering look. "Heard your brother was selling some of his fancy crossbreeds to the Army."

Jack shrugged. The horses were Brady's business and Jack didn't feel comfortable discussing them.

"Breeding stock too?" the old man prodded.

"You'll have to talk to my brother about that. How much do I owe you?"

After they'd settled up, Jack said he'd need his horse saddled and ready by nine the next morning, told Clem good night, and went to the hotel.

It hadn't changed much either, although Jack was surprised and pleased to note that with their newfound wealth, the Wilkins family got first choice on the best suite in the house — no extra charge.

He was going to miss being rich.

Since the hotel dining room was closed for the night, he headed down the boardwalk to the saloon he had frequented in the past whenever he was in town, and ordered a bowl of chili and a shot of whiskey. The chili was rank and the whiskey raw — no change there either — and recognizing neither of the two drifters at the bar, nor any of the three old men playing poker at a table in the corner, as soon as he finished eating, he paid up and headed back to the hotel.

He wondered if Val Rosa had always been this boring, or if he was just showing his age.

Morning came in a blast of light. Since the town backed up to an east-facing bluff, daybreak seemed to come from all sides — sunshine from the east, and the reflection off the caliche bluffs from the west. In summer, it felt like being trapped in an oven.

But at nine o'clock, as Jack headed to the livery after a robust breakfast in the hotel dining room, the sun felt welcome and warm in the chilly morning air. After exchanging a few words with Clem, he rode on to the telegraph office, where he sent a wire to his bank in San Francisco. He wasn't sure how much was in his account there, but it had been growing rapidly over the last three years due to his investments in cargo and shipping.

He was even part owner of the clipper he'd come in on, and the bales of wool it had carried back from the sheep stations in Australia would bring a tidy profit. But today, he only requested a thousand dollars, figuring that would be enough to start. After waiting until he got back a telegram confirming the money was on the way, he rode on to the bank.

It hadn't changed much either, Jack thought as he stepped out of the morning glare into the cool silence inside. Harold Lockley had been the bank manager when Jack had left, and apparently he still was, judging by the black lettering on the door behind the teller's cage. Jack wondered why he had sold their smelter loan to Blake, then pushed the thought aside. It wasn't his problem. Brady had made that abundantly clear.

This early, the bank was empty except for a thin-necked, bespectacled fellow wearing an open-crowned visor on his head and protective cuffs on his sleeves, who was watching him warily from behind the barred teller window.

The bars, Jack supposed, were to give the illusion to customers that their money was safe. But the way banks were wobbling since Grant had signed the Coinage Act, and the way the railroads were faltering due to overbuilding and corruption, the bars might come in handy to protect the tellers as well.

"Morning." He leaned forward to read the

engraved brass nameplate pinned to the man's suspender, then straightened. "Mr. Lomax. I'm Jack Wilkins. I'd like to open an account, using this to set up a line of credit until the rest of the money gets here." He slipped the confirmation telegram into the tray below the bars.

The teller read it carefully, then looked up to give Jack a thorough study through eyes that looked huge behind his spectacles. "Jack Wilkins? Of Wilkins Cattle and Mining?"

"The same."

Lomax frowned. With an ink-stained finger, he pushed the wire-framed glasses higher up the bridge of his nose. "Your brothers have already set up an account —"

Jack held up a hand to stop him. "This is separate, Mr. Lomax. It has nothing to do with the ranch or mines. And I'll need five hundred dollars in cash today."

The huge eyes disappeared then reappeared as the man blinked at him. "Out of this account and not the other?" The man looked confused, but maybe that was just a distortion caused by the spectacles.

"This account. Will that be a problem?" Jack glanced at the closed door behind the teller. "Maybe I should talk to Lockley."

"Oh, no," Lomax said hurriedly. "It's just, well . . . never mind." He smiled, showing a lot of small, perfectly aligned teeth. "I'll get it for you now, sir."

Five minutes later, with the five-hundred-dollar bribe tucked safely in his pocket, Jack headed back to the ranch.

It was just past two when he rode up to the barn. After tending his horse, he went inside to find the house quiet, as it usually was in the early afternoon in deference to the sleeping babies. Knowing Daisy was probably upstairs putting Kate down for her nap, Jack stopped by the kitchen first and cajoled Consuelo into fixing him a plate of ham and eggs.

She seemed upset with him, but he didn't ask why. Consuelo had been with the family since they took over RosaRoja, and she sometimes forgot she wasn't his mother and he wasn't still the little kid she used to sneak cookies to. Besides, she'd eventually tell him what had her peeved. Consuelo was a hell of a talker and silence was unnatural to her. He was into his second slab of ham when she finally broke, spouting Spanish so fast he could hardly understand anything other than he was in trouble for sending Daisy away.

"Away?" He froze, a forkful of eggs hanging in front of his open mouth. "What do you mean away? She's not gone, is she?"

Consuelo menaced him with a wooden spoon. "*Mañana. Qué le hizo a ella?* What did you do to her?"

Hell and damnation. The fork clattered to his plate as Jack shot from the chair. Consuelo was still fussing at him as he bounded up the stairs.

He checked Kate's room first. She was sleeping. But the room was stripped bare of the toys that usually littered the floor, and the hooks on the wall where her clothes usually hung were empty. He crossed to the open connecting door that led into Daisy's bedroom.

She was standing at the bed, folding garments and putting them in a worn valise. The pouch she'd taken on their picnic sat beside it, bulging with Kate's belongings.

She was really leaving.

He stood frozen as that realization circled in his mind.

His life could go back to what it had been. Carefree, unencumbered. He could give them the money and send them on their way. He wouldn't have to worry about them anymore. Or see them. Ever again. He could do whatever he wanted, whenever and wherever he wanted.

No Kate. No Daisy. He'd be free.

Jesus. That wasn't what he wanted at all.

Battling panic, he stepped into the room.

She looked up, and for a second, before she masked it, he saw relief.

That was all the encouragement he needed. "I've come to apologize. Again." He smiled.

She didn't smile back.

Undaunted, he moved to stand beside her. Not close enough to crowd her, and definitely out of swinging range, but near enough to stop her if she tried to escape before he said what he came to say. "I didn't mean what I said about taking Kate. I would never do that. Ever."

She continued to study him, her expression guarded.

Reaching into his pocket, he pulled out the wad of money and set it carefully onto the bed between them. "This is not for Kate. It's for you."

She stared at the money. Her lips pursed. Amused or disgusted? He wasn't sure. "You're thinking to buy me now?" she asked.

If only I could. The thought seemed to come from nowhere. It rattled him and revealed to him how much he wanted Daisy — and not just because of Kate.

And why wouldn't he? She was a beautiful woman. And smart. And so full of life, just being around her gave him a lift. In a lot of ways.

He liked the way she made him laugh, and how she kept him guessing, and how she held him accountable when he made mistakes — rather than dismissing him as not worth the effort to keep him in line, like he suspected Brady often did. He liked that she expected more from him than carefully practiced smiles and easy charm, and that she seemed to genuinely admire the man he usually kept hidden behind the laughing mask. She understood him as no other person ever had, yet she seemed to care for him anyway.

How could a man not be attracted to a woman like that?

And how could he not do whatever was necessary to keep her?

"I'm just trying to buy time, Daisy. That's all. Just a little more time with you and Kate. But if you can't give it, the money's yours anyway. To help you start over wherever you want. No strings." It was a lie, of course. Now that he'd decided he wanted her, there was no way he would give up on Daisy that easily.

But he couldn't blame her for having doubts. He'd broken trust with his foolish remark about buying Kate. He hadn't meant it, even when he'd said it. He knew Daisy was too devoted a mother to ever part from Kate. He'd just been angry and scared of losing them and had said the first thing that had come into his mind.

She touched the bills, then spread them out. "This is too much."

"Stay. Please, Daisy. Don't go yet."

Instead of responding, she turned away from the bills scattered on the bed and walked to the window. For what seemed a long time, she stared out, arms crossed, back stiff, her small, perfect form framed by white-capped mountains and endless sky.

He sensed she was weighing his words, trying to find her trust again. He didn't push her or try to force an answer. This decision had to be hers, and he would accept it, whatever it was. Probably.

But her silence was killing him.

Finally, she faced him. She wasn't smiling, but she wasn't frowning either. She looked almost weary. Resigned. As if she had no expectation of this turning out well, but had no other choice except to give it a try. "I have to be in New Orleans by the end of May. I can give you two more weeks."

Jack nodded, his relief so great he couldn't even summon a smile.

Two weeks should be time enough.

Despite the lingering tension between them, Jack continued the riding lessons, much to Kate's delight and Daisy's dismay.

She was still angry with him, but found herself too weak-willed to maintain that anger for long. Every hour spent in his company diminished the hurt a little more, and each day further eroded her determination to stay aloof. She was pitiful.

Two more weeks. Why had she done that? So that Kate would become more attached to him, and she would become more hopeful? How many times must she be disappointed before she learned her lesson?

And yet, she stayed. And hoped. And the days slid by.

Each afternoon, as soon as Kate awoke from her nap, he would arrive to escort them to the barn. His timing was uncanny. Kate would start bouncing with excitement, waving her kitty and calling "horsy" as soon as she saw her father at the door. A half-hour lesson, then they would either check on the new foals, count the calves, pet the barn kitty, or take a walk.

No mention was made of marriage, or Elena, or Daisy's looming departure. It was as if a truce had been called and nothing mattered before or beyond the hours they spent together . . . almost as if they were a family.

An illusion. Daisy knew that. But she enjoyed it nonetheless.

Yet it troubled her that as time passed, she found herself thinking more about Jack and less about going with the troupe to Rome. She had the money she needed, so why didn't she leave? She felt like she was betraying herself but wasn't sure if it was because of her confused feelings for Jack or because the dream of training with Madame Scarlatti seemed more distant every day.

But she had given her word, so she had to stay. Or so she told herself.

At dinner a few days later, Brady announced that workers would be taking a wagon into Val Rosa to get supplies, and if anyone needed anything brought back, they were to give him a list by the end of the evening.

"Perhaps I should go with them," Elena suggested. "It is time I returned to the abbey."

Before the words were out, an uproar ensued. Even though everyone knew she would have to leave soon, no one was ready yet to let her go. Jessica and Brady insisted she stay a few days longer, since they would never see her again. Molly suggested she stay at least until all threat of the horse flu was past, and Hank nodded his agreement. Jack watched but said nothing, his expression giving no clue to his thoughts.

Against such strenuous entreaties, Elena eventually relented. "But only for a few more days," she told them.

The ladies smiled in satisfaction. Brady asked Hank to pass the roast beef, and Jack resumed eating, regarding Elena from time to time with thoughtful eyes.

Daisy wondered what he was thinking. Or what he would have done if Elena had decided to leave despite the protests. Would he have gone with her? She wondered why just posing that question in her mind opened a hollow place in her heart.

The following afternoon the wagon returned from Val Rosa, bringing a packet of mail, a month's worth of foodstuffs and supplies, and Jack's sea trunk.

He made a grand production lugging it into

the house, hinting that it contained all manner of curiosities from his travels, which he
would reveal — "but only to the stout of
heart" — in the big room after supper.

The children weren't the only ones in a
dither of excitement. Brady's foreign travels
were limited to England and Scotland. Neither Jessica nor Molly had been west of Santa
Fe, and Hank had never seen an ocean. They
were all curious to see oddities from other
lands — especially Elena, since she would be
spending the rest of her life on islands Jack
had visited.

Supper was devoured in record time, then
Jack herded them all toward the main room
and the trunk that waited before the crackling
fireplace.

"Gather around if you dare," he said ominously.

Promising unimaginable shocks and thrills,
he waited for the children to settle in a circle
before the trunk and for the adults to take
their seats. The hush of expectation settled
over the audience. When the pop and snap of
the fire were the only sounds in the room, he
took one last look around, then with a flour-
ish that would have made a carnival magician
proud, flipped open the trunk. The lid
cracked on the hearth, making the audience
jump. The children surged forward.

"Stay away!" he warned loudly, sending
them scurrying backward on their knees. He

waited for them to settle again, then peered down into the round eyes staring back at him. "Inside are dangerous things — vile, frightening things that no child should view without first knowing the risks." He dropped his voice to a menacing whisper. "Are you prepared, my lovelies, to take those risks?"

"Yes!" the children squealed, their high-pitched voices bouncing off the rafters.

"Me first!" Ben shouted.

"I'm oldest," Charlie, Hank's stepson, argued.

Reaching into the trunk, Jack whipped out a round thing decorated with dangling wisps of hair and knotted twine. "Then behold!" he boomed, holding it high. A moment of stunned silence. Then shrieks of horror — and not just from the children.

"Hellfire," Ben shouted.

Daisy grabbed for Kate.

Jessica tried to hide Abigail's eyes.

Elena clapped a hand over her mouth.

"Good God," Brady choked out. "Is that a human head?"

Slipping out of his carnival role, Jack grinned, apparently oblivious to the shock he had caused. "Either that or a monkey. Hard to tell. Want to see it?"

"Christ, no!" Brady shrank back, hands upraised. "Keep that thing away from me."

Charlie made a face. "What's that smell?"

"Must be Welch," Dougal muttered and left

the room.

Charlie edged closer then jerked back. "It smells like feet."

While Molly tried to pull her nephew away from the trunk, Hank absently patted Penny's back as she crowded against his knee, her eyes as round as marbles in her ashen face. "How come it's so small?" he asked.

"They shrink it. After they pop out the eyes, they peel the skin off the skull, then they sew the eyelids and mouth shut, pack it with sand, and cook it real slow. Takes about a week."

"Madre de Dios," Elena gasped.

Daisy swallowed back her supper, and Penny lost hers on Hank's boots.

"Enough!" Jessica shot to her feet. "Children upstairs. Now! And, Jack, if I ever see that vile thing in my house again, I will make you rue the day. Children, come." In an instantaneous headlong scramble to escape both the hideous head as well as Penny's mess, children and women pounded up the staircase.

As the noise overhead receded, Jack sighed. "Hell."

Hank laughed. "Oh, don't be too hard on yourself, Jack. Let us do it."

Jack looked ruefully at his brothers. "I'm in trouble again, aren't I?"

Hank nodded. Brady was more vocal. "I can't believe you'd show that thing to kids. They'll be having nightmares for a month."

"How was I to know? I grew up with older brothers, I've been stuck on a ship for the last three years, and I've only known I was a father for two weeks. What do I know about kids?"

"Enough to make one apparently." Shaking off his boot, Hank pointed at the remains of Penny's supper. "You going to clean that up?"

"She's your kid."

While they argued responsibility, Consuelo came in with a bucket and a rag, cleaned up the mess, including Hank's boot, then left, muttering the whole time.

After the air settled, Hank leaned forward and peered into the open trunk. "Got anything else in there? Maybe something useful?"

Jack grinned. "I do. Something I think both of you will appreciate."

Hank grinned over at Brady. "French postcards."

"Let's hope."

After rummaging for a moment, Jack pulled out a flat four-inch-wide piece of wood with a dogleg bend in the center. "What do you think of this?" he asked, tossing it to Brady.

Brady studied it a moment. "It's a stick."

Hank took it and turned it in his hands, studying it from all angles. "Definitely a stick." He looked up at Jack. "No French postcards then?"

"This is better." Reclaiming the piece of

252

wood, Jack gripped it at one end and popped his wrist in a throwing motion. "It's called a boomerang and it's the damnedest hunting stick you'll ever see."

"Hell," Hank said.

Brady sighed. "I know. Postcards would have been nice."

Even so, after Jack gave a lengthy demonstration in the yard the next morning, the boomerang soon proved to be a grand success.

Hank got the hang of it right away, but only after he made a careful study of the "physics of the thing" — whatever the hell that was. He was calculating the "loft to spin ratios" when his older brother finally lost patience and told him to just throw the goddamned thing. Brady had never been very good about waiting his turn.

Charlie did fairly well when his chance came, until his dog, Buddy, grabbed it and ran off. Once they got it back, Penny gave it a try, but soon decided it would make a fine stick horse for her doll, Miss Apple. Ben was less interested in throwing it than in using it to smash ants, and Kate just wanted to eat it. Abigail had no interest in it whatsoever, and the twins slept straight through.

In an attempt to buy himself back into the good graces of the ladies, Jack brought out some of the less controversial items in his trunk. Skirts made of long blades of grass, garlands of dried flowers, feather headdresses, a stuffed baby crocodile — not that well received — and several musical instruments from the wilds of Australia — a drone pipe, a bullroarer, and clap sticks — although Brady said the bullroarer didn't sound like any bull he'd ever heard, and Charlie almost took Molly's head off with it when he got it spinning around and around. Still, everybody seemed to enjoy looking over the items, and no one puked, and Daisy didn't hit him a single time, so Jack figured it was a fine day all around.

THIRTEEN

The days grew longer, the sun hotter. While Elena made preparations to leave, and the ranch workers looked ahead to spring roundup, and the cottonwoods unfurled new leaves, Jack continued the daily riding lessons and afternoon walks with Daisy and Kate. As their hikes ranged farther and became more strenuous, Daisy's initial soreness gave way to renewed energy. But as her body strengthened, her will weakened, and thoughts of Jack haunted her nights.

She felt suspended in time, moving furiously, but going nowhere.

Several days after the "head" incident, Jack took them to the creek to see if it had risen still higher with the warmer weather and increased snowmelt. It had, and to the point that it was now overflowing the banks by several feet.

Slipping off the pouch of spare jackets and slickers they always brought along on their walks, Jack picked up a stick then knelt beside

Kate. "Look, Katie-girl." He tossed the stick into the rushing current. "See how the water swept the stick away?" Looping a protective arm around her narrow shoulders, he gave a gentle squeeze. "That could happen to you, little one. So you must never go into the water without your mama or me. Understand?"

"Titty too?"

"Kitty too."

"Bad water."

"Not bad. Just water. But when it's moving fast, it's not safe. Never, ever go into fast water. Promise?"

Kate nodded solemnly.

"That's my girl." He rose, picked up the pouch, and taking Kate's hand in his, led her along the bank toward a huge boulder. As they drew closer, Daisy could see markings etched into the stone . . . symbols, names, dates, initials.

"This is a message rock," Jack explained. "People have been carving on it for hundreds of years. There's even a marking left by a Spanish soldier that goes back to the fifteen hundreds. Look, Kate." He bent and ran his fingers over a crude rendering of a deer. "An Indian put this here a long time ago. And these are names of pilgrims passing through. Want me to carve your name here?"

"Titty too?"

"Kitty's too." He glanced at Daisy. "And

256

Mama's, if she wants."

Feeling suddenly that in agreeing she might be sending a message she didn't want to give, Daisy tried to laugh it off. "You'd be carving for days."

But he was already digging through the rocks for a piece of flint. "Your initials, then. I'll do all our initials."

It took him a while and the results were crude, but knowing her initials would be there for all time gave Daisy an eerie feeling, as if she were permanently attached to this place and this family by a few simple markings on a rock.

They continued their hike up through a stand of tall pines, following a clear trickle of icy water that wound down from deeper in the canyon. Their footfalls barely sounded against the thick carpet of pine needles, and here and there, patches of snow still clung in the shadows on the north sides of big boulders and under tangled blowdowns of toppled trees. Seeing that Kate was growing weary, Jack picked her up and let her doze against his chest as they followed a faint path that climbed steadily upward.

Hearing an odd noise coming from Jack, Daisy looked over at him. He seemed lost in thought, pleasant thoughts, judging by the smile tugging at his lips.

"What was that?" she asked.

He glanced at her over Kate's head. "What

was what?"

"That sound. Are you well?"

He flashed a sheepish grin. "I was humming a tune."

"That was a tune?"

"What'd you think it was?"

"Tunes normally have more than one note."

He chuckled. "In my head, they do. It just doesn't always come out that way. You don't recognize it? You used to sing it at the Silver Spur."

So he'd noticed her singing, after all. Daisy smiled, pleased and a little sad. Most of her songs had been for him, whether he knew it or not, and even though it no longer mattered, she was gratified he'd taken note.

"I liked your singing."

"Did you? You never said."

"It was a bad time for me," he admitted without looking at her. "But even when I was so drunk I could hardly think or form a thought, I heard your voice. It was like the bell of a buoy sounding in the darkness, pulling me back."

"Back from what?"

He shrugged. "My own destruction, I suppose. Hell, you probably saved my life." Abruptly he stopped and faced her, forcing her to stop beside him. The laughter was gone from his eyes, replaced by an intensity that seemed to add substance to the still, pine-scented air.

"Marry me, Daisy."

She felt something twist in her chest. "For saving your life?"

"For that, and Kate, and the good times we shared. And there were good times, Daisy. I remember that. And laughing. And reaching for you in the night when holding you was the only thing that kept me from giving up."

"No." Desperate to put distance between them, she turned away. *Why now?* After she'd worked so hard to pull herself back together, why was she letting him tear her apart again?

His hand grabbed her arm. "Why not?"

She pulled free. "I am not your savior, Jack. Besides, you're in love with another woman, remember?" How many times did she have to remind him of that?

He didn't deny it. She didn't expect him to. It was too late for that anyway.

She started up the path again. They didn't speak again until they reached a high, open plateau that overlooked the valley. It was a beautiful view, stretching from a large flat-topped formation at one end of the valley to the cluster of ranch buildings at the other. From this distance, the flooded creek looked like a shiny brown ribbon laced through the trunks of the budding trees, and the cattle dotting the grassy flats seemed no bigger than drops of dark paint on a stark green canvas.

Warm from their uphill trek, Daisy removed her shawl and spread it on a soft spot in the shade of a boulder. Then motioning for Jack to hand down Kate, she settled her daughter on the shawl and gently rubbed her back until she drifted to sleep again.

"I've loved Elena since I was seven years old."

She looked up to find Jack leaning against a boulder several feet away, staring down at them with a pensive look. She didn't respond. She didn't want to talk about Elena. Jack owed her no explanations, and she certainly didn't want to hear any.

But he continued, unmindful of her pain, his gaze focused inward, his voice flat and distant.

And she listened.

"She was six and her brother Sancho was using a whip on her. Brady stopped him. No one had ever stood up for her before, not even her own father, and from that moment on, Brady was her hero." He smiled ruefully. "I wanted her to look at me like that. I wanted to be the one to save her. But Brady was there first. He always was. In everything."

Daisy didn't want to hear this. But she didn't ask him to stop. She sensed Jack was revealing a part of himself he had probably never shown anyone else, and perhaps if she had the courage to listen, she might under- stand the hold Elena had on him.

Bending over, he picked up a pinyon cone. With his folding knife, he dug out a seed and set it on the boulder near his shoulder, then dug for another. "For years I thought there was something special between them. There was — there still is. But not in the way I thought. I didn't realize that until Jessica came."

Motion caught her eye, and Daisy watched a small striped ground squirrel inch across the top of the boulder toward the seed.

"At first I figured Brady was using them both," Jack went on. "We almost came to blows over it. But he denied there had ever been anything between him and Elena, that she was like a sister."

The squirrel grabbed the seed and skittered out of sight.

Jack put another in its place. "I didn't believe him at first. I thought maybe Elena wouldn't have him and he was just making excuses. Then I saw the way he looked at Jessica. It was different from the way he looked at Elena. And I thought, 'Here's my chance.' I could take her to San Francisco to get her hip fixed, care for her during her operation and recovery, and be her hero at last. I could win what Brady couldn't."

Daisy frowned, trying to understand. Was this about Elena, or a rivalry with his brother?

Having dug out all the seeds, he tossed the pinecone away, scooped the seeds into his hand, and rested his upturned palm on the rock.

"Hank said something to me the other night. It didn't make sense at first, like most of what Hank says, but I've thought about it a lot and I think I understand what he meant."

The squirrel appeared again, saw Jack's outstretched hand, and froze.

"He said if a man has feelings for a woman, he should know why. So I've been asking myself . . . do I want Elena because I love her? Or to prove to Brady I'm the better man?"

Daisy wondered the same thing but said nothing.

The squirrel inched forward, its tail flicking, its nose twitching. Moving in fits and starts, it skittered to Jack's hand, grabbed a seed, then scampered out of sight. Another poor creature charmed by Jack Wilkins.

"And your answer?" she asked, trying not to hope.

He dumped the remaining seeds onto the rock then dusted his hands. His gaze met Daisy's and in his eyes she saw doubt and confusion, and maybe sadness. "I've loved her since I was seven," he said again. "But I never slept with her and I hardly ever kissed her. I'm not sure why."

Disappointment left a bitter taste on her tongue. "And you think marrying me will provide an answer?"

For a long time Jack didn't reply. "I think

we suit, Daisy," he finally said. "I think Kate needs us both. And I think we can make this work."

And what of love?

Beside her, Kate began to stir. Reaching out, Daisy gently stroked her daughter's cheek to reassure her as she awoke. Anger and resentment seeped out in a long sigh. Nothing had changed. Nothing ever would. Elena would forever be the perfect, unattainable, unrequited love, and Daisy would be . . . what? Jack's consolation prize? The woman who waved him off on his adventures and patiently waited for his return? Was she to give up her dream of singing for so little?

"I know you mean well, Jack. You always do. And I know you care for Kate. But a child is a forever thing, not something you can lavish attention on one moment then ignore the next. She needs an everyday father, and you're not suited to that. You want to travel the world. So do it." Picking up Kate, she rose, shook out the shawl, and threw it over her shoulder. She turned to face him so he could see the determination in her eyes. "Gamble, drink, pine over Elena, or chase after women to your heart's content. Do what you do, Jack. We'll be fine without you."

"Then why are you here, Daisy?" he challenged. "If things were so fine, why did you come begging for money?"

Heat rushed into her face. "I didn't come

begging! I thought you might want to help your daughter."

Kate whimpered, blinking sleepy eyes against the harsh words and bright sunlight. Clutching her tightly, Daisy started down the path.

Jack fell into step beside her. "I don't want to fight with you, Daisy," he said in a low voice so he wouldn't alarm Kate. "And I don't know how I feel about Elena right now. But I do know I want you and Kate in my life, so don't expect me to let you go without a fight."

"You're wasting your time. I won't marry you."

"I can be pretty persistent."

She whipped around to face him. "Why? Is it just the chase then?"

His eyes narrowed in confusion. "What chase?"

"Think about it, Jack." Wrapping both arms around Kate so she wouldn't give in to the urge to punch some sense into his hard head, Daisy asked, "Why did you want Elena? Because you thought Brady did. Why did you run off to sea? Because after you got what you wanted from me, you lost interest. And now you're after me again. Why? Because I won't have you. With you, the chase is everything."

As she spoke, his face had flushed to an angry red. "You're wrong. I'm not that kind of man."

"Aren't you?" She gave a brittle laugh, all the hurt she had hoarded over the last three years pressing against her throat. "If I said yes, what would you do? Run off on another adventure and leave me and Kate behind, that's what. Face it, Jack. You're no more the marrying kind than I'm the waiting-around kind."

She started to turn away when he grabbed her shoulders. Pulling her toward him, he brought his mouth down on hers.

Daisy froze, hardly aware of Kate wiggling between them. Hurt died as old yearnings arose in a hot, shivery rush. Long-suppressed need flooded her body even as her mind struggled to resist. *Not again,* she thought in panic as she felt herself sinking into the magic that was Jack Wilkins. *Never again.* With a gasp, she pulled back, knowing if she didn't stop this now, she would be lost forever.

"That's why I'm after you," he said in a strained voice. "It's still there, what we had. You felt it too. Admit it."

"Titty too." Kate thrust her kitty in Jack's face. "Kiss Titty."

"W-What? Ah . . . sure." Befuddlement fading into amusement, he kissed the bedraggled toy, then Kate, then went for Daisy again.

"No." She brushed a shaking hand over her face, as if that might rid her of the feelings still coursing through her. Thank God Kate had interrupted them. Daisy was still shaking inside. "I won't let you do that to me again, Jack."

His smoky eyes seemed to darken. A slow smile split his face. "Oh, I'll definitely do it to you again, Daisy," he said in a voice caught somewhere between desire and menace. "I'll do it until your eyes roll up in your head, then I'll rest up and do it again. Count on it."

"I must go, *querido*."

Brady looked up from his breeder's journal to see Elena standing in the doorway of his office. Immediately he rose and crossed to her. Waving aside her protests, he took her arm and led her to one of the chairs in front of his desk.

She felt brittle in his grip. Her face looked tired and drawn, but against the severe black of her habit, it still seemed too beautiful to be real. Almost unearthly, like one of those religious paintings he had seen when Jessica had dragged him to a museum in England.

"Go where?" he asked, once he'd helped her into the chair.

"Where I belong. Back to my sisters in the abbey."

He wanted to argue with her, tell her she belonged here too. But he no longer believed that. Even though he still saw in her a shadow of the little girl he had rescued from San-

266

cho's whip all those years ago, the Elena he had protected for the last quarter century was in other hands now, hands more powerful than his.

Moving back behind his desk, he settled once more in his chair. "Because of Jack. That's why you're leaving, isn't it?"

"I leave because it is time to begin the work God has given me to do."

He hated all this pious talk. It stifled logic and argument and half his vocabulary. But he didn't say anything, since they'd been through this already. Twice. And he'd lost both times. For such a gentle, meek woman, Elena could be as unyielding as stone. "When?"

"Soon. But before I go, I must speak to you of my concerns."

"About Jack." Conversations with Elena always came around to Jack.

"And about you. You must mend this rift between you."

Brady blinked in surprise. "What rift? There's no rift."

Elena gave him a look of exasperation he was sure she never let loose in the abbey. "For as long as I have known the two of you, there has been anger between you. If you do not end it, *querido,* it will cost you this brother too."

"Anger about what?" Brady thought he'd done a good job of keeping his temper in

267

check. He'd barely berated Jack for his long absence and failure to write. He hadn't asked his brother for money, although admittedly, he hadn't told him about the money he and Hank had set aside for him out of the mine profits either. Other than the one time, he hadn't called him to accounts over Daisy and Kate, and had been careful not to badger Jack about how long he'd be staying. He figured he'd been damn near saintly about the whole thing.

"You are too hard on him," Elena said. "You are pushing him away."

"If he leaves, it'll be by his decision, not mine."

"But you have taught him to do so. You make him think he is not important, that he has no place in your life, so why should he stay?"

"Of course he's important, Elena. He's my little brother."

"*Ves?* That is what I mean." She sighed and shook her head. "You speak of him as if he is not yet a man. As your *little* brother. Has he not earned the right to be more to you than that?"

"But he *is* my little brother." Brady spread his hands in an encompassing gesture. "And all this — the ranch, the house, the mines, the years of endless work to carve something out of nothing — it's for him and Hank, our wives and kids, for you and even those souls resting in the graveyard on the hill. I don't know what else to do, Elena. So tell me. What other proof do you need that each of you, including Jack, is important to me?"

He didn't mean to lose his temper, but he was weary of trying to justify the way he lived his life and the hard choices he'd had to make. But indignation died when he saw tears fill her eyes. Jesus, he hated it when women cried.

"Oh, Brady. Forgive me for making you think we are not grateful. You have been the rock of this family for so long. But we cannot all be like you — so strong and sure and steady. Some of us have to take a different path. But that does not mean we reject you or the life you have built for us."

Maybe not, but sometimes it sure felt that way. "I know I may seem hard on Jack." He gave a rueful smile. "Truth be told, I often envy him. It's all so simple for him. So uncomplicated. And even if sometimes I want to beat the sass out of him, I admire his hardheaded independence."

"Have you told him that?"

Brady smirked at the idea. Admitting such a thing to Jack would be like giving his wild little brother free rein to get himself into all sorts of mischief. "I know I seem a little heavy-handed at times, but I walk a thin line here, Elena, trying to keep the ranch going and my brothers safe. And believe me, it takes its toll. So much so, that sometimes I find myself wondering what it would be like to ride past those mountains and never come back. But then I realize this is the work I've been given to do. This is what I am, and this is where I belong. I won't apologize for that."

"*Por supuesto que no.* Of course not. But let Jack seek his place, too, *querido.* Maybe he will find it in some faraway place, or maybe he will realize it is here at RosaRoja. But let him choose." A stern look came over her face. "And let him choose what to do about Daisy and Kate as well. You must not force that issue either."

Brady would make no promises on that score. He'd give Jack time to do the right thing, but if he didn't, Brady would step in. Little Kate was part of his family now. And he looked after his family.

"And finally, *hermano,* you must forgive yourself."

An unseen hand seemed to grab at his chest. He didn't want to talk about Sam. It was old history. Almost fourteen years old. He'd learned to live with it and didn't want it dragged out again.

"Sancho killed him, Brady. Not you."

"Elena —"

"You gave him peace," she cut in. "Now allow yourself that same grace."

He sat frozen, waiting for the pain to roll over him, for that cloying guilt that never

270

seemed to go away to rise in his throat like bile.

"Sancho killed him," she said again.

"Let it rest, Elena. Please."

He saw worry in her eyes, but she said no more. "Then I will pray for you, my brother. And I will never forget all that you have done for me."

He watched tears roll down her cheeks and felt an answering sting in his own eyes. "I'll never see you again, will I?"

"Si Dios quiere." She gave him a watery smile. "If God wills it."

Brady thought of the little girl with the bloody legs who had run across the courtyard and into his heart. Letting go of her, he realized, was going to be much harder than he'd ever imagined.

FOURTEEN

The day after Jack kissed her — *kissed* her, for heaven's sake — and she *let* him — what was she thinking? — Daisy stepped out onto the front porch and into another beautiful day. Cloudless. Pleasantly warm. Perfect.

Then why did she feel like running from this place as fast as she could?

Because of Jack, of course. Because he had kissed her. And because she had let him and it had been every bit as wonderful as she remembered. *Ninny.*

Setting Kate and her basket of toys in a sunny spot near the rockers, Daisy stretched onto her toes and filled her lungs with sage-scented air. A refreshing change from San Francisco.

For one thing, the air she drew in here was so clean she couldn't see or taste it — no coal soot or fish smell here, and no gray clouds hanging so low the world seemed wrapped in cotton batting.

The sounds were different too. Birdsong

instead of foghorns, cattle lowing instead of people shouting, nights so quiet she could hear crickets chirping, and mornings so hushed that without the clatter of wagon wheels on cobblestones, she could even hear distant voices throughout the house.

Happy voices. Children laughing. The occasional song.

It didn't feel right to her. Something was missing. Instead of calming her, all this peace and quiet only reminded her of those long, long days on the farm when she would pause in her chores to look down the road stretching away from her and wonder if she would ever know what lay at the end of it.

She missed the city. An awful thing to admit, but there it was. Despite the danger and hardship of her life in San Francisco, she missed it — the rush and bustle, the unpredictability, the vitality of so many people crowded into so many buildings doing so many different things. And the longer she stayed removed from it, the more her energy waned. But what troubled her most was that with each passing day in this calm and peaceful place, Jack took over a little more of her heart and the dream took up a little less.

She couldn't allow that. Singing was like breathing to her, and without it, she would die. Pressing a hand to her mouth, she stifled a sudden urge to laugh. Or cry. She wasn't sure which and that frightened her. She was becoming an emotional fool, she realized in dismay. She had to gain control of herself, put Jack Wilkins from her mind and concentrate on getting through the next ten days.

"I think this is my favorite time of year," a voice called.

Startled, Daisy dropped her hand and looked around to see Jessica at the other end of the porch, peering up through the railing. Grateful for the company, she walked toward her. "What are you doing down there?"

As she neared, Daisy realized Jessica was working in the flowerbed, supervising a middle-aged Mexican worker — although judging by the impatient looks he aimed at her, the Englishwoman was mostly getting in his way.

Jessica grinned up at her. "It's always so exciting to see what has survived the winter. Rather like opening a long-awaited gift, don't you think?"

Daisy smiled. *Her Ladyship, indeed.* With her vibrant tavern red hair tumbling about her shoulders, her apron muddied, and dirt smeared across her freckled cheeks, Jessica looked less like the lady of the manor than a happy, dig-in-the-dirt gardener. And Daisy liked her all the more for it.

"Are those roses?" she asked, looking over the railing at the leafless sticks poking through the dirt like grasping fingers.

Jessica beamed at her stick-plants, as proud

as a new mother. "They are. Yellow, for the most part — Enrique, don't forget to trim that one, *por favor* — although I've begun adding a white or pink here and there."

"No red?"

Jessica pushed back a curl with a dusty glove. "There's a red in the cemetery that Brady transplanted from this bed when he rebuilt the house." With a dismissive shrug that was at odds, Daisy thought, with the sad look in her soft brown eyes, she added, "It was the only survivor. There was a dreadful fire, you see, that destroyed the original house and all the lovely roses."

"How many did you have?"

"A hundred, but they weren't mine actually. They were originally planted by Elena's mother. That's how RosaRoja got its name — Red Rose Ranch." Her smile seemed forced, but Daisy wasn't sure why. "They endured for over a quarter century, poor dears, until fire destroyed all but the one Brady found when he began excavations for this house. Since he moved it onto the hill, something about the soil up there has caused the blooms to darken to a deep crimson. Almost a blood red." She looked up with a wry smile. "A fitting color for a cemetery, don't you think?"

Unsure how to answer, Daisy moved to a safer subject. "Would you like help? I may not know much about roses, but I'm a farm girl from Quebec, so I definitely know how to dig in dirt."

Jessica laughed and glanced back at the worker. "I'm not sure Enrique could tolerate more help. But there's always the vegetable garden. Let me send for the twins, and a blanket for the children to play on, and I'll show you."

It was more like a walled fortress than a vegetable plot, Daisy decided later when they walked around the side of the house. Apparently this family had a gift for overbuilding. Once she'd settled Kate beside the twins on a blanket by the fence, Daisy left her to Rosa Ortega's care and followed her hostess on a tour.

"I know it's rather much." Jessica swept a hand in a gesture that encompassed the sprawling acre of garden. "But Brady always says, 'Why build for today, when a century would be better?' "

At least a century, Daisy thought, looking around in amazement.

Built in stockade fashion, the fence was constructed of standing ten-foot-tall posts stuck in the ground and lashed together with stout rope. At one end of the enclosure was a heavy gate hung on horseshoe hinges. At the other end stood a log and stone outbuilding next to a railroad-style water tank on stilts. Budding fruit trees, their trunks wrapped to protect them against frost, stood along the fence. Lined up before them like troops awaiting inspection were rows of elevated beds separated by flagstone walkways. The beds were just budding now, showing the merest green tops of emerging seedlings. There was also — if Daisy surmised correctly from the grid of earthen pipes bordering the walkways — an elaborate gravity-fed watering system that linked the water tower to each bed. "How clever," she remarked, studying it as they walked, not sure how it worked, but admiring the ingenuity. "Did you do this?"

"Hank." Jessica paused to pluck out a weed that had dared send up shoots between the stones. "He's quite the innovator, you see. One is never sure what he'll come up with next." This last was added as a murmured afterthought.

"Does it work well?"

"Eventually." Straightening, Jessica tossed the weed aside and continued down the path. "The first year, the shutoff mechanism between the tank and pipes broke and the ensuing flood washed out everything, even the dirt." Another pause, another weed torn from the earth. "The next year, carpenter ants damaged one of the posts supporting the water tank and it tipped over, taking down a section of fence. What didn't wash away in that flood was quickly devoured by deer and rabbits. But last year, I am pleased to say, it worked beautifully."

"You have rabbits?" Daisy had noted evidence here and there on their walks with Jack, but hadn't seen any yet. Kate would be delighted.

Jessica shot her that wry smile again. "Another of Hank's ideas. We have quite a few mouths to feed at RosaRoja and he thought rabbit would be a nice change of pace from the usual beef and venison."

"That didn't go well either?" Daisy wondered what new catastrophe this latest scheme of Hank's had brought about. Apparently the poor man had everything going for him but luck.

"It did. At first. But then one of the children left the cages open, and several dozen rabbits escaped. And now," she shrugged, "in addition to being overrun with rabbits, we also have packs of plump coyotes running about. Do keep an eye on Kate."

Daisy stopped midstride. "Would they attack her?"

Her voice must have shown her fear. Jessica reached out and patted her arm, leaving dirt smudges on her sleeve. "They're not that bold," she assured her. "And there are always dogs about the place to warn us if they come too close. It's just that . . ." Taking her hand from Daisy's arm, she looked around as if expecting to see . . . what?

Frowning, not sure what she was looking for, Daisy looked around, too, wondering what other dangers could be lurking. "It's just *what?*" she prodded.

Jessica chewed her bottom lip for a moment then sighed. "I don't want to worry you. Truly, I don't. But since you're unfamiliar with the area and Kate is so small —"

"What?" Fully alarmed now, Daisy had to struggle not to snatch Kate from the ground and flee into the house. "What else should I be watching for?"

It had to be snakes. She'd heard the West was full of snakes. And poisonous spiders. And scorpions and giant lizards and wild pigs that attacked for no reason, and bears and wolves and mountain lions and crazed buffalo.

At least in San Francisco she only had to be wary of rats and villainous humans.

"I don't want you to become overly concerned," Jessica began in a voice that concerned Daisy mightily. "But I should probably mention a few things of which you should be aware."

Her list of horrors seemed enormous and included every threat Daisy had imagined, in addition to the occasional Indian war party, drunken desert dwellers, flash floods, rock slides, frostbite, and heatstroke.

Even as Jessica spoke, Daisy was mentally packing her valise.

"Try not to worry." This time Jessica patted Daisy's shoulder, no doubt smearing it with dirt as well. "As Hank often says, 'Being aware is the best defense against the unexpected.' And don't forget" — she gave Daisy a bright smile — "Molly is a remarkably gifted nurse."

"I think I frightened Daisy today," his wife said as Brady came out of the dressing room, wearing nothing but a damp towel and high hopes.

"Why?" He paused to check his chin in the vanity mirror. He didn't want to give her whisker burn. "Want me to shave?" he asked, hoping not.

"I don't care." She flipped back the counterpane so hard it almost sailed off the bottom of the bed. "She needs to be aware, that's why. Especially with Kate toddling about."

She *should* care. She had a redhead's sensitive skin, after all. Everywhere. Gaze pinned to the mirror, he watched her shrug out of her robe, admiring every familiar dip and hollow that showed through the thin cloth of her gown. The towel hanging at his waist twitched in expectation. "Aware of what?"

"Snakes, tarantulas, whatnot." She began her normal bed preparations, but with more vigor than usual — fluffing the pillows with grim-faced efficiency then shaking out the quilt so hard it snapped like a billowing sail. By the time she was done, the bed would be a shambles, at which point she would spend

280

the next quarter hour righting the mess she had made until nary a wrinkle showed.

He knew the routine well. She was upset, for sure.

Sensing trouble but not knowing the cause or how it might impact his bedtime plans, Brady settled a hip on the corner of the vanity, folded his arms over his damp chest, and waited her out. As he watched her assault the bedding, he mentally sorted through the day's events for any blunders he might have made. He couldn't think of a one. All in all, it had been a good day. Even the Army had cooperated, sending word they would take as many of their horses as they could get. In fact, as far as Brady could tell, other than his concerns over ranch finances, Jack, and losing his herd of prized horses, it had been a damn near perfect day.

But not, apparently, for his wife. She was definitely fretting about something. And if not him, then what?

"You were right to warn her," he said, tossing out a line.

"Of course I was. That's all put to rights. It's Molly who concerns me."

Molly? He must have missed something. But rather than admit that, he kept his mouth shut. She would eventually tell him what was worrying her. Then he would fix it and she would be happy again, which would make him happy again.

Climbing into bed, she began smoothing out all the wrinkles she had made. "She's so melancholy of late, Brady. I scarcely hear her laugh anymore."

Ah. Now he understood. If there was one thing that could upset his wife faster than him, it was problems with her family. Or Hank's family. Or now even Jack's family. Or any one of the dozen families that made up the bigger family of RosaRoja. She was the mother of them all.

"It's Hank," she said with conviction. "He's done something or said something to upset her. You need to find out what it is and fix it."

Brady bit back a smile. A brother telling him to butt out and a wife telling him to butt in. And they wondered why he seemed arbitrary sometimes. Pushing away from the vanity, he walked toward her. "It's not something I can fix."

"You can try."

Sitting on the edge of the bed beside her hip, he smiled down at her, thinking how beautiful she looked to him with her hair spread across the pillows like fiery wings and her whiskey brown eyes so full of trust and love. Through all the violence and turmoil in his life, how had he found his way to this remarkable woman? Even after almost four years, it was still a wonderment to him.

"Please, Brady, just give it a go. If anyone

can make it right, you can."

When she looked at him like that, he almost believed it. She had a way of making him think anything was possible and there was nothing he couldn't do. Which was mostly true most of the time. Hell, he was here, wasn't he? Wearing nothing but a towel and a hopeful smile, sitting beside the most exciting and beautiful woman in the world. He must be pretty damn good to deserve all that.

Leaning down, he kissed her brow then straightened. "Don't say anything to her, okay? You know how private Molly is, and this is between her and Hank." He waited for her reluctant nod, then said, "She's upset because there's no baby."

He watched surprise give way to understanding. She let out a sigh of relief. "Of course. How silly of me. She's mentioned how much she looks forward to adding to their family. I should have known that was what was bothering her."

"But if you still want me to fix it, I could ask Hank if he needs any help."

"Dolt." She punched his shoulder then laughed, letting her fingertips trail down his bicep and across to his chest.

His skin prickled. He saw something change in her eyes as she watched the way his muscles flexed beneath her touch, and it sent blood pumping through him.

"On second thought . . ." She glanced up

at him through her cinnamon-colored lashes. "Maybe you should shave after all."

Grinning, he pulled back the covers. "Too late."

"A mustang's bigger and stronger," Brady said, carrying the argument from the kitchen table to the big room where the family had congregated after supper.

"Aye, but the garron is more surefooted," Dougal countered from his spot in front of the hearth, where he was toasting his backside.

Daisy relaxed on a couch, watching Jessica read a picture book to Ben and Abigail and Kate, who gathered by her rocker. Charlie and Hank sat shoulder to shoulder on one end of another couch drawing plans for a three-wheeled scoot-along, while Molly sat at the other end, helping Penny bandage Miss Apple's arm.

"So are burros," Brady pointed out, dropping into one of the chairs beside the hearth. "But you wouldn't want to ride one. Unless you're a stump-legged Scotsman, of course."

"Haud yer wheesht, ye craiker numptie. Yer lettin' yer feet outrun yer shoes."

Brady looked around. "Does anyone know what he's saying?"

"Best not ask," Hank advised without looking up from his tablet.

"I think you've been told to shut your geggie." Molly ran another loop of gauze around Miss Apple's arm then grinned over at the old man. "Do I have that right, Dougal?"

"Aye, lass. No tha' 'twill dew any guid. Easier tae kiss a bolt o' lightnin' as talk sense intae the yammerin' trout."

"Jack kiss Mama," Kate piped in. "Kiss Titty too."

Brady's brows shot up. "Good God. In front of his daughter?"

Daisy smothered a laugh. "She was talking about her toy kitty."

"Ye're a sick mon, ye are, tae think such a thing," Dougal said in disgust.

"Gentlemen." Jessica paused in her reading to send them chiding smiles. "Carry it outside if you must argue."

"Tae cold," Dougal mumbled, hiking his kilt higher to the fire.

"Wouldn't be if you wore pants instead of a dress," Brady reminded him, which set them off again, but thankfully at a lower volume, until finally Dougal gave up the fight and stomped out, calling for Consuelo.

"I thought he'd never leave," Brady said with a labored sigh.

"Don't you like Mr. Dougal?" Charlie asked him.

"I do. Especially when he's in another room."

"Make it tighter, Aunt Molly," Penny instructed, waggling the doll's arm. "Or it'll fall off."

Daisy sighed with contentment, enjoying the ebb and flow of conversation and the comfortable camaraderie of this big, rowdy family. It had been a long but lovely day. Even though the evenings were still quite cool, the afternoons were growing steadily warmer. On their hike earlier, she had seen tiny flowers bursting through the damp soil, heralding the end of winter even though the spring equinox wasn't due for another few days. The cold fog of San Francisco seemed such a distant memory, she could scarcely remember the chill of it soaking into her bones.

The couch sagged as Jack plopped down beside her. "Been looking for you," he said. "I thought you'd be upstairs putting Kate to sleep."

"Later," she mumbled around a yawn.

"Tired?"

"A bit."

He leaned closer until his hard-muscled shoulder touched hers. "Why don't you take off your clothes and hop into bed for a while?" he whispered. "I could watch over you to be sure you weren't disturbed."

"But I'd be disturbed anyway, just knowing you were watching me."

"Then I'll keep my eyes closed. Promise."

She tried to stifle a laugh but choked a bit instead.

"That's a nasty cough," Jack murmured

once she'd caught her breath. "Maybe I should take a look at your chest."

"Hush!" She glanced at the others, but they all seemed engrossed in other things. Too engrossed perhaps. "You love another woman, remember?" A tired refrain, but true nonetheless.

"I love lots of women," he whispered back. "But I'm marrying you." He took her hand in his. "You've captured my heart, my little desert flower. You've found a warm place inside me that's yours alone. I'm just trying to do the same." He waggled his brows. "Want to go upstairs and try to find it together?"

She snatched her hand back. The man was incorrigible and growing more so ever since he'd thrown down the gauntlet of marriage again a few days ago. His attentions were unrelenting. And flattering. And impossible to ignore. Especially after that kiss. Daisy smiled, remembering. Even though she doubted the sincerity of his pursuit, Jack was so charmingly outrageous about it, she couldn't take offense.

"Where's Elena?" she asked, hoping to pull him off track.

He looked around in surprise, as if he'd only just realized she was absent from the room. "Probably at prayers. Now where were we?" He leaned close again. "Oh yeah, you were thinking about taking off your clothes."

"I was not." He was so near she could smell the sandalwood soap he had used in his bath before supper. She had heard him in there, splashing and humming in his monotone. It had aroused all sorts of images in her mind — sleek, wet, honey-colored skin — muscles bunching and —

Suddenly aware that Jack had spoken and was waiting for a response, she faked another yawn to cover her inattention.

"Am I boring you?" he asked.

"No more than usual."

"We can't have that. Hmm, here's an idea." His lips brushed against her ear as he whispered, "Why don't you take off your clothes and sit on my lap and I'll read to you?"

She reared back to give him an arch look. "You can read?"

That slow grin. Mercy, the things it did to her stomach.

"Oh, I'm an excellent reader, Daisy. Come upstairs and I'll show you."

"Are you whispering secrets?" Penny called, studying them with curious brown eyes. "Aunt Molly says secrets aren't nice. Isn't that so, Aunt Molly?"

Molly made a garbled sound but didn't look up from her bandaging.

"No secrets," Jack said. "I was worried Daisy might have picked up some ticks on our hike today and was just asking if she wanted me to check."

"Ticks?" Daisy squeaked.

"They're itchy," Penny explained. "Aunt Molly found one on my bum once and it itched me forever. Isn't that so, Aunt Molly?"

Molly didn't — or couldn't — answer. Jessica seemed to be stumbling over the words of a simple picture book, and Jack's older brothers stared into the fire, as stony faced as cigar-store Indians. Daisy felt her skin tickle and hoped it wasn't tiny feet.

Her distress must have shown. Jack reached over and patted her hand. "If she won't let me check for ticks, maybe we can get our little Daisy to sing for us."

Jessica jumped on that like a hen on a pill bug. "You sing, Daisy?"

"She does," Jack answered before Daisy could. "She was the star of the Silver Spur Saloon."

"You sang in a saloon?" Jessica's smile faltered. "How splendid."

"Oh, it *was* splendid," Jack assured her. "Magical even. Especially the high notes." He gave Daisy an angelic smile. "Remember those high notes, Daisy? How you rattled the rafters night after night when —"

"I have no music," she blurted out, heat rushing into her cheeks.

Grinning, Brady turned to Hank. "One-Track-Jack. He never gives up."

Hank grinned back. "Better than a peep show."

"And what do you know about peep shows?" his wife challenged.

Hank's grin froze. "Only what Brady told me."

"I never told you —"

"Does a peep show have baby chickens?" Penny cried in delight.

"Do sing," Jessica said loudly. "Anything from memory would be fine."

Daisy put up a token resistance before graciously agreeing. In truth, she was relieved to escape Jack's whispered taunts, *that cad,* and was thrilled to be able to sing before an audience again.

Since she couldn't control her breathing as well sitting down, she rose and went to stand beside the fireplace, hands clasped at her waist. She was surprised at how excited and nervous she felt.

Ignoring the way the action drew Jack's gaze to her breasts, she took several deep breaths to fill her lungs, then began with a lively Irish ballad about a scorned woman's revenge. With sound being somewhat diffused by the high ceiling and overhead beams, she was able to release the full power of her voice, which she joyfully did. After transitioning into one of the milder saloon songs, she followed with an English lament about a rowan tree, and concluded with the same French lullaby she had sung for her audition at the Elysium. Despite the poor acoustics and being a bit out of practice, she thought she did well, and finished with a smile.

But when the last notes faded, it was to utter silence.

Confused, she scanned the faces staring up at her and saw varying expressions — sleepiness from the children, tearfulness from Jessica and Molly, grins from their husbands, and slack-jawed shock from Jack.

Then the room erupted in applause.

Daisy beamed, absurdly touched. She hadn't realized how much she had craved their approval until they'd given it.

"Hell, Daisy," Jack said in an awed voice. "I'd forgotten how beautiful your singing was. You put wings to sound."

Brady looked at her with new respect in his ice blue eyes. "That's amazing, Daisy. You have a gift."

Hank nodded in agreement.

"Goodness." Jessica sighed and dabbed at her eyes. "If I'd known, I would have insisted you sing every night. I've never heard a more beautiful voice."

"You should be on a stage," Molly added. "A real stage."

Daisy flushed with pleasure. "I hope to be. Someday."

"What a lovely way to end an evening. Certainly better than with one of Jack's ghastly revelations about shrunken heads and whatnot." Rising, Jessica motioned the chil-

291

dren to their feet. "Come along, dear ones. Time for bed."

As the women ushered the protesting children out, Brady went to his office, returning a few moments later with the whiskey decanter and three glasses. He poured, passed the glasses around, then settled into his chair with a sigh.

"That's a helluva voice for such a little person," Hank said once the first sip had settled warmly in his stomach.

Brady nodded. "It's those fine lungs, I suspect."

"They are nice." Hank smiled at the rafters. "I've always admired nice lungs on a woman."

"Shut up. Both of you. She'll be your sister-in-law, for Crissakes."

Brady gave Jack a surprised look. "You asked?"

"I did."

"And she accepted?"

"Not yet."

"Not ever," Hank amended with a smirk.

"For sure not after the way he went at her tonight," Brady agreed.

"What'd I do?"

"I thought she was going to hit you again."

"Why? I was just teasing."

Hank laughed. "Christamighty, Jack. And you call yourself a charmer?"

Brady raised his glass in mock salute. "I have to hand it to you, little brother. You really stepped on your John Thomas this time."

"I'm flattered you think such a thing is possible. Apparently Daisy was thinking about it too. She was blushing."

"Blushing mad," Brady corrected. "I know the look."

"I bet you do. But not to worry, girls. She'll come around."

"You're a dimwit." Setting his empty glass on a table beside the couch, Hank picked up the plans he and Charlie had been working on, then rose. "But a lucky one. If I pulled those shenanigans on Molly, she'd come at me with a scalpel." He frowned in the direction of the staircase. "Hell, she may anyway after that peep show remark." Things had been difficult enough lately without him adding fuel to the situation with some ill-advised comment.

"I owe you for that." Brady glared up at him. "Jessica is probably honing her tongue even now."

Jack shook his head in mock dismay. "You two are pathetic. Cowed by a couple of skirts. I'm embarrassed for the both of you."

"And yet, oddly enough," Hank countered, "we won't be sleeping alone tonight. How 'bout you?"

"Soon, girls. Soon."

FIFTEEN

Molly wasn't waiting for Hank with a scalpel in hand. In fact, she wasn't waiting in the bedroom at all.

Not that he'd been that concerned, despite what he'd told his brothers. Molly was a sensible, even-tempered woman and far too intelligent to get emotional over some chance comment. Usually. But when she was nearing the onset of her monthly cycle, which his calculations indicated she was, it was always a difficult time for her. And him.

Over the last year, he'd learned to read the signs. First, nervous anticipation. Then, fretful worry. Then, bitter disappointment when she realized she wasn't breeding. It near broke his heart every time.

Stripping by the unlit fireplace, he grabbed his sketchbook and a lead pencil from his bedside table then slipped under the covers.

Fifteen minutes passed as he worked on drawings for a modified railroad handcar that could be propelled by foot pedals or rigged with a sail. After a half hour, he was starting to worry when he heard the creak of the bedroom door opening. Peering over his sketchbook, he watched a tangled mop of blond curls inch around the edge of the door.

With a sigh, he set the book aside and made sure he was properly covered. "What do you want, Penny?" he called out.

The door swung open the rest of the way to reveal his stepdaughter standing hesitantly in the threshold. She held out the china-faced doll Jessica had given her and Molly had just repaired. "Miss Apple is thirsty."

"There's water in the cup in your room."

"Oh." Her shoulders sagged. Miss Apple dropped to her side. "I forgot."

Hank studied her, wondering what was wrong. She wasn't bursting through the door like she usually did. Nor was she racing across the floor to bound onto the bed like a wiggling puppy. She just stood there, looking worried and maybe a little sad.

The women in his life confounded him. He didn't understand them, couldn't fathom how their minds worked, and hadn't a clue how to negotiate the emotional quagmire that surrounded them. But he would give up his life for them, and he would do everything in his power to see that their days were filled with smiles rather than tears.

He held out his hand. "Come here, Penny. Tell me what's wrong."

Once he had her settled between the counterpane and the quilt, her little body snuggled by his side and her head tucked against his neck, he asked her again what was wrong.

"Aunt Molly is crying again."

Again?

"Why is she sad, Papa-Hank?"

Hank stared up at the ceiling, not sure how to answer. He knew why Molly was sad. Her inability to conceive was devastating to her. They'd never spoken of it, as if by not acknowledging there was a problem, they could pretend it wasn't there. But it was there and it wouldn't go away. Not unless they faced it and dealt with it. Which meant he would have to tell her what Doc said.

"Is it my fault, Papa-Hank? Did I do something wrong?"

"No, Penny." Hank pressed his lips against the crown of her head then drew back, wondering at the odd smell. Then he recognized it as the perfumed talc Jessica used on Thomas Jefferson and Little Sam, despite Brady's strenuous objections. They were boy twins, after all. Penny, being enthralled with babies, was constantly fooling with them. She would have made a grand big sister. "You did nothing wrong," he told her. "Maybe she's just tired."

"Or cranky. TJ and Sam get that way when they miss a nap."

"I bet that's it." He lifted the counterpane.

"Go back to bed, Penny. Everything will be fine in the morning."

Sitting up, she gave him a hopeful gap-toothed grin. "Read me a book?"

He looked at her.

She sighed. "Yes, Papa-Hank."

After kissing both Penny and Miss Apple one last time, Hank sent them on their way and settled back to wait for his wife to finish crying and come to bed.

It didn't take long. A few minutes later, she came through the water closet door. The tears were gone and in their place was a smile that looked as if it had been cut there with a chisel. "I thought I heard voices," she said, pulling off her robe as she padded across the room.

He admired the way the golden light from his lamp played across the shiny fabric of her gown, highlighting every jiggling movement beneath it. Even after a year of nights, she was a wonder to him.

But tonight, he reminded himself, they had to talk.

"That was Penny. She heard you crying. She's worried about you."

His wife made a shooing motion. "It's nothing." Lifting the covers, she slid in beside him. But she didn't roll toward him or reach for him as she usually did. Instead she lay flat on her back, blinking fast at the rafters overhead.

He watched her swallow hard and knew she was fighting tears again. "Molly," he said.

She didn't respond.

Reaching out, he gathered her in his arms then rolled onto his back, taking her with him so her fine body draped over his. "Talk to me, Molly."

For a moment she resisted him. Then the stiffness eased from her shoulders and her head drooped in surrender. As she pressed her cheek against his chest, he felt the wetness of fresh tears. "I don't think it's going to happen this time either. I won't know for sure for a few days yet, but — oh, Hank, I'm so sorry."

"Don't be." He stroked the long silky curve of her back, filled with self-disgust that he was failing this woman who deserved so much. "You have nothing to be sorry for, Molly."

"I don't know what's wrong," she said in a quavering voice. "I've taken tonics, restoratives, I've done every —"

"Shh. It's all right."

"How can it be all right?" Lifting her head, she looked down at him, her face twisted in anguish. "I'm barren, Hank. Don't you understand that? We can't — I can't —"

"It's not you." Reaching up, he brushed her hair aside, pinning the soft, glossy waves against her temples with his big hands. "It's not you. It's me."

Confusion, then disbelief moved across her expressive face. Then finally, understanding. "No."

"I talked to Doc."

"Dr. O'Grady? He's a quack and a drunk."

"He thinks it's me. Because of the derailment."

"No." Her eyes filled with more tears. She shook her head. "You're just trying to take the blame to make me feel better. Train derailments don't cause sterility."

"High fever might." He waited for her to refute his words.

She didn't. And that told him she had thought about it. And had maybe even wondered if his raging fever after the derailment when she had worked so hard to save his arm could have killed his seed. But being Molly, she'd clung stubbornly to hope, either because she wanted a child so badly she wouldn't accept that he couldn't give her one, or because she was trying to shield him from his own inadequacy.

It tore him apart. Even with all his strength and wealth and love, he still couldn't give her the one thing she wanted most. That was the failure that was hardest for him to accept. "I'm sorry, Molly."

This time it was she who comforted him, feathering his face with salty kisses, telling him it was okay, it didn't matter.

Which of course was a lie.

He withstood it as long as he could. A man could tolerate just so much pity. Besides, it wasn't as if he couldn't function — thank God. And they still had Charlie and Penny. And sterility was a whole lot better than the alternative.

After talking to Doc, and when Molly wasn't around, he'd looked through some of her medical books. In addition to learning more about male sterility than any man should know, he'd found out some disturbing things about childbirth mortality. Thousands of women died every year — young women, bearing normal-sized babies. Molly was thirty-three and he was anything but normal in size. Odds were against them, and Hank would gladly accept sterility rather than take that bet.

"Maybe it's a good thing, Molly." Lifting her hand, he twined his fingers with hers, clasping them palm to palm. "Look at you and look at me." His hand dwarfed hers. His wrist was almost double hers in size. "You breed a fine-boned Arabian mare to an eighteen-hand Clydesdale, you're just asking for trouble."

"You're comparing me to a horse?"

He smiled. "A really beautiful horse."

She tried to smile back, but the sadness was still there behind her beautiful almost-green eyes.

He pushed on. "And look at Brady and Jessica. He's smaller than me and she's bigger than you. Look at how difficult it's been for her. She almost didn't make it."

"That doesn't signify."

"It does to me. It's a real risk, Molly. You could die struggling to bring my child into the world and I couldn't live with that. So maybe it's a good thing."

Releasing his hand, she brushed tears away. "But I wanted to have babies, Hank. *Your* babies. I wanted —" Her voice broke.

"I know." Pulling her back down against his chest, he wrapped his arms tight around her, as if that might shield her from the pain he knew she was feeling. "But we need you, Molly . . . Charlie and Penny and I. And the world needs you for all the good you can do and the people you can help. You're too important to risk."

She cried a long time. He said nothing more, just held her and waited for the indomitable spirit that was Molly to reassert itself. It might take a while, weeks even, but when it did, maybe she'd be ready to hear what he'd found out about a thing called the Orphan Train.

"Tell me about your travels," Daisy said.

Jack laughed. "I wouldn't know where to start."

He had reversed the schedule for the day, moving Kate's riding lesson to late morning so they could have a picnic lunch. Now they sat on the blanket amid the remains of their feast, Daisy with her arms around her up-raised knees, Jack, stretched on his back, his heels propped on the lid of the picnic basket, Kate by his shoulder, digging happily in the dirt.

Daisy had tried to stay mad at him after his horrid teasing the previous evening when he'd coerced her into singing for the family. But by morning her pique had faded to reluctant amusement. He did that so easily — changed frowns into smiles. Just another part of his charm. And anyway, today was too lovely to waste in anger . . . fleecy clouds overhead, the breeze pleasantly cool, the sunshine like a warm hand against her back. Besides, thinking back on his comments, she couldn't help but be a little flattered. He'd called her voice beautiful, after all.

"Start with the favorite place you've been," she suggested.

"I guess that would be Katoomba in the Blue Mountains," he said after giving it some thought. "That's in Australia."

"Why is it special?"

"It's a place of mystery. Misty and wild, filled with plants, and reptiles, and birds you'll never see anywhere else. It looks a lot like that." He pointed to the flat-topped mountain at the west end of the valley. "But much bigger, and littered with caves, and strange rock formations, and gorges that drop down over two thousand feet." His smoky eyes took on a distant look. "It's something to see."

Daisy suspected that for Jack to stay in one place for long would be as torturous as a slow death.

"But I liked Tasmania too," he went on. "And New Zealand and the islands of the South Pacific. It's a big world and I've only seen a small corner of it."

Resting her chin on her knees, Daisy watched the play of sunlight across his handsome features. Had he always had that small lump on the bridge of his nose? And that mole on his cheek? She studied him, noting a new scar cutting through one eyebrow and more squint lines than she remembered fanning out from his remarkable eyes. Were the grooves bracketing his mobile — and talented — mouth deeper? It struck her that despite the intimacy they had shared, in many ways they were strangers. Who was Jack Wilkins really? What drove him?

"Where do you intend to go next?" she asked, seeking clues to this familiar stranger beside her.

"North," he said without hesitation. "To see a polar bear and the aurora borealis and listen to the crack of ice breaking on the Yukon River. Then maybe east and across the Atlantic. I've always wanted to sail the Irish coast where Grandpa Brady lived and stand on the battlements of an ancient fortress."

As he spoke, his features livened and his hand gestures became more enthusiastic. "From there I'd go south. Maybe ride across the Pyrenees on an elephant like Hannibal did. Or walk where the gladiators fought, and rest my hand on the cold face of Michelangelo's *Pietà*. I want to go to Egypt too. And race an Arabian stallion through the shadows of the pyramids, and visit the tombs of the great pharaohs. Or maybe float down the Zambezi into the rainbow mist of Victoria Falls." He seemed to catch himself, then turned his head toward her and flashed an embarrassed lopsided smile. "You asked."

And she was glad she had. This was a side of Jack she had never met. She had never realized how knowledgeable he was. She had to wonder why he hid his intelligence behind a careless smile and presented such a flighty, haphazard image to the world.

"What's a *Pietà*?" she asked.

Rather than commenting on her ignorance, he became earnest again. "A statue of the Virgin Mary holding the dead Christ. I saw a picture of it in a museum in Sydney. It's amazing, Daisy. Snow-white marble polished smooth as glass, carved hundreds of years ago by a man barely in his twenties. It's in Rome. There are a lot of places in Italy I want to see. And Greece. And in Africa and South

America. Do you know they eat humans there, and in the jungles are tribes of people no taller than three and a half feet?" He laughed aloud, attracting Kate's attention. "Katie-girl, you would fit right in," he told her as he scooped her up and held her over his head. "And I'd be a giant, wouldn't I? Big enough to eat tasty little morsels like you."

Daisy watched them tussle for a moment, smiling in spite of her concerns over their closeness. Jack was a high-spirited, openly affectionate man, unlike his reserved middle brother and his stern, intimidating oldest brother. And he was certainly not the empty-headed drifter he made himself out to be. She wondered why he would cultivate such a shallow image, and if his family knew the true man beneath the façade. She wondered if she knew him any better.

Once he'd lowered Kate and she'd settled down on her back beside him to watch cloud figures drift across the sky, Daisy asked, "How did you learn about all these places you want to visit?"

"At sea. Look, Katie, doesn't that cloud look like a frog?"

"See fwog," Kate said, pointing her kitty at the sky.

"There's a lot of free time on a ship," he went on, his smile giving way to a frown as he studied the sky. "And our captain had a trunk full of books. Reading occupied my mind and kept me from drinking."

"You quit drinking?" That was a surprise. As she recalled, drinking and gambling were two of Jack's three favorite things.

"Mostly. Until I got back anyway." He shot her a crooked grin. "Between the fine Scotch whiskey that Jessica imports and needing a crutch to get me through my brothers' interrogations, I've started the habit again."

"That's too bad," Daisy murmured. Jack, when he was drinking, was a funny, passionate, playful clown. But this sober Jack was much more interesting.

"Not to worry," he added, apparently catching her unspoken censure even though his attention remained focused on the clouds crowding the peaks to the west. "I'll never be the drunk I was. That was a bad time. I don't want to make mistakes like that again."

She wondered if he thought of her and Kate as part of those "mistakes" but hadn't the courage to ask.

"See those puffy clouds, Kate? The ones with the pouches along the flat bottoms? If they get bigger and darker, it'll mean rain."

"Wain," Kate said.

Daisy watched Jack's big hand idly stroke Kate's stomach and felt a quiver of remembrance move beneath her own skin. Despite his size and strength, Jack was one of the gentlest men she'd ever known.

And those hands held magic.

Forcing herself to look away, she cleared her throat and said, "It's very quiet and peaceful up here, isn't it?"

Jack snorted. "Too quiet for me. Sometimes the silence in this country carries such weight it smothers. In the jungles and rainforests it's as raucous as a cage of birds. And aboard ship, even if no one says a word, it's still noisy. The snap and flutter of the sails, wood groaning, the slap of water against the hull . . . it's like a whole different kind of music. Except when we're becalmed. Then it's like here, so quiet you can hear your own heartbeat. And when it's that quiet, it means you're just sitting there, doing nothing."

Daisy smiled. "And that's unacceptable to you."

He looked over and grinned. "Damn right."

She felt that flutter again, and knew if she weren't careful, this man would break through all her carefully erected barriers. "Do you know the time?" she asked, needing to pull herself back to safer ground.

He reached into his pocket and pulled out a watch. As he did, something small and shiny tumbled down onto the blanket. Kate immediately reached for it.

Instead of taking it away from her, Jack leaned over and kissed her forehead. "Keep that for luck, Katie-girl, but don't eat it."

Knowing whatever her daughter had in her hand would eventually end up in her mouth,

Daisy asked what it was.

"Just a trinket." He studied his watch. "It's a quarter past four. We'll have to start back soon." With a sigh, he sat up and stretched.

Freeing the object from Kate's resisting grip, Daisy saw it was a silver cross intricately engraved with twining roses. "This is beautiful. Did you pick it up in your travels?" As she spoke, she turned it over and saw letters engraved on the back: "EMR to AJW." Anger clutched at her throat. *Elena.*

Quelling the urge to fling it at Jack's head, she handed the cross back to Kate, then looked up to see Jack studying her, his expression guarded and somber.

"It's just a trinket, Daisy. One I no longer need."

Somewhat mollified, as well as embarrassed that he had seen her angry reaction, she asked what the "A" in his initials stood for.

"Andrew. Andrew Jackson Wilkins."

"You're named after 'Old Hickory,' the president?"

He shrugged. "My father thought if he named his sons after heroes, they might act like heroes. Hank is named after Patrick Henry, and our little brother Sam, after Sam Adams. Brady, being eldest, carries our mother's maiden name."

Sam? "There's another brother?" She had only heard of three.

A shadow came into his eyes. "Was. Sam

died when he was twelve. Tortured by Elena's brother, Sancho. Brady . . . found him."

Daisy was shocked at the tangled web that bound these people together. It was too fantastical to be true, yet the sadness in Jack's face told her it was.

He must have sensed her curiosity and hurriedly answered her questions before she could voice them, as if wanting to get the subject behind him as quickly as he could. "We were feuding with the Ramirez family over the ranch. We won. Sancho went crazy, killed his folks, and set everything on fire before Jessica set *him* on fire." He smiled grimly. "Rough justice, don't you think?"

Daisy was astonished. Prim and proper Jessica had killed a man too? A sudden image of Bill Johnson exploded in her mind, and for a moment her whole body seemed to clench in reaction. Then she remembered that Johnson had come to steal Kate so he could sell her to some pervert, and fury swept regret and guilt aside. Justice deserved and served. She wasn't sorry she'd rid the world of vermin like that.

"And yet Elena stayed," she observed, going back to what Jack had said. "Why?" What kind of woman would align herself with the family that had taken her home and killed her brother?

Jack shrugged. "She had nowhere else to go. Besides, she's been like part of the family since she was six. Like a sister, almost."

Except a man didn't fall in love with his sister. Pushing that disturbing thought away, she said, "But Jessica killed her brother. Didn't that cause strife?" Daisy had no siblings, but she was sure if she did, and he or she had been killed, she wouldn't have become "almost a sister" to the killer.

"There was no love lost between Elena and Sancho." His voice had turned cold, his tone clipped. "He was the one who crippled her. Nearly kicked her to death. But that's all in the past." Abruptly he stood, ending the conversation as well as the easy companionship of their hilltop picnic. "It's late. We better get going. I don't like the look of those clouds."

"You think it'll rain?"

"I'm more worried about lightning. We're too exposed up here."

Left with more questions than answers, Daisy had no choice but to let the subject drop. But she was beginning to realize that simple, lighthearted Jack Wilkins was a much more complicated man than she had thought. And this new Jack would be far harder to walk away from.

As she tossed the remains of the picnic lunch into the brush, a sudden gust swept over the hilltop, whipping her skirts around her legs and peppering their faces with grit. The sun disappeared behind dark billowing clouds, and the air felt suddenly chilly and damp.

Kate began to cry, Kitty hugged close in her arms.

"Damn," Jack muttered. "Forget the food. Where's the pouch with our jackets?"

Daisy tossed it to him, alarmed by the urgency in his voice. As she tried to stuff the blanket back into the picnic basket, another gust almost wrenched it from her grip.

Jack pushed her hands aside. "I'll do that. Put a jacket on Kate. We need to be across the bridge before the water rises."

Daisy looked up at the sky, which seemed to have grown darker within the last few moments. "Why would it rise? It's not even raining."

"It is up there." Jack nodded toward the slope rising behind them. "And it'll be running downhill fast. Hurry."

Daisy had just finished fastening Kate's coat when cold, heavy drops slapped the ground around them, driven almost horizontal by the gusting wind.

Jack picked up Kate and Kitty, tucking them tight against his chest. "Leave the pouch," he called, the wind snatching his words away. "Come on. Now."

Fully alarmed, Daisy slipped and slid after him down the rain-slicked trail. Already the footing was treacherous, and Daisy's wet skirts clung to her legs, making it hard to balance in the howling wind. Before they'd gone a hundred yards, water was running down the path between their feet, cutting deep grooves in the sandy soil.

The suddenness and ferocity of the storm appalled Daisy. Had it been only five minutes ago that the sun was shining? Lightning flashed, almost blinding her. Then a deafening boom of thunder. Out of reflex she ducked, half expecting one of the trees whipping back and forth overhead to explode in flames, or a limb to come crashing down on her head.

"Maybe we should stop until it blows over," she yelled at Jack's retreating back.

"Can't," Jack shouted back. "If we don't cross now, we could be stranded on this side without food or shelter for days."

Daisy stumbled doggedly on, trying to ignore the cold rain stinging her face and seeping under her collar. It was coming down so hard and fast now she could scarcely see Jack's hunched form only a few yards ahead. Water rushed over the laces of her walking boots, and all around them limbs snapped and trees groaned against the onslaught of wind. Above the thunderous deluge she heard Kate crying.

Then the icy rain turned to hard pellets of hail.

Sixteen

It was late afternoon and Hank was working on his calculations of how many square feet of sail it would take to move a five-hundred-pound railcar along a track at ten miles per hour when Brady threw open the door to his office.

"Where are Jack and Daisy?"

Hank continued to scribble. "Haven't seen them. Why?"

When there was no response, he looked up to find his brother still standing in the doorway of his office, his gaze fixed on the window.

Curious, Hank turned. His jaw dropped in astonishment.

Dark thunderheads boiled out of the west, racing down the valley ahead of a hard, driving rain. Lightning bounced between the clouds. Thunder rumbled. A sudden gust drove grit pinging against the windows and sent the branches of the mesquite tree on the hilltop behind the house into a thrashing frenzy. As Hank watched, a limb snapped off and crashed against a grave marker so hard the stone toppled over. Another flash, then a blast of thunder so loud it made him flinch. An instant later the skies opened, dumping hailstones the size of elk droppings that clattered across the porch floor to bounce against the panes of the French door like crazed white bees.

"Sweet Jesus," Hank muttered, rising to his feet. "Where'd that come from?" And why hadn't he been aware of it?

"Did they go for a hike?" Brady demanded. "Are they still out there?"

"I don't know."

"Christ." His brother ducked into the hall.

Hank went after him.

"Check the barn," Brady ordered as he took the stairs three treads at a time. "I'll see if Jessica knows where they are."

A few minutes later, soaking wet, his black hair plastered to his head, Brady rushed into the barn. "Did you find them?" he asked, dumping an armful of slickers and dusters into the straw.

Hank shook his head and turned back to the horse he'd been readying, just in case. In other stalls, other men were doing the same.

"Damnit to hell!" Freeing a duster from the heap, Brady struggled to pull the oiled canvas over his wet jacket. "They're out there somewhere. I know it."

Lightning bolted from the sky. Thin bars of light flashed through the gaps between the planks of the exterior walls, then thunder boomed, making the horse lunge and snort, white showing in its eyes. The air crackled and buzzed.

Murmuring softly, Hank calmed the frightened sorrel then tossed the saddle onto its back. With brisk movements, he slipped the girth strap through the D-ring, pulled it tight, and secured the dangling end. After tugging on his own duster, he rolled the remaining jackets in a slicker and tied it across the back of the saddle.

As he worked, the part of his mind not churning with worry stayed alert to his surroundings — the distant sounds of men saddling up, the clink of bits and stomp of restless horses, the frightened mewl of a barn cat. He checked the air for smoke in case the lightning had set something ablaze, but smelled none.

Overhead, the loft door crashed open, then banged on its hinges until finally it slammed shut so hard the timbers shuddered. In the near darkness, the air grew still and thick with the smell of alfalfa and manure and wet horses. But outside, the storm raged and hail hammered the roof and the wind howled like a wounded cougar.

It's just a spring storm, Hank told himself. *It'll pass soon. They'll be fine.*

"Jessica said they went on a picnic," Brady shouted as he fumbled with a strip of rawhide he'd looped over the crown of his Stetson and under his chin to keep his hat from blowing off. "Why would they go on a picnic? Didn't he see there was a storm coming?"

Hank didn't argue with him, knowing his brother's bluster was a cover for his fear. Anyone familiar with this country knew these mountains could spawn thunderstorms in a moment's notice. Jack wasn't a fool. He might not see a storm coming, but he wouldn't go into the mountains unprepared in case one arose. Especially with his daughter.

He handed the reins of the sorrel to Brady then untied the bay gelding he'd saddled first and left hitched to a stall door. "Kate with them?" he asked as he stepped into the stirrup and threw a leg over.

"Hell, yes. How could he go wandering off like that?"

"He's not stupid, Brady. He'll know what to do."

Brady spun toward him. "No, he'll try to outrun it, goddamnit. He'll take chances like he always does." His face grim with worry, Brady swung into the saddle. Turning to the other men leading saddled horses from the stalls, he shouted orders above the rattle and roar of the storm buffeting the walls.

"Go in twos. Check along the creek first. If

there's lightning, dismount and find low ground. Fire two rounds if you find him, three if you're in trouble or need us to come. Be back by dark."

At his signal, two boys ran forward to wrestle open the barn doors. Wind roared into their faces as they rode out into a lashing torrent of rain and hail under a sky that had turned twilight dark.

Daisy was growing frantic. Then as quickly as it had begun, the deluge ended. An eerie stillness descended, magnified by the sudden absence of howling wind and clattering hail. Lightning still flashed and thunder rumbled, but growing more distant as the storm moved down the valley toward the eastern peaks. Above the wind-battered trees, the clouds thinned then broke apart here and there, showing patches of blue sky tinted pink by the setting sun.

She sagged in relief, not realizing how frightened she had been until the crisis was over. "Is it past then?" she called ahead to Jack, who hadn't slowed his pace down the trail.

"The first squall is. But more's coming."

She looked up and quailed to see another dark band of thunderheads racing toward them out of the west, bursts of light streaking between the clouds.

"Hurry, Daisy. We're still a long way from

the bridge."

Skirting fallen twigs and branches, she worked her way down the slippery trail and over deepening ruts as water continued to pour down the steep slopes. She started to shiver, her wet jacket and skirts cold against her skin, her waterlogged boots rubbing raw spots on her chilled feet. Thankfully, Kate had stopped crying, so Jack must have been able to keep her dry.

It began to rain again, but with less wind this time and the lightning stayed far down the valley. But the runoff continued to cut into the ground beneath their feet.

It seemed an eternity before they reached the bridge. Daisy almost wept in gratitude to see it still standing, even though the creek had risen to the cross struts and was now a swirling, foamy cauldron of debris and broken tree limbs. She had no doubt that within minutes it would be lapping at their feet.

"Hurry," Jack called, waving her on. "It's coming up fast."

Eyeing the water churning around the rocks at the base of the abutment that supported the huge spanner logs, Daisy skidded down the last few feet and onto the bridge. It shuddered under her, buffeted by rushing water, the planks slick with wet pine needles. A broken limb slammed into a support, almost knocking her off balance, but she managed to stay upright and keep moving after Jack.

They were halfway across when she heard a crack as loud as a pistol report. Clinging to the railing, she looked back to see one of the spanner logs separating from the abutment. The downstream side of the bridge began to sag.

She cried out, grappling for a handhold as her feet slipped across the planks toward the icy water.

Jack's hand clamped over her arm and jerked her back. "Take Kate!" Thrusting the terrified child into her arms, he shoved them both past him toward the far side of the creek. "Run!"

"Titty!" Kate shrieked, straining to reach the waterlogged toy that had fallen to the planks.

"I'll get it!" Jack shouted behind her. "Just go!"

On the bank they had just left, a rope gave way and a shattered timber shot into the air like a broken twig. More ropes snapped and twanged, slapping the water like angry snakes.

"Run!"

Daisy tried, but the bridge bucked and contorted beneath her feet like a wild thing, making her stagger and reel for balance. Over Kate's wails, she heard Jack pounding behind her, urging her to go faster.

The embankment loomed ahead. She was almost there. Battling to keep her footing, she lurched toward it, Kate thrashing in her arms. She heard Jack curse and looked back. He was several yards behind her, tugging at his leg, trying to free his foot where it had crashed through and gotten caught on a splintered plank.

"Jack!" she yelled.

When he saw her starting back toward him, he frantically waved both hands. "No! Keep going! There's no time!" He pointed upstream.

Daisy looked, saw a huge uprooted tree bearing down on them, its twisted limbs flailing like a demon's arms. "Jack —"

"No!" His face suddenly white with fear beneath his rain-plastered hair, he waved her on. "No, Daisy! Go on! RUN!"

Holding her daughter tight against her thundering heart, Daisy ran.

With a deafening roar, the tree slammed into the supports, the impact almost lifting her off her feet. Timbers groaned and twisted. Metal spikes shrieked as they sheared off. She scrambled on, the planks sinking lower with every step. Water washed over her boots and pinned her wet skirts around her ankles.

The ropes tying the logs to the abutment in front of her began to unravel with a high-pitched whine. A huge chunk of the embankment broke off, leaving a crumbling wall of wet earth and exposed roots. With a loud crack, the last rope gave way and the huge spanner logs began to roll off the side of the abutment.

In blind terror, Daisy pinned Kate tight against her chest and jumped.

She seemed to hang in the air forever. Then her feet slammed onto the steep wall of the bank. Earth rained down. She started to slide backward.

Clawing for a handhold with her free hand, she found an exposed tree root and clung to it until she regained her footing. Shielding Kate as best she could, she clambered up the muddy bank, grasping at rocks and roots to pull them up.

Once clear, she fell to her knees, gasping for air. With shaking hands she checked to see if Kate was all right.

Mud-spattered and terrified. But safe.

Fighting tears and laughter, Daisy rocked her wailing daughter in her trembling arms, chanting her name over and over and thanking God that they had made it.

When that short rush of terror and relief had passed, she gathered what courage she had left and made herself look back toward the water.

The uprooted tree was gone. The bridge was gone.

Jack was nowhere in sight.

Hank rode hunched against the rain, following a muddy trail that ran parallel to the flooded creek. Brady searched farther up in the trees in case Jack and Daisy had made it to higher ground and were hunkered down out of the wind.

It was slow going over ground littered with toppled trees and broken branches. The trail was six inches of sucking mud that pulled at the horse's hooves with every labored step, and the light was starting to fade.

Hank seethed with impatience.

They had started the search at the bridge, which was now no more than a few pieces of splintered timbers spinning in a foamy backwash. Only the half-submerged log and rock abutments remained to mark the place where the structure had been, and they would probably wash away soon too. That was two hours ago.

And still no sign.

Cursing in frustration, Hank pulled the bay to a stop. He tried to listen in case Jack had seen them and was calling out, but all he heard was Brady moving through the brush on his left and the thunderous roar of the creek on his right. It was well beyond the banks now, running as high as he'd ever seen it. Even the message rock had been almost entirely under water when they'd passed it an hour ago.

Where are they?

Through the rain streaming from his hat brim, he studied the far bank but saw nothing other than a gray squirrel scurrying back and forth along a tree trunk, trying to find a way to dry ground.

Grimly determined, Hank kicked the weary horse forward.

Hopefully Jack had seen the danger before they'd tried to cross. But if that were the case, they would have been waiting by the bridge abutment. No matter what Brady said, Jack wouldn't have taken chances with Daisy and his daughter by leading them off somewhere on his own. He would have kept them close and stayed someplace safe where help could find them.

Like the abutment.

So why weren't they there? The rain continued and the sky grew darker. In another couple of hours they would have to send back for lanterns and torches and continue the search on foot. But where? How far could the current have carried them? Were they even looking in the right place?

It was almost dusk and they were at least three miles downstream of the bridge when he saw movement along the near bank. Heart thudding, Hank rose in the stirrups for a better view through the brush.

He saw Daisy, stumbling along with Kate in her arms. But not Jack.

"Got Daisy and Kate," he shouted to Brady over the rush of water. "Alive."

"Jack?"

"No sign. Signal the others."

Brady nodded and rode back out of the trees toward the flats.

As Hank dismounted, he heard three gunshots in rapid succession, then Brady shouting and distant voices shouting back.

Daisy seemed not to hear, and continued staggering over rocks and reeds at the water's edge. Both she and Kate were crying.

After quickly untying the bundle of dry jackets lashed behind his saddle, Hank hurried toward her. "Daisy?" he called, shoving through brush and over fallen branches.

She whirled. "Hank! Th-Thank God you're here! I can't f-find him! I've looked everywhere! We h-have to find him!"

As he drew closer, he looked them over for signs of injury. They were both filthy and soaking wet. Kate's hair was caked with dirt and her eyes were puffy from crying; otherwise, she seemed fine.

But Daisy looked ravaged. She was shivering, her clothing torn and muddy. Her hands bled from a dozen scratches and her eyes, when they finally focused on him, were twin pools of terror.

Hank jerked a slicker from the bundle and slung it over their heads, but Daisy was shaking so badly, it kept sliding off, so he grabbed her shoulders to anchor it and keep her still.

"Where's Jack?" he demanded.

"Bad water get Jack," Kate cried, tears running through the mud on her cheeks. "Take

Titty gone too."

Daisy tried to calm her, but she wasn't doing that well herself, and her teeth were chattering so hard Hank could hardly understand her.

"W-We were on the b-bridge. He was r-right behind me — then h-he . . ." Her voice rose to that squeaky high-pitched gibberish that women spoke when they talked and cried at the same time.

He gave her shoulders a squeeze. "Slow down, Daisy. Take a breath." He tried to keep his voice calm, but fear had him in such a tight grip it was all he could do not to shake her. "Just tell me what happened."

In fits and starts she told him how they were halfway across when the bridge started to break up and Jack's foot got caught. She tried to go back to help him but a huge uprooted tree was heading toward them and Jack told her there wasn't time and to take Kate and run.

"We r-reached the other side j-just as the tree hit," she said in a quavering voice. "When I l-looked back, it was gone — the bridge — J-Jack — everything. Gone." With a shaking hand, she swiped at her eyes, leaving muddy streaks on her scratched face. "I've been l-looking and calling but I c-can't find him. H-He's a good swimmer. He s-should be here, b-but I can't — I can't —"

She started to crumble.

Hank caught her and anchored her against his side with an arm around her shoulders. "We'll find him, Daisy," he said. "I swear we'll find him."

Hearing an approaching horse, he looked over her head to see Brady working his way back through the brush.

"A tree hit the bridge," Hank told him when his brother reined in beside them. "Jack went down with it. He could be miles downstream by now."

"Sonofabitch." Brady frowned at the roaring river that was normally a meandering creek. "I've never seen it this high."

"It'll get higher." Hank looked up, blinking against the rain. "As long as those thunderheads stay caught on the peaks and the rain keeps coming down, it'll keep rising."

With a muttered curse, Brady rode off to tell the men to move farther downstream and look for a way to cross.

Daisy didn't want to stop searching, but Hank insisted that Kate needed dry clothes and Molly should look them both over for injuries. After his repeated assurances that they would keep searching as long as they could, she agreed to let him take them back to the house.

Impatient to return to the search as soon as he could, Hank quickly remounted then had Daisy hand up Kate. After tucking the exhausted child under his duster against his chest, he helped Daisy swing up behind him. The scratched hands gripping his waist felt like ice, and he could feel the cold dampness of her shivering body against his back even through his duster and the spare slicker he had insisted she pull over her wet clothes. He headed home as fast as he dared.

As soon as they rode into the yard, Langley came out of the barn to meet them. A moment later, Jessica flew out the front door, Molly close on her heels. As they rushed down the steps, Elena waited on the porch, her rosary clutched in her hands.

"Where's Jack?" Jessica asked, reaching up for Kate while Molly helped Daisy dismount.

Hank quickly relayed what had happened, then told Langley to hitch the buckboard and load it with ropes, pulleys, chains, axes, harness parts, anything they could use to rig a way to cross.

"I'll gather blankets and food," Molly called back over her shoulder as she helped Daisy up the porch steps.

"Lanterns too. And bandages," Hank added. Turning back to Langley, he instructed him to bring the wagon three miles downstream of the message rock. "And hurry. It's getting dark fast."

Jack exploded out of the void in choking terror.

He couldn't breathe. Something was on his

back, shoving his face into the mud. In mind-less panic, he thrashed and bucked with all his might.

The weight shifted, then rolled away.

Clawing dirt from his mouth, he sucked air into his starving lungs. Deafened by the thud of his own racing heartbeat, he flopped onto his back, gasping. After a while, his breathing slowed and awareness crept over him.

He opened his eyes.

Dusk. Water splattering in his face. More water rushing nearby. The creek. So he was still by the creek. But where?

And where were Daisy and Kate?

He yelled for them, heard nothing, and ter-ror engulfed him again. He called over and over until his voice grew hoarse and his head was spinning so badly he was afraid he would pass out again.

But no voice called back.

Oh God oh God . . .

He lay shivering, battling to bring his panic under control so he could think.

He remembered the bridge breaking up and his foot falling through. The tree hurtling toward them. Sending Daisy and Kate on. He closed his eyes and tried to picture what happened then, but his last image of Daisy was of her at the end of the bridge just as the tree hit. Did she make it to the bank?

His heart started pounding again. *Think! Are they okay? Did they make it?*

The impact of the tree had freed his leg. He remembered falling, grabbing for a log, missing, and going under. When he fought his way through a crush of shattered timbers and splintered planks to the surface again, he was long past where he'd last seen her. Then his endless battle to stay on top of the water as the current swept him away.

How far? How long had he been lying here? Where was he?

And where were Daisy and Kate?

Fear drove him to action. He tried to roll over, couldn't. Something heavy — blinking against the rain, he lifted his head to see a broken tree trunk pressed against his side. The weight that had rolled off his back. He tried to kick it away but something was wrong with his leg. He looked down again, realized his jacket and one boot were missing, and saw blood seeping out of a long tear in his right trouser leg. More blood stained his tattered shirt, but it wasn't spreading.

With shaking hands, he unbuckled his belt and pulled it through the loops. Then groaning with the effort, he sat up and slid it around his thigh above the bleeding gash. He pulled the belt tight, almost crying out at the searing pain. Swallowing against a wave of nausea, he slumped back to the cold mud, his chest pumping like a bellows, pain coming at him from all sides.

Fury burned through him. Why had he

tried to cross? Why hadn't he checked the ropes better? Why hadn't he been more careful of the planks breaking apart beneath his feet?

Did they make it?

"Daisy!" he shouted, fear rising again. "Are you there? Can you hear me?"

Nothing but the roar of the water. In despair, he pounded his fist against the muddy ground and felt something wet and soft against his arm. He lifted it up.

Kate's kitty, matted with mud, one front leg dangling by a thread.

Something twisted in his chest. His eyes burned. Clenching his teeth against a howl of anguish, he squeezed the battered toy as hard as he could, as if somehow that might hold Kate fast to his side, where he could keep her safe.

"Daisy? Are you out there?"

Nothing. Blinking against the misty rain, he struggled to bring the fear under control. He had to do something. He had to find them. Slowly a feeling of calmness stole over him, and he could think more clearly. He had to move. He had to tend his leg. Then he would start searching.

Loosening his grip on the toy, he carefully tucked it into the waistband of his trousers.

He was alive. He was breathing and he was alive.

He would find them.

Seventeen

Daisy stood shivering while Molly helped her out of her wet clothes and checked for injuries. Jessica had already stripped Kate and had taken her into the water closet to give her a quick bath. The sounds of their voices and Kate's splashing seemed absurdly commonplace after the horrifying events of the afternoon.

Daisy's sluggish mind was still unable to grasp it all. It had been such a lovely day. A beautiful day for a picnic. How could it have so suddenly turned deadly? She tried to make sense of it, but all she could think about was the look on Jack's face as the tree hurtled toward the bridge.

Let him be alive. Please let him be alive.

Molly's voice broke through the cocoon of despair Daisy felt wrapped in. "None of these seems serious," she said, studying the scratches on Daisy's arms and hands. "Let's get you cleaned up first, then we'll tend them."

As they crossed through the dressing room, Jessica came out of the water closet with a wiggling bundle of blankets in her arms. "How is she?" Daisy asked.

"She appears fine." Jessica smiled at the scrubbed face peering up at her.

"No bruises or scratches? It was so treacherous, I was worried she might have gotten bumped or scraped." In truth, Daisy remembered little of that terrifying scramble up the bank, only her desperate need to get away from the tumbling logs and churning water.

And Jack.

Guilt twisted in her stomach. Should she have gone back to help him?

No, she sternly told herself. She'd done the right thing. Kate was her first responsibility, and she wouldn't have been able to save them both. In fact, if he hadn't sent them on ahead, they might all have gone down with the bridge.

But, God, what a terrible choice to have to make.

"While you wash, Molly can look her over, just to be sure."

Nodding her thanks, Daisy went in to draw a bath. She soaked until the water cooled and her fingertips puckered, but she still felt chilled to the bone. After pulling on the fluffy robe Molly had left on the stool beside the tub, she went back into her bedroom to find Consuelo setting a table in front of the roaring fire. Jessica was already seated in one of the two chairs beside it, and Kate, dressed in her night clothes, squirmed in her lap, staring hungrily at the bowl of oatmeal Consuelo was placing on the table before her.

Molly rose from the other chair when she saw Daisy in the doorway. "Feeling better?" she asked, crossing toward her.

Daisy nodded. "Is Kate all right?"

"Not a scratch. You protected her well."

"Not just me. Jack too. He saved our lives." The thought of Kate disappearing into that churning water reawakened such a feeling of terror Daisy could hardly draw a breath. "Any news?"

"Not yet."

Glancing at the window, Daisy saw only the reflection of lamplight on the panes of glass. "It's dark. Shouldn't they be back by now?"

"Soon. Come eat something. Consuelo made soup for you."

At Molly's urging, Daisy took the chair across from Jessica and Kate. She stared numbly at the steaming bowl of beefy broth, her stomach rolling. "I don't think I can."

"Try." Molly pushed a spoon into her hand, then moved her medicine satchel and the tufted vanity stool over beside Daisy's chair. "You'll need your strength."

For what? But Daisy hadn't the courage to ask. Knowing Molly was right, she forced herself to take a spoonful. Then another. She managed to finish half the bowl before pushing it away. "We should have heard by now," she said, speaking aloud the thought that kept circling and circling in her head.

Jessica gazed anxiously at the window, a spoonful of oatmeal suspended in her hand. "Not necessarily. These things take time."

Kate grabbed at the spoon, spilling a glob of oatmeal down the front of her nightgown. Kate was never patient where food was concerned.

"Have you checked?" Daisy persisted. "Maybe they came back and we —"

"They're not back," Molly cut in gently, sharing a worried look with Jessica. "They'll send word as soon as they have news."

Daisy watched Kate finish her meal, grateful her daughter seemed unbothered by the ordeal, and also grateful these kind women had temporarily taken on the task of tending her. Daisy doubted she would have had the strength.

Molly cleared the table of dirty dishes, setting them outside the door to take to the kitchen later, then returned and began pulling jars from her medicine satchel and setting them on the tabletop.

"He's a good swimmer," Daisy said. "He used to swim in the bay even though the water was cold and —" Her voice faltered. She waited for the tightness in her throat to ease, then continued. "And he would have made it to the bank. I know he would. Don't you think he would have made it to the bank?" She looked at Molly then at Jessica, seeking agreement.

Instead, she received forced smiles.

Molly spoke in a calm voice that belied the worried crease in her brow. "I'm sure he did. But he may have been carried miles downstream before he was able to. It will take the searchers a long time to cover so much ground, so we must be patient."

Patient? He could be dying. Dead. How am I to be patient about that?

Pressing a hand hard to her forehead as if that might drive out that terrible thought, Daisy said, "Yes. You're right. They could already be on their way back."

God, let it be true. Let him be alive.

"Well then." Sinking down onto the vanity stool, Molly reached for Daisy's arm. "Let's tend those cuts, shall we?"

Daisy stared into the fire as Molly spread ointment on the dozens of cuts and abrasions crisscrossing her hands and arms. None needed stitching, although a few were deep enough to require bandaging. After tending the blisters left on Daisy's feet by her wet boots, Molly smeared a sharp-smelling salve on a long scratch up Daisy's left shin.

Jessica rose, Kate still bundled in her arms. "Finally asleep, poor dear." She swayed gently back and forth, smiling down at Kate's round face. "Shall I put her down in her crib, Daisy, or would you prefer to keep her in here with you?"

When Daisy hesitated, unable to make even that simple decision, Jessica added, "I can send one of the Ortega girls to sit with her, if you'd like."

"Yes, please." Daisy gave a weary smile. "Thank you."

After Jessica left, Molly recapped the salve and began moving the various jars and bottles back into her satchel. "I know what you're going through."

Daisy glanced up from the fire. How could anyone know the terror that consumed her? The utter helplessness, the anguish of waiting until it was too late to acknowledge the feelings that had been building within her? How could anyone feel this pain and survive?

"I almost lost Hank," Molly went on, without looking up from her satchel. "Twice, really. The first time to injury. The second, to my own hardheadedness. And pride, I suppose."

Daisy heard the hesitation behind the words, and suspected it was difficult for a person as reserved as Molly was to reveal such personal things.

"He was injured in a train derailment," Molly explained. "He wasn't expected to survive. In fact, the doctor tending him had already given up. But I wasn't ready to

336

abandon hope. Faith never hurts."

Daisy was trying desperately to have faith. She wouldn't give up on Jack. She *wouldn't.* But she remembered the look of fear on his face, and the sound the tree had made when it hit the bridge, and how from one minute to the next everything had simply washed away. It was hard to remember that and have faith.

The fire crackled. Rain tapped gently at the windowpanes, and the air in the warm room smelled of carbolic ointment, beef soup, and the gardenia-scented soap Daisy had used in her bath. Rain at the window, a fire in the hearth, footsteps in the hall. Odd, how things could sound so normal even in the midst of such turmoil.

"The second time was after a misunderstanding," Molly continued. "I broke his trust, and in his anger, Hank treated me badly. I almost gave up on him then."

"Why didn't you?"

She looked up and smiled. Molly's smile was a revelation. It always started hesitantly, moving gently across her well-defined features until it burst from her face like a bright beam of sunlight on a cloudy day. She was attractive without it, but when she smiled, she was beautiful. "Because he deserved a second chance," Molly answered with a distant look in her hazel eyes. "We both did."

Daisy wondered why Molly was telling her

this. Did she think Daisy wouldn't give Jack a second chance? She would do so without hesitation if she thought he no longer held Elena first in his heart. At this moment, she might even overlook that, if he would just come through that door.

Tipping her head back against the chair, Daisy closed her eyes and wondered if it was already too late for second chances. "Do you think Jack still loves Elena?" When no answer came, she opened her eyes and looked over.

Molly's expression was perplexed now, and Daisy could almost see the wheels turning in her head. Molly always thought before she responded. She considered and reasoned and plotted her words carefully, giving a question her full attention before answering. "Yes. I believe he loves her, but perhaps not in the way he once thought he did."

"What do you mean?"

Molly gave a half-shrug. "It's all mixed up with the land, I think. Perhaps the brothers thought if they could protect Elena from her brother, Sancho, and give her a home here with them, it would make everything all right."

"Make what all right?"

"How they got the land and what they did to keep it." At Daisy's questioning look, Molly made an offhand gesture with one graceful hand. "Oh, their father obtained it legally," she assured her. "He paid the back taxes and filed the claim just as the law required. But I think it smacked of trickery, and that never sat well with his sons. And whether it was because of guilt or their innate sense of fairness, they've continued to protect and look after Elena ever since."

That still didn't answer the original question of how Jack felt about Elena now. Perhaps there was no answer. Perhaps it no longer mattered.

"He's alive," she whispered. "He's got to be alive."

Molly buckled the strap closure on her satchel then rested her hands across the top. She studied Daisy, her expression one of kindly concern. "I'm new to this family. I know neither Jack nor Elena very well, and you even less. But I believe Elena is content with her choice to become a nun. And I think Jack is coming to accept that, and perhaps question what his feelings for her truly are. I also think you're not a woman who makes commitments lightly, so at one time, you must have cared about him a great deal."

Tears threatened, but Daisy blinked hard to hold them back. "I did," she admitted in a strained voice. "I still do."

"Then does it truly matter now whether he once loved Elena or not? Can you not give him the benefit of the doubt? And maybe one more chance?"

God, she wanted to. Leaning forward, Daisy

propped her elbows on her knees and pressed the heels of her hands against her stinging eyes. She loved Jack — still and forever — and right now, all she truly wanted was for him to survive and come back through that door.

A commotion downstairs brought her head up. Voices, then heavy footfalls coming down the hall. On shaking legs, Daisy rose just as the door swung open.

Hank. Only Hank. Looking wet, exhausted, discouraged. And behind him, Elena, her face ashen, her rosary in her grip.

God . . . no. Daisy clasped her hands over her heart in a futile attempt to slow the thunderous rhythm within. She opened her mouth, but no words came out.

"Did you find him?" Molly asked.

Hank shook his head.

Not dead. Daisy thought her legs might buckle. Somehow she managed to stay upright. "Nothing?" she choked out, her whole being begging for a different answer. "You found nothing?"

"A boot. His jacket."

Daisy stared at him, her mind unable to grasp the significance of that. A boot and a jacket? How could he lose his jacket? And why only one boot?

"Where?" Molly asked.

"About four miles down. Caught in some brush on the bank."

"Four miles?" Molly looked thoughtful. "They wouldn't have floated that far on their own, so he must have been wearing them at least that far."

Hank's gaze fastened on his wife's. Daisy sensed silent messages bouncing between them, messages she didn't want to know.

"That's what we figure," Hank agreed. "There's a log pileup there. He might have lost them trying to get past that."

Daisy pressed a hand to her mouth as terrible images rose in her mind — Jack being impaled on branches, splintered planks — Jack being dragged down in a swirling backwash — Jack being crushed by tumbling logs.

Be alive. Please, God, let him be alive.

"We'll start farther downstream tomorrow. At least it's quit raining." Hank turned toward the door. Picking up her satchel, Molly followed after him.

"Wait," Daisy cried, panic rising again. "You can't stop looking. He could be hurt —"

"It's too dark," Hank cut in with weary patience. "We could miss him."

"But —"

"The men need rest, Daisy. We'll start again at first light. I promise we're not giving up."

Knowing he was right, Daisy choked back her pleas and nodded.

Hank and Molly left. As their footfalls faded down the hall, a voice said, "God will keep him safe."

Daisy had forgotten Elena. Turning toward her, she saw the same terror she battled mirrored in those dark, slanted eyes. She wanted to believe Elena's words. She wanted to believe this holy woman had the ear of God, but hope was starting to fade. "Do you think so?"

"*Sí*. I do." Elena came toward her, her long black skirts swaying with her lurching gait, the silver cross bouncing against her thigh. "He will come back to you. He must."

Stopping before Daisy, she reached out and brushed a tendril of damp hair from Daisy's brow. Despite her reticence with this woman, Daisy felt a sense of peace move through her at the gentle touch. A connection almost.

"I love him," Daisy whispered, finally saying aloud the words she had kept hidden, even from herself, for so long.

"*Lo sé*. I know." Elena smiled, her dark eyes bright with unshed tears. "That is why God sent you to him, *mi hermana*. To heal him. To calm his restless spirit and give him the love he deserves."

"Do you think he'll ever love me back?" Even as the words came out, Daisy wondered why she had asked them, especially of the woman who had held Jack's affection for so many years. But wounded pride was a paltry thing when death loomed close. And somehow she knew Elena would understand, and perhaps even empathize with the pain and yearning that gripped Daisy's heart.

"Love you back?" The question seemed to amuse the beautiful nun. She laughed softly, her smile serene and untroubled, despite the tears glistening in her lovely eyes. "He already does love you, *querida.* Do you not know that? Can you not see it in his face when he looks at you and little Kate?"

Anguish squeezed Daisy's chest and long-suppressed tears flooded her eyes. Tears of love, of gratitude, of a longing so desperate it seemed to burn inside her. She wanted so badly to believe Elena's words were true.

"God will send him back to you." Tears coursing down her own cheeks, Elena opened her arms. "I swear it."

Feeling her brittle defenses crumble, Daisy stepped into that comforting embrace. And as the rain stopped and moonlight broke through thinning clouds, the two women who most loved Jack held each other and wept.

Jack awoke shivering and disoriented. He blinked into darkness that was as dank and cold as a cave, wondering why he was so wet and sore and thirsty. He tried to swallow, but his tongue felt alien in his mouth, and when he licked his lips, he tasted dirt and blood.

Memory came flooding back.

Water rushed nearby. The creek. The bridge had failed and he'd been swept downstream.

To where? Wincing at the pain in his ribs and side, he tried to sit up then fell back when his head collided with something rough and hard that hung just above his face. He reached up and felt a tree trunk, the bark wet and gritty. More timbers pressed against his shoulders. A blowdown.

He remembered crawling, trying to find shelter, but he'd only made it to this tangle of downed trees because of his leg.

His leg.

Reaching down, he touched the belt around his thigh and the gash below it. The belt had come loose and the wound was seeping again, but not as badly as before. He needed to find moss to plug it and stop the bleeding. Clean water. Something to eat.

A snuffling noise at the back of the blowdown caught his attention. He froze and listened. Then a rank, animal smell assailed him.

Bear.

Fear shot through him. Groping frantically in the dark, he found a stick. Cursing and shouting, he banged it against the logs, making as much noise as he could. With a snort, the bear retreated through the brush, its claws digging up a clatter of loose stones as it lumbered up what sounded like a steep slope rising behind the blowdown.

Jack sagged back, his body shaking, his mind spinning. He'd been so worried about finding shelter and tending his leg, he hadn't thought about predators. What if they were after Daisy and Kate too?

In sudden terror, he yelled for them again and again, but heard nothing over the roar of the creek.

Maybe they'd made it off the bridge. Maybe they were safe and back at the ranch.

He wouldn't consider any other alternatives.

He must have dozed off. When next he opened his eyes, bright light filtered through the snarl of limbs overhead and the roar of rushing water didn't seem as loud as it had in the night. Leaning up on one elbow, he peered through the logs.

A line of debris on the far bank indicated the creek had gone down at least a foot, although it was still a churning froth of sticks and branches. He wouldn't be able to cross it any time soon, especially if more rain came. He needed to find a better shelter and water that was safe to drink while he figured out where he was and what he should do. But first, he had to assess the damage in his leg and find a way to stop the bleeding.

To cushion the wound when he crawled through the logs, he made a pad from pieces of his shredded shirt then buckled the belt around his thigh to hold it in place. He peered through the logs, but didn't see the bear, nor did he hear anything but the rushing creek.

He hoped it was a black bear and not a grizzly. A grizzly was unpredictable. Once it had you in its mind, it wouldn't give up until it had you in its mouth. And a grizzly would be strong enough to pull apart this blowdown if it wanted to.

Careful not to drag his injured leg over the rough bark, Jack pulled himself out of his log shelter. Once clear, he lay gasping on the muddy bank and waited for the pain to ebb. His leg burned. His ribs ached with each breath, and dozens of cuts and bruises protested every movement he made.

But he was alive. And it had stopped raining. His lucky day.

Grabbing a nearby branch, he used it to pull himself up onto his good leg. He tested the injured one. Despite the pain, it moved when he told it to. It looked straight, and it didn't fold when he put a little weight on it, so he figured it wasn't broken.

He could also move his torso and breathe without bringing up blood, which told him his ribs might be cracked but not broken enough to puncture a lung. But since they were bruised on the same side as his injured leg, it would make using a crutch difficult, as well as painful. But he'd do it. He had no choice. Daisy and Kate might be out there somewhere, waiting for him.

Using the stick for balance, he hopped over

to a boulder and leaned against it, his leg outstretched so he could assess the damage. Carefully, he unbuckled the belt and lifted the pad.

The gash was maybe an inch deep, eight inches long, running up the outside of his right thigh. It looked fairly clean — the seepage had probably kept it that way. But he couldn't afford to lose any more blood. He felt weak enough as it was.

With the stick, he dug around the base of the boulder and nearby tree trunks until he found a spongy spot with moss growing on top. Moss was supposed to stop bleeding and prevent festering. He hoped it would work. Pulling up a wad, he rinsed it in a nearby puddle, and gingerly laid it over the gash.

A shock of pain arced through him. The moss looked soft enough, but the prickly surface hurt like hell against his raw flesh. With shaking hands, he replaced the pad he'd made from his shirt and buckled the belt over it.

Air hissed through his clenched teeth as he waited for the pain to ebb. Once it did and he could think again, he looked around to see where he was.

A high-walled canyon. One he recognized. And one that ended with the aptly named Dead Horse Falls. He would have laughed if he'd had the strength.

Except for the muddy patch where the

blowdown was, there was no bank, either upstream or down, just sheer rock walls funneling the swollen creek into a forty-foot-wide chute of boiling rapids that roared over the cliff onto rocks fifty feet below. The only reason he hadn't gone over himself was because of a huge logjam perched on the edge of the falls just a few yards from where he'd washed ashore. From what he could see, the only ways out of this canyon, other than going over the falls to certain death, would be across the logjam — a dangerous undertaking for a whole man, much less one with a wounded leg — or up the sharp incline rising behind him. The one the bear had taken.

He was trapped like a rat in a maze.

Strength deserted him. He sagged against the makeshift crutch, his head hanging in despair. How would he get to Daisy and Kate now? They could be out there, needing him, but all he could do was wait for the creek to go down, or sit here until help came, or try to find a way across the logjam.

Lifting his head, he stared numbly at the twisted pile of shattered timbers that had probably saved his life by keeping him from going over the falls. He could never cross that. Not without guide ropes and two good legs.

Then recognition came, and he laughed bitterly.

Caught in the logjam were ropes and splintered planks and shattered two-foot diameter logs. Apparently, he hadn't gotten that far from the bridge after all. But maybe there was something in that pile he could use to find another way out.

He scanned the steep walls for a place to attach the ropes. Instead, he saw water seeping out of a long split in the rock face, and suddenly he was so thirsty he could hardly swallow. Hobbling over to it, he brushed away grit with his tattered shirtsleeve, then pressed his open mouth to the fissure and greedily sucked up the trickling water. After drinking his fill, he turned and studied the steep grade rising behind the blowdown, wondering if he could climb out that way.

Deep gouges scored the muddy soil where the bear had clawed its way up the slope. A big bear, by the looks of the tracks and depth of the gouges. A sense of defeat moved through Jack when he realized even if he could scale that incline with his bad leg, the bear could very well be up there waiting for him.

Or maybe it wouldn't wait. Maybe the scent of blood that had attracted it the previous night would bring it back again tonight.

He checked his pocket and was relieved to find he still had his folding jackknife. Small, but it might do some good. With painful slowness, he hobbled over to the logjam, intent on salvaging anything he could use to defend himself or strengthen his blowdown shelter in the event help didn't come today and he had to spend another night.

Help didn't come.

But long after dark, when the moonlight spilled silvery bands of light through the gaps in the logs and planks Jack had tied over the blowdown, the bear did.

EIGHTEEN

Brady awoke with a gasp, his heart pounding in his chest. Not sure what woke him, he listened but heard nothing unusual . . . the tick of the day clock on the mantel, a coyote howling down the valley, Jessica breathing softly at his side, her arms and feet flung wide in an attitude of careless abandon she allowed herself only when asleep.

Gently removing the arm thrown across his chest, he rose and padded across the thick rug to the window that overlooked the front of the house. Pushing the drape aside, he looked out.

The sky had cleared except for a few wispy clouds moving east ahead of a three-quarter moon. A pale gray wash highlighted the landscape, creating odd shadows but giving some visibility. Across from him the barn was a dark, looming mass, its sharp angles and long, flat planes softened by moonlight. In the paddocks, horses rested quietly. No dogs barked. Nothing moved.

Then what had woken him? Awareness burst into his mind.

Jack.

Not an image, or even a fully formed thought — but a feeling, a certainty — that Jack was alive and in trouble and needed him.

Now.

He quickly gathered the garments he'd thrown over one of the wingback chairs by the cold fireplace and slipped into the dressing room. Without taking time to light the lamp, he hurriedly dressed, the sense of urgency so strong it made him clumsy, and his shaking fingers fumbled with the buttons on his shirt.

They'd searched all yesterday from dawn until full dark. Still no sign. The nights were cool, too cool for an injured man or one without shelter or dry clothes. If they didn't find Jack today . . .

No! He wouldn't even consider that possibility. They would find him. And Brady had an idea of where they should start looking. It was a long shot, but with the creek running as fast as it was, Jack might have drifted that far. It was the only place he could think of that they hadn't already searched.

A moment later, he stepped back out of the dressing room to find the lamp lit and Jessica sitting up in bed.

"What's wrong?" she asked, as unerringly

attuned to him and his moods as he was to hers.

He considered lying to her. Not just to shield her from worry, but because he didn't want to waste time in explanations. But lying to Jessica had never come easy, so he decided to go for partial truth.

"I couldn't sleep," he said, avoiding her eyes as he sat in one of the chairs to pull on his boots. "Thought I'd get an early start."

"It's the middle of the night."

"There's plenty of moonlight yet."

"Brady."

Clenching his teeth in impatience, he lifted his head and looked at her.

"What's wrong?"

He continued pulling on his boots, speaking hurriedly, his tone daring her to argue. "He's alive, Jessica. I know he is. I have to go."

"Can you not at least wait for daylight?"

"No. He's in trouble. I feel it. And he's running out of time."

He stood, lifted his gun belt from the hook behind the door, and slid it around his waist. As he buckled it on, he could feel her watching, could feel the press of all her unasked questions and her doubts and fears for both him and Jack.

"I won't give up on him, Jessica," he said curtly. "I won't lose another brother. By God, I won't."

When she didn't respond, he looked over to find her studying him, her eyes dark, luminous pools in her worried face.

"Then what can I do to help?" she asked.

Gratitude flooded him. He loved her for that — for understanding, for letting him do what he had to do without pulling him down with her doubts and worries. Crossing the room in two strides, he cupped her face in his hands and gave her a hard, quick kiss. She tasted of sleep and her hair smelled like flowers and his love for her was like a living, breathing thing lodged in his chest.

He straightened and gave her a look he hoped would reassure her. "I can't wait on Hank. Tell him I'm going to Dead Horse Falls. Have him bring the wagon of supplies and meet me there. I'm sure that's where Jack is."

"Find him then, Brady. Bring him home."

"I will." He left the bedroom and hurried down the hall. As he came around the curve of the staircase, he saw a figure silhouetted against one of the moonlit entry windows. Daisy.

She turned to watch him come down the last of the stairs.

Even with the dim light, the woman looked like she'd been dragged behind a horse. But despite her haggard, scratched appearance and the terror he saw in her eyes, he sensed within her the same unyielding resolve that seemed to afflict all the women in his family. He and his brothers were lucky that way.

"Why aren't you asleep?" he asked as he stepped onto the entry landing.

"Why aren't you?"

He paused and looked down at her, thinking again his brother would be ten times a fool to let this woman get away from him. "I'm going to get Jack."

Hope trembled in her voice. "You know where he is?"

"I think so."

Air rushed out of her. Reaching a shaking hand into her pocket, she brought out something that glinted in the shaft of moonlight coming through the window. "When you find him, give him this. For luck."

It was a silver cross. Nodding, Brady took it and slipped it into his pocket. As he started toward the coat hooks on the other side of the entry, she reached out and caught his arm.

"You bring him back to me, Brady," she said in a wobbly voice. "Promise me you won't come back without him."

"My word."

Stanley Ashford dressed carefully. He hadn't seen Jessica Thornton for almost four years, and it was important to him that he looked his best.

Not *Thornton,* he reminded himself. Wilkins now.

Stupid woman.

Careful to avoid looking at his face in the mirror, he made sure the points of his collar were perfectly straight and aligned, then reached for the new tie he had bought expressly for this occasion. Slipping it around his neck, he lined up the loose ends before tying it.

Wilkins Cattle and Mining, he called himself now.

Pretentious bastard.

At least the new name was easier to say than *RosaRoja Rancho.*

The last time Stanley had been to the ranch, Wilkins had been a hard-luck rancher living in a worn-out adobe house with his two idiot brothers — one of whom looked like a damned cave dweller. Now he heard they lived in a grand log and stone mansion. They had mines and their own spur line and fancy crossbred horses and cattle. Now they were rich.

But not for long. Stanley took some satisfaction in that.

Pleased with the width and fluff of the bow tie, he crossed to the small wardrobe that passed for a clothes closet in this dismal hotel room. He pulled out the black gabardine jacket he'd had the coolies in the laundry down the street clean and press. After inspect-

356

ing it carefully for wrinkles and scorch marks, he hung it on the door then made the same thorough examination of the brocaded vest he intended to wear under it.

Hate for Brady Wilkins churned in his belly. He'd despised the cocky bastard from the moment Wilkins had walked into the stage stop where Stanley had been gagging down a bowl of chili and enjoying the admiration of Jessica Thornton. *Widow* Thornton, she had assured him and her other fellow passengers on the westbound that day.

But the *Widow* Thornton had fooled them all, hadn't she?

He had known who Wilkins was, of course. The Wilkins brothers were notorious throughout the area, and not just because of their feud with Sancho Ramirez over their ranch. They were admired, actually *admired,* for being hardheaded, clannish, uncompromising sons of bitches who would rather live in prideful squalor than allow the railroads access across their land.

Idiots. The West was full of them.

But advance work for the railroads was Stanley's business, and he had dealt with men like Wilkins before. In fact, Wilkins was the reason Stanley had been in the area that day — to secure the RosaRoja water rights for his employers, the Texas and Pacific Railroad. And when Wilkins, whose horse had died somewhere between the stopover and El

Paso, had climbed onto the stage for the last leg into Val Rosa, Stanley had considered it a lucky break.

Then their stagecoach had fallen over a cliff. By the time Stanley had recovered — at the Wilkins ranch, that pesthole — the T&P had decided upon an alternate route to San Diego, and Stanley was out of a job. Oh, he soon got another one, of course. In this wasteland, men of his refinement and education and experience seldom lacked employment for long. But working for a small group of investors on a branch line was not as lucrative as working for one of the big railroads or the transcontinental, and Stanley had soon found it difficult to maintain his style of living. So using that education and experience his employers had so vastly undervalued, he'd augmented his meager salary by using the money his employers had set aside for the purchase of water rights to make his own investments in the Union Pacific Railroad.

And it would have paid off handsomely except for the Credit Mobilier scandal. Now the railroads were toppling like a house of cards, and the Union Pacific was looking at bankruptcy, as were most of its investors.

Except in Stanley's case, it would be embezzlement charges and prison as well.

Smoothing his hands over the front of the vest, he savored the slickness of silk against his palms then pulled on his jacket. He smiled, liking the feel of it too. A perfect fit and well worth the outrageous price he'd paid for it.

Stanley liked looking his best. He liked living well and enjoying fine things. Perhaps that small weakness was what had led him down the treacherous path he found himself on today.

No matter. Soon he would be back on track and all would be as it should be.

Either Wilkins would repay the smelter loan that Stanley had forced that banker, Lockley, to sell him — which would then enable Stanley to return the borrowed funds to the railroad account before the auditors came. Or if Wilkins couldn't pay, then Stanley would take the deed to the ranch instead, and as the new owner of RosaRoja, he would hand over the secured water rights to the auditors and he would be saved.

Either way, he couldn't lose.

And just to be doubly sure, he had an ace up his sleeve. The Widow Thornton. She would do anything for her husband, he'd been told. And Brady Wilkins would do the same for her. All Stanley had to do was apply the right pressure on the right spouse.

A perfect plan.

After dusting his coat sleeves for stray lint, he straightened his lapels, then moved to stand before the full-length cheval mirror beside the bureau. Bracing himself, he looked at his reflection.

As always, there was that instant of shock when he first saw his ravaged face, followed almost immediately by a feeling of such fury and disgust it bordered on nausea. Only a handful of people in the entire country were unable to tolerate the smallpox vaccine, and he had to be one of them.

Goddamn Indians. They're the ones who kept the virus going. They should all be shot.

Frowning at his scarred image, he tried to see himself through Jessica's eyes. She had looked on him with approval at one time. Even interest. Certainly admiration. Would she even recognize the handsome man she had once esteemed?

No matter. She was used goods anyway. He knew all about her now.

Several years ago when he'd first read the notice tacked to the board outside the sheriff's office in Socorro seeking information about a lost Englishwoman with red hair, he'd known exactly to whom it referred. The sheriff, a garrulous old man missing his right ear, had confirmed it.

The *Widow* Thornton had never been married at all, it seemed. And a man in England named John Crawford was offering a huge reward for her return.

Her lover perhaps? The father of the child she carried?

No, *children.* Twins, he'd heard. One still-born, and the other very much alive. He wondered if Brady Wilkins knew the truth about lying *Widow* Thornton and her bastard son?

Stanley smiled. He had hoarded her dirty little secret for years, waiting for the perfect moment to bring it to light. How gratifying that the time had finally come.

Lifting the tin of Orland's French Hair Dressing and Restorative from the bureau, Stanley scooped a dab more pomade and smoothed it over the blond strands covering his bald spot. Then returning the tin to the bureau, he straightened his jacket and made a final check.

Perfect.

Satisfied, he left the room, ready to go visit the esteemed Mrs. Jessica Thornton Wilkins and her lout of a husband. He laughed softly, looking forward to bursting their happy little bubble of domestic bliss.

Just a few more days. Then, either Wilkins would have somehow found a way to repay the loan, at which time Stanley would be able to put back the money he'd borrowed from the railroad account. Or the ranch and all those lucrative water rights would be his.

And if that were the case, the best part, the part he would relish the most, would be booting that English slut and her turd-kicking husband to the road while he toasted his toes by the fire in their fancy new house.

He laughed softly, picturing it. What a treat that would be.

A purplish pink glow was just backlighting the eastern ridges when Brady neared Dead Horse Canyon. After a day and a night without rain, the creek had started back down, but it was still running so full and fast he could hear the roar of the falls even though it was still fifty yards upstream.

He reined in and dismounted. Because of the canyon's sheer walls, he would have to leave the horse here and climb on foot down to the base of the falls. He had decided to check there first, before working his way back upstream. If Jack had made it this far, and had gone over the falls, then that was where he'd be. Dead or alive.

That sense of urgency grew stronger.

Jack had to be somewhere in this canyon. They'd looked everywhere else. Brady wouldn't even consider that his brother might be dead and the reason they hadn't found him was because his body had gotten caught on a submerged log, or trapped in a logjam, or might even now be lying at the bottom of a swirling backwash waiting to be exposed when the creek went down.

Moving quickly, he loosened the coils of rope lashed to the front of the saddle and untied the bulging saddlebags attached behind the cantle. Knowing he might have to cross to the other side, and not wanting to have to backtrack later, he loaded himself up with the supplies he'd brought. In addition to a hundred feet of stout rope, the long knife in his boot, the Colt with five rounds — he never carried a live round under the hammer in case of accidental discharge — he'd also stuffed his saddlebags with a hatchet, a small shovel, an extra jacket for Jack, heavy gloves, a box of safety matches wrapped in oilcloth, a packet of dried meat, and assorted medical supplies like cotton batting, gauze, carbolic ointment, and pads suitable for dressing wounds. The saddlebags felt like they weighed fifty pounds when he slung them over his shoulder.

Leaving the horse tied to a tree, he picked up the rope and with the saddlebags slapping against his back, worked his way as fast as he safely could over tangled brush and downed limbs toward the base of the falls.

Thoughts of his brother haunted him with every step.

He couldn't imagine life without Jack. As much as he'd butted heads with his brother in the past, and even resented and envied him at times, there was something about Jack that had such a stranglehold on Brady, to lose him would be to lose part of himself.

Maybe even the best part.

They'd always fought. Jack could try the patience of a saint, and Brady was no saint.

On the farm in Missouri, before they'd come west, whenever there had been a task to be delegated or a reprimand to be given, it had fallen on Brady. Never Jack. Pa always had excuses.

Jack's too young. Jack's head is too far in the clouds. You're stronger, more responsible. You do it.

And Brady had done it because he was oldest and that was the way it was. And also, whether he'd let on or not, because he'd liked being the one Pa had depended on or turned to when he'd needed help. Brady had gotten a taste of running things in '48 when Pa had gone off to fight the Mexicans, leaving him to watch over his brothers and Ma and baby Sam. Brady had barely been twelve at the time, but he'd liked being the man in charge. He was good at it. And still was.

But managing Jack was like shoveling manure — a thankless, never-ending chore that brought more aggravation than reward. And being charged with that task throughout their growing years had left Brady with a well of resentment. Mostly because he had never been fooled by Jack's antics. He knew his brother wasn't the dimwit he pretended to be because he'd seen him come up with some astoundingly creative ideas, especially when a woman or a prank was involved. Like the time he'd danced a jig on the courthouse steps wearing nothing but a red bandana and wooly chaps, just to impress the judge's wife. Or when he'd dusted the personal papers in the outhouse with ground chili peppers.

Crazy maybe, but not stupid. Brady knew that beneath the charm and big grins was a good brain, but like Hank's, it just didn't work the way everybody else's did.

After Pa had died and the huge task of running the ranch and watching over his brothers had fallen on Brady's shoulders, Jack had become his biggest burden, his chief aggravation and tormentor, and certainly his greatest worry. Yet throughout the years, no matter how much he had silently railed at the unfairness of having to do his job and Jack's too, or how much he had resented the way his brother charmed his way out of chores or accountability, or how often he had wanted to knock some sense into that seemingly empty head, Brady couldn't help but love the little bastard. There was something about Jack that made you forgive him, and laugh and shake your head, and let him go on chasing his rainbows and talking his dreams, simply because he was . . . well, Jack.

In other words, he was everything Brady wasn't allowed to be when he was a kid, and a lot of what he wished he could be as a man.

And Brady couldn't imagine a world without him.

That sense of impending doom that had dogged him ever since he'd awakened in a cold sweat that morning now hardened into a grim determination. He would find Jack. He would find him and bring him home. Then he would probably have to watch him leave again, but at least he would know his little brother was out in the world someplace . . . alive.

When Brady reached the base of the falls, the roar of water cascading fifty feet down onto the rocks drowned out all other sound. A fine mist collected in his eyelashes and mustache and dampened his shirt until it stuck to his back. The air smelled cool and wet, like the inside of a dank cave.

Stopping at the edge of the rushing water, he let the saddlebags slide to the ground and flexed his shoulders. He stood a moment, scanning both sides of the creek, but saw only piles of limbs and debris lining the banks, indicating last night's high water mark.

"Jack," he yelled, but his voice was lost in the thick mist and didn't even bounce back at him off the rocky walls. He didn't see Jack, or any evidence that he had gotten this far.

Brady told himself that was a good thing. At least he hadn't been swept over the cliff.

Picking up the saddlebags again, he started the hard climb over tumbled boulders crowded against the sheer walls rising up to the top of the falls. It was hard going, loaded down as he was, and the leather soles of his boots kept slipping on the damp rocks. He was sweating like a muleskinner when he stopped to catch his breath about a dozen feet below a tangled logjam that hung out over the top of the falls, stretching from the far bank almost halfway across to his side of the canyon.

Pushing back his hat, he studied the pile of timbers, recognizing remnants of the bridge in the snarl of ropes and broken planks. He wondered if it would be stable enough to hold him if he tried to cross on it — assuming he could get over to the logjam without being sucked under it or washed over the falls.

It would be dangerous, but with guide ropes stretching across for him to hang on to, he could do it. There was no other place to cross unless he went at least a mile upstream past the steep walls to where the bank flattened out a bit. But even then, with the water running this high, there was no guarantee that crossing there would be any less treacherous than crossing here.

He resumed his climb. At the top, crawling over boulders and loose stones, he worked his way farther upstream and past the logjam so he could get a better view of the other side of the canyon.

Stopping to catch his breath, he looked around. All he saw were rocky walls hemming in a small, muddy stretch of bank with a blowdown at the bottom of a steep slope. No sign of Jack. He was about to turn away when movement caught his eye.

He stopped and squinted through the early-morning gloom.

There. Behind the blowdown.

A big black bear, clawing at the logs, trying to pull them apart. It was so intent on its task it hadn't even noticed Brady.

But no sign of Jack.

Discouraged, Brady turned and studied the rocky walls stretching upstream, wondering if he should continue along the boulder-strewn bank, or climb back on top where he could move faster and get a wider view. Then a strange noise barely heard over the rush of water drew his attention back to the bear working the blowdown.

It was an old bear, by the looks of it. And half-starved. Even from sixty feet away, Brady could see the white on the bear's muzzle and ruff, and the hang and sway of loose flesh at its belly.

Then Brady noticed something else — something odd about the blowdown.

Dropping the saddlebags, he stepped to the edge of the churning water, his heart thudding.

It wasn't just a tangle of downed trees. There were also planks like those from the bridge, and they were tied over the gaps in the logs with the same thick rope that he'd seen tangled in the logjam. There was no way those boards and ropes had gotten there by chance.

Christ. It was Jack under there! The bear was trying to get at Jack!

Brady yelled and waved his arms, the sound of his voice almost lost in the roar of the falls.

The bear stopped digging and looked up. Rising on its back legs, it lifted its snout to test the air.

Brady prayed it would catch his scent, even though he was downwind of the animal. Most bears avoided humans. If they saw them in time and weren't on a blood trail, or weren't so old they could no longer hunt and were forced to eat whatever they could find, they usually ran off.

But this bear was old. And looked to be starving.

Brady yelled again, jumped up and down, and waved his arms.

But the bear, being poor of eyesight, as most bears were, took no notice of him. After a last look around, it dropped back onto all fours and returned its attention to the blow-down.

Cursing himself for not bringing his rifle, Brady drew the Colt. A pistol, even with a perfect shot, wouldn't take down a bear at this distance. In fact, it might just make it angry and more determined. But maybe the sound of it would scare it off.

Lifting the revolver, Brady aimed at the

bank behind the animal's head, hoping the bear could hear the sound of the bullet passing close. What bears lacked in vision, they more than made up for in the ability to hear and smell.

Brady squeezed the trigger.

The bear shook its head and swatted at its ear with a front paw as if to chase off an annoying insect.

Teeth clenched in frustration, Brady fired off two more rounds, loosening a cascade of small rocks on the slope behind the blowdown.

This time, the bear jerked fully upright. It looked around, nose sniffing the air. Then, maybe because it had finally caught Brady's scent or perhaps because the sharp smell of spent powder had alerted it, the bear roared in challenge and began to run.

Jesus, Brady thought, scrambling back as the bear charged toward him. He'd forgotten that bears were hellishly good swimmers, too.

NINETEEN

It had been another rough night for the women awaiting news, and the morning had been little better. Now lunch was over, the dishes washed and put away, and the kitchen tidied. The younger children were upstairs napping, and the three older ones — Penny, Charlie, and Ben — were off somewhere with Dougal practicing with the boomerang.

With nothing left to do, the four women sat at the kitchen table and waited.

There was no conversation, no idle chatter to lighten the somber mood, just the silent, patient suffering of women who, like their sisters throughout history, sat and waited for their men to come back to them.

It was a unique kind of suffering that only females had the strength to endure. The ability to wait — for the last breath, for the fever to break, for the summons to come or the news to arrive. Such patience in the face of crisis was unbearable to men, who were ever driven to action. But females tolerated it well,

Molly had found, especially when there were other women with whom to share the endless hours. It was a silent bonding wherein each was the glue that kept the others from falling apart. Alone, a woman might crumble. But together, women could withstand anything.

Nonetheless, judging by the puffy eyes and weary faces, it had been a long night and morning. Molly, having attended more bedside vigils than she wanted to recount, was more accustomed to it. But she could see the toll the waiting was taking on the others. Elena seemed lost in prayers, her fingers working the rosary beads. Jessica stayed busy pouring more coffee or refilling the teapot. But Daisy seemed to deflate a little more with each passing hour. Molly wished she could do or say something to reassure her, but she was beginning to lose hope herself.

Jessica had risen for the tenth time to check the teapot when the back door slammed open, making the women jump in their chairs.

"Mama, Mama! Somebody's coming!" Ben yelled, racing into the room.

"It's Jack! Or maybe Brady sent word!" Jessica rushed into the entry, Molly and the other two women close behind. Crowding at the window with Ben, they all craned their necks to watch a black buggy splashing through the puddles in the lane that led to the house.

An unfamiliar buggy, carrying two people

— men. Neither was Jack.

With a discouraged sigh, Daisy stepped back. "It's not him."

"Hellfire," Ben muttered, echoing her disappointment.

"Adrian Benjamin!" Reaching around the other women, Jessica gave her son's ear a tweak. "I told you no cursing."

"Hellfire's not cussin'. Papa said — ow!"

"Why aren't they back yet?" Daisy said, ignoring the ruckus behind her. "Shouldn't they be back?"

Molly patted her shoulder but had no words of comfort to offer. Hank had left over seven hours ago. If Brady had found Jack in the canyon where he thought his brother might be, it seemed they should have sent word or been back by now.

Unless Jack wasn't there. Or they'd had problems. Or any one of a hundred other things that might have gone wrong had gone wrong.

"Goods heavens!" Jessica leaned closer to the window to stare at the two men in the buggy talking to the ranch hand who had come out of the barn to meet them. "Do you see who that is?" she asked Elena, a frown of confusion puckering her brow. "What would he be doing here?"

Elena peered out then drew back with an expression of distaste. *"Serpiente."*

Daisy recognized one of the men too.

"Blake," she muttered in a tone of equal disgust.

Jessica looked at her in surprise. "Blake? Franklin Blake? You're sure?"

Daisy nodded and stepped away from the window. "The same polecat who brought me and Kate to the ranch and almost tipped over our buggy when he tried to run through the quarantine. He's insane. I wouldn't let him in."

Jessica turned back to the window. "I wonder why they're here?"

"Probably about the loan. Come along, Ben." Daisy headed back toward the kitchen with Ben in tow. "We'll be in the garden if you need us. Ben promised to watch for snakes while I thin the seedlings."

"I will join you." Elena limped after them. "I dislike snakes also. Human ones, *especialmente. Y zorrillos, también.*" She wrinkled her nose. "Polecats."

As they walked away, Jessica turned to Molly. "What loan?"

Molly shrugged. "The one on the smelter?" She was as much in the dark as Jessica seemed to be. Neither Hank nor Brady was very forthcoming about ranch business. "I guess we'll find out soon enough." She studied the two men climbing down from the buggy. "Which one is Blake?"

"The bigger one. I've never met him, but I certainly know that other man. Stanley Ashford. He was on the stage when — my word! What has happened to his face?" Pulling back from the window as the men started up the steps, Jessica frowned in consternation, then shrugged and brushed a palm over her hair in a futile attempt to smooth the springy wisps that had escaped her topknot to curl around her face. "I must look a fright."

Molly had always thought Jessica's curls charming and wished her own unremarkable brownish hair was as lively, but Jessica seemed to think her flyaway tresses a monumental bother.

"Thank heavens Brady isn't here," Jessica muttered. "They despised each other. No, don't go," she said, grabbing Molly's wrist before she could retreat to the kitchen. "If this is about some ranch loan, then it concerns you too. And if it's something of a more personal nature — God forbid — then I definitely don't want to face the man alone."

"Who is he?" Molly asked, surprised by Jessica's addled reaction. She was usually so unflappable. Unless her temper was up, of course.

"Just someone I knew several years ago. He was on my stagecoach when it crashed. Didn't I tell you about that? Brady saved his life, although the little ingrate would never admit such a thing. Keep an eye on him. He bears watching."

A knock sounded on the door.

Jessica shot Molly a brace-yourself look, then took a deep breath and hiked her chin. And instantly she ceased being a flustered mother and ranch wife and became prim and proper "Her Ladyship."

An amazing transformation, Molly thought, filled with admiration.

Jessica opened the door.

The smaller man, who stood to the fore, doffed his bowler hat and made a mocking half-bow. "Jessica, old friend, how pleased I am to see you again."

Slim and well dressed, with thinning blond hair and a narrow, precisely trimmed mustache, Ashford might have been handsome at one time, Molly realized, but now his face was marred by bitter eyes, a down-turned mouth, and deeply cratered scars.

"Why, Stanley Ashford," Her Ladyship said with such a gracious smile and haughty British accent that Molly almost laughed out loud. "What a surprise. Do come in."

As they stepped inside and Mr. Ashford introduced Mr. Blake, Molly studied both men.

After only a few moments, it was apparent Mr. Blake was the subordinate of the two, despite the barely veiled looks of contempt he sent Mr. Ashford. Molly had seen his ilk before — surly, mean-spirited, and judging by his dismissive attitude toward Jessica and herself, not particularly respectful toward women. Or anyone other than himself, Molly suspected.

Ashford, however, was much more complex. It was apparent he had suffered a severe case of smallpox. The scarring was immense. Perhaps that was the reason for the anger Molly sensed was simmering just below the surface. And even though he sounded educated and cultured, the smooth smiles and honeyed words didn't hide the menace behind his brown eyes when he looked at Jessica. Jessica might think they had been friends at one time, but Molly suspected Ashford was not her friend now. She wondered if Jessica sensed that, too, and hoped she would keep up her guard.

Leading the guests to the big room, Jessica invited them to take seats on the couch facing the cold fireplace. As Molly took a chair beside the hearth, Jessica moved to stand with her back to the fireplace, hands clasped lightly at her waist — taking the dominant position, as well as indicating she did not expect the visit to be of long duration.

"And how may I help you, gentlemen?" she asked.

Stanley Ashford crossed one leg over the other, straightened the crease of his trousers, then looked up with a smile that was as cold as his eyes. "On the contrary, dear Jessica. It is I who came to help you."

Jessica's rust-colored brows rose in twin

arcs. "How so?"

Instead of answering, Ashford made a show of looking around. "Is your husband available?"

"He is not."

An elaborate sigh. "Just as well. As I recall, he was a bit volatile. Perhaps it's best if we handle this just between us old friends."

"Handle what, may I ask?"

Ashford, who seemed to have an inordinate interest in neatness, dusted his cuff and said, "It's about a loan I hold. Full payment is due in a few days and I was just checking to see how things were progressing."

If Molly hadn't known Jessica so well, she would have missed the tightening of her lips, the slight flare in her nostrils as she drew in a sharp breath. All signs of a temper on the rise. Hoping to avoid a messy scene, Molly stepped in with a guess. "I assume you're referring to the loan on the smelter?"

Ashford shot her a look of disapproval for interrupting. "Yes."

"I thought the bank held the loan," Molly persisted.

Ignoring her, Ashford directed his answer to Jessica. "Lockley, at People's Bank, sold it to me."

"Indeed." Jessica's expression showed polite interest, although Molly could see fury behind her brown eyes. "I wonder why?"

"I can be very convincing."

"You misunderstand." Jessica gave a condescending smile. "I was wondering why you would have such a deep interest in the business of Wilkins Cattle and Mining that you felt the need to buy our loan?"

A dark flush spread across Ashford's scarred cheeks. "I have long had an interest in the doings of RosaRoja, ever since I was a reluctant guest here almost four years ago."

"Have you? How odd. I scarcely remember that time. Although, I suppose I have been too busy to dwell on such inconsequential things."

The flush deepened. "I, too, had forgotten. Until I saw that poster at the sheriff's office in Socorro. Tell me, Jessica, my dear, did John Crawford ever find you? He was offering such a large reward for your return."

What poster? Molly glanced at Jessica. And who was John Crawford?

Apparently, the poster was news to Blake too. Up until that comment, he had been the picture of bored impatience — stifling yawns, jiggling the foot crossed over his knee, drumming his fingers on the arm of the couch. But with those words, his gaze sharpened and the fidgeting stopped.

"He did," Jessica answered, her lips scarcely moving as she spoke.

"At first," Ashford went on with that oily smile, "I thought Crawford might be part of your widowed husband's family. But the

379

sheriff assured me you were never married. Imagine my surprise, dear Jessica, after that elaborate story you gave us about your poor deceased husband. Although, considering you were *enceinte* at the time, I can certainly understand why. And how is your son, by the way? The one you were carrying when you first came to RosaRoja?"

Molly had a hard time hiding her shock. She knew Ben wasn't Brady's natural son, but it had never been an issue worth exploring. Brady was as devoted to the boy as he was to all his children, and Molly had always assumed Ben was Jessica's son from a previous marriage. Not that it mattered. Such mixed-matched families were not uncommon. Weren't she and Hank raising her sister's children? What was odd was that Ashford would be so boorish as to make mention of it.

And that Jessica would be so angry that he had.

Blake grinned, all but salivating at the prospect of drawn blood.

Ashford feigned surprise when he saw the thin-lipped fury on Jessica's face and the surprise on Molly's. "Oh, dear. I hope I haven't misspoken. You *have* told your family that he's a bastard, haven't you, Jessica?"

If the little weasel had hoped to send Jessica into a dithering tizzy, he had sadly underestimated the woman he was trying so hard to intimidate.

"Oh, Stanley." Jessica's chuckle almost sounded sincere. "You were always such a small-minded, ineffectual little man. Of course Brady knows. But I wonder why you dwell so on past history that is absolutely no concern of yours? Surely you didn't harbor some small hope of you and I . . ." The words trailed off into another chuckle. "How absurd."

Then, as abruptly as it had come, the laughter died. Drawing herself up to her full height, Jessica leveled at Ashford the steely-eyed glare that could freeze children in their tracks. "You dare to come into my house with your sly innuendoes and call my son — and Brady's son — a bastard. Do you think to humiliate me? Frighten me? Make me bow my head in shame? You pathetic creature."

Mr. Ashford opened his mouth, but Jessica cut him off with a dismissive wave as if she were shooing away some small bothersome insect. "Do please leave, gentlemen. We have nothing more to say to each other."

Blake ended his long silence. "But what about the —"

"The loan will be repaid," Jessica cut in with another wave. "Have no fear of that."

"I do hope so." Ashford uncrossed his legs, smoothed his trousers over his knees, then rose. "Because there's more at stake here than just a smelter."

"Indeed?"

Blake stood too. By the smirk on his bulldog face, Molly guessed he was enjoying watching Ashford do battle with Jessica and lose.

"The future ownership of the ranch hangs in the balance, as well, Jessica." Ashford gave a reptilian smile. "As part of the loan, the deed to the ranch was given as surety. So if you don't pay on time, your husband will lose both the smelter and the ranch."

Some of the color left Jessica's face, but her bland expression didn't falter. "That doesn't signify, does it? Insomuch as the loan will be repaid in full on time. Now, I say again. Please leave. I would dislike having to pull our workers from their more important tasks just to come in here and throw you out."

Anger flashed behind Ashford's cold brown eyes. He turned away then stopped, fished something from his inside coat pocket, and turned back. "By the way, the woman my associate here, Mr. Blake, brought out to the ranch a while back . . . is her name perchance Desiree Etheridge?"

When Jessica didn't respond, Ashford pushed on. "Because if it is, you might be interested in this." He held out the folded piece of paper. "Mr. Blake found this notice tacked to the board outside the sheriff's office in Val Rosa. Quite a surprise, I must say. Well, then." Another mocking nod. "I'll look for you in a few days." Then he turned and, trailed by Blake, left the room.

"That vile, malicious little popinjay," Jessica railed as soon as the door closed behind them. With shaking hands, she unfolded the paper he had given her and quickly read it. "Oh, my word." Thrusting the paper toward Molly, she sank into the other chair by the hearth, a stunned expression on her face. "I can't believe this."

Molly studied the paper, then looked up at Jessica in shock. "Daisy? A murderess? That's ridiculous."

"Blast! What a mess. Jack going missing, then some loan of which I know absolutely nothing, and now this." Taking back the paper, Jessica read it over again then slumped against the cushions. For a minute or two she stared up at the rafters, a discouraged, resigned look on her face. "I'm sure you have questions," she finally said. "About Ben."

"Not a one." Molly smiled. "But I'm always willing to listen."

Leaning forward, Jessica reached out and put her hand over Molly's and gave it a brief squeeze. "I bless the day you came to us, dear sister. And not just because your nursing skills enabled you to save Hank and the twins, but because you have brought so much to my life." Another squeeze, then she sat back again, her eyes suspiciously bright. After a moment, she cleared her throat and said simply, "I was raped."

Molly had suspected it ever since Ashford had called Ben a bastard. Now hearing the words and seeing the pain in Jessica's face brought up a well of anger for her friend. "John Crawford?"

Jessica nodded. "My sister's husband. He's dead now. It's a long, sordid story. Brady knows. His brothers too. I would have told you, but —"

"You owe me no explanations," Molly cut in. "I'm sorry you suffered such a thing. But I'm happy to see you've put it behind you. Not all women can."

Jessica gave a watery smile. "I owe that to Brady. He saved my life as well as my soul." Then she took a deep breath and hiked her chin, transforming into yet another Jessica — the one who had survived rape and killed Sancho Ramirez and brought such order and joy to this chaotic family. "But now we have another sister to save. I don't believe this rubbish for a moment." Crumpling the poster in her fist, she stuffed it into her pocket and rose. "But just in case that despicable bounder Ashford comes back, we must come up with a plan."

Waving Molly along, she marched toward the kitchen with long, purposeful strides. "Let's go find Daisy. Between us we'll figure out what to do to keep her safe. And then, by God, before this day is over, I intend to have a long talk with my dolt of a husband."

The bear rushed to the water's edge, then stopped, bellowing in rage.

"Come on, you bastard!" Desperate to keep the animal focused on him rather than the blowdown where he was certain Jack was hiding, Brady threw rocks as fast as he could. "Come on!"

The bear swung its massive head side to side, growling and snapping its jaws.

"Come on, you sonofabitch!" Brady grabbed more rocks, then stopped when he noticed movement at the blowdown.

A figure crawled through the logs.

"Jack! Jack!" he yelled.

His brother took no notice and continued hobbling around and behind the piled timbers.

Brady noted the bloody rag belted to Jack's thigh and more blood staining his torn shirt. But he was moving. He was alive. Elation gave him new strength. Redoubling his efforts, he moved back and forth along his side of the creek, yelling and slinging rocks.

But the bear had seen Jack, too, and had turned to look back at the blowdown. Rising on its back legs, it lifted its snout to test the air.

Brady yelled louder, throwing with both hands.

Ignoring the rocks bouncing off its matted fur, the bear dropped onto all fours and started toward the logs where Jack crouched, partially hidden by timbers and boulders.

What the hell was Jack doing? Why didn't he stay in the blowdown?

With a shaking hand, Brady whipped out the Colt and emptied the last two rounds directly into the bear. He knew they hit true because the animal flinched as the slugs slammed into its side. Yet the bear continued toward Jack.

Frustration and fear sent Brady's mind spinning in circles. He started to reload, then cursed when he realized he hadn't brought a spare cylinder. Maybe if he jumped into the water, the current would take him into the logjam and he could work his way to the other side from there.

But the bear had caught sight of his brother behind the blowdown. It started to run.

Brady watched, dread hammering in his chest. Then to his utter astonishment, he watched Jack rise up, yelling and waving his arms over his head, almost as if he actually wanted the bear to charge.

Christamighty! What is he doing?

In helpless panic, Brady raced up and down the bank, watching the bear draw closer and closer to where his brother stood waving him on.

"Jack! Go back! GO BACK!" Driven to do

something — anything — Brady tore into his saddlebags until he found the hatchet. A useless thing, but it was all he had. He couldn't just stand there and watch a bear maul his brother.

Rushing back to the water, Brady hefted the hatchet in his hand. The bear was almost at the blowdown. Praying his aim was true, Brady drew back his arm and threw as hard as he could.

Then oddly, time seemed to slow.

Flipping end over end in a high, looping arc, the hatchet seemed to float across the water while the bear lumbered on, its movements slowed to a dreamlike pace.

Jack stopped waving and sank back down into the rocks behind the blowdown.

The hatchet reached the peak of the arc and started its slow downward tumble.

All of Brady's senses seemed to sharpen. Details became acutely distinct — the flash of sunlight off the hatchet blade with each rotation, the smell of wet earth, the hollow sound of his own heartbeat inside his head.

Then the hatchet struck.

And bounced off the bear's back with as much effect as the rocks had done.

And time speeded up again.

Brady roared in anguish as the bear charged Jack, claws raking the air, its huge jaws open on a snarl. And only then did Brady see the thick lance that his brother held, one end braced in the rocks, the sharpened tip of the other end pointed up toward the bear's chest as it lunged through the air.

Brady froze, staring in dumbfounded terror, his heart beating so hard he could feel it kicking against his ribs.

He saw the tip of the lance pierce the bear. Saw the bear jerk, then fold, as its weight and momentum impaled it farther onto the lance. Saw it slam into Jack, the lance protruding from its back as they both went down behind the timbers.

Then nothing.

"Jack!" Brady shouted, running forward and almost falling into the rushing current before he caught himself. "JACK!"

No answer. Nothing moved.

Cursing in panic, Brady rushed over to the rope, thinking if he could lasso one of the logs in the logjam, he could use it as an anchor and pull himself across. But his hands were shaking so badly, he couldn't even tie the knot.

Then he heard a muffled sound, like a shout. Dropping the rope, he rushed to the edge of the water to see movement where the bear and Jack had gone down.

"Jack!" he yelled, his voice so hoarse now it came out more of a croak.

For a moment, nothing, then his brother's bloody head appeared over the top of the timbers. Brady's breath caught as Jack slowly straightened. He was drenched in blood, his head, face, shirt. He came slowly around the blowdown and hobbled toward the water, using a stick for a crutch, and gripping the hatchet in his free hand.

"Jack, are you all right?" Brady yelled.

Jack swiped the arm holding the hatchet across his bloody face. He looked at Brady and said something, but Brady couldn't hear it.

Seeing that his brother was alive and moving brought up such a swell of emotion within Brady, his eyes burned and his throat grew so tight he could hardly draw in a breath.

Jack stopped at the edge of the water. "Kate and Daisy?" he yelled.

Brady nodded vigorously. "Okay. They're okay and back at the house."

Jack closed his eyes. The hatchet slipped from his hand to flop in the mud. Brady thought his brother might fall down, too, but he staggered and seemed to catch himself. After several deep breaths, he bent over, and using the crutch as a brace, slowly lowered himself down onto his knees. Planting his hands in the water, he plunged his face into the current, shook his head several times, then came up blowing and spitting.

Brady watched blood wash down Jack's face in pink rivulets and realized none of it was his brother's. The lance must have pierced the bear's heart, just as Jack had intended.

He'd had it planned from the start — the sharpened lance, bracing it in the rocks, taunting the bear into attacking. An amazing thing, and damned clever. Brady grinned, filled with pride. A wonderment, that's what it was.

It took two more dunks before Jack's head and arms were clean of blood. Careful not to put too much weight on his injured leg, he levered himself back onto his feet, then bent and picked up the hatchet. He glared across the water at Brady. "You threw a damn hatchet at me?"

They were close enough now that Brady had no trouble hearing the words, or recognizing the furious accusation in Jack's voice.

"I threw it at the bear," Brady yelled back.

"A goddamned hatchet? What the hell good was that supposed to do?"

Brady grinned, delighted to be arguing with his little brother, rather than burying him. "I was out of cartridges and didn't have a spare cylinder."

"You could have killed me."

Brady shrugged.

Which only seemed to fuel Jack's anger. "Well, here. I don't need it anymore." And hauling his arm back, he heaved the hatchet across the creek.

"Christamighty!" Brady sputtered, ducking as the blade skimmed by. "What are you doing?"

"Same thing you did to me, you idiot!"

"I was trying to help you, not kill you!"

"Having fun down there?" a voice called out.

Brady whirled to see Hank and several ranch hands grinning down at them from the bluff rising at his back.

"See you got dinner," Red yelled, pointing at the dead bear. The other hands dissolved in laughter.

"If you girls are through playing catch with that hatchet," Hank called, "why don't we haul Jack out and go home. I'm hungry."

TWENTY

Jessica and Molly found Daisy alone in the garden, down on her knees, vigorously digging up beet starts. She'd already made a shambles of half a row, and was starting into a second when they arrived.

It was a lovely afternoon for gardening, Molly thought, as they moved down the flagstone walkway. After two blustery days, it was a relief to see the sun again and feel a warm, dry breeze instead of that chill dampness that seemed to soak into her very bones. There wasn't a cloud in sight and the clear sky was such a vibrant blue it would be an almost exact match to Brady's eyes. Although, to be honest, Molly had always found her brother-in-law's icy stare a bit disturbing. She much preferred the warm, velvety brown of her husband's.

"Daisy," Jessica called, weaving around the raised beds toward the woman attacking the ground with a spade.

Daisy's head jerked up. "Any word?"

Jessica shook her head. "Not yet. But soon, I'm sure. Where are Ben and Elena? Weren't they out here with you?"

As they drew closer, it was obvious that Daisy had been crying. Swiping a wrist over her eyes, she rocked back on her heels. "They went to the pasture. Dougal said the wind uprooted a tree and Ben wanted to see. Oh, look what I've done," she said, apparently only then aware of the decimated seedlings she'd left in her wake. "I'm so sorry. I just started digging and I — I . . ." Her voice broke.

Tucking up her skirts so they wouldn't drag in the dirt, Jessica crouched beside her. "It's all right, dear. We always have more beets than we can eat, and we can certainly plant more if need be. Come." Taking Daisy's arm, she helped her stand. "There's a bench by the fruit trees. Let's sit over there so you don't ruin that pretty dress."

In truth, it was an ugly dress. Even though Molly had little fashion sense, she could see that brown wasn't Daisy's color. Yellow would be better with her lovely hazel eyes. And the fit was atrocious — at least a size too big for her small frame. Molly suspected Daisy wore oversized clothing to distract from her full bustline. Not that it did so. The woman had a form any man would look at twice, no matter if she wore burlap or satin. Molly, with her own slim, less-endowed figure, tried not to feel too gawky around her. It was Jessica, with her flair for style and color, who was the fashion plate of the family, although her hats were sometimes a bit overwhelming.

Once Jessica had Daisy settled between them on the stone bench under the greening fruit trees, she gave her one of the lace-edged hankies she always seemed to have hidden somewhere on her person. Daisy mopped up, then gave a shaky smile. "I'm sorry. I wish I could be brave about all this, but I keep thinking —"

"Then don't," Jessica cut in, and rather curtly, Molly thought, which was a clear indication of how worried she truly was. "Tears will avail you nothing. And in any event, we have something to discuss with you." She pulled the crumpled poster from her pocket. "Are you aware of this?"

Daisy read it then groaned. "Oh, God."

"You knew him?" Jessica pressed. "This Bill Johnson person?"

"Yes. I knew him." Daisy looked up with a grim, humorless smile. "I killed him."

Molly met Jessica's look of shock. Trying to keep her voice from betraying her alarm, she asked, "Why, Daisy? What happened?"

"He was after Kate. He intended to sell her to a brothel." Daisy explained about finding Edna Tidwell dead at the bottom of the stairs at her boardinghouse, and how when she went upstairs to the room she shared with

Kate, she caught Johnson bent over Kate's bed. Ignoring their gasps of shock, she added in a flat, unemotional voice, "When I pushed him away from her, he tried to choke me. So I shot him. Twice."

"My word!" Jessica put an arm around Daisy's shoulders. "You poor dear."

Molly rose, unable to think as well sitting as she did standing. Movement fueled her mind. "Then what happened?"

"A friend was with me. A d-dear friend." Daisy's voice grew more animated and tears again flooded her eyes. "She took care of . . . everything." In a faltering voice she told how they had packed hers and Kate's belongings, then put Daisy's bloodied coat on Edna Tidwell and the pistol in the dead woman's hand. "So it would appear that Edna had killed him. Then my friend took us to a nearby church where the pastor hid us until we left to come here."

"Smart woman," Molly mused, pacing before the bench.

"I don't know what I would have done without her help."

Stopping before her, Molly held out her hand. "May I see the poster again?"

Daisy handed it over.

After skimming it, Molly nodded. "I thought so. There's nothing here that actually accuses you of Bill Johnson's murder. They only want to question you about it, perhaps to see if you witnessed anything." She returned the paper to Daisy. "It sounds as if your friend's ploy worked."

"Do you think so?" Daisy asked hopefully.

"No matter," Jessica cut in, waving that aside. "We can't know for certain you're not a suspect, so we can't take the risk of responding to the inquiry. What's important is that we figure a way to keep you and Kate safe."

"I thought we were safe. San Francisco is over a thousand miles away." Daisy stared down at the poster in her hands. "How did you even get this?"

Plucking the paper from Daisy's lax grip, Jessica folded it and slipped it back into her skirt pocket. "Stanley Ashford. That bloody bastard."

"Jessica!" Molly gasped in astonishment. Even the stricken Daisy gaped at the usually oh-so-proper-Englishwoman's use of harsh language.

Jessica gave a dismissive shrug. "Well, he is."

Molly sent Daisy a wry smile. "She's right. He is."

"Think, ladies," Jessica persisted. "We must devise a plan."

Molly resumed pacing. Jessica pursed her lips and frowned into the distance. Daisy seemed more deflated than ever, and even the flies circling the compost pile in the corner of the garden appeared to have lost their vitality.

"I'll simply have to go back," Daisy announced after a lengthy pause. "I'll have to tell them what happened and that I killed him in defense of my daughter."

"Absolutely not," Jessica protested.

"Too big a risk," Molly agreed.

"Then I'll leave."

"And go where?"

"New Orleans."

"Have you family there?"

"No."

"Then why New Orleans?" From what Molly had heard, New Orleans was no more safe than wild San Francisco. Perhaps even worse, with all the carpetbaggers and Reconstruction troubles. And hadn't they been having riots there between freedmen and Southern sympathizers?

"I — well — it's complicated." Daisy let out a weary breath and seemed to deflate even more. "There's something I need to do in New Orleans. I have to get on a ship, you see."

"No, I don't see." Jessica sounded curt again, but this time, rather than showing impatience, she sounded a bit angry. "We're trying to help you, dear. But you must be open with us so we can. Ship going where? And why?"

"Rome." Daisy seemed to be at war with her own thoughts, but after twisting Jessica's fine lace hanky into a wrinkled knot, her need to confide in them apparently overcame her reluctance to speak. "You said I should be singing on a stage — a real stage."

Molly nodded. "And so you should."

"Well, I have a chance to do that. And train with Madame Sophia Scarlatti in Rome."

Jessica reared back in surprise. "The Sicilian Songbird?"

"You've heard of her?"

"I actually heard her sing once, although I was a child and have no memory of it. My mother said she was phenomenal. But I thought she no longer sang."

"She doesn't. But she trains others, and she's offered to train me."

Molly heard a note of pride in Daisy's voice. And no wonder. She had heard of the Sicilian Songbird, too, and although she had never heard her sing, Molly knew the woman was renowned for her exceptional voice. That she would acknowledge Daisy's gift by offering to train her was high praise indeed. "Daisy, that's wonderful."

"It's been my dream to sing on a stage for as long as I can remember. I-I can't just let it go."

"Certainly not," Jessica said.

Molly nodded her agreement. "And it's actually the perfect solution to this Bill Johnson debacle. By the time you complete your training, the whole thing will have probably blown over. How long is the training, by the way?"

"Two years. Then for three years after, I tour with Madame Scarlatti's troupe."

"Even better." Jessica beamed, as if everything was all settled. But when she saw Daisy's spirits hadn't lifted as well, she tilted her head to study the younger woman's face. "Something is still bothering you, isn't it?"

"Jack," Molly guessed.

Daisy nodded. "Yes, Jack."

"What does this have to do with Jack?"

Daisy gave a brittle laugh. "Nothing. That's the problem."

"You've fallen in love with him," Molly surmised. "And you don't want to leave him."

Daisy stared down at the fingers twisting in her lap.

"Then don't leave him," Jessica said in exasperation. "Take him with you."

"It will be difficult enough trying to manage the training and traveling and tending Kate, without having to worry about Jack too." That laugh again, with an edge of pain and despair that caught at Molly's heart. "Not that he would be there to worry about. Jack has his own dreams, and I wouldn't ask him to give up his plans for me, any more than he could expect me to give up mine for him."

"Have you asked him?"

Daisy shook her head. "I've told him nothing. Jack is . . ." She paused, a sad look in her eyes. "Impulsive. He would want to go along with us. And he would. For a while. Then that need to escape, to explore, to keep moving, would pull him slowly away from us, and one day we'd look around, and he'd be gone. I know this because it's happened once already and it nearly killed me. I can't put Kate through that. I won't." With trembling fingertips, she brushed fresh tears from her cheeks. "Better to go our separate ways now before she becomes too attached. Although it may be too late already. Jack's absence has upset her more than I thought it would."

"What a mess," Jessica said with a sigh.

Molly idly watched two sparrows flit among the branches of a tall pine outside the fence and thought about dreams, and taking chances, and making hard choices. Everyone thought being a healer was her dream, but it wasn't. It had been her father's hope, not hers. Thinking back on it, Molly wondered if she'd ever had dreams of her own. No doubt at one time she had, but they'd been buried so deep so long ago, she'd never really had a chance to explore them. Now her dream of having her own children would have to be buried too. Not out of choice but circumstance. In neither case was the decision hers to make. How much harder it must be for Daisy to have to decide between a lifelong dream and taking a chance on Jack.

Molly turned back to her friends. She wished she knew Jack better and how deeply his feelings for Daisy ran. She knew so little about men. The only one she had ever truly known was Hank, and he was such a rock and so steadfast in his emotions that Molly had no doubt of his feelings for her. If Daisy didn't have that same unquestionable belief in Jack, then perhaps she was right to pursue her own dreams rather than live in the shadow of his. A terrible choice, though, and one Molly was grateful she had never had to make.

"So what are you going to do?" Jessica asked.

Daisy took a deep breath and let it out. She seemed to re-inflate a bit, as if in having discussed her problem with Molly and Jessica, she had gained the strength to make a decision. "Now that Jack has so generously provided the money I need, I'll go on to New Orleans. I'll find someone to come with us on tour to watch over Kate. Then by month's end, Kate and her nanny and I will be off to Rome." She gave them a brave smile, and added, "I can scarcely wait."

Then promptly dissolved in tears.

Hauling Jack out was more complicated than Hank had expected.

Getting him across the creek was easy enough, although judging by the amount of coughing and cursing from Jack, being towed across the current with two ropes tied around his chest was hard on his bruised ribs.

Then once they got him across and pushed the water out of him, they found getting him out of the canyon wouldn't be any easier, since Jack was adamantly opposed to hiking out, citing his injured leg as the reason.

An understandable concern, Hank supposed, but it posed the new problem of how they were going to get him up to the wagon on top.

Luckily they had plenty of rope. And after a careful study of the situation, and a bit of rummaging through the spare harness parts and hardware he'd had the foresight to add to the sundry supplies in the wagon, Hank was able to rig a sling apparatus to haul Jack straight up the rock wall.

Well, mostly straight. There were a few jut-outs here and there, and a cluster of prickly pear cactus they probably should have avoided, but Jack made it to the top in better shape than he would have if he'd had to walk out. Although his little brother had some harsh opinions about that too.

Kind of a baby, Jack could be. But then, he had had a rough couple of days.

When they finally got him settled down enough so they could tend him, they plucked out the remaining cactus spines, then Brady held him still while Hank doctored the cut on his leg. After cleaning it as best he could with Jack thrashing around, he slapped on some of Molly's carbolic salve, wrapped the leg tight and tidy, and tossed him in the back of the wagon.

Hank figured if they hurried, they could make it home in time for supper.

Jack prayed for death.

His or his brothers'.

He didn't care which.

He just wanted them to either finish killing him, or take him home so he could see for himself that Daisy and Kate were all right. Then once he was assured of that, he would commence killing them.

What a pair of peckerheads. They'd damn near crippled him for life in their zeal to rescue him. Biting back a groan, Jack pulled the blankets closer around his shivering body and tried to ignore the jostling of the wagon over rocks and ruts. And they wondered why he was always so anxious to get away from them. Still, once he recovered, if he hadn't done them in by then, he would probably be grateful they had come to rescue him. Maybe.

But for now at least his belly was full of water and dried meat — and getting fuller by the minute it seemed, almost as if an entire cow was rehydrating inside him — and the blankets were keeping him mostly warm and soaking up the lingering dampness in his clothes — and he knew Daisy and Kate were safe. So despite the shivering and exhaustion and the gut ache and soreness and constant throbbing in his leg, it was turning out to be a pretty good day after all.

The ride home seemed to take forever, although it was still light when they rolled up to the house. By the time his brothers dragged him out of the wagon, people were swarming down the porch steps like ants from a burning anthill.

Jack couldn't help but be touched that they'd been that concerned about him. But the two faces he was most anxious to see were absent. Then he saw Daisy running around the corner of the house from the garden with Kate on her hip.

Daisy was grinning. Kate just looked bewildered. Then she saw him and her face split in a toothless giggle and she started bouncing on her mother's hip the way she did when she was impatient and excited.

And suddenly all his aches and pains and worries faded away.

He wanted to laugh out loud, scoop them up in his arms and dance them across the yard.

But he was too dirty and sore, and he was afraid his leg would give out and they'd all topple into the dirt. So he just watched them come, filling his mind with the sight of them while something almost like pain moved through his chest and up into his throat.

By God, he needed this woman. Maybe he even loved her. He wasn't sure if he knew what love was, but the feeling that gripped him now as he watched her come toward him was the most powerful, consuming, undeniable emotion he'd ever experienced. He'd certainly never felt that way about Elena. About anything.

It felt bigger than his mind could encompass.

It felt right and strong and true.

It felt like . . . flying.

By the time they reached him, Kate was holding a little tighter to her mother and acting shy again, probably not fully sure who he was under the whiskers and bruises and matted hair.

But Daisy knew him, and her smiling face was the prettiest thing he'd ever seen. "Jack," she said with a catch in her breath. "Oh, Jack," she said again, and burst into tears.

He almost did, too, but masked it with a broad grin that felt as wobbly as his balance on his makeshift crutch. Then he saw the cuts and bruises on the arm holding Kate, and his grin faltered. Reaching out a grimy hand, he cupped her wet cheek. "Are you all right?"

Smiling through her tears, she nodded. "We're all right. How about you?"

Before he could answer, Kate poked a finger against a tender lump on his forehead.

"Jack alwight?"

He tried not to flinch. "I'm all right, Katie-girl. Just dirty."

"Bad water take Jack gone. Make Mama cry. Katie too."

Blinking hard, he forced a smile. "Well, I'm back. And look who I brought with me." Reaching into the waistband of his denims, he pulled out the battered toy he'd guarded like gold over the last days.

"Titty!" Kate shrieked. "Titty come back!" Then before Daisy could stop her, she threw herself at Jack and her toy.

Laughing, Jack caught her. Ignoring his filth and the ache in his ribs, he pinned her tight against his chest with his free arm. She smelled like flowers and sunshine and berry jelly, and the feel of those little arms going around his neck was the sweetest welcome he had ever known. That unnamed emotion rose again and pressed against his throat so hard he could scarcely breathe. "Katie-girl," he whispered. And closing his eyes against a sudden sting of tears, he breathed in the clean baby scent of his beautiful daughter, and lost his heart forever.

Something that sounded like a collective sigh penetrated his brain, and he opened his eyes to find a crowd of grinning people standing around them.

Embarrassed, he tried to cover his unmanly display of emotion with another big grin. "So what's for supper?"

The house had finally settled down for the night.

It had been an emotional evening — for everyone but Jack, that is, since Molly had given him enough laudanum to put him out while she tended his injuries. She was still working on him an hour later when the rest of the family sat down to a late supper. The children had all been fed, read, and put to bed, so only the adults sat around the big kitchen table.

Daisy felt so emotionally and physically drained she could barely lift a fork. But the others were in high spirits, and soon the meal became another of those everybody-talking-at-once gatherings that seemed to be the normal routine for this boisterous family. Brady and Hank took great delight in recounting Jack's epic battle with the bear and his rescue across the flooded creek and out of the canyon. And although they made it sound comical and had them all laughing, Daisy could see the lines of weariness and strain on their faces, and knew Jack's ordeal had taken its toll on his brothers as well.

No one actually put it into words, but she sensed each of them was thinking the same thing. They'd come within a hair's breadth of losing Jack, and they were all immensely thankful he had survived. Daisy sent Elena a silent look of gratitude, certain that her prayers had had a big part in bringing Jack back to them.

When Molly joined them, leaving Jack doctored and dozing peacefully, they were relieved to hear that after some fancy stitching on his leg, the removal of a stray cactus spine or two, and some ointment spread on various cuts and scrapes, he was doing remarkably well for all he'd gone through.

"Other than a lingering soreness from his bruised ribs and having to be careful of his leg, he should be feeling up to his old self within a couple or three days," she announced.

Daisy felt a tightening in her stomach. Three days. During their talk in the garden earlier that afternoon, despite their loudly voiced doubts that Daisy was doing the right thing in leaving Jack, Molly and Jessica had decided that if she was determined to leave, she should do so as soon as they were certain Jack was on the road to recovery. Daisy had agreed, stipulating only that Jack not be told about her impending departure; she knew if given the opportunity, he would probably talk her into forgoing the dream of singing and staying with him . . . which she was certain would last only until the lure of the wandering life drew him away from her again.

But three days. That hardly seemed any time at all.

And now, with supper over and the house quiet, the hollow echoes of her footfalls as she moved down the hall seemed to Daisy like a bleak foreshadowing of the lonely days to come. She would miss this family. She would miss the chaos, the banter and teasing, the laughter and energy. It had been nice feeling like part of a family again and having women around her she could talk to and trust.

And then there was Jack. All those wonderful hours with Jack.

She would miss those most of all.

As she passed Jack's door, she heard movement within, and paused to listen. Was he up? He should be sleeping. Seeing that the door was ajar, she gently pushed it open.

Molly was bent beside the bed, smoothing sticking plaster over a thick bandage on Jack's leg. He appeared to be asleep, although he flinched when Molly pressed against the bandage, and Daisy could see small restless movements in his hands and legs.

"Is everything all right?" she asked from the doorway.

Molly looked over with a reassuring smile. "I'm just checking his bandage. He's doing well."

"Anything I can do?"

Molly straightened, studied her patient for a moment, then nodded. "You can sit with him while I get the laudanum and some food.

He's starting to wake up, and I'm afraid he may try to get out of bed. I hate giving him so much opiate, but if we can keep him down for another day and night, he'll heal much faster."

"Of course." Stepping aside as Molly left the room, Daisy studied Jack's long form. It was odd seeing him so still. Usually his energy and vitality seemed to fill the air around him. She remembered how restive he had always been even when he was drunk or asleep, as if his mind had begrudged even those few hours of inactivity.

Sinking into the chair beside the bed, she took his big hand in hers. It was scratched, the knuckles scraped and bruised. Now that he was clean, she could see his poor face had fared no better. What must he have suffered? Tears burned in her eyes when she thought of how close she had come to losing him. The world wouldn't have been the same without Jack Wilkins wandering through it, so full of life and laughter and boyish dreams.

She wouldn't have been the same.

"You wretch," she whispered, smiling as she wiped away a tear with her fingertips. "You've made me love you again, haven't you?"

The restless movements accelerated. He sighed. His dark lashes fluttered, and beneath his closed lids his eyes jerked and darted.

Daisy watched, entranced. She could almost feel awareness flow through him, as if a beautiful statue were slowly coming to life.

He took another deep breath, frowned, then opened his eyes.

Daisy waited for that smoky gaze to find her. When it did, she smiled. "Hello."

He blinked groggily, then his brow cleared and he smiled back. "Daisy," he said in a rusty voice. "You're all right."

"Thanks to you, I am."

He tried to roll over, then winced and looked down at his leg. "Am I?"

"You are. Bruised and battered is all. Nothing cracked or broken. Molly stitched your leg and wants you to stay off of it for another day or so, then you should be up to your old shenanigans."

"Shenanigans?" That crooked smile. "You mean courting?"

Brady was right to call him One-Track-Jack. The man could be half-dead and still try to flirt.

"What's that smell?" He looked clean, so she knew it wasn't him.

"Stinky. Behind you."

Daisy turned to see a huge form in a shadowed corner. She reared back in disbelief. "Is that a buffalo?"

"It is. And don't ask."

Before she could, Molly returned, carrying a tray loaded with thin-sliced roast beef, cheese, bread, a cup of applesauce, a pitcher of water, and a brown medicine bottle of laudanum.

After helping him sit up, Molly and Daisy watched in amazement as he drank three big cups of water, then gobbled down everything on the tray but the laudanum. When Molly tried to administer it, he shook his head.

"It makes me feel strange," he complained, pushing aside the brown bottle.

Molly pushed it back. "One more day. That's all."

He looked to Daisy for help.

"Just one more," she seconded.

With a great deal of shuddering and gagging, he took his dose. "I suppose now you'll want to carry me into the water closet and help me relieve myself too," he said petulantly as he tossed the empty spoon onto the bedside table.

"It's been my fondest dream," Molly said sweetly.

He shot Daisy a crafty look. "I'd rather she do it."

Instead, both women helped him into the water closet, and once they had him balanced before the stool, they promptly deserted him with instructions to call when he was ready to come back into the bedroom.

By the time he was back in bed, his face was pale and it was apparent the opiate was starting to take effect. Satisfied, Molly scooped up the tray and headed toward the door, saying she would be back in the morning.

When Daisy started to follow her out, Jack grabbed her hand. "Stay," he said sleepily. "Just for a while."

"A while" lasted no more than five minutes before he was snoring softly and his big body was completely relaxed. Daisy watched him a minute more, then exhaustion overcame her, too, and she left.

TWENTY-ONE

Early the next morning, Jessica stood at her bedroom window, watching her husband walk across to the barn. She was still furious with him about the loan he hadn't seen fit to mention, but she hadn't yet had the opportunity to confront him about it. He had been so exhausted the night before that by the time she had come into the bedroom after checking on the children, he was already sprawled in the bed, snoring.

Just as well. She had been weary, too, and what she had to say could wait until they were both rested. But now he had escaped her again, and she was having none of it. Grimly determined, she headed into the hall and down the stairs, primed for battle.

Bright sunlight assailed her as she stepped outside. It was a beautiful crisp, cool morning, and even though a sharp breeze whipped at her skirts as she crossed to the barn, the cloudless sky promised a warm afternoon.

She caught up to him in the paddocks. He

stood alone, arms crossed along the top rail of the fence, his chin resting on his forearm as he studied the gangly Thoroughbred-cross foals cavorting about their mothers. It looked to be a good crop, and he should have been encouraged by the progress of his breeding program, yet his expression seemed more melancholy than pleased.

But she couldn't allow herself to be distracted by whatever was bothering him. She had issues of her own.

"Brady, I need to talk to you, if I may."

Lifting his head, he turned, one elbow still resting on the rail. His welcoming smile didn't entirely mask a hint of sadness in his vivid eyes. "What's got you out so early? When I left, you were snoring like a buffalo."

She raised her brows.

"A really small buffalo," he amended.

"I do not snore," she said, lifting her chin. "And don't change the subject."

"What subject?"

"Stanley Ashford came out to the ranch yesterday."

All humor left his face. He came away from the fence. "The railroader?"

"And Mr. Blake."

Menace turned his eyes to ice. "Those sonsofbitches. What did they want?"

"To discuss a loan that's due in a few days. One you apparently didn't see fit to mention to me."

"It's not important," he said, looking away. "Just ranch business."

"Indeed?" Anger made her voice vibrate. She took a step closer until the tips of her shoes almost touched the toes of his boots. Planting her fists on her hips, she glared up at him. "Am I not part of ranch business?"

"I didn't want to worry you."

"If it's not important, why would I worry?"

With a labored sigh, he took off his hat, raked a hand through his hair, and replaced the hat, giving it a tug on the front brim. Hooking his thumbs in his belt, he looked past her, his gaze distant, his lips pressed in a thin line below his dark mustache.

She knew the look. He was trying to find a way to answer without revealing more than he wanted or shading the truth too much. Brady was so predictable. And so incapable of lying to her. That he would even consider it now only increased her worry.

"Is this about the loan on the smelter, Brady?" Experience had taught her that the way to get direct answers from her husband was to ask direct questions.

He sighed again, then nodded.

She remembered sitting in the big room, sewing pouches to distribute after Christmas on Boxing Day, while Brady and Hank lounged in the chairs by the hearth, discussing the smelter and how they could defray some of the huge cost by selling shares to other mine owners in the area. "I thought that was in partnership."

"It was. But Blake was pressuring the other owners to sell, and rather than lose controlling interest to that weasel, we borrowed enough to buy the other owners out."

"By putting the ranch up as surety?"

He made an offhand gesture. "Just a formality."

"Why didn't you come to me, Brady? You know I have money from the coal —"

"That's for renovations to the Hall."

"Oh, bother the Hall! This is more important and you know it!" For the last four years, ever since she had allowed the mining consortium to mine the coal beneath her land in England, Jessica had funneled her share of the proceeds into an account to maintain Bickersham Hall, which Abigail would inherit one day. But *this* home was the more important of the two.

"So you borrowed the money from Stanley Ashford?" She couldn't imagine Brady going to Ashford for anything, much less money.

"No. From Lockley, at the bank. Apparently he sold the paper to Blake. I'm not sure how Ashford's involved, though."

Jessica had forgotten about Lockley. She now also recalled how Ashford had taken charge of their meeting while Blake fidgeted in boredom. "I think Blake works for him. Ashford is behind all this."

"Why? What would any of this matter to him?"

A frisson of fear moved through Jessica. She pictured the look on Ashford's face when he said there was more at stake than just the smelter. And suddenly she realized this wasn't just business to Stanley Ashford. This was personal. For some reason she didn't understand, he wanted to hurt them. Hurt her.

Fear escalated into full-blown panic.

"He wants the ranch," she said. "That's what this is about. He doesn't care about the smelter. It's the ranch." Fear ignited fury. "Brady, you did this! You put the ranch up to secure the loan and now he's just waiting to take it over!" She wanted to strike him, slap him, shove him into the fence. How could he have put everything — their home — their lives — in such jeopardy?

Strong hands gripped her upper arms and gave her a gentle shake. "Calm down, Jessica. Calm down. It's all right. I've got it taken care of."

She didn't realize she was crying until she felt the trickle of tears down her cheeks. Angrily, she swiped them away. "How? The loan is due in a few days!"

"And I'll pay it when I take the horses in."

Hope blossomed, then wavered as his words sank in. "What horses? Take them in where?"

"To Val Rosa." He released her arms. That guarded look returned, but not before she glimpsed sadness again in his eyes. "I'm selling the Thoroughbreds to the Army."

She blinked in disbelief. "*All* of them?"

He nodded.

Jessica was aghast. She looked past him at the foals in the paddocks. Such beautiful foals. "But what about your breeding program? All the work you've put into it? All the —"

"I'll start again. You've been talking about going back to England to check on the Hall and visit your sister. I'll just get more breeding stock then." He finished with a smile that was more sickly than reassuring.

Another jolt of rage shot through her. "This is my *home,* Brady. This is where my children were born. Where my daughter is buried. These are my horses too. How could you put all that at risk?"

He drew back, clearly perplexed by her outburst. "It's not at risk. I told you I'm paying off the loan."

"With what? Your dream? Four years' work? And what if something happens to the horses?"

"Nothing's going to happen."

"How do you know?" She was crying again but was too furious to care. "Why didn't you come to me, Brady? Why couldn't you, just this once, trust me enough to come to me?"

He spread his hands in a gesture of frustration. "I didn't want to worry you. I was trying to protect you."

"I don't need your protection, you big dolt! I need your trust!"

"I do trust you, Jessica." He reached out to her again.

"Don't!" Taking a step back, she raised her palms in a hands-off gesture, afraid if he touched her when she was this upset, she might act on the anger churning inside. "Don't you even talk to me. I'm so furious with you right now I could strike you and not feel a bit sorry for it."

"Jessica."

"Don't!" Whirling, she fled toward the house, scarcely able to see the ground for the tears clouding her eyes. Even after all they'd been through, all they'd shared, she still hadn't proven herself worthy enough to have his trust.

Cursing under his breath, Brady watched his wife slam into the house. He started to go after her, then stopped, not sure what he would say once he caught up with her. Why couldn't she understand that everything he did, every action and decision he made, centered around her and the family? Why couldn't she see he was just trying to protect her?

Women. Hell.

Scowling, he turned back to the paddock. He couldn't think about that right now. He had horses to get ready, a brother to take care of, Elena to send off, and this mess with Daisy and Kate to figure out. He didn't have time right then to worry over his wife's misguided concerns.

But now she had him fretting too. The whole goddamn day was ruined.

Hell.

It was nearly noon by the time he finished his tally on the horses and gave Langley instructions for moving them to Val Rosa. He'd decided to send them a day early. Because of the foals, they would have to take it slow, and instead of a five-hour trip, it would take a full day. Langley and several men would hold them north of Val Rosa overnight, then take them into town the next afternoon after the deal with the Army was finalized.

Brady had planned to go with them but now decided against it. He was afraid if he went himself and came face-to-face with Ashford, he might get himself in worse trouble. Maybe even in jail. Besides, he needed to straighten out this thing with Jessica, and Christ knew how long that might take.

As he headed toward the offices to ready the paperwork for the sale of the horses, Daisy waylaid him in the hall.

"I need to talk to you," she said, a look of worry in her eyes.

Jesus. Just what he needed. Another fretting female. But he smiled gamely and motioned her into his office, wondering if in addition to having his day ruined for a second time, he was about to miss his lunch too.

"What can I do for you?" he asked once she'd settled into one of the leather chairs and he'd taken his position behind the desk, arms folded on the blotter.

"Is that a grizzly?" she asked, staring askance at Bob.

"It is. What do —"

"Why do you have a grizzly in your office?"

He curbed his impatience. "Jessica won't let me keep him anywhere else." He'd accommodated his wife on that, hadn't he? Why couldn't she accommodate him on the horses — or whatever it was she was so upset about? A reasonable question, he thought. And one he happily stored away for their argument later.

"You wanted to talk to me?" he prompted.

She finally gave him her attention. He noted she looked only marginally better than she had before they brought Jack home, her face drawn, her eyes puffy. Obviously she'd been crying. *Hell.*

Moving his elbows from the desk to the armrests, he sat as far back in the chair as he could in an attempt to distance himself from this latest emotional female. He told himself if she got weepy, he'd leave. He had a low tolerance for crying women, especially today.

"I can't stay," she said.

Relief soared through him. He bolted to his feet. "Well, all right then. Maybe later, when you feel you can talk to me, you —"

"No," she cut in. "I mean I can't stay at the ranch."

Caught and penned. Sighing, he sat back down. "Why not?"

"I have to go to Rome."

He blinked. "Rome. The one in Italy."

She nodded and went on to spin a convoluted tale about training with some Italian singer and how it was a wonderful opportunity and maybe her one chance to be on a real stage and she'd been dreaming about it all her life and now that Jack had given her the money she needed, she'd be able to go and take Kate with her. Finally pausing for breath, she gave him a teary smile. "So you see my problem."

He didn't, of course, but knowing his little brother, took a guess. "Jack."

"Exactly." Her lips quivered in a smile. Tears started down her cheeks.

How did women do that? he wondered, pressing deeper into his chair. Cry and smile and laugh all at the same time? It was confusing. A man never knew if he was in trouble or not. Jessica called them "happy tears," which made no sense whatsoever.

But Daisy looked anything but happy.

He took another guess. "He doesn't want

you to go."

She wiped a hand over her blotchy, tear-streaked face. "Worse. He wants me to stay here and marry him."

Worse? How could staying at the ranch be worse? RosaRoja was the best place in the whole world, the perfect place to raise kids and cuddle by the fire and . . .

Brady smiled, remembering the night he and Jessica had stripped down on a moonlit hilltop and made love under the stars while meteors shot in fiery arcs across the —

"It's not funny, Brady."

Blinking away those wondrous images, Brady found Daisy glaring at him. He put on a thoughtful expression. "Why don't you want to marry him?"

She gave him one of those how-can-you-be-so-stupid looks. "And if I did, what then?"

He had no idea.

Luckily she pressed on before he had to admit that.

"How long before his itchy feet send him on his way again?" she demanded, as if somehow Jack's itchy feet were Brady's fault. "You know Jack. He can't stay in one place long enough to cast a shadow. He'll leave like he always does, and then what'll happen to me and Kate?" She started crying again.

Pulling a clean kerchief from his desk drawer — after near four years of marriage to an emotional woman, Brady had learned to

424

keep a stash on hand — he passed it over to her.

While she mopped up, he wondered what she expected him to do.

She was right, of course. It wasn't in Jack's nature to stay in one place for long. Brady had known that when his little brother had run off the first time twenty years ago to be the capper for a traveling patent medicine salesman. And again later when they'd caught him trying to tag along with a fellow who ran a touring magic lantern show. Jack probably would leave — he couldn't help it. But on the off chance that Daisy and Kate were the exact thing his little brother needed to settle him down, Brady wanted to see that he was given the opportunity to figure that out. Not that he intended to interfere. He just wanted to point out all the possibilities. That's all.

"What does Jack say about you going to Rome?"

Wadding his kerchief into a sodden ball, she carefully set it on the corner of his desk, then took a deep, hitching breath. "I haven't told him."

Well, that's typical. Brady rubbed a hand over his bristly chin to hide his look of disgust. Keeping a fellow totally in the dark, then getting mad at him for *not* doing what she thought he should do, or for what she thought he *might* do if she had ever bothered to tell him what she expected in the first place.

Women. Hell.

"So what do you want me to do?" he asked. If marriage had taught him one thing, it was the value of those eight words.

"I want you to help me get away."

"From Jack?"

Nodding, she picked up the kerchief and dabbed at her eyes again.

"He'll notice." And be mad as hell.

"I'll leave a letter for him. It'll explain everything."

Another female tactic. Drive a man to a confrontation, then avoid it by leaving a letter instead, giving him no way to answer the charges. Thank God Jessica had more courage than that. Although he had to admit that when she came at him head-on like she'd done this morning, it was a bit unsettling.

Glancing out the window, he thought about what his wife had said earlier. How could she doubt he trusted her? She knew him better than anyone in the entire world.

And yet . . .

That last niggling doubt prodded him like an imp with a pitchfork.

He pushed it away. She was still here, wasn't she? Despite all his mistakes and failures, she was still here.

But no matter how often he reminded himself of that, the lingering doubt always remained. For how long? When would she realize she deserved better than a rough-edged rancher with big clumsy hands and a violent past?

Daisy's voice brought him back. "So will you help me?"

He looked at her, thought about it for a moment, then suddenly knew exactly what he had to do. Interfering or not, he couldn't let these two make a mistake of this magnitude without at least giving his little brother a chance to get it right.

"When do you want to go?" he asked.

"As soon as possible."

Brady worked it out in his mind. He would send the horses out with Langley tomorrow. Then early the following morning, assuming his little brother was up to the trip, Brady would have him take Elena into Val Rosa to catch the stage. And while Jack was there, he could also take care of the horse sale to the Army and pay off the smelter loan to Blake — or Ashford — or whoever. And by the time Jack got back to the ranch, Daisy and Kate would be well on their way to Redemption. An excellent plan, Brady thought.

"You're sure this is what you want?"

"No." Daisy blotted away tears again. "But I don't know what else to do."

"Then be packed and ready day after tomorrow. You can always back out if you change your mind. If not, as soon as Jack and

Elena leave for Val Rosa, Hank will take you to Redemption."

"Where's Redemption?"

"In the opposite direction from Val Rosa. A little mining town on our northwest boundary. There's a spur line that goes from there directly up to the transcontinental." Brady didn't mention there was no locomotive left to make use of the spur line and Redemption was all but a ghost town. He'd leave those details to Jack.

As soon as Daisy left, he went looking for Hank.

"How's your sail-rig coming?" he asked his brother when he tracked him down behind the barn, where he was testing his new gyroscope-auger-post-hole-drilling thing.

Hank stopped digging and wiped a sleeve over his sweating brow. "Why?"

"We may need it."

"Why?"

Brady told him how Jack had asked Daisy to marry him but she'd said no because she'd rather go study singing with some foreign lady, although she'd never told Jack any of that, and now she wanted Brady to help her sneak away while Jack was taking the horses and Elena to Val Rosa, which Brady didn't think was fair at all. "So I figure it's our duty to our little brother to do something about it. You with me, or not?"

Hank just looked at him.

"Good. Here's what we'll do." Brady explained that after Jack and Elena and the horses left for Val Rosa, Hank was to take Daisy and Kate and the sail-rig to Redemption. With the spur line shut down and no locomotive, the only way to reach the transcontinental would be to ride twenty miles on horseback over a treacherous mountain pass, which Daisy wouldn't be able to manage on her own with a little kid — or to take a handcar, which she wouldn't have the strength to pump uphill. "In other words," Brady concluded, impressed with his own ingenuity, "she'll be stranded in Redemption until Jack gets there."

"How will Jack know to go there if he's not supposed to know she's gone?"

"I'll tell him, of course. Just as soon as he gets back from Val Rosa. And don't look at me like that. If Molly ran off and I knew where, wouldn't you want me to tell you?"

Setting down the auger, Hank pulled a kerchief from his back pocket, wiped his hands, and muttered something under his breath.

"I know, I know." Brady waved a hand in impatience. "You think I'm interfering. But I'm not. I'm just giving Jack the opportunity to make his case — if, of course, that's what he wants to do — although he'd be a fool not to. Plus, I'm providing a nice, quiet, safe place where they can hash it all out in the privacy of your little house there." Brady grinned. "Sort of like putting two wolverines in a burlap bag, shaking it up good, then sitting back to see who comes out first."

"You're an idiot."

"And once they've worked everything out," Brady went on, "they can decide to either return here and set up house in Jack's wing, or go join up with Daisy's singing teacher. Which is where the sail-rig comes in. If they decide to go on up to the main line, it would be much easier to get there by sail than pumping a handcar for twenty miles."

Hank sighed and shook his head.

"Well how else can they get over the pass to the transcontinental?" Brady argued. "We sold the locomotive, remember?"

"Whose idea was that, I wonder."

"The point is," Brady pressed, "after what he's been through, Jack is in no condition to pump the handcar over a pass. The sail-rig is their best bet."

"It's never been tested," Hank reminded him.

"What's to test? The wind blows, the sail fills, the handcar moves. Simple."

"And if there's no wind?"

"Then Jack can pump until there is."

"What if there's too much wind? Or a gust lifts it off the tracks?"

"Then he can cut the sail. He'll know what to do. He was a sailor for Crissakes. Now quit whining and get it ready."

"And if the wind dies before they clear the top?"

A sudden picture filled Brady's mind — the sail going limp, the car losing momentum and rolling back down the long incline, moving faster and faster as it picked up speed, metal squealing, Jack frantically yanking on the smoking hand brake. That'd be something to see, he thought with a grin. But his amusement abruptly faded when he remembered Daisy and Kate would be on the railcar too. "I guess you'd best test it first," he told Hank.

"I'm not testing it. You test it."

"It's your damn contraption. Have you so little faith in it?"

Hank glared at him.

"Good. Have it ready day after tomorrow. I've got to go talk to Jessica."

Muttering under his breath, Hank picked up the auger again.

TWENTY-TWO

"Will you sew something for me?"

Molly lowered the pamphlet she'd been reading and looked up from her chair beside the unlit bedroom fireplace to see Hank standing in the doorway with a huge wad of canvas sheeting under his arm.

"Making a covered wagon, are you?"

"A sail."

"For what?"

"A handcar." Stepping into the room, he dumped the cloth onto the bed. "It's got to be done by day after tomorrow. Just one seam. A six-inch flap that I can run a rod through. Then maybe a dozen tabs. Really sturdy. It's not complicated." He gave her that dazzling smile that made women titter.

She barely refrained from doing so herself, even though she was aware he was using it to manipulate her. As if.

"If it's not complicated," she said, picking up the pamphlet again, "then you do it."

He blinked at her. "I don't sew."

She loved his eyes. They were the color of the richest, darkest chocolate. And every bit as addictive. "I only sew people," she reminded him.

His mouth tipped up at one corner. "This won't be as messy."

"One would hope not." She studied him a moment, then held up the pamphlet she had been reading. "I found this on the bureau. Do you know how it got there?"

"I put it there."

"So I would find it?"

He shrugged. Leaning his shoulder against the tall post at the end of the bed, he crossed his arms over his wide chest and looked down at her.

She studied the pamphlet. "It's an interesting concept, the Orphan Train — sending parentless and abandoned children to the West to find new homes."

He didn't respond. But she felt him watching her.

"I didn't realize there were so many children without families," she went on, flipping a page. "Thousands, it says."

When he still didn't speak, she looked up to find him studying her, a thoughtful, almost sad look in his eyes.

"Were you thinking to adopt an orphan or two, Hank?"

This time she waited him out, turning back on him the silence he so deftly used on her.

Several moments passed before he spoke, and when he did, she watched him closely to decipher the emotion behind the words.

Hank wasn't much of a talker and he rarely showed expression. But over the last year she had learned to read the subtle changes in his facial muscles, especially around his eyes and mouth, and she was beginning to understand what each quirk of his lips meant, and how his eyes widened when an idea caught his interest, and his voice deepened when he spoke of something intensely important to him. And from what she deduced now, this Orphan Train idea was very important to him.

Pushing away from the post, he walked over to hunker beside her chair. He took her hand in his and said, "You're a good mother, Molly. I know you were unsure when you first took on Penny and Charlie. But look at them now."

Unsure? She had been terrified. Having spent most of her youth training with her father, she had little experience with young people. And when she had unexpectedly found herself responsible for two bewildered and frightened children, she had felt utterly overwhelmed and out of her depth. She might have learned how to be an adequate healer, but she knew little else. She had been an awkward, socially inept woman who hadn't the slightest idea how to interact with healthy people — especially men and children.

Then Hank had come into their lives.

"That's because of you," she said. "The children adore you. They have from the first."

He said nothing, but she could see the softening in his eyes. He loved her niece and nephew. He loved children. He deserved to have them in his life.

But it was *his* children Molly wanted. And even though that now seemed an impossibility, it was hard for her to abandon the notion altogether.

Besides, there was no telling what these poor children had suffered, or how damaged by their circumstances they might be. They could be diseased, or incorrigible, or perhaps had fended for themselves in street gangs for so long they wouldn't be able to fit into a normal, ready-made family.

Then she thought of Charlie, and how angry and frightened he had been when his mother died and Molly had whisked him and Penny away from their vicious stepfather. But today he was a happy child again. A hopeful child. She and Hank had given him that. Perhaps there were other children out there they could help. Other children they could love.

"Is this what you want, Hank?" Reaching out with her free hand, she brushed a fall of dark brown hair from his brow. "To adopt one of these homeless children?" Before he could answer, she let her hand drop back to

435

her lap and gave him a stern look. "I won't have an indentured servant. I won't take a child on those terms. If children come into this house, it will be as members of the family, not as servants."

Hank nodded, a smile in his eyes.

Molly studied the pamphlet again. "There's a name here. Charles Loring Brace of The Children's Aid Society. Have you contacted him?"

"Not yet."

Molly looked toward the window, which was open to the beautiful spring day. Children's laughter drifted in with the fresh breeze. She recognized Ben's voice and Penny's shout and Abigail's squeal of delight. Charlie was off somewhere with Dougal, Kate was on the other side of the house with Daisy, and the twins were probably running the Ortega girls ragged in the nursery. Was there room for another child in this crowded household?

She turned back to her husband. "It says they send the children to specific towns where people are waiting for them. After checking them over, they pick the one they want, and take them home."

Hank continued to watch her, his thumb gently stroking the back of her hand.

"It sounds rather cold, doesn't it?" she said, feeling a prick of sympathy. "Almost like a livestock auction." She knew what it felt like to be on display, to be judged and found wanting. She could still feel doctors and other medical men scrutinizing her, wondering what kind of woman would venture into their male domain, wondering when she would falter or make a mistake.

And what if a child wasn't chosen? Perhaps was too ugly, or crippled, or deemed unlovable? Was he or she sent back?

That would be unbearable.

She remembered always being on the outside looking in. She remembered how it hurt to feel like she didn't belong.

Until Hank.

And this lovely family.

They had given her back herself and, in accepting her as she was, had allowed her to become the person she was meant to be.

How could she not do the same thing for someone else? Especially a child?

She looked into her husband's wise brown eyes and saw the acceptance and unquestionable support he had always given her. How could she deny him anything?

She would pick the homeliest, most awkward, most seemingly unlovable children on the train. Then she and Hank would make them shine.

Leaning over, she gave her husband a quick kiss, then straightened. She held out the pamphlet. "Then write to him," she said. "While I sew your sail."

He took the pamphlet and set it aside, then smiled at her in that familiar way that made the nerves beneath her skin quiver in anticipation. "Maybe later."

Brady didn't catch up to Jessica until late that afternoon.

He hadn't exactly avoided her, but with so many things to settle before the horses left for Val Rosa, and Elena left, and Daisy and Kate went on their way, he barely had time to think, much less come up with what he wanted to say to his wife.

And why should he have to explain himself anyway?

She should know him well enough by now to realize how intolerable it would be to him to have to ask her for money. He might as well hand her his balls on a plate. He would try to explain that to her — not in those exact words maybe — no use giving her ideas — but somehow he had to get it across to his wife that he had everything under control and she had nothing to worry about.

The ranch was secure.

Her home and her family were safe.

He trusted her.

Always.

He found her up in the hilltop cemetery, sitting on the little stone bench beneath the mesquite tree, where she always went when she was upset or needed time and space to think. The sun was sinking toward the mountains to the west, and the tombstones, silhouetted against the last bright rays, looked edged in gold. Tattered pinkish-purple clouds clung to the mountain peaks, and the breeze out of the east was warm and fragrant and alive with the music of RosaRoja — crickets, cattle lowing, distant voices and laughter from the bunkhouse and cabins.

It was his favorite time of day.

Stepping through the iron gate, he let it clang shut behind him to warn her that he was there. As he wove through the markers of all the people who had lived and died on this patch of land called RosaRoja, he wondered how Jessica could ever think he would put it at risk. This was his home too. And these were his family and friends resting here.

Maybe *she* was the one who lacked trust.

Brady sighed. He was kidding himself and he knew it. This wasn't about trust. It was about fear. His fear of losing her.

But pigs would frolic like nighthawks in the twilight sky before he would ever admit that to anyone but himself. A man had his pride.

She looked up when she heard him approach, but said nothing. He was relieved to see she wasn't crying. Stopping beside her, he thrust his hands into the front pockets of his denims and said, "I made a mistake with the smelter loan. I should have told you but I didn't want to worry you and I . . . I was afraid if you knew, you'd be disappointed and, well . . . upset."

Christ. Why had he admitted that? He almost reached down to check that his balls were still there. Instead, he stood in embarrassed silence and waited for her to speak.

It was a long time before she did.

"You're such a dolt."

Relieved, he sank onto the bench beside her. Lacing her fingers through his, he said, "The ranch was never at risk, Jessica. I wouldn't have let it go that far. But you have enough to deal with and I didn't want to add to your worry."

"It's my home, Brady."

"As you once told me," he reminded her with a smile, "it's just dirt."

"But it's *our* dirt." She took in a deep breath. When she let it out, he felt some of the stiffness leave the fingers in his grip. "I know it's against your nature to ask for help, Brady, but in refusing to do so, whether you intend it or not, you tell those around you they're not needed."

Brady had to laugh. "Not needed? Hell, you're the reason for everything I do. You, the children, my brothers. Without you, there's nothing."

She didn't respond, but he sensed a softening in her posture.

Gently stroking the hand he held in his, he watched evening creep down the slopes, sending long shadows across the valley floor as the sun slipped behind the peaks. Bobwhites would be out soon. Coyotes and crickets would add their voices to the night music that had lulled him to sleep for a quarter-century. He would sooner die than let it all go. "Besides," he said after a time, "how can you think you're not needed? I let you tend all the important things, don't I?"

She turned her head and looked at him, the side of her face stained pink by the dying sun. "What important things?"

"Me, for one." He grinned. "And the kids, of course."

She cast her gaze at the darkening sky. "You're absurd."

Undaunted, he added, "And I went all the way to England for you, didn't I?"

"*After* a whole year," she reminded him. "And *after* you sent me there."

He couldn't argue that.

"And as I recall" — she gave him an arch look — "when you arrived, you said you would never push me away again, and that you wouldn't shut me out of your life, and we would share our problems and concerns with each other. Remember?"

Not exactly, but he nodded anyway. After kissing her hand to show his sincerity, he lifted his head and gave her what he hoped was a stern, manly look. "But don't expect me to come belly crawling to you every time

I have a problem."

"Belly crawling!" She reared back to look at him, an imp dancing in her eyes. Her smile was positively evil. "Oooh. I like that picture."

The sassy woman was laughing at him. "You want pictures? I've got your picture right here." Releasing her hand, he reached for his belt buckle.

"What are you doing?" she asked, her eyes pinned to his hands as he undid the top button on his denims.

"I thought you wanted to share."

"Brady!" She looked around. "It's daylight. Anyone could see us!"

"It's dusk. And no one can see us."

"But we're outdoors! Cover yourself!"

Instead, he opened his trousers all the way and undid the tabs on his drawers. "Remember those riding lessons we shared? Time for another lesson." And before she could protest further, he swung a leg over to straddle the bench, grabbed her around the waist, and lifted her astride his lap.

"Brady!"

"Help me out here," he muttered as he tugged and wrestled her skirts aside. "Shift to the right . . . yeah . . . there."

"Oh."

"Oh, *yes.*"

Jack had not been an easy patient.

He had insisted he be allowed up that

morning, but Molly had been adamantly against it, afraid that if he walked on his leg too much too soon, he might pull his stitches loose and they would have to start all over again. It had been an ongoing battle throughout the day, but with liberal doses of laudanum and Molly and Daisy and Jessica and Elena all taking turns browbeating him, they had managed to keep him in bed.

Daisy had needed that extra time to figure out what she was going to do. The moment for a final decision on Brady's plan was drawing close, but no matter how much she argued with herself, she remained mired in confusion. She loved Jack. But the dream was so much a part of who she was, she was certain if she let it drift away, she would lose the better part of herself.

It was an intolerable situation.

That evening, as she headed up to check on Kate before retiring for the night, she still had not reconciled herself to leaving Jack, and she was so weary of fretting over it she felt like curling into a ball in a corner and crying until there were no more tears left. Which would accomplish nothing, of course, other than to give her puffy eyes and a raging headache.

Stepping into Kate's room, she raised the lamp she had brought from downstairs high enough to light her way through the toys and books strewn across the floor. Except the floor was clean — she had forgotten she had packed everything away that afternoon. Seeing the stripped room reminded her that she no longer belonged here, that soon she would be gone from this place and these people she had grown to care for so much. Then she realized Kate wasn't in her crib.

Had she crawled over the slatted sides? It wouldn't be long, Daisy knew, but she hadn't expected it to happen so soon. Kate wasn't yet two, although she was very agile for her age and had always been an energetic climber.

Frowning, she crossed to the water closet. Not finding Kate there, she went on to her own room. She wasn't there either. Retracing her steps to her daughter's room, she checked the wardrobe and behind the chair. Nothing. Starting to become concerned, she went out into the hall and listened. The house was as quiet as a church on Monday.

Then she saw that Jack's door was ajar. She crossed over to it and knocked softly, not wanting to awaken him if he was asleep. When she heard no answer, she gently pushed it open.

Jack lay sleeping on his good side, the thick lump of his bandage outlined by the thin coverlet. Kate was sprawled beside him, one arm flung wide, the other holding her battered toy cat.

Daisy felt a knot of emotion tighten her throat. They were so beautiful. So perfectly matched. Was she doing the wrong thing, forcing them apart?

But if she didn't, and Kate became even more attached, and Jack left . . .

If only . . . she thought for the thousandth time.

If only she were different and didn't have this dream burning inside her.

If only Jack were different and less . . . Jack.

Ah, but then she wouldn't love him so much, would she?

With a weary sigh, she tiptoed toward the bed. After setting the lamp on the bedside table, she reached down to pick up Kate.

"Don't."

Startled, she straightened to find Jack watching her through drowsy eyes.

"Don't take her." He spoke softly so he wouldn't wake Kate. "Let her stay for a while."

"How did she get in here?"

"I woke up and there she was."

"I'll raise the sides on her crib." Then she thought, *Why?* She'd soon be gone.

She stood in awkward silence for a moment, a little addled by the intimacy of being alone with Jack in his bedroom. Which was absurd, of course, considering they had shared rooms in San Francisco, and she'd been here alone with him last night after Molly had left. But somehow tonight it felt different. Perhaps because when he looked at her that way, she reacted to the man, not the patient.

"Why don't you join us?" He gave her a sleepy smile.

Although he hadn't shaved, he'd bathed again — she could smell soap, and in the lamplight, his clean, sun-streaked hair glinted like threads of spun gold. He was wearing a new nightshirt, too, and she wondered where he'd gotten it, since she didn't recall him ever using one in San Francisco. But that sleepy, beckoning smile she remembered all too well.

"Stay," he prodded. "It gets lonesome in here all by myself."

"You're supposed to be sleeping."

"I've been sleeping. I've never been in bed so long . . . except for that time you and I —"

"Hush."

The grin widened. "So you remember too."

Oh, she remembered. She remembered more than she wanted to. Even now her clothing chafed against her tingling skin.

"Please, Daisy. Stay and talk to me. Tell me about your day."

"Well . . ." Turning, Daisy looked in the shadows for the chair.

"No, here." Reaching over, he patted the mattress on the other side of Kate. "There's plenty of room." His expression changed subtly — his right brow rising in an arc, a lazy smile quirking one corner of his mobile

446

mouth. She recognized the challenge behind it. "Stretch out, Daisy. Just for a bit." His voice dropped to a husky whisper. "Unless you're afraid."

For a moment she blinked at him in astonishment, then clapped a hand over her mouth to stifle a startled burst of laughter. "My God, you're unbelievable," she choked out. "Do you ever think about anything else?"

"Not around you."

"So now I'm supposed to rip off my clothes and leap into bed, is that it?"

His smile seemed to waver. "Only if you want to."

"Oh, Jack." Still fighting laughter, she leaned over and gave his whiskered cheek a quick kiss. "You do know how to make me laugh."

The smilc was completely gone now, and she knew she had tweaked his feelings. But really. The man was a drugged invalid, for mercy's sake.

"I wasn't trying to be funny."

"I know." Stretching out on top of the covers beside Kate, she carefully tucked her skirts around her legs. "That's why it was."

Aware that he was leaning on one elbow, his head propped on his fist, looking at her, she stared up at the ceiling and tried to think of something to say to restore his good mood. The poor man had had a rough enough day. He didn't deserve ridicule.

"How do you feel?" she asked in a kindly tone.

"Rejected. Hurt. But still willing."

She looked over and found him grinning at her again. The man was unrelenting. "One-Track-Jack" indeed. "I meant how does your leg feel?"

"Rejected. Hurt. Still willing. Oh, that leg."

He knew how to provoke her, he surely did. When she started to sit up, he chuckled and put his hand on her shoulder. "Relax. I'll behave."

She doubted it, but lay back anyway.

Silence stretched between them, and Daisy's teasing mood became melancholy as she thought of all that had transpired over the last days and all that she owed this man beside her. With so many people around all the time, she hadn't been able to talk to him about it and she needed to let him know how grateful she was.

"Thank you," she said softly. "If you hadn't sent us on — I keep seeing that tree heading toward you — and I —"

"I know." Reaching over with his free hand, he tucked a stray curl behind her ear. "I keep seeing you and Kate running toward the end of the bridge. Until Brady told me, I didn't know if you'd made it to the bank or not."

His fingertips stroked down her cheek. Unable to stop herself, she turned her face into his touch, and found his smoky eyes studying her with an unfamiliar intensity. "If I'd lost you, Daisy . . . either of you . . ." His gaze moved over her face, following the path of his fingers as they traced the arc of her jaw and down the long column of her neck. "It would have killed me."

She felt a clenching deep inside as his fingers moved across the front of her worn dimity dress to cup the swell of her breast. "You're a wonder, is what you are," he said softly. "You were made for my hands. Made for me."

Closing her eyes, Daisy struggled to focus her mind away from the fingers that were slipping the buttons free. But sweet memories floated through her mind. And long-checked needs arose. And when he opened the front of her dress and pulled down the thin chemise and his fingers brushed the arc of her bare breast . . . they left fire in their wake.

"Your heart's beating as fast as the wings of a little bird. For me, Daisy? Because of this?" His fingers moved to stroke her other breast.

She arched into his hand. Her nerves sang. She wanted to melt into him. Taste his skin.

If only . . .

Time spiraled backward. The empty years faded away and all the hurts and disappointments and pain of the past eased under his stroking hand.

"Ah . . . Daisy," he said. "I've missed you. I've missed the feel of you."

Sensing she was slipping back where she couldn't allow herself to go, Daisy forced open her eyes. Sounding calmer than she felt, she said, "Elena is leaving."

The gentle stroking stopped. His hand slid away as he rolled onto his back. She heard him take a deep breath and let it out in a long exhale. "When?"

"The day after tomorrow."

"I'll miss her."

"As will I."

She was aware that he'd turned his head to watch her refasten the buttons on her dress.

"I like her," Daisy admitted. "She's a lovely woman. A good woman. I can see why she means so much to you and your brothers."

He looked up at the beams overhead. "Elena was the one beautiful, untainted thing throughout those long blood-soaked years. Keeping her safe was our salvation. I'll always love her for that."

"I know."

"But like a sister. Nothing more."

When Daisy didn't respond, he turned his head and gave her a sad but open smile. "I should take her to Val Rosa to see her off."

"Yes, you should," she agreed, and realized at that moment, with those words, the decision had been made. He would go one way. And she would go the other. That was the only chance they had of escaping this tangled web of hopes and dreams and what-ifs. But already she was dreading the moment he and Elena rode out the gate — the last moment she would see him — maybe forever.

Anger curdled in her stomach. What a coward she was to slink away like a thief in the night. Surely she owed him at least a good-bye.

Abruptly, she sat up, feeling trapped by her weakness. She should have ended this earlier. She should have left the moment Jack gave her the money. Instead, she had let herself fall in love with him all over again. *Fool.*

Swinging her legs over the side of the bed, she sat with her back to him, her hands gripping the mattress beside her hips. When she saw the brown bottle of laudanum on the bed table, she looked back at him over her shoulder. "Have you taken your evening dose?"

"Just before you came in," he said around a yawn. "But that's it. I'm done with that swill so don't expect me to take more tomorrow."

Tomorrow. The last full day before she left. Tears clogged her throat. Feeling herself weaken and fearing that if she didn't speak now she might change her mind, she blurted out the words she had avoided all day. "I can't stay."

There, she'd said it. She'd found the strength to put her foot back on the right path. Now all she had to do was keep going.

"Stay where?" he asked behind her.

"Here. Kate and I can't stay."

"Sure, you can. You can stay here as long as you want."

She looked back at him over her shoulder. "No. I can't stay. I have to go."

Frowning, he leaned up on his elbow. "*Have* to go, or *want* to?"

She wouldn't answer that. To do so would shatter the resolve she was struggling so hard to maintain.

"You can't leave," he argued. "You need to stay right where you belong. Both of you. With me."

She looked away, her throat so tight she could barely breathe.

"Jack —"

"We'll work something out," he said, yawning again. "I promise." She felt the mattress shift as he lay back down again. "Just as soon as I get back from Val Rosa, we'll figure everything out. I promise."

She should have spoken then. Told him about the dream and a lifetime of yearning and hope. But she couldn't form the words. So she sat by his side and watched him as the drug took effect, memorizing the planes and angles and textures of his beautiful face, tucking the images safely away for all the lonely years ahead. When finally he slept, she wiped the tears from her cheeks, lifted Kate from his side, and tiptoed from the room.

TWENTY-THREE

The next morning, Jack awoke a new man. It was amazing what a warm, dry bed; a full belly; and a bottle of laudanum could do for a fellow. He'd even managed to get through another gouging and poking examination by his new sister-in-law and now here he was standing on both feet and shaving all by himself without his hand shaking or that woozy feeling from being drugged and kept in bed so long.

It was going to be a grand day.

He paused, the straight razor poised above his jaw, and wondered if Hank knew his pretty little wife's hands had been all over his injured leg. His injured *upper* leg. *And* sore chest. Grinning, he resumed shaving. He'd have to tell him.

He was limping out of the water closet when Brady came in, wearing his usual scowl. "Good. You're up," he said distractedly. "I need you to take Elena to Val Rosa and take care of the horse sale."

"When?" Hopefully not today. He might be feeling better, but not well enough to take an eight-hour buggy trip to town and back.

"The horses go this afternoon. You and Elena will meet Langley in Val Rosa tomorrow. As soon as the fellow from the Army hands over the money, hunt up Blake and pay him off. Be warned, he may have Ashford with him."

"Ashford? The railroader?" Jack remembered him well. A small man with a cold smile and the manners of a schoolmarm. He also remembered that he'd seemed taken with Jessica. Maybe that was the reason for Brady's scowl.

Brady explained about Ashford and Blake coming out to the house. "Jessica thinks he's after the ranch, so be sure to get everything signed and marked 'Paid in Full' so he'll have no reason to come after us. If there's any problem, talk to Lockley at the bank."

Jack snorted. "The same guy who sold our loan to Blake in the first place?"

"Don't worry. I've spoken to him. He understands he did a wrong thing and he's anxious to show he's sorry." Brady smiled as he said that. It was the kind of smile that made men back up a step. "He'll cover any shortages."

Brady started for the door, then stopped and turned back. "How long are you staying?"

454

"In town?"

"At the ranch."

Jack blinked, taken aback by the question. He'd expected it would come sooner or later and should have been prepared with an answer, but he wasn't. That familiar smothered feeling rose in his chest. "I don't know," he hedged. "Depends on what Daisy wants, I guess."

"And if she wants to stay?" Brady pressed.

Stay here? Forever? Surely not.

Suddenly Jack found it hard to breathe. "I don't know."

"That's not much of an answer."

"It's all you're getting. Where is Daisy, by the way?"

Instead of responding, Brady studied him from the doorway, his gaze intense and intrusive. "How's it going with you two?"

Jack's guard went up. "Why?" Brady was a meddlesome sonofabitch, and Jack knew better than to freely give out personal information.

"She decide yet if she's going to marry you or not?"

Jack forced a laugh. "I've been sort of busy the last few days."

"So that would be a 'no'?"

Jack's smile faded. He leveled his gaze at his brother. "For now."

"She's in the garden." Turning, Brady left the room.

It took Jack a while to get down the stairs, and he was glad no one was watching because with every step he had to cling to the handrail like an old lady with a bum knee. By the time he made it to the bottom, he was regretting he'd foregone use of the crutch he'd brought all those weeks ago when he'd arrived at the ranch with a busted foot. Pride could be a burdensome thing.

After a brief rest to shore up his waning strength, he worked his way out through the kitchen and into the garden.

No rain today, thank God. In fact, a month without rain would suit him just fine. But the storm had definitely brought on spring. Distant hillsides were tinted yellow with mountain balsam flowers, and the pockets of aspens trailing out of the canyons showed the pale green of new leaves. Spring roundup should be starting soon, always a busy time at the ranch, and even though it involved a solid week of noise and dust and backbreaking work, it had always been one of Jack's favorite times. There was an excitement about it as the tally mounted and each pair of riders vied with the others to earn the bonus Brady paid for the team who flushed the most cattle out of the canyons. But once the cattle were gathered in huge milling throngs, the real work began — cutting, branding, culling. That wasn't as much fun, and Jack definitely wasn't looking forward to the flies and stink and bawling of the calves.

He found Daisy bent over a raised garden plot, thinning something green. Pausing by the gate to watch her, he admired the way her light brown hair shone in the sun, and how that calico dress showed off her round little butt, and how when she bent over, the hem rose and exposed her slim calves. Strong calves, too. He smiled, remembering how they had once felt locked around his waist, pulling him in.

Tonight, he promised himself. Tonight he'd feel that again, by God.

Kate squatted beside her, talking up a riddle and digging in the dirt with a bent spoon. They were a pair, his ladies. And so beautiful they took his breath away. Smiling, he limped toward them.

He wasn't sure when it had happened, but they'd both moved right into his heart. He had thought he would never feel about another woman the way he'd felt about Elena. But with Daisy, it was . . . different. Stronger. More comfortable. And he wanted her in a way he had never wanted Elena.

Stopping beside her, he waited for her to notice him and look up. When she did, he smiled and said, "Stand up."

Hesitantly, she did.

Capturing her face in his hands, he leaned down and kissed her. Kissed her like he'd been wanting to since he'd come home the evening before last, so relieved to see them safe and unharmed he'd almost unmanned himself. Like he'd wanted to when she'd looked at him over their sleeping daughter last night. And like he planned to tonight after the house was quiet and he laid her out like a feast across his big four-poster bed. He'd give her a kiss then like none she'd ever had before. Because this time he wasn't drunk, and this time he knew what he was doing and who he was doing it with, and because this time it would mean a whole lot more to him than it ever had before.

"Good morning," he said when he finally stopped for air.

She blinked up at him, her eyes round and slightly out of focus, her lips parted and pink and plump as berries. "You're up," she said.

He had to grin. "Oh, I'm definitely up."

"Me, too, up," Kate demanded, lifting her arms. Grinning, Jack picked her up and held her in one arm while he wrapped the other around Daisy so he could hug them both.

"Well, pretty ladies. Tomorrow I have to go into Val Rosa, but today we have all to ourselves. What shall we do?"

"Horsy!" Kate cried.

"No hikes," Daisy added.

Jack laughed and kissed them both once more because it felt so good.

It was definitely going to be a grand day.

And an even better night.

■ ■ ■ ■

It was long after supper. Molly and Jessica had said their goodnights and ushered their children up to bed several hours ago, and the brothers had retired to Brady's office to discuss the sale of the horses tomorrow. The house was quiet except for the scratching of the pen across the paper as Daisy sat at the small secretary in her bedroom trying desperately to form her scattered thoughts into written words.

Muttering under her breath, she tore another sheet of paper from the tablet, wadded it into a ball, and tossed it into the small fire crackling in the fireplace. Words had deserted her. Everything she wrote read like a bumbling list of excuses. Good-bye letters were so coldly impersonal.

Sighing, she rose and walked to the window.

The moon was full and bright, painting the world below in such stark shades of gray and cloudy white she could make out the horses in the paddocks, rocks in the yard, the individual boards on the side of the barn.

Leaning her forehead against the cool glass of the window, she sighed again.

Maybe she should just talk to him. Explain about the tour and her chance to train with Madame Scarlatti and sing on a real stage. Jack would understand.

459

Wouldn't he?

She let her thoughts drift back through the lovely day — their last full day together. After Kate's riding lesson and a visit with the barn kitty, they had spent the rest of the morning in the nursery with Kate and the twins and little Abigail. They read, they painted, they sang. The two little girls danced while Daisy played the piano and Jack accompanied her on the tom-tom drums and the twins shrieked out a song. It was chaos. After the noon meal, exhaustion had claimed Kate, and Daisy had left her napping in the care of one of the nursery girls, and had gone on a buggy tour with Jack. He seemed so carefree and happy, showing her all his favorite haunts and relating stories of pranks and scrapes he'd gotten into with his brothers. It was almost like he was reacquainting himself with his childhood . . . or else telling his special places good-bye. But Daisy would let no melancholy thoughts intrude on the lovely day — the last day. She enjoyed every moment.

Supper had been more boisterous than usual. With Jack able to join them again and Elena leaving the next day, it was a lively celebration with a great deal of laughter over Jack's ordeal and fond remembrances of Elena as a child. No sad thoughts or regrets intruded, and even though Daisy sensed an underlying poignancy about Elena's departure, the family seemed to have accepted her

460

decision to devote her life to the church. Brady was the only one who knew Daisy and Kate would be leaving the next day, too, although headed in the opposite direction, but other than a few thoughtful glances cast her way, he gave no indication. It was a lovely gathering and a perfect ending to a perfect day.

But now it was over. And here she sat in her lonely room, with a letter to write and a night of regrets and "what-ifs" to get through, and with every breath she took, she felt herself weaken a little more.

At the creak of the door behind her, she turned to see the very person she had been fretting over limp into the room.

She raised a brow. "I didn't hear your knock."

"That's because I didn't." Grabbing her coat off a peg behind the door, he held it out. "Here, put this on."

"Why do I need a coat?"

"Because it's cool outside." After she slipped on her worn gabardine, he took her hand and pulled her toward the door. "Come on. It's a full moon and there's something I want to show you."

"What if Kate wakes up?"

"I sent one of the Ortegas to sit with her. Come on."

"It's dark," she protested, even though she offered no other resistance as he led her out into the hall. "What do you expect to see in the middle of the night?"

He grinned back at her. "The inland ocean."

"The what?"

"You'll see."

They left the house and crossed through the barn and out the other side, where two saddled horses stood tied to a rail by the double back doors.

"You do ride, don't you?" he asked, stopping before a small mare with a blaze running down her face that looked almost silver in the moonlight.

"Yes, but not frequently. And you shouldn't be riding at all with that leg."

"We're not going far." After helping her into the saddle, he untied the mare and handed up the reins. "She'll follow. Just keep a light hand on the leathers."

Luckily Jack's injured leg was his right one, and he was able to swing into the saddle without putting a strain on it. Still, she could see it bothered him until he slipped the toe of his boot into the stirrup and let his knee take most of the weight. Without a word, he reined his big gelding toward the valley and kicked it into a mile-eating lope. Daisy's mare followed smoothly behind.

They rode for less than a quarter hour before Jack pulled his horse to a stop on a small treeless knoll that rose out of the flats.

Daisy reined in beside him. For a moment they sat quietly, looking out at the moon-gilded vista.

"Look," Jack finally said. He stuck out a hand, palm down, and drew it in a slow, sweeping arc, mimicking the roll of the landscape. "Squint your eyes and feel the wind and let your mind drift."

Daisy did, and there it was. The inland sea. The combination of rain and warm sunshine had sent the spring grass shooting up, and with every gentle gust, the tall blades bobbed and shimmered and rippled like waves on a rolling sea. The sense of movement was uncanny, and with the rhythmic shushing of wind through the grass, it truly sounded like water lapping against the shore.

On either side of the valley, pine-covered hills rose out of the silvered plain like dark islands stretching high into the sky to where the last patches of snow on the peaks gleamed white in the frosted light. Somewhere in a far canyon, a cow bawled, but to Daisy it sounded like it could have been the muffled blast of a distant foghorn. Other than that, and the soughing of the wind, and her own pulse beat in her ears, the silence was complete and eerie and magical. It was like being transported to another world of wind and water and endless stars.

He turned toward her. "Do you see it?"

He was smiling, his teeth a white slash

against his darker face. The angles and planes of his strong features were so perfectly sculpted by moonlight she wanted to reach out and touch him and feel the warmth of his skin to assure herself he was real.

"Yes," she said. "I see it."

Jack's ocean in the mountains.

Still smiling, he closed his eyes and lifted his face to the sky. His lips parted. She watched his chest rise and fall on a deep breath and could almost feel renewed energy flowing through him.

He needs this, she realized. *He needs this openness and space around him. Without it, he's like a caged bird.*

And with that realization came another.

She didn't want to be another bar in the walls of that cage. She didn't want to be the one who held him back from his soaring dreams. And she could do it, she knew. If she stayed and bound him to her side with marriage, she could clip his wings forever. Jack would always be torn between her and Kate and the beckoning beyond. But since he couldn't be two men at the same time, he would end up being neither. And the Jack she loved would be lost forever.

She couldn't do that.

She had to let him go. *God, give me the strength.*

His voice broke the long silence. "I used to

464

come here as a kid."

Braced against the searing emptiness, she turned toward him, praying for the courage to say what she must. "Jack."

But his attention was turned toward the valley, his face softened by moonlight and memories. "On full moon nights, I'd sneak out and come here. I'd run the whole way. I would stand right here on this little hilltop and pretend I was on the bow of my own ship on my way to some other place, some other adventure." He fell silent for a moment.

She watched him take in another deep breath and let it go in a rush.

"I could breathe here. I could be someone other than Brady and Hank's little brother. I could be someone different. Someone grand." Turning his head, he looked directly into her eyes. "I still can. If you and Kate stay with me."

To watch you wither away?

"Jack," she began, still not sure what she was going to say.

Again, he cut her off. "Or we can go adventuring together. The three of us. Go anywhere in the world we want."

And give up singing forever.

"It would be an adventure, Daisy."

She could hear the laughter in his voice. The joy and yearning.

"There's a river in South America. It's called the Amazon and it's so big some have

465

named it the River Sea. It can even handle steamboats. Huge Anaconda snakes live there and man-eating piranha fish and a species of river dolphin called a Boto that the natives say can turn into a man. Kate would love it. You too. I've got enough money to take us anywhere we want, so why not see it all?"

"Jack, I —"

"First we'll go north, all the way to the Yukon, another great river. Did you know they train dogs to pull sleds across the ice up there and they have mountains that are so tall the snow on top never melts? They call them glaciers. And the rainbows in the night sky" — he waved a hand toward the moonlit dome overhead — "hell, you won't believe the colors, Daisy. They say they're almost alive. The natives call it the 'dance of the spirits'. It's magical."

He laughed, his teeth white in the moonlight. "I want to show it all to you. And what I haven't seen, we can see together. The world's a wondrous and astounding place, Daisy, and I want our daughter to know there's more to it than just this valley."

Our daughter. *But what of me?* Could she live a life without music? The breeze gusted and Daisy trembled as a cold draft cut through her thin coat like the blade of a knife. "I wish . . ." *What?*

To stay? To go? To hear him say he loves

me? Would that be enough to give up the dream?

"You're cold," he said, frowning over at her. "I didn't mean to keep you out in the wind so long. I just wanted you to see it." He reined his gelding toward the house, Daisy's mare trailing behind.

"Want to race?" he called over his shoulder, and before she could answer, he kicked his horse into a gallop. Her mare lunged after him.

Laughing like carefree children, they raced across Jack's inland sea, while the waving grass shimmered around them, and the moon lit their way, and the breeze tugged Daisy's hair from her braid and stung her eyes. And if Jack had looked back and noticed her tears, she would have laughed and told him it was just the wind.

But he didn't look back.

Jack felt the shiver of her body when he lifted Daisy down outside the barn, and berated himself for not getting her a better jacket. But he wasn't sorry they'd gone. It was the first time he'd ever told anyone about his "mountain sea," and even though he knew it was just a child's fantasy, he was glad he'd shared it with her. It had always been easy to talk to Daisy. She never mocked or judged, and when he was around her, he felt he could let the masks drop for a while.

"You go on in and warm up," he said. "I'll take care of the horses."

He watched her walk through the darkened barn and out again into the moonlight. Her hair had come loose and lifted in the breeze, fanning around her shoulders like a silver veil. She looked smaller to him. Diminished somehow. And Jack had a sudden odd premonition that she would keep walking away from him until she disappeared altogether. But that was probably just a trick of the moonlight.

Tonight, he thought, laughing softly as he unsaddled the horses. Was there ever going to be a grander night than tonight?

After he'd brushed the animals and turned them out into the back pasture, he put the tack away, secured the barn, and headed toward the house.

He took the stairs as quickly as he could. His leg was sore from the ride, but not as painful as yesterday, and certainly not troublesome enough to put him off his plans. He paused outside Daisy's door to catch his breath and realized his hands were sweating and his heart was racing like a schoolboy's. Which was stupid. He'd been bedding women for almost half his life. He'd bedded this woman. Many times. Probably. But this was different. This time it was important.

He pushed open the door. The room was dark, but he could see by the moonlight coming through the French door that Daisy wasn't there. Then he heard movement in the water closet and smiled, picturing her in the tub, naked and soapy and sleek with water, her skin rosy from the heat. He wanted to go in there and strip off his clothes and climb into the tub with her. But he decided not to. She was still holding back for some reason and he didn't want to rush his fences. Even as young as she was, Daisy was headstrong. She wouldn't like being pushed too hard.

Stepping across the hall to his bedroom, he went through the dressing area and into the adjoining water closet. Quickly, he washed off the horse dirt, changed his shirt, and checked his teeth. When he went back into the hall, he almost plowed into the nursery girl as she came out of Kate's room.

"Everything all right?" he asked, peering past her into his daughter's room.

"*Sí.*" The young woman nodded and stifled a yawn. "*Todo está bien.*"

After thanking her for staying with Kate, Jack sent her on to bed then stepped through the door, closing it softly behind him.

Daisy was bent over the crib, humming softly as she stroked Kate's back. He could smell the same flowery soap she used on Kate and saw that she had changed into a long flannel gown that seemed to hang on her small frame. She'd replaited her light brown hair, and the thick braid hung down her bent back, the end brushing against the rounded bottom that showed pink through the worn cloth.

His heart pounded even harder.

Grinning, he walked up behind her and slid his arms around her slender waist. He felt her startle, then relax as he pulled her back against the length of his body. She clasped her arms over his, and they stood in silence, looking down at their daughter. "We made a beautiful baby, didn't we?" he finally said.

"Yes, we did."

"Before you came, I never thought of being a father. Now I can't imagine a life without her." He pressed a kiss to the crown of Daisy's head. "Thank you for bringing her to me."

He felt tension move through her. He thought she was about to say something, but she didn't, and slowly relaxed back against him again. Her body felt small and soft and warm next to his. Lowering his head, he kissed her temple and whispered, "I want you."

"I can tell."

Chuckling, he slid his hands up and cupped her breasts. Her perfect breasts. "My room or yours?"

Turning within his arms, she faced him. She looked sad, and he could almost feel her pulling back even though she hadn't moved away. "Jack," she began hesitantly.

He cut her off, recognizing in her tone that

same finality he'd heard in Elena's voice when they had talked in the cemetery weeks ago. "I know you have things you need to do. But can't we do them together?"

"I can't —"

"Or is it the words?" He drew back to see her face, still holding her, but loosely, so she wouldn't feel trapped. He put on a smile. "I can say them if you want, even though I'm not exactly sure what they mean or if there really is such a thing, but if there is, then I guess I come closest to it with you."

Hell. That made no sense whatsoever.

Her frown of confusion told him she agreed. "What words?"

He shrugged. A different kind of heat moved through him and up into his face. "You know. The words."

"Oh. *Those* words." She smiled.

Encouraged, he added, "I only said them once and that was in anger, so I don't think it counts."

"To Elena?"

"I'm not sure why I said it. Or even if I believe in it." He gave a laugh that sounded odd in his own ear. "God knows there weren't a lot of tender feelings floating around here when I grew up."

Her smile faded. She drew back as far as she could within the circle of his arms. "How can you say that? Your brothers adore you."

"Adore? I don't think they even know the word."

Pulling all the way free, she crossed her arms over her chest. "Perhaps not the word, but the feeling is there. Just look at their faces when they're with their wives. Or their children. Or you."

"Fine. Okay." He waved the notion aside, embarrassed to be talking about his brothers in such a way. But before he could get back to what he meant to say, she cut in again.

"I would give anything to have a family like yours. To have brothers or sisters, to have my parents back. You have no idea what it's like when there's no one left in the world who really knows you, or knew you as a child, or has the same memories you do. It's like losing a part of yourself."

"I do care about my family, Daisy. But I'm ready to make another family. One with you and Kate."

"Even though you don't love us."

"I didn't say that." He had to work hard not to let his frustration show. "I said I didn't know exactly what those words meant. Does it mean wanting to spend time with you, share your bed, protect you? Talk to you about childhood memories, or hopes, or plans that stretch into old age? I don't know."

He had her full attention now and he sensed that this was his one and maybe only chance to break through that wall she had been keeping between them. And this time, a smile wouldn't do it, or even a touch. It had to be words straight from his heart. *Christ.* He was starting to think like a girl.

Taking a deep breath, he let it out, then tried to put voice to all the confused emotions churning inside him.

"But what I do know, Daisy, is that I want to wake up each morning with you beside me. I want to be able to touch you every day, hear you sing and laugh, look into your eyes when I make love to you. I never wanted that before. Not with Elena. Not with anyone. Is that love?" He spread his clumsy hands in a gesture of confusion. "I don't know."

Surprised to see his hands were shaking, he dropped them back to his sides. "When I thought I'd lost you and Kate" — he hesitated, his throat going tight, his mind struggling to put those terrifying moments into words — "it was like all the breath and color and light went out of me. I felt . . . empty. Like there was nothing left — no reason to go on. And I knew without any doubt that you and Kate and I belong together. Without each other, we're like lost pieces of a puzzle that will never make sense on their own. Whether it's here or in San Francisco or somewhere else, it doesn't matter. You belong with me, Daisy. And I belong with you. I'm just trying to show that's how I feel."

"By taking me to bed."

473

He nodded, hope sparking. "That's the best way I know how."

She continued to study him.

"I'll even say the words, if you want," he added lamely.

"Will you? How generous." A smile played at her lips. "Say them."

"Now?"

She raised her brows.

"Yeah. Okay." For a moment that smothered feeling returned. He felt like he was back on the bluff, with the open sky above him and the ranch spread below, and all he had to do was lift his arms wide and take a step and he'd be flying.

But what if she didn't love him back? What if saying the words and opening up his heart wasn't enough and she still left?

He would fall like a stone.

But for a few moments, at least, he would know how it felt to fly.

He cleared his throat, took a deep breath, and stepped off solid ground into thin air. "I love you, Daisy."

Oddly, it wasn't as difficult to say as he'd thought, although it did sound peculiar hearing those words spoken aloud in his own voice.

"I love you," he said again.

Her gaze didn't waver, but he thought he saw a look of sad resignation come into her eyes. It bothered him because he didn't know what he had done to put it there.

"Okay," she finally said.

Okay? What the hell did that mean? "Okay what? That I love you?"

"Sure." Pushing past him, she walked across the room and opened the door. In the doorway she stopped and turned back. There was challenge in her smile and devilment in her eyes. "You do know how to do this sober, don't you?"

He did. And excellently so, even if he said so himself. It was something a man never forgot, since it was the first thing he thought about when he woke up and the last thing he thought about before he went to sleep . . . and most of the time in between. He looked forward to showing her how much better he was at it sober.

"How do you expect to do this with that bad leg?" she asked a moment later when he slid under the covers beside her.

"Oh, I'll manage. Besides, that's not the leg I plan on using."

"Don't be crass." But he heard the laughter under the reprimand. Then the way her breathing changed when he loosened the tiny bows holding her gown closed.

"Ah, there you are, my beauties," he murmured, pushing the flannel aside so he could kiss one soft, warm mound, then the other. "I've missed you."

"Are you talking to my breasts?"

He looked up with a sheepish grin. "I know I'm not supposed to notice them, but they're so round and jiggly and —"

"Who said you couldn't notice them?"

"My brothers." Bending his head, he returned to his task. "They said women didn't like it when — Ow!" he muttered when she bolted upright so unexpectedly her shoulder cracked his nose.

"You discussed my breasts with your brothers?"

He blinked at her through watery eyes. "Not *discussed* . . . exactly."

"Then what *exactly* did you say to them?"

Lifting his fingers to his nose, he felt for blood and was surprised to find none. "Remember the night you came to the ranch and I accidentally looked at your . . . em, chest, and you hit me for it?"

"I hit you," she reminded him in an unfriendly tone, "because you didn't remember who I was until you looked at my . . . *em* . . . chest."

"But I did remember you," he defended.

"And accidentally? How do you accidentally look at a woman's breasts?"

It happened all the time, but he didn't mention that. "My brothers said I shouldn't ogle." Like that would stop him.

"They were right."

He didn't debate that either.

She flopped back with a labored sigh. "I

just wish when God was passing out parts, He'd given the breasts to men. The world would be a lot simpler."

But not as much fun. "If he had," he quipped in an effort to put things back on a friendly track, "nothing would ever get done. We'd still be sitting under the ole apple tree fiddling with them and having a grand time." He grinned.

She scowled back.

"That was a joke, of course," he lied. "Now where were we? Oh, yeah. I was about to do this." And before she could start another argument, he ducked down under the covers and commenced doing what he did best. And with grand results, judging by Daisy's reaction. She was panting like a racehorse when he finally came up for air. "You're right. This may be too much for my leg."

"W-What?" She lifted her head off the pillows to stare dazedly at him. "Really? You're sure?" Was that disappointment in her voice?

"Here's an idea," he said as if suddenly inspired. "If you were on top, it probably wouldn't bother me as much." He pulled her closer.

She rolled away. "I wouldn't want to hurt you."

"I'll be fine. Not to worry."

"But, still, I —"

"Damnit woman," he cut in, trying to sound severe but ruining it by laughing. "Will you just shut up and climb on."

She did, and it was a wonderment.

With a sigh, Daisy smiled up at the ceiling as the first glow of dawn tinted the exposed beams a soft pastel pink. What a night. What a lovely, astounding, exhausting night.

She should have regrets, but she didn't. When she and Jack parted this time, it would not be in anger or panic or drunken confusion. And the memories they would carry away with them would not be shameful or despairing. She had made the choice to bed the man she loved, and she was glad she had. Oddly, sharing these beautiful hours together seemed to make the prospect of leaving him a little easier. Like closing the back cover on a good book, or finishing a satisfying meal, or hearing the last notes of an exquisite aria. Tonight was a perfect memory and it would linger in that perfection forever.

Oh God. Who was she trying to fool? It would kill her to leave.

But it was over. Finished. The night was done.

Turning to the window, Daisy saw the light was growing stronger. Beyond those pink-tinted panes, life was awakening to the day. But inside the house, all was quiet except for the soft snores of the man sprawled on the bed beside her.

She breathed deep, filling her mind with

the scents and sounds and memories of their lovemaking. Memories sent heat into her face. The man had played her like a lute, orchestrating her every response until she arched beneath him, gasping and shivery with delight. He could make music with those hands.

She glanced over at him.

He had made a shambles of the covers; Jack, in sleep, was as full of life and energy and vitality as he was when awake. But he should be tired now, since he hadn't slept that much during the night. He wouldn't notice if she left.

Quietly pushing back the covers, she rose and retrieved her gown from the floor. As she was tying the bows down the front, restless movement on the bed told her Jack was awake. Turning, she found him smiling sleepily at her.

"Don't go," he said in a gravelly morning voice. "It's early yet."

Reaching up, she pushed loose hair out of her face, aware of the way the action drew his attention to her breasts. The breasts that had once embarrassed her and she had tried to hide. The breasts that now tingled under his gaze, as if he were actually touching her and not just looking. Amazing how he did that.

"You and Elena will be leaving in a couple of hours," she reminded him. "It'll be a long day. You should rest while you can."

"I don't want to rest. Come here."

Jack had always been especially amorous in the morning. In the past, she had thought it was because by morning he had finally sobered up enough to appreciate what he was doing. But seeing that familiar look in his eyes now, she realized it was more of a personal preference. Not that she minded. But today was going to be one of the most difficult of her life, and every moment she spent in Jack's arms would only make it worse.

Thank God he was departing first. She didn't think she would have had the strength to be the one to leave him.

"Go back to sleep," she said, bending down to give him a kiss, then laughing and moving out of reach as he made a grab for her breasts. "I'll see you later."

"Damn right," he muttered, his eyes drifting closed.

Daisy didn't bathe right away, afraid the knocking of the pipes would awaken the house. Instead, she forced herself to write the letter she had left unfinished the night before when she had thought she might simply tell Jack everything.

She was glad she hadn't. Although a letter was more cowardly, it was easier, and Daisy hadn't the conviction or will to say this to his face.

She told him everything, even how broken she had been when he'd left her before. She wrote that no matter how much he might want to stay with them, she feared his drive to keep moving would eventually pull him away. She understood that and didn't blame him for it. She explained about the dream she had cherished for most of her life, and how because of Madame Scarlatti and the money Jack had so generously given her, she now had a chance to make it come true. She added that if he still wanted them after her training was complete in two years, he could contact her through Mr. Peter Markham of the Elysium Theater. And finally, she wrote that she cared for him with all her heart, and would always treasure their time together and think fondly of him. She closed with the promise that even if they never saw him again, she would make certain Kate remembered him as the father who loved her so much he almost gave his life to keep her safe.

Then with trembling hands, she folded the letter away, curled into a ball, and wept until Kate awoke and called for her.

TWENTY-FOUR

"I can't believe she's gone forever," Jessica said.

"I know." Brady thought he'd prepared himself, but the finality of seeing Jack and Elena's buggy pass under the high arched gate was like a blow to his chest.

Was it really forever?

He couldn't fathom it. Elena had been a part of his life for so long he couldn't imagine never seeing her again. But if that's what she wanted . . .

Beside him, Jessica gave a wobbly sigh. "First the horses, now Elena, and soon Daisy and Kate. I feel as if my family is breaking apart."

Her grip on his hand was so tight Brady's fingers tingled. "It's not." Leaning down, he pressed his lips against her temple, drawing in the flowery scent that was his wife's alone. It calmed him. Just having her within reach restored his balance. Even as he straightened to watch the buggy roll over the last rise and out of sight, some of the emptiness of Elena's leaving was already fading.

"Families have to spread to grow," he told her. "We can't keep everything the same forever."

"I wish we could."

"I know."

His wife was a strong, forceful woman. In many ways, Brady figured she was stronger than him. But because her father had left when she was young, and her brother had abandoned her and her little sister and their dying mother for the gold fields of the American West, she still battled feelings of abandonment, which made her as tenacious about the family as he was about the ranch. So he understood the emotion behind her tears, and knew that for now he had to be the strong one.

"If I ever lost you —"

"You won't," he cut in. "I'll never leave you. Ever."

She turned her face into his arm. He could feel the dampness of her tears soak into his sleeve. A lesser man might have gotten weepy himself.

Instead, he waited stoically while she shed her tears, having learned over the few years of their marriage that there was nothing he could say or do to stop them. Like tick fever and blizzards, they had to run their course, and all he could do was offer what comfort he could and wait for them to pass. And sometimes, if he comforted her just right, one kind of soothing might lead to an even better kind, and he would find himself the lucky recipient of her lusty gratitude.

He wondered if this might be one of those times. He could use some soothing too.

"I love you so much." Her voice was muffled against his arm. The hand in his felt small and fragile.

"I know."

He felt her waiting, but didn't speak. When she lifted her head and looked up at him, he was hard-pressed not to smile. She was so predictable.

"And you love me too," she prodded.

"I know."

"Then say it."

Instead, he took her inside and showed her.

By the time they cleared the gate, Elena had stopped crying, for which Jack was heartily grateful. It wasn't that her leaving didn't bother him. But his feelings for the woman riding beside him had changed drastically over the last few weeks. He still cared about her. Loved her, even. Just not in the way he had before. And it saddened him that he would probably never see her again. But that terrible sense of loss that had hounded him for the last three years had softened into acceptance.

He would miss her.

And worry about her.

But he was ready to let her go.

They rode for an hour without speaking. But it wasn't the awkward silence that had persisted between them ever since he had come back. Now that the pressure was off, he was more comfortable with her, and more attuned to her feelings rather than worrying so much about his own. And he could see she was hurting.

As they rattled along, she seemed to be taking it all in like she was seeing RosaRoja for the first time. Or the last. He sensed she was saying her good-byes to this place where she had lived for most of her life. Jack understood the difficulty of that. How could you not love this wild and beautiful land? And even though both of them were reaching for something beyond this emerald valley, it was still hard to leave it behind. At least Jack could always come back. Elena never would, and there was sadness in that.

But he didn't want to feel sad today. He was still flying high on memories of the most amazing night he'd ever spent. Just thinking about it sent blood pumping through his veins.

"I worry about you and Daisy," Elena said after a while.

"Don't." Jack shot her a grin. "She's coming around."

"Is that why I heard her crying early this morning?"

Jack's smile faded. *Crying?* Frowning past the horse's ears, he wondered what Daisy would have to cry about. He'd said the words, hadn't he? And he'd backed them up with some pretty astounding bedsport, even if he did say so himself. What could she possibly have to cry about?

Then he remembered the poster Brady had given him just before they'd left, and a feeling of dread dampened his cheery mood.

He and his brothers had been standing by the buggy waiting for the women to say their good-byes to Elena when Brady had pulled a crumpled piece of paper from his pocket. "Jessica gave me this an hour ago. Said Ashford had been waving it around when he was out here last week. I'm not sure what to do about it, but figure while you're in town you can stop by Foley's office."

"Foley?"

"Rikker passed on a year or so ago. Foley — you remember him — used to be the Deputy US Marshal — anyway, he wanted to stay closer to his wife and kids, so after Rikker died, he took over as sheriff in Val Rosa. Apparently this came off the board outside his office." He handed the paper to Jack.

Jack read it, then looked at his brother in shock. "Murder? They think Daisy is a murderer?"

"Keep your voice down," Brady warned. "If Daisy sees you're upset, she'll get upset. Besides, they just want to talk to her."

Hank craned his neck to read over Jack's shoulder. "That thing's over a month old," he said, pointing to the date printed in the lower right-hand corner. "It might already be straightened out by now."

"Probably," Brady agreed. "But you ought to check with Sheriff Foley just to be sure."

"Sure of what?" Jack challenged, his mind still reeling. "You can't think Daisy had something to do with this."

"Hell no. But you ought to check and make sure she's in the clear, that's all I'm saying. And if she's not, find out what we have to do to take care of it."

Thinking back on it now as they climbed out of the valley and turned onto the stage road linking Val Rosa to points east, Jack wondered if that was what Daisy had been crying about. But if she was that worried about the poster, why hadn't she discussed it with him? Surely she wasn't afraid he would believe such nonsense.

But when he remembered that odd, stricken look on her face when he'd climbed into the buggy beside Elena, an uneasy feeling crawled along his spine. He'd thought she'd just been caught up in the emotional good-byes to Elena. But maybe it was more than that. Maybe this murder was what was behind her

487

insistence on leaving.

Fear trickled into his mind. Was she thinking to go back on her own to clear her name? And what if they didn't believe her? What if they did more than just talk to her? What if they put her in jail and Kate —

The trickle became a flood. What would happen to Kate?

Jack slapped the reins on the horse's rump, pushing him into a trot. He needed to get this over with so he could get back to Daisy before she did something foolish. He had to make her understand that there was nothing she couldn't tell him, or discuss with him, or ask him. They were connected now, and not just because of sex or Kate or the past. They had found their way back to each other and there was nothing that could separate them now.

Elena's hand on his arm pulled him back from his dark thoughts. "Do you mind going slower, Jack?" she asked, a strained look on her face. "The bouncing hurts my hip."

Instantly regretful, he pulled the horse back to a running walk. "Sorry," he said with an apologetic smile.

"Are your thoughts so troubling?"

He shrugged, unwilling to burden her with his worries. "It's a sad day with you leaving, and all," he hedged.

"But there were so many days that were not. Let us think of those instead."

So they spent the next two hours reminiscing about the past and some of the scrapes he and his brothers had gotten into as kids, like the time Hank had built a flying apparatus that almost got the three of them killed, or how Elena's first batch of chili had left them all gut-sick and blistered in unmentionable places. They didn't talk about Sam or Sancho, or the pain both their families had inflicted on each other. Even now, some things were too painful to put into words.

Talking helped pass the time. But the worry festered in the back of Jack's mind.

A few miles shy of Val Rosa, they came to the box canyon where Langley and a half-dozen hands were holding the horses until the Army sale was finalized. Jack still couldn't believe Brady was selling off his whole herd. He had offered money from his San Francisco account, but being the prideful, hardheaded sonofabitch his brother was, Brady wouldn't take it. Apparently he had as low an opinion of Jack's money as he did of Jack's help. Some things never changed.

The horses had overnighted well, and were contentedly grazing on fresh grass bordering a small creek. The three studs were in separate rope enclosures deeper in the canyon well away from the mares and foals, and their constant whinnying echoed along the canyon walls. After exchanging words with the men, Jack told Langley he'd send the Army fellow out that afternoon, then he and Elena went on into town.

The Army buyer was sitting on a bench outside the hotel, waiting for them. Major Billingsly. He seemed a straightforward, honest fellow with a decisive handshake and the stiff bearing and weathered countenance of a career soldier. His questions indicated he also knew his horseflesh, and when he said he wanted to see the herd before he made his bid, Jack gladly gave him directions to the canyon where the horses were being held. With assurances that they would talk later at the bank, Billingsly left and Jack escorted Elena next door to the Overland office to get her voucher.

They had an hour to spare before the westbound came through.

It was a long hour. They spent most of it over a quiet meal in the hotel dining room — with all the good-byes behind them, there wasn't much left to say — and soon the awkwardness Jack had felt in the hilltop cemetery returned full force. He found himself checking the front window more often as the minutes passed, and was relieved when he finally spotted the telltale cloud of dust that signaled the stage had arrived.

They were still too early and had to wait on the boardwalk while the horses were changed for fresh teams. But when the passengers finally started loading, Jack felt a rush of panic, as if all those unspoken words had clogged up in his throat, and this would be his last chance ever to get them out.

Which it was.

Elena started toward the coach. On impulse, he reached out and grabbed her hand. "Elena," he began, then couldn't think of what else he wanted to say.

For a moment they stared at each other, then she smiled, tears glistening in her dark eyes. *"Yo comprendo, hermano.* I love you too. *Para siempre."*

When she turned away, he said, "Wait," and reached into his pocket for the silver cross she had given to him, and he had given to Kate, and Brady had given back after they had pulled him out of the canyon.

"Take this," he said, thrusting it into her hand. "It protected me at sea, and it protected Kate and Daisy on the bridge. Hopefully it'll protect you in Kalawao." Leaning down, he put his cheek against hers. "When you look at it," he whispered into her ear, "remember how much you mean to me. Always."

Then she was gone.

Jack stood alone on the boardwalk as the dust of her leaving settled around him, then he whirled and headed to the nearest cantina for a drink. He felt like a part of his life had ended and the finality of that left him a bit shaken. Normally, neither the past nor the future greatly concerned him. But seeing

Elena roll out of his life forever made him re-alize that changes happened all the time, whether he marked them or not, and even the richest life was no more than a long series of hellos and good-byes.

He was on his second drink when Langley came in. "The major's working out his bid." As he spoke, Langley motioned to the bar-keep to bring another glass. "Says he'll meet you at the bank in an hour."

Jack curbed his impatience. Leaning his elbows on the counter, he shifted his weight to ease the ache in his leg, which was hurting like a sonofabitch from sitting in a bouncing buggy all morning. He was tired of waiting and wanted to get back to Daisy. Then he remembered the poster in his pocket.

Pushing away from the bar, he told Langley to find out where Blake was, then come to the bank in half an hour. "If you need me before then, I'll be at the sheriff's office," he added as he limped toward the door.

"Expecting trouble?" Langley called after him.

"I hope so." He was in the mood to hit someone. The banker, Blake, Ashford — he didn't care which. They all deserved it.

He found Sheriff Foley sitting outside his office with his chair propped back against the wall, studying the inside of his eyelids. "Howdy, Sheriff," he said, giving the chair a nudge with his foot.

Foley awoke instantly but without noticeable concern. Calmly pushing back his hat, he glared up at Jack. "What do you want?"

"Two things. First, I'd like to find out what you know about this." Fishing the worn poster from his pocket, Jack passed it over.

With a labored sigh, the sheriff let the front legs of his chair thud back to the boardwalk. He took the paper, studied it for a moment, then shot Jack a hard look. "Where'd you get this?"

"From my brother. He said it sort of showed up with a weasel."

The sheriff's eyes narrowed. "Then he must have taken it off my board here, since that's where it was last."

Jack shrugged. "You know weasels."

Foley studied the paper again, then pointed to a notation on the bottom. "This is dated over a month ago."

"Yes, it is."

Foley looked up with a frown. "I guess you want me to wire San Francisco. See if it's valid."

"I do."

"Why?"

"I might have information."

"What kind?"

"The pertinent kind."

"Christ." Folding the paper, the sheriff slipped it into his vest pocket. "And the second reason you came bothering me?"

"I'd like to post my bail."

Foley blinked. "For what?"

"Beating the stink out of a weasel. It'll happen about an hour from now. I'll let you know for sure once I find him."

"Oh, hell." Foley sighed wearily. "You're a Wilkins."

"I am. And proud of it."

"You're the one who left, aren't you?"

"I am. And proud of that too."

Foley took off his hat, scratched the top of his graying head, then replaced the hat. "Who's the weasel?" he asked in a bored voice.

"Stanley Ashford."

That perked him up. "Ashford. I know him. Works for the El Paso and Pacific Railroad. Pockmarked face, girlish manners. Definitely a weasel."

"That'd be the one."

"You're too late. He's gone." Tipping his chair back against the wall, Foley added, "Bastard cleaned out the EP&P account and left this morning. Pinkerton detectives are already heading out of Chicago, hot on his trail. I'm hoping the Apaches get him first."

Jack's good mood faded. Then he remembered Blake. "How about his cohort, Franklin Blake? He still in town?"

Anger flashed in Foley's eyes. "Bastard's here. Hangs out at the Palace. Wish the Indians would get him too."

Spirits happily restored, Jack grinned. "Then as soon as I pay him the money I owe, I'll be beating the stink out of him."

"Why?"

"He acted harshly toward the woman I'm going to marry." Just picturing Daisy's bruised face after Blake tried to run their buggy through the quarantine made Jack's hands clench. "Elbowed her in the face."

"Sounds like Blake. He purely loves beating on women." Foley smiled as he said it, but it wasn't a pleasant expression. "Just don't kill him. I know how you Wilkins boys are." Tipping his head back, he closed his eyes. "I'll send the wire to San Francisco after my nap."

The major was waiting with his bid when Jack arrived at the bank. After talking horses for a minute, Billingsly made his offer. It seemed reasonable, but Jack countered on principle, then left the major to mull it over while he excused himself and stepped into the bank manager's office.

Harold Lockley wasn't a robust man, so Jack didn't consider using force to get his point across. It would be like slapping around a maiden aunt. And judging by the look of terror on the bookish man's face after Jack introduced himself and plopped down in the chair in front of his desk, Brady had already explained the Wilkins position on selling loans to a third party. Still, Jack felt he should do something, since he'd come all this way and was in town anyway.

He decided to get right to the point. "You shouldn't have sold our paper."

"N-No, sir."

"You won't do it again."

"N-No, sir."

"Ask me why."

"W-Why?"

"Because we won't like it."

"Y-Yes, sir."

Hell, this is no fun at all. Then inspiration struck. Reaching into his pocket, Jack pulled out the shrunken head he had planned to use on Ashford. Idly he passed it from one hand to the other, enjoying the way Lockley's eyes bulged as they tracked it. "Know what this is?" Jack asked pleasantly.

Lockley made a garbled sound.

"Right. A shrunken head. Ask me where I got it."

"W-Where d-did you g-get it?"

"I don't remember. Here." Leaning forward, Jack placed the fist-sized head in the center of Lockley's desk. "As a show of trust, I want you to have it. No, I insist," he added with a wave of his hand when the little banker tried to distance himself by pressing as far back in his chair as he could. "Ask me why."

"W-Why?"

Jack showed his teeth in a wide grin. "Because if I need to, I can always make another." He waited for that to sink in, then ignoring the banker's rapid breathing, got down to business. "How much is in my account?" On the ride in, he'd decided to get Daisy a ring. Something special that would show her just how serious he was. Something so pretty she wouldn't be able to refuse.

"W-Which one?" Lockley asked, his gaze still pinned to the stringy-haired head, which would have been staring back at him if it had eyes and its lids weren't sewn shut.

Jack frowned in confusion. "Which one what?"

"W-Which account. You have t-two."

"I do?"

Finally Lockley glanced up. Some of his color had returned and he seemed pathetically eager to answer Jack's questions as quickly as possible. "You have the account you transferred money into from the bank in San Francisco. And you have the account your brother set up several years ago. Which one?"

"What the hell are you talking about? What account my brother set up?"

A fine sheen of sweat glistened in the fuzz on Lockley's top lip. "The, ah, one from the mine profits." He gave a sickly smile. "He didn't mention it to you?"

"No. He didn't." Confusion gave way to disgust. Did Brady think he was some good-for-nothing spendthrift who had to be put on an allowance?

Something in Jack's expression caused color to fade from Lockley's face again. "Your brother, Brady, set up accounts for each of you as soon as the mines starting producing. His and Hank's accounts have been seriously depleted by capital expenditures like equipment purchases, the cost of the spur line, a locomotive, and such like. But yours has remained untouched. In fact, it's grown quite rapidly over the last couple of years."

Jack was so stunned he just sat there, his mind spinning, his anger building with every heartbeat. "How much is in it?"

The banker didn't know exactly, but offered to go check.

"Take a guess," Jack said through stiff lips.

Lockley did, and Jack felt as if the floor had bucked beneath his feet. It was a substantial amount. At least as much as the horses would bring in. More than they owed Blake. More than enough to cover any debt they'd ever had.

So why hadn't Brady used it to pay off the smelter? And why hadn't he told Jack about it? Did he think Jack wouldn't want to help?

Then realization came, and a sick feeling moved through Jack's gut. Was Brady really so pig-headed he would rather put the ranch at risk than turn to his little brother for help?

Goddamn him.

Jack didn't realize he'd spoken aloud until he saw Lockley's startled expression. It took him a moment to bring his temper under control, then in a voice he barely recognized as his own, he said, "Exactly how much do we owe Blake?"

"Well, em, actually Blake was acting as agent for another gentleman. A Mr. Stanley Ashford."

"So how much do we owe Ashford?"

"Well, em, that's the thing." With a wrinkled kerchief, Lockley mopped his top lip then his damp brow. "Apparently, Ashford stole the money from the railroad account to buy the paper from us. So in effect, you owe the EP&P — the El Paso & Pacific Railroad, that is."

"How much?" Jack asked for the third time.

"W-With interest? I-ah-have to check."

"Do it." Jack realized he was gripping the armrest so tight, his fingers had gone numb. Forcing them to relax, he said as calmly as he could, "Take whatever we owe out of my mine account, and move the rest into the ranch account."

"All of it?"

"All of it. Then close the account my brother set up for me and never open it again. Understand?"

"Y-Yes, sir."

"Then draw up papers marked 'Paid in Full.' "

When Lockley just sat there, blinking and

sweating, Jack leaned forward and said softly, "Now."

The banker shot to his feet. "Y-Yes, sir." A second later, he was out the door.

Jack waited, drawing in deep breaths to calm the cyclone of fury and disbelief and disappointment whirling through his mind.

He was done. This was the final insult. He wouldn't subject himself to his brother's highhanded arrogance any longer. Now that he knew with certainty that Brady held him in such low esteem that he'd rather lose the ranch than accept — or even *ask* — for his help, Jack saw no reason to stay.

But *Jesus,* it hurt to realize his brother held him in such contempt.

He had reached a level of icy calm by the time Lockley returned with the papers and a packet of cash to repay the loan. Jack counted it, made sure the papers were in order, then, moving stiffly, rose from the chair and went back into the lobby, where Billingsly and Langley waited.

"Change of plans," he said tersely. "Major, you can have the colts that are ready this year, and first option on those that will be ready next year. But we're not selling the brood mares or studs, or anything younger than three years."

Langley's mouth fell open.

When Billingsly started to argue, Jack held up a hand. "Forget my counter. I'll take your

500

first offer on the colts and discount it ten percent because they're still green. But it's not negotiable. Think about it, and if the offer is agreeable to you, have Lockley draw up the bills of sale."

He turned to the old cowhand. "Langley, if the major takes the deal, hold the three-year-olds until his men come for them, but send the mares and studs and foals back home as soon as possible."

Then without waiting for a response, he spun on his heel and walked out of the bank.

TWENTY-FIVE

"Think it'll work?" Brady asked, watching over the side rails as Hank slid the sail-wrapped mast into the back of the wagon.

"Probably."

"Seems small."

"It only has to move eight hundred pounds."

"Still."

Mumbling to himself, Hank tossed in the box of tools and extra parts with more vigor than necessary.

Brady could see he was still mad. They'd had words earlier, but Brady was convinced it was their brotherly duty to help Jack any way they could. "Maybe you should test it. You know, just to be sure."

Hank threw in the ax and his saddlebags, then turned to glare at him. "Have at it then."

"It's your invention." Seeing the set of Hank's jaw, he quickly added, "What's the ax for?"

"You, if you don't get away from me." Back-

502

ing that up with a surly look, Hank resumed loading items into the wagon bed — a water cask, a basket of food, extra slickers and jackets, his repeater, a pouch of toys, a fluffy blanket with bunnies sewn on it, Daisy's valise. "Or in case they need to stop quick," he added as a mumbled afterthought.

Alarmed, Brady reared back from the rails. "I thought the handcar had a brake."

"It does. Probably."

"Probably?"

Hank lifted his head and looked at him.

Brady recognized the warning and changed the subject. "Our wives are planning something."

Hank went back to loading.

"Jessica asked when Jack would be back from Val Rosa, then she asked how soon he would leave here for Redemption. When I told her, she kissed me, put on a big smile, and asked where my good boots were. Sounds suspicious, don't you think?"

"I think you're an idiot. That's what I think."

"Then I saw her whispering to your wife," Brady went on. "Furtive like. And when they saw me seeing them, they shut up. Something's not right."

"Probably you."

"Still."

A commotion drew Brady's attention, and he turned to see his wife step out of the house. Behind her came Daisy, leading Kate by the hand, followed by Molly. They clustered on the porch, talking and hugging and looking overwrought. Daisy looked especially weepy, but after careful study, Brady could see Molly was almost smiling. Furtively.

Women. They loved their secrets.

As the ladies started down the steps, the door banged open again and kids stampeded across the porch, trailed by the overworked Ortegas, each with a wiggling twin on her hip. Charlie held back a little, being too mature now for emotional displays, and Abigail just tagged along for the hell of it. But Ben and Penny seemed genuinely concerned that their cousin was leaving.

"Kate!" Penny shouted, waving a rag doll she must have made herself, judging by the off-kilter eyes and mismatched arms. "You forgot Prissy!"

While the children gathered around Kate at the foot of the steps, all talking at once and giving pats and shoving toys in her face, Brady watched Jessica and Molly pretend to be sad about Daisy's departure.

It was a poor performance. In truth, he suspected they were both happy as larks with his brilliant plan to force Jack and Daisy together in Redemption. He hadn't wanted to admit his scheme to Jessica, but she'd wormed it out of him, and seemed to think it was a fine idea. Hank was the only one who seemed disturbed by it — insisting Brady was meddling — but then if Hank had his way, there wouldn't ever be a need for secrets or any kind of interaction, since they would never speak at all.

Folding his arms along the top wagon rail, Brady studied the women who had brought such change to their lives. Beautiful, intelligent women, with fire in their eyes and courage in their hearts.

"Look at Daisy." He kept his voice low so it wouldn't carry to the ladies. "She's suffering. You know what that means."

Hank dug through the parts box.

"It means she cares about him. Which means we're doing the right thing."

"Doesn't matter. It's none of our business."

Brady frowned, a bit put out by Hank's ability to remain aloof in the face of such exciting doings. "Don't you have any brotherly concern? You know she's right for Jack."

"You're starting to sound like an old lady matchmaker. And if it's so right, then why all the secrets and lies?"

"So you think we should just let her leave. Make no effort to keep them from making a mistake that could ruin their lives." Brady threw up a hand in aggravation. "Hell, you'd probably prefer it if we all rode off in different directions and never saw each other again."

Hank looked up and smiled.

Aggravated that his brother's righteous attitude was starting to make him feel guilty, Brady allowed meanness to take ahold of him. Striking back with the only weapon he could find, he said, "Besides, you ought to be glad we're sending them off. Jack said when he was too drugged to fight her off, Molly had her hands all over him."

Hank picked up a rusty bolt, studied it, then dropped it back into the box. "She's a nurse."

"So she is. And a fine one, at that. I guess when you were hurt after the derailment, she had her hands all over you too." Looking over his folded arms, he smirked at his brother. "Nothing like a woman's soft touch to soothe a man's troubles, don't you think?"

Finally Hank looked up, and the look in his eyes almost made Brady back up a step. "I think you better shut the hell up."

Brady sighed, no longer enjoying himself. Much as he wanted to vent his concern over Jack and his frustration over losing the horses, he knew picking a fight with Hank would bring more pain than release. "You want me to drive Daisy and Kate to Redemption?" he offered in an effort to smooth things over.

Hank snorted. "And have you hook up the sail and make sure everything is running right?"

"I guess not." With another sigh, Brady

dropped his chin onto his folded arms. He stared into distant clouds as wispy as horses' tails rising above the mountaintops where the last patches of snow glistened in the late morning sun. Already the balsam blossoms on the hillsides had faded and white-faced daisies were pushing up through the rich, moist earth beneath the aspens. Summer was coming. Same as it did every year. But even though it all seemed business as usual, Brady sensed change lingering just past the horizon and that made him uneasy.

"We should start gathering the cattle soon," he said.

Hank walked to the front of the wagon to check the harness.

Brady turned to watch him, one arm resting on the top rail. "Looks to be a good crop of calves." At least with roundup they'd be so busy he wouldn't have time to fret over the horses. Then the dry season would be on them, and they'd have to patrol the water holes and keep an eye out for wildfires and scarlet locoweed and blackleg and tick fever. Then fall would come and it would be time to bring the cattle down from the mountains and send the culls to market and gather the fattest steers for the reservation bid. And by the time that was done, the first snow would cover the sun-browned hills with a blanket of white and everything would settle in for the winter and the cycle would start all over again.

Except Elena would be gone to her lepers.

And Jack and Daisy would be off God-knows-where.

And no leggy foals would be crowding the paddocks.

Feeling suddenly as if things were slipping from his grasp, Brady glanced at his brother, regretting some of the things he'd said earlier. He didn't want to lose Hank too. Besides, Hank couldn't help being a stiff-necked sonofabitch. He was the family conscience, after all. "Jack didn't say he actually *enjoyed* having her put her hands on him," he admitted by way of apology. "He just said it was disconcerting, her being your wife, and all."

"Leave it, Brady."

"I'm just saying."

"Well, don't."

"Okay."

Daisy just wanted to get on with it.

Having made her decision to leave, she was ready to go. Parting from this family was difficult enough without adding to the pain with prolonged good-byes. Besides, with every moment's delay, the urge to forget about Rome and stay at RosaRoja grew stronger.

"You'll let us know when you reach New Orleans," Jessica said, clutching Daisy's hand in both of hers.

"I will."

"You have enough money?" ever-practical Molly asked.

Daisy nodded. "Jack was most generous." Just saying his name aloud sent tears clogging her throat.

"Be sure not to wave it about," Jessica warned. "Put it in a safe place. I always used my corset. Back when I wore one." Her grip on Daisy's hand tightened. "Oh, just look at me. I'm getting maudlin and I promised myself I wouldn't in front of the children." She smiled, looking anything but maudlin.

"Well, Daisy," Brady said, coming up behind her. "Ready to go?"

No. I'll never be ready.

Instead, she forced her trembling lips into a smile and nodded. "All ready." Taking Kate's hand, she walked with Brady across the yard. But when they reached the wagon, she paused and put a staying hand on his arm. "Brady, I appreciate all you've done. For helping me. For . . ." Her voice faltered.

He waved her thanks away, an uncomfortable expression on his rugged face. He might even have been blushing. "You and Kate are welcome anytime," he said gruffly. "With or without Jack."

Without Jack. Alone. Lonely.

Such was the dismal future that loomed ahead.

How will I bear it?

Before her courage failed her, she pulled the letter she had agonized over from her pocket. "Give this to Jack," she said, handing it to Brady. "It explains everything. I hope he'll understand and forgive me."

"He will. I'll make him." Brady slipped it into his pocket, then in what seemed an afterthought, he bent down and kissed her cheek. "You take care now," he muttered, and stepped back.

Then suddenly the good-byes were all said, and she was sitting with Kate in the wagon, and all the faces she had come to love were staring up at her. She wished she were eloquent, and had something profound and moving and elegant to say. But words deserted her. And as their faces blurred behind a sheen of tears, all she could do was wave a shaking hand as the wagon rolled away.

Jack paused inside the swinging doors at the Palace Cantina and looked around. He'd never met Franklin Blake, but none of the men sitting at the tables or the desert rats leaning on the bar matched the description Brady had given him. He approached the bar, which was manned by an unfamiliar fellow, a crooked old man missing his right eye and most of an ear.

"Where's Blake?" Jack asked him.

"Who wants to know?" the barkeep lisped, apparently missing most of his teeth too.

"Me." Jack smiled to show friendly intent, although he was still so mad it may have come across more like a snarl.

"He's upstairs," a woman said.

Jack turned to see a whore sitting at a table in a shadowed corner. He knew she was a whore because he recognized her. Sort of. Her face was so swollen and bruised it was hard to be sure. "Millie?"

The woman studied him through dark-shadowed, puffy eyes. "I hope you've come to kill the bastard."

"He do that to you?"

"You shut your mouth, girl," the barkeep warned. "I won't have you spreading tales about a paying customer."

Ignoring him, Jack nodded toward the doors lining the open second-story hallway that overlooked the bar area. "Is he up there, Millie?"

"I don't want no trouble," the barkeep cut in, and Jack turned to see he had a length of cordwood in his hands and a challenging look in his one eye.

"Then quit bothering me, old man. Which room, Millie?"

Before she could answer, two men came in. They wore suits and round bowler hats and hardly any dust on their shiny city shoes. Behind them came Sheriff Foley. "Blake still alive?" the sheriff asked at large, although Jack had a feeling the question was directed more at him than anyone else.

"What if he is?" the barkeep bristled.

Foley sighed wearily. "Just get him, Calvin. I don't have time for your foolishness."

When the muttering barkeep stumped off — seemed he was missing part of a foot too — Foley motioned the other two fellows on toward an empty table, then veered to where Jack stood at the bar.

"Heard back from San Francisco," he said without preamble. "Drunk by the name of Edna Tidwell did it, then fell down the stairs and broke her neck. Case closed. Talked to Blake yet?"

Relieved to be able to put his worries over the poster to rest, Jack shook his head. "No, but I'm hoping to before you arrest him."

"Arrest him for what?"

Jack sent a meaningful glance over the sheriff's shoulder. "For beating on whores, that's what."

Foley turned and studied the battered woman watching them from the corner. "Blake do that, Millie?" he called out.

"Do what, Sheriff? I just fell down the stairs, is all."

"Damnit, Millie. How can I help you if you won't talk to me?"

The whore laughed bitterly, then grimaced and pressed her fingers to a barely healed split on her lip. "Like you helped Rosella? No thanks, Sheriff."

With a look of disgust, Foley turned back to Jack. "They're afraid of him. They know I can only hold the bastard so long, and when he gets out, he'll come for them. So they just take it."

"What happened to Rosella?" Jack asked.

Foley shrugged. "Dead or gone. No one's seen her for a month."

Movement drew Jack's gaze to the cracked mirror behind the bar. In the reflection he saw a middle-aged man in a tailored suit follow the limping barkeep down the staircase. He didn't appear to be armed. Jack smiled in anticipation.

Foley noticed and gave another of his big sighs. The man was a helluva sigher. "It wouldn't be prudent to kill him in front of witnesses. You know that."

"I have no intention of killing him, Sheriff." With his size, Blake might have been a physical presence at one time, but easy living had put a belly on him and now his swagger was more show than substance. Jack was a bit disappointed.

"Then what're you going to do?"

Turning his head toward the sheriff, he shrugged. "Just talk. Share a drink. Maybe arm wrestle a little."

"Before you get started, you ought to speak to those fellows over there." Foley nodded to the two city slickers. "They're auditors for the EP&P Railroad, and are interested in talking to Blake about the missing money."

"It's not missing. I got it right here." Jack patted his coat pocket. "And I'll be glad to give it to them soon as I finish with Blake."

"Finish what?" Franklin Blake asked, coming up behind them.

Jack turned with a friendly smile. "Our drinks." He motioned to the barkeep. "A bottle of your best," he said. "Three glasses. And make sure the bottle's really thick."

Blake blinked at him, clearly surprised by the offer of a drink. "Do I know you?" he asked with a frown.

"I'm the man who's going to save your life."

Surprise gave way to a smirk. "That right?" Blake had small eyes, set deep in the soft, puffy face of a heavy drinker. They were hooded and cold like the eyes of a sunning lizard. "And how do you plan to do that?"

"By offering you a choice."

The barkeep plunked three glasses down on the counter. He started to uncork the bottle, but Jack raised a hand. "I'll do it," he said, taking the bottle from the old man's grip. He smiled at Blake. "You favor your right hand or left?"

"Right," Blake answered with a confused look. "Why?"

"I'll show you. Trick I learned in Australia." Jack nodded toward the bar top. "Put it out there. Palm down would be best."

Blake hesitated then did as instructed.

In a motion so sudden the other man had no time to react, Jack brought the thick heel of the bottle down on the back of Blake's hand.

Bones snapped. Blake shrieked. The barkeep whooped. As bar rats scattered in a headlong rush for the door, Blake howled and lurched back, clutching his arm to his chest. "You bastard! You sonofabitch!"

Foley took the bottle from Jack's hand, uncorked it, and poured two drinks. After shoving one toward Jack, he downed his own, then smacked his lips.

Jack did likewise, then unperturbed by the vile curses coming from the injured man, set his glass back on the bar and calmly looked around.

The men at the tables sat without moving, eyes round in their slack faces. Jack anticipated no trouble from them. The barkeep's grin told him there would be no trouble there either. And the city slickers wouldn't have dared. Setting his empty glass down on the counter, Jack motioned to the furious man reeling and cursing behind him. "Come back here, Blake. We're not finished."

More curses. And of a variety and ingenuity that would have impressed even the most hardened sailor. "You see what he did, Sheriff?" Blake sputtered, cradling his smashed hand.

"See what?" Foley asked.

515

"Damn you, he broke my hand! You better do something!"

"You're probably right," Foley said and poured himself another shot.

"Aw, quit whining, Blake," Jack said with weary patience. "Let's get this done so I can get home before dark."

"You're crazy, you sonofabitch! Who the hell are you?"

Jack smiled pleasantly. "I'm Millie's friend."

"Who?" Blake looked confused, then caught sight of the woman grinning at them from the corner. "You bitch!"

Jack lashed out, catching Blake on the side of his head with enough force to send him crashing into the bar. "I don't have time for this." Turning to face the other men in the room, Jack said loudly, "Anybody willing to help me out here?"

No one moved.

Jack pulled a handful of coins from his pocket and slapped them onto the bar. "There's at least ten dollars here and most of a bottle of fine rye whiskey. All you have to do to earn it is hold him still."

Immediately chairs scraped across the wooden floor.

"Sheriff, do something!" Blake cried, scrambling for the door as men descended.

Foley poured another drink.

With so many helpers, they had Blake corralled and pinned to the bar in no time. Once he quit struggling, Jack leaned down and looked directly into the frightened man's lizard eyes. "Remember the woman and little kid you took out to the Wilkins place a while back?"

Blake gaped up at him, his breath coming in short, shallow gasps.

"That was my woman," Jack said. "And my daughter you tried to harm."

"I didn't do any —"

Blake's words ended in a high-pitched shriek as Jack brought the bottle down on the back of his left hand.

After the wailing stopped, Jack waved the helpers away. Putting his hand on Blake's neck to hold him still, he bent to whisper in his ear. "Now here's where I give you advice that'll save your life, so pay attention." He straightened and waited until Blake stopped whimpering, then said with careful enunciation, "Don't hit women. This time it was only your hands. Next time it'll be your balls. You understand?"

Blake made a choking noise.

"Good." Jack shoved him away. "Now leave."

Blake reeled for the double doors. After they swung closed behind him, Foley pushed away from the bar. "Have fun?" he asked Jack.

"Not particularly." Jack could hold his own in a fight — except against Hank — but with his size, and the training he'd received at his brother's hands and in various ports here and there, it wasn't that much fun anymore. Too easy.

Foley belched. "Well, I did. Now I gotta go hide from my wife 'til I sober up." And with a backward wave, he made his way unsteadily toward the door.

"Helluva show," the barkeep said as he cleared away Foley's glass.

Jack noticed he was missing two fingers on his right hand. "Jesus, man. What got ahold of you? Apaches?"

"Cougar." The old man showed pink gums in a big grin. "Got him back, though."

And in the nick of time, Jack thought, afraid to ask what other parts the poor fellow might have lost. Tossing enough coins on the bar to settle his bill, he nodded his thanks to the barkeep and walked to the table where the city slickers sat watching him with worry on their faces.

"I understand Wilkins Cattle and Mining owes your employee, Stanley Ashford, some money," Jack said, after he'd introduced himself. "But I figure since he stole the money he loaned us from you in the first place, it's really the EP&P we owe." Pulling the packet of cash from his pocket, he dropped it onto the table. "This ought to cover it."

They blinked at the packet, their eyes as bright and round as shiny new coins.

"I don't care how you handle it with Ashford," Jack said. "Hopefully the Apaches have taken care of him by now. But as far as we're concerned, if you'll just sign this" — he unfolded the loan paper and spread it open before them — "then we'll be fair and square and I can be on my way home."

And ten minutes later, he was.

Daisy decided Hank was the perfect escort for the long ride to Redemption, since he didn't try to engage her in conversation, or talk her out of her melancholy, or offer false assurances that she was doing the right thing.

But after the first hour, the silence she had so appreciated at the onset grew tedious in the extreme. Even Kate grew so bored she fell asleep on her blanket in the back.

And as the miles rolled past to the monotonous clop of the horse's hooves, with no conversation to distract her, Daisy found herself reliving over and over those hours with Jack from the night before.

She had taken a huge risk. Even now she could be pregnant. And if she had thought making love to Jack would make this parting easier, she was woefully mistaken.

Yet she had no regrets.

Instead, it was her decision to go on without him that brought her the most distress.

Just once, she thought. If just once she could stand before the flickering lights in a

grand hall that had been created solely to
glorify music — if she could look out at the
expectant faces, hear the lilting strains of the
orchestra all around her as she sent her voice
soaring to the rafters — then she would be
satisfied. She would know the dream could
have been a reality, that she could have done
it.

Just one chance. That's all she wanted.

But was it worth giving up Jack?

It was all so unfair. *Damn it all.*

"You say something?"

Glancing over, she found Hank studying
her with a questioning look in his brown eyes.
He had such kind eyes. Wise and watchful, as
if she could find all her answers hidden within
them if she only knew which questions to ask.
"Have you ever had a dream, Hank? A burning drive to be something else, or reach for
something else?"

He turned back to the road and thought
about for it a while. Then he said almost
reluctantly, as if he were revealing a deep
secret, "I always wanted to be an inventor."

She almost snorted. "But you *are* an inventor," she reminded him.

"No. I'm a tinkerer. There's a difference."

Leave it to Hank to be that precise. "So
why did you settle for tinkering?"

"Molly."

"Ah . . . so you're a romantic," she teased.
"You must love her a lot."

"She'll do." The corner of his mouth quirked as he stared at the road ahead. "But mostly I realized it can be more satisfying to watch other people find their dreams than to get too caught up in my own. And tinkering suits me fine."

Could she do that? Settle for half measures? She'd tried singing in a saloon, and that hadn't been satisfying at all.

Daisy lapsed into thoughtful silence as the horse plodded on, the land around them changing as they climbed higher into the mountains. The trees weren't as tall now, their limbs stubby and slightly bowed from spending long winter months under a burden of snow. The road, which had dwindled to a narrow trail cut into steep slopes, wound through huge boulders, with rocky walls rising on one side and sudden drop-offs on the other. Aware of the precariousness of their path, Daisy didn't look down, praying Kate remained asleep and the horse didn't stumble and Hank stayed calm.

Which, of course, he did. She had never seen Hank anything but calm. She had a feeling she didn't want to, either.

When they finally cleared the ridge and started down the other side, the road improved somewhat, and Daisy was able to breathe easier and enjoy the incredible views of this magnificent country. It was as wild and rugged as any place she had ever seen and she had to admire the men of this family who worked so hard to tame it. But soon they were back in the trees once more and without the wide-open vistas to distract her, she began fretting again.

"Do you think I'm doing the right thing?" she asked after a while.

Hank was leaning forward, his elbows on his bent knees, the reins loose in his big hands. He smiled but didn't respond.

Not that she expected him to. Hank was too crafty to fall for such a loaded question.

"Wise man, not to answer." She gave his strong profile a rueful smile. "No wonder they say you're the smartest brother."

He shot her a dazzling grin that would have made her heart falter if she weren't so in love with his brother. "Not the best looking?"

She laughed. "Sorry. I'd have to give Jack my vote on that."

His smile faded. He faced forward again. "Don't underestimate him, Daisy. There's more to Jack than his face. He's smarter than he lets on."

"I've noticed. So why does he play at being the carefree gadabout?"

Hank thought it over. Like his wife, he carefully considered before he spoke. Daisy had to wonder if they were as deliberate in the bedroom as they were outside of it. Then she thought of the look she had sometimes seen in Hank's eyes when he'd glanced at his wife, and the answering blush on Molly's cheeks, and realized whatever they were doing seemed to suit both of them just fine.

"That was his place in the family," he finally said. "Brady was the responsible one. I was the tinkerer and workhorse. And since Jack was too young to wrest those jobs from either of us, he took what was left. The prankster and the dreamer." Hank shrugged. "I might be able to work numbers and figure how something works, but I can get lost in the details. Brady, he sees the bigger picture, like this ranch and what it takes to keep it going. That takes a different kind of smart. But Jack's a little harder to figure out, since he puts up so many false trails. He may not know yet who he is or what he wants. I think because he's had to play catch-up to his big brothers all his life, sometimes he forgets why he's running and where he's headed. But he's learning."

"What would he be running from?"

"Us. The ranch. It's a heavy burden."

"Yet you stay."

He shrugged. "Brady needs reasons for what he does. Since he took over the ranch, Jack and I have been his reasons for working it and us so hard. But he's got a wife now, and kids, and it won't be long before he realizes they give him all the purpose he'll ever need. Then I can leave."

Daisy tried to imagine the ranch without

Hank and Molly and their stepchildren. Jessica would be devastated.

As they turned a bend, Daisy saw a doe in the road ahead, her belly distended with the fawn she would drop soon. For a moment, the deer froze and stared at them with dark, unblinking eyes, then, having made her decision, she bounded into the trees. Daisy wished she could reach her own decisions as easily. She sighed, so confused her stomach was working itself into knots. "I wish I knew if I was doing the right thing."

"How does it feel to you?"

"Wrong."

"Well, then."

"But it feels wrong to give up on singing too."

"Well, then."

" 'Well, then'?" She gave a broken laugh. "That's all the advice you have?"

"You want advice, go to Brady. He's so overrun with it, if he didn't give some away from time to time, it would probably send him into a choking fit."

Laughing, she reached over to pat his muscled arm. "He just worries about you. He's your big brother."

"I know." Hank sighed. "And it's a curse."

TWENTY-SIX

Jack bounced between fury and disbelief as he headed home in the buggy.

He might not admit it to anyone but himself, but he looked up to his big brothers. Yet even as a kid, he'd felt little more than a tagalong behind them, never smart enough to have anything important to add, or big enough to do his full share of the heavy work, or experienced enough to be given the same amount of responsibility his brothers carried. So after a while he'd quit trying and had gone his own way. But until today, he'd never realized they thought less of him for not fitting the family mold, or considered him so incapable that they wouldn't even come to him if they needed help.

Even Hank. He'd always known he didn't measure up to Brady's idea of what he should be, but he thought Hank had higher regard for him than that.

Apparently not.

Well, now he knew.

And finally knowing exactly how he stood with them would make it a lot easier to move on without feeling guilty about leaving the ranch, or fearing he was letting them down. He could make a clean break. He had Daisy and Kate now. He didn't need any other family but them. It was time to ride away from this place and never look back.

As he approached the canyon where the horses had been held overnight, he saw Major Billingsly and his men bringing out the three-year-olds. Luckily their earlier two-day jaunt into town had made them trail wise, so they were herding up well. The mares and foals and studs had already left for home. Jack suspected Langley would push straight through this time, rather than drag it out two days.

After exchanging words with the major and adding his signature to the bills of sale, Jack turned the buggy toward home. He was anxious to get there before dark so he could have it out with his brothers, change horses, then load up Daisy and Kate and head back to Val Rosa. It would be late by then, but there should be enough moon that they could see their way. He didn't want to stay at the ranch any longer than he had to, and he had a feeling once he said his piece, his brothers wouldn't want him to hang around either.

Even so, and even feeling the way he did now, it would be hard leaving them forever.

They were his brothers. And despite everything, he would miss them.

Langley and the horses had made good time, and Jack passed them about two miles shy of the arched gate. It was still early, not yet six o'clock, so Jack was confident he could do what he had to do and be on his way to Val Rosa with two hours of daylight left.

As he drove the buggy around to the back of the barn, Curly came out to meet him. Jack told him the mares and foals were headed in so he needed to open the paddock gates. "The studs will be along later," he added, wincing as he stepped down onto his sore leg. It was stiff from all the sitting he'd done. He wasn't looking forward to another four-hour trip after doing eight already, but he sure as hell wasn't staying here another night.

"Have one of the Garcia boys check the buggy over then hitch a fresh horse," he said over his shoulder as he limped through the barn. "I'll be back directly."

As he went out the double front doors into the yard, he saw the horses trotting through the gate. They had perked up, being so close to home, and were kicking up enough of a ruckus to bring Brady out onto the front porch.

"When did you get back?" his brother asked, then turned his attention to the horses filing past. "And what are they doing here?"

"I sent them." Jack stopped in the yard and waited for his brother to come down the steps to meet him, preferring to do this in neutral territory rather than in Brady's office.

"Why?"

"Because I didn't sell them. The loan is paid off. Here's the paperwork." He held out the signed paper when Brady stopped before him.

After reading it over, Brady looked up, a frown of confusion drawing his dark brows together. "I don't understand."

"I don't either, Big Brother. So why don't you explain it to me."

"Explain what?"

"About the account you set up for me." When his brother just stared at him, Jack's anger caught fire. "Did you think I couldn't earn my own way, Brady? That I was so helpless you had to coddle me like a baby on a sugar tit?"

The blue eyes widened in surprise. "We all got equal shares, Jack. This is your ranch too."

"Is it?" Jack gave a bitter laugh. "Well, I've said it before and I'll say it again. I don't want it. I don't want anything to do with it — or you — anymore. Just stay the hell out of my life." He started toward the house.

Brady yanked him back, almost sending him toppling when his weight came down on his bad leg. "What the hell's wrong with you, Jack? What did I do this time?"

"It's not what you did. It's what you didn't do." Yanking his arm free, Jack thrust his face close to Brady's, forcing him to look directly into his eyes and see the fury he didn't bother to hide. "You damn near lost the ranch rather than come to me for help. Why is that?"

"What are you talking about?"

"Why didn't you pay off the loan with the money in that account you set up for me?" Jack demanded.

"It wasn't mine to use. It's your money."

"You could have asked me for it. Or were you afraid I wouldn't give it to you?"

"I was afraid you *would.*"

Jack took a step back. Now he was the one confused.

"You have Daisy and Kate now, Jack," Brady snapped, obviously struggling to keep his own temper in check. "You need it for them. Besides, it was my mistake that got us into trouble and I wasn't going to let you trade your future to get us out of it."

"*Let* me? It wasn't your decision." Jack wanted to shout in frustration. Why did his brother think he had to manage everyone? When would he stop deciding what was best for all of them without even giving them a say-so? "Damnit, Brady, I'm almost thirty years old. I don't need you taking care of me, or making decisions for me, or paying me a damn allowance."

"I was just trying —"

"Well, don't!" Jack cut him off with a savage slash of his hand. "I've got plenty of money. I don't need yours." He laughed bitterly. "Hell, I'm part owner of a trader. I've got a warehouse full of merino wool in San Francisco that has probably already sold for a small fortune, and I have shares of two more ships working the China trade. It's time you started taking me seriously and quit treating me like your idiot little brother."

"But you *are* my little brother."

Jack threw his hands up in exasperation. "Well, not anymore. I don't want the job, so I quit. I'll never be you and I'm tired of trying. Soon as I load up Daisy and Kate, we're going to Val Rosa. I'm done here."

Whirling, Jack started toward the barn again.

Brady's voice stopped him in midstride. "They're gone."

Another wave of anger rose in Jack's chest. Slowly he turned. "Gone?"

"I sent them to Redemption."

That was it. The final, tiniest blade of straw, the weight of which snapped the last thread of Jack's frayed temper.

Bracing against his good leg, he drove his right fist into Brady's jaw with enough force to send his brother's Stetson flying.

Brady fell back, staggering for balance.

Jack came after him, ignoring the ache in his leg and the blood on his knuckles, no longer aware of anything but the decades of anger and festering resentment that demanded release. "You sonofabitch!" he shouted, swinging again as Brady ducked and threw an arm up to block him. "You had to take them away from me too?"

"I gave them back to you, you stupid bastard." Dropping his right shoulder, Brady drove his fist into Jack's stomach.

Air whooshed out. Jack doubled over.

"I sent them to Redemption for you!"

Momentarily distracted by Brady's words, Jack didn't see his brother's leg shoot out and hook his ankle. A moment later, he was toppling backward. He hit with a thud that drove the air from his lungs a second time, and all he could do was gape up at his brother, who stood over him shouting.

"They were leaving, you dimwit! I sent them to Redemption because there's no way out of there, and you'll be able to catch up to them before they get too far. Christamighty!"

Once he caught his breath, Jack rolled over and, using his good leg, pushed himself back onto his feet. He leaned over to spit the dust from his mouth, then straightened. Resting his hands low on his hips, he scowled at his brother. "What do you mean, they were leaving?"

"Christ." Brady swiped blood from a cut on his top lip, then bent and snatched his

Stetson from the ground. "It was the singing thing."

"What singing thing?"

"Jesus. Don't you two ever talk?"

"What singing thing, damnit!"

"Ask her." Shoving dark hair out of his eyes, Brady put the hat back on, then reached into his pocket. "Or read this." Pulling out a folded sheet of paper, he passed it over. "She said it would explain everything."

"You haven't read it?"

"Hell no, I haven't read it! How low do you think I am?"

Jack let his glare answer for him. Opening the paper, he started reading. By the time he'd finished, he was mad all over again. "Hell and damnation! Does everybody in the world think I'm a damn fool?"

Wisely, his brother didn't answer that.

Muttering under his breath, Jack whirled and started toward the barn. If he left now, he could be over the pass before dark. And when he caught up to Daisy . . . *damn her.* Did she think he would just let her and Kate go?

"What are you going to do?" Brady called after him.

"None of your goddamned business."

A moment later, he heard his brother coming up behind him. "Jack, wait."

"For what?" he said without slowing. "More talk? You're never going to change and I'm

532

never going to be more than your little brother. So I'm done talking." With a backward wave, he continued on into the shadowed barn, speaking as he went. "Adios, Brady. Give my good-byes to Hank and the ladies and the kids. I'll leave the horse and buggy in Redemption." Having a better idea, he stopped and reached into his pocket. "Or I can pay you for them now if you'd prefer."

Before he could pull his hand from his pocket, he was on the ground again.

Brady loomed over him, his face red with fury. "You'll stay until I have my say. Then if you still want to go sniveling off, I'll hitch your goddamn horse myself. Now get up!"

Jack got up. Slower this time, but still game if his brother preferred to use fists rather than words. He just wanted it over with. "Go ahead then," he said, once he'd regained his feet. "Say your words."

Brady's eyes seemed to snap fire. His chin jutted belligerently and his teeth were a white snarl beneath his dark mustache. "You want to be taken seriously? Then be serious. Commit to something — anything. Take a chance and believe in something bigger than yourself. Don't be a drifter all your life — you're a better man than that. I know, because I helped raise you."

When Jack started to interrupt, Brady held up a hand. "Maybe you don't want to hear that. But the fact is, Jack, I *am* your big brother, and I do worry about you, same as I worry about Hank and Jessica and Molly and the kids and Daisy and Kate and everyone else in my family."

"I don't need your worry."

"Well, that's too bad. Because even if you ride off tonight and never come back, I'll still be your big brother, and I'll still worry about you."

Not sure how to respond, Jack studied dust motes drifting through a beam of sunlight shining down through the open loft door. They looked like tiny golden flecks suspended in space, like stars hanging in a twilight sky. He let out a weary breath and watched them scatter in swirling chaos.

He wanted to stay mad. He had a right to his resentments.

But in truth, he was weary of them.

"I may have been hard on you," Brady went on, sounding as drained as Jack felt. "But I never gave up on you, and I never disrespected you. Hell" — he gave a rueful laugh — "sometimes I even envied you."

Jack looked over, certain that his brother was mocking him.

But Brady seemed sincere. Embarrassed, even. And really, really tired. The grooves bracketing his mustache seemed to have deepened overnight, and there was a weariness in his eyes that Jack had never noticed before. It was unsettling. Brady had always seemed so sure and unshakable, so abso-goddamn-lutely convinced of his own right-ness. But maybe that arrogant high-handedness was as much for show as Jack's carefree I-don't-care attitude was. Maybe Brady had his worries, too, and was just try-ing to do the best he could with what he had, and making his own mistakes along the way.

A lot of mistakes.

"Envied me, why?" Jack asked, not con-vinced such a thing was possible.

Brady made a dismissive motion. "You had everything, Jack, yet you always wanted more. The ranch wasn't good enough. We weren't good enough. And you were ready to toss us all away for places you'd never been, places you'd never seen. On top of that," he added with a half-smile, "you got away with shenani-gans we couldn't. No matter what foolishness you pulled, Pa always favored you." He sounded almost embarrassed, as if admitting such a thing, much less saying it aloud, would sound unmanly and pitiful.

Which it sort of did.

"Favored me?" Jack tried to laugh the no-tion off. "You were the one he talked to."

"The one he ordered around maybe." Jack heard a derisive tone in Brady's voice that seemed out of character for his forceful big brother. "I was just his errand boy. But you made him smile."

I did? He didn't remember Pa hardly noticing him. Had he been wrong all these years? And if he'd been wrong about Pa, could he have been wrong about Brady too?

It was disconcerting. Like a familiar door had opened in his mind, but what he saw behind it was altogether different from what he had expected to find.

"It wasn't easy on me either," Brady added. "Or Hank. You weren't the only one who thought about leaving."

Jack stared at his brother as if seeing him for the first time. Which in many ways, he was. "So why didn't you?"

Brady gave a crooked smile. Motioning out the open barn doors toward the grasslands stretching like a green sea across the valley, he said, "I'm a rancher. That's what I am and what I do. And after doing it for as long as I have, I realized one day I actually liked it. And even more important, I'm damn good at it."

Jack couldn't argue that. Despite this mess over the smelter and the horses, Brady had kept RosaRoja running strong through lean years and good.

Feeling suddenly embarrassed by the softer turn of the conversation, and fearing he and his brother were about to step into emotional areas that would be better left to weaker minds, Jack gave him a grin and moved back to safer ground. "I'm Hank's favorite too. Told me so himself."

"He counts in his sleep," Brady reminded him. "And talks to horses."

"Yeah, well . . ."

To hide his sudden awkwardness, Jack studied the letter again, still confused and a little hurt by what Daisy had written. How could she go running off after the night they'd had? Hell, how could she move at all? He was still a bit sore himself. "I can't believe she told you about the singing thing but not me."

Brady prodded his toe at a dung beetle crawling through the straw at his feet. "Seems like a poor excuse for running off, just to sing on a stage."

Jack shot him a hard look. "She deserves to be up there."

Thrusting his hands into his front pockets, Brady rocked back on his heels and looked at him.

"She's a damn good singer," Jack defended. "She should have her chance."

"So you're going after her?"

"Of course I'm going after her."

"Good."

His brother's smug look brought Jack's hackles up again. "But not because of you. Don't think you talked me into it, because you didn't."

"Of course not."

"You're an interfering sonofabitch."

"I know."

"All right, then." Jack turned toward the waiting buggy.

Brady fell into step beside him. "You ought to go by horseback. Hank won't be able to drive both the wagon and buggy home by himself. Unless you're planning to bring Daisy and Kate back here. Which I'm guessing you're not."

Jack stopped and looked at his brother. "Hank's in Redemption? With Daisy?"

"I couldn't send her alone. Since we closed the mines and shut down the spur line, most folks have already left. Place is a damned ghost town."

Hank. The man who turned women into simpering simpletons. Alone with Daisy. In a ghost town. *Grand.* "Then how are we supposed to get from there to the transcontinental?" The idea of being trapped in a ghost town seemed only marginally better to Jack than being trapped at the ranch.

"We still have the handcar. Hank's figured a way to attach a sail to it so you won't have to pump all the way up the pass. In fact, he's probably already rigging it up."

"Hell."

"I know. But he's not one to hold a grudge, so I'm sure he'll do his best."

A different kind of alarm moved through Jack. "Grudge about what?"

Brady looked sheepish. "I accidentally told him what you said about Molly having her hands all over you."

"Accidentally?"

"And there's something else I should probably warn you about."

"Christ." Jack was tired of standing — or falling — on his bad leg, he was hungry, and he wanted to go after Daisy. "What?"

"The ladies are planning something. Big secret. But whatever it is, me and Hank had nothing to do with it. Wanted you to know. And I don't think Daisy knows anything either." Brady patted his shoulder in commiseration. "Thought you should be warned, you know, in case it's something like that thing with the Henshaw sisters."

"Oh, hell."

"I know." Brady grinned. "But maybe this time, you'll like it."

Daisy bounced her hungry daughter on her knee and stared in confusion at the shuttered storefronts and near-empty streets and the small number of people walking along the boardwalks in Redemption.

"Where is everybody?" she asked as Hank reined the team down a back street that looked like it hadn't been traveled since the last rain. Even the train track that paralleled it was sprouting weeds between the rails.

"Gone."

"Gone," Kate echoed.

"Why?" Daisy asked.

"No work. Same with most mining towns since Grant changed the country from silver to gold."

Several derelict types came out of the back door of a saloon to watch them as they came down the street. Hank nodded, but didn't stop. After the wagon rolled past, Daisy turned and looked back to find them still watching, their eyes dulled by drink and disappointment. A shiver of unease went through her. She faced forward again, wondering if she and Kate would be safe here. And how would they get out? It was obvious the train wasn't running. "Is there a stage office?" she asked.

"Nope."

"Then how will we go on to New Orleans?"

"We'll think of something."

Not much of an answer. As they passed a one-room church with an empty steeple, a man straightened from a small vegetable patch inside the unpainted fence. "Hello, Hank," he called with a wave.

Hank waved back. "Howdy, Reverend."

"Got time for a visit?"

"Later," Hank called without slowing. "After supper."

Supper. Daisy's stomach rumbled just to hear the word. They had finished all the food they'd brought hours ago.

"Hungwy," Kate said, looking up at Hank.

"Soon." Reaching over, he ruffled her blond

curls, his big hand dwarfing her small head. "Got your daddy's appetite, don't you, Katie-girl?"

"Katie-girl," Kate said and grinned.

Daisy's worry grew as they left the deserted buildings of town behind and passed cabin after cabin that looked to be abandoned. Finally, at least a hundred yards past the last dwelling, Hank pulled the wagon to a stop in front of a small clapboard house with a wide front porch. A horse that was still harnessed to an old-fashioned carriage was grazing in the side yard. As Hank stepped down to tie the team to the hitching rail beside the walk, a gray-haired woman came out the front door.

"Got word, I see," Hank said by way of greeting.

"Ya, I did," the woman answered in a heavily accented voice as she stood on the porch, smiling and wiping her hands on a faded calico apron tied around her equally faded calico dress. "And supper is waiting."

The woman, Hank explained as he helped Daisy and Kate out of the wagon, was Anna Strobel. Her husband, Hans, had been a shift foreman in one of the Wilkins mines. His job now was to watch over what equipment was left, and to ready the house whenever it was needed.

"Is this her home?" Daisy asked, following him up the walk.

"No. It's mine." He told her that since he

was in charge of the mining aspect of Wilkins Cattle and Mining, he had needed a place to stay whenever he was in Redemption, which had been fairly frequently when the mines were flourishing. Now the place was closed up most of the time unless someone from the ranch sent word they'd be needing it.

It was a cozy little house. Three rooms — a kitchen and eating area with a stone fireplace, with a small alcove that held storage items and an unmade cot — a single bedroom dominated by an oversized bed — and adjoining it, a water closet built along the same design as those at the ranch, complete with a big hot water tub and an indoor water stool, Daisy was pleased to note.

But she was a little concerned about the sleeping arrangements. She wondered if Hank intended to stay at the house with her and Kate, and if so, would he take the bedroom, or the alcove off the kitchen?

Anna, in addition to being a welcoming grandmotherly woman, was also an excellent cook, and the supper she set out was a treat — a rich, beefy stew loaded with vegetables, warm black bread straight from the oven, and a tart berry pie. Once she was sure they had everything they needed, Anna loaded supper plates for her and Hans into a basket, then left, promising to check back tomorrow.

Kate did most of the talking over supper, her comments directed to Kitty, who sat beside her. Hank attended his meal with single-minded dedication — the Wilkins brothers certainly took their food seriously — while Daisy ate and worried and fretted.

She figured Elena was on her way to San Francisco by now, and Jack had returned to the ranch and had probably read her letter. Was he disappointed? Furious that she'd left without saying good-bye? Relieved?

He'd said he loved her. At the time, he probably meant it. But did he love them enough to come after them? Did she want him to? And if he did show up, did she love him enough to put aside her dream and stay with him? Pushing her empty plate away, she sighed, still no surer of her decision to leave than when she had made it hours — no, days — ago.

"I'll be stepping out for a while," Hank said, watching her over his coffee mug. "You and Kate take the bedroom. When I come back, I'll stretch out on the table here."

She looked at him in surprise. "The table? Not the cot in the alcove?"

"Too short."

Of course it was, she realized. Most beds or cots were only six feet long, and Hank — in fact, all the brothers — were taller than that. "Then Kate and I will take the alcove. You use your own bed."

"I'll be fine." His tone discouraged argument, even though his eyes smiled.

A few minutes later, he left. Daisy shared a bath with Kate, then rocked her by the unlit fireplace until she drifted to sleep.

As she climbed wearily into bed beside her daughter, Daisy wondered where Jack was, and if he was thinking about her, and if she'd ever stop thinking about him.

Odd, but now that she had chosen music over a life with Jack, she had no desire at all to sing.

TWENTY-SEVEN

The moon was fast slipping behind the western ridges when Jack finally rode into Redemption.

He'd come by horseback, as Brady had advised, and had made it through the rough spots before dark. Now the moon was lighting the rest of his way down into the little canyon that had once been Sancho's hideout, and later was his tomb, and finally after the landslide, became the site of the first Wilkins mine.

The town was all but deserted. A single window glowed in the hotel, and only two horses were tied outside the one saloon that wasn't boarded over. Following the directions Brady had given him, Jack went straight through town and out the other side.

He'd spent most of the trip going over what he would say to Daisy when he finally caught up to her. He was no longer mad that she had left him without even a good-bye — hadn't he done near the same thing when he'd sailed off to Australia? Of course, at the time, he'd been drunk and confused.

He wondered what her excuse was.

Not that it mattered. He'd find a way to convince her to stay with him. If he wanted to give his life any meaning, he had to have Daisy and Kate by his side.

Hank's house was easy to spot because the ranch buckboard was sitting out front. There was an odd, long, canvas-wrapped pole hanging out the back, which was probably the sail for the handcar. Relieved to have his travels over, he reined in the tired horse beside the wagon. As he swung down, careful to put most of his weight on his left leg, a figure rose out of a chair on the darkened porch. He was too big to be anyone but his brother.

" 'Bout time," Hank said, coming down the steps.

"Where's Daisy and Kate?" Jack asked as he untied the saddlebags from behind the saddle.

"Asleep." Hank waved him aside. "I'll tend your horse. If you're hungry, there's leftover stew on the stove."

Jack perked up at that. "You'll join me?" he asked, almost hoping he wouldn't. Hank had a formidable appetite.

"I could use a bite. Besides, you'll want to tell me what happened in town."

"I will?"

Hank looked at him.

Jack sighed. He'd hoped to avoid long explanations tonight. Slinging the saddlebags over his shoulder, he glanced at the darkened house. "You have a water closet in there? One with a tub?"

Securing the loose strap in the D ring, Hank lifted the saddle from the horse's back as if it weighed less than a feather. "Through my bedroom. But be quiet. Daisy and Kate are in there."

Jack whipped his head back toward his brother. "In your bedroom?"

"There's only the one." Hank's teeth showed white in the faint moonlight. "But don't worry. I managed to keep her from — how did that go? — oh, yeah — from putting her hands all over me."

Too weary to get into it with this brother, Jack let that pass. "How is she?"

Grabbing a rag from the back of the wagon, Hank began rubbing down the weary horse. "Tired. Confused."

"Me too." Jack nodded toward the pole sticking out the back of the wagon. "That the sail for the handcar?"

Hank nodded.

"Think it'll work?" Jack didn't relish the thought of pumping uphill for ten miles.

"Probably."

"Probably?"

"You'd prefer to walk?"

Grand. Jack limped on toward the house.

In the kitchen, he paused to light the lamp in the center of the table, then added a couple of sticks of kindling to the stove. When he lifted the lid on the pot simmering on top of it, he was delighted to see there was more stew than even Hank could eat. The smell of it made his stomach rumble, but he replaced the lid, wanting to wash off the dust before he ate.

And he needed to make sure Daisy and Kate were really here.

Saddlebags in hand, he moved toward the door on the far side of the kitchen. He eased it open. When his eyes adjusted, he saw two quilt-covered lumps in the middle of the big four-poster bed. He smiled, recognizing Daisy's soft exhales and Kate's snuffle. Knowing they were finally within reach aroused such an onslaught of emotion, for a moment he felt weak and wobbly.

He wanted to shake her. He wanted to hug her. He wanted to climb in beside her, wrap her in his arms, and sleep for a week.

Moving quietly, he went to the side of the bed and looked down at them.

His beautiful ladies.

How could Daisy even think he would let them go off on their own? Or that he would prefer the life of a nomad to a life with them? They were a family. They were meant to be together.

Closing his eyes, he took a deep, calming

breath that filled his head with the smell of new wood, burnt kerosene from the doused lamp, Daisy's soap. And as the scent of her moved through him, all the turmoil inside his mind quieted. He felt balanced again, stronger, less . . . scattered. It was as if he'd been missing a vital part of himself for so long he hadn't even been aware that he had been without it until he found Daisy again. She was his lifeline, his buoy in the darkness. Being with her was better than flying.

Opening his eyes, he smiled down at her. Then resisting the urge to touch her, he moved on into the water closet, which he was gratified to see held not only a Hank-sized tub, but also a sink and a modern flush stool.

Luckily, the pipes weren't as noisy here as they were in the water closet at the ranch. Probably because there wasn't a boiler here, but an elevated metal tank atop a small woodstove. Pipes running through the wall filled the tank with cold water, which was heated by the stove, then more pipes out the bottom of the tank delivered the hot water into the tub or sink. Drainpipes through the floor emptied the wastewater. Hank and his innovations.

Although the fire in the stove was down to glowing coals, the water in the tank was still hot. Jack let it run until it emptied all the heated water, then climbed in, bad leg and all. He settled back with a long sigh.

Before he left, Molly had checked his leg and said the cut was healing well, but insisted he keep the stitches in for another few days. The massive bruising from hip to knee would take a lot longer to go away, which she said was a good thing, because the lingering soreness would keep him from overworking the leg before it was fully healed. The logic of that had escaped Jack, but after his twelve-hour jaunt today, he conceded she might be right. Thankfully, the hot water eased the stiffness a lot.

He soaked until hunger forced him out, then he toweled off, pulled clean clothes from his saddlebags, dressed, and went back to the kitchen.

Hank was already sitting on one of the benches at the table, gobbling stew. Jack was pleased to note that a bottle of Jessica's fine Scotch whiskey and two mugs sat on the table by the lamp.

They ate in silence until Hank finally pushed back his empty plate. After pouring a healthy dose of whiskey into each mug, he took a deep swallow from his, then looked at Jack's hand. "Where'd you get the tooth marks?"

Jack glanced at his swollen knuckles. "Brady."

"Figures. Who won?"

Jack thought it over while he chewed. They'd both cleared some long-standing problems between them and he felt easier about his big brother than he had in a long time. So maybe he won. Or maybe not. "Neither."

"What set you off this time?"

"The account he opened for me at the bank." Spearing a bite of potato, Jack studied his second brother. "Why didn't you tell me about it, Hank? Or use it to pay off the loan?"

"It wasn't my call. It was yours." Tossing back the last swallow of whiskey, Hank plunked his mug onto the table. "And if you brought the horses back, you made the right one."

"Kind of a risk, wasn't it?" He could have just taken the money and left, although, thinking back on it now, Jack realized that idea had never occurred to him.

His brother smiled.

Did Hank really have that much faith in him? If so, then Jack had been wrong about him too. As he mopped his plate with a slice of black bread, he thought about all the angry years and bottled resentments. No wonder his brothers lost patience with him.

"And this way," Hank added after a moment, "you made the offer all on your own. You weren't asked to do it, or pushed into doing it, or told to do it. You just did it."

"Like you knew I would," Jack said dryly, a little disturbed that his brothers seemed to know him better than he did.

"Like I knew you would," Hank agreed, looking smug. "I am the smart brother, after all. Your pretty little wife said so herself."

Not wanting to trade blows with this brother too, Jack ignored the jab. Pushing back the bench, he rose and carried both their plates to the sink. "Thanks for watching out for them," he said, anxious for Hank to leave so he could go back to Daisy.

"They're my family too." Rising with a yawn, Hank cleared the rest of the table and returned the whiskey bottle to a cupboard. "You leaving tomorrow?"

"I am. But not because of Brady."

"The singing thing."

Christ. Did everybody in the territory know about the singing thing but him? Jack glanced over, saw his brother watching him, and shrugged. It didn't matter who knew. He would end up with Daisy, and that was all that mattered.

Hank stretched, his hands brushing the ceiling. Taking his hat and jacket off the rack of pegs by the door, he said, "There's a cot in the storage area behind the fireplace, if you're interested."

Jack wasn't. Nor did he care to reveal to his brother that he had no intention of sleeping anywhere but next to Daisy. Now that he'd caught up with them, he wasn't letting either her or Kate out of his sight until he'd settled this singing thing once and for all. "Where are you staying?"

"There's still a couple of rooms open at the hotel." Hank crossed to the door. When he opened it, a cool draft swept in, making the lamp light flutter and bringing with it the smell of wood smoke and the lonely call of a whippoorwill. Jack saw stars hanging above the mountain peaks before his brother stepped into the doorway and his broad form blocked the view. "Come to the depot in the morning. I'll need your help attaching the sail to the handcar."

After the door closed behind him, Jack stood in the kitchen for a moment, wondering if he should go into the bedroom. Stupid question, he chided himself. But he'd be careful not to wake Daisy. He was too weary to do anything anyway, and right now, all he wanted was to lie down beside his woman and go to sleep. Words could wait until tomorrow.

The dip of the mattress brought Daisy from deep sleep to drowsy confusion. For a moment she lay still, disoriented and not sure where she was or what had awakened her. Then strong arms reached from behind to pull her back against a hard, warm body.

She came instantly awake. "Jack?"

Her answer was a weary yawn.

She tried to look back over her shoulder to see his face, but he was wrapped around her so tightly she couldn't turn far enough. The scent she recognized, a lingering hint of Jack's spicy soap, overlaid with the smell of beef stew and whiskey.

He'd come after her. He had actually come after her.

She smiled into the darkness.

Warm breath fanned her nape as he yawned again. Then in a voice roughened by exhaustion, he said, "You're not leaving me, Daisy."

A heartbeat later, he began to snore.

Warmth flowed through her, bringing with it such a swell of contentment tears stung her eyes.

He had come after her.

He had read her letter, and knew what she felt she had to do, and he had still come after her. Did that mean he intended to give up his wandering life and stay with her and Kate?

Cocooned in his warmth, she watched the stars move past the window, growing brighter as the moon slipped behind the mountains. By the time early dawn stained the window-panes pink, she knew what she had to do.

"Go horsy! Go horsy!"

Jack groaned and covered his head as a small body began bouncing up and down on his back.

"Kate, no," Daisy whispered, lifting the squirming imp away. "Let him sleep."

Too late for that.

"Horsy!" Kate insisted at a pitch that would have deafened him if his head hadn't been under the pillow.

"Later, Kate." Daisy's voice and Kate's protests faded, then stopped altogether with the click of the door latch.

Jack sighed. Muscles relaxed and his mind grew sluggish. His body felt heavier and heavier . . .

With a gasp, he lurched up onto his elbows. Bright afternoon sunlight seared his eyeballs.

How long had he slept? Where was he?

Hank's. With Daisy and Kate.

Still bleary with sleep, he slumped back, listening for sounds beyond his closed door. But the house was so quiet the only thing he heard was the thud of his heart against his ribs.

Too quiet.

Panic sent his mind into another flurry.

Goddamn. They'd left him again.

Rising too quickly on muscles that weren't yet awake, he collided with the bedpost in his stumble across the room. When he reached the door, he flung it open so hard it banged against the wall. "Daisy!"

"What? What's wrong?"

Blinking groggily, he saw her standing at the stove, staring at him with worried hazel eyes. "Jack?"

"I —" He let out a rush of breath. His heart resumed a less frantic rhythm. "I thought you were gone."

Her face cleared. Smiling, she walked over and put her arms around his neck. "I'm right here," she said against his cheek.

Shaky with relief, he grabbed on to her, pulling her so close he could feel those perfect breasts flatten against his chest and the steady beat of her heart within. She smelled so good to him — flowers, lemons, yeast, bacon? *Bacon?* Glancing over the top of her head, he saw a pot of coffee on the stove, bread rising, fatback sizzling in a pan.

His stomach growled.

Still only half-awake, he lifted his head and scanned the room. "Where's Kate?"

She gave him a quick kiss then stepped out of his arms. "With Anna."

"Anna?"

"Anna Strobel," she said over her shoulder as she went back to the stove. "She made the stew you ate last night. She sometimes watches the children when your brothers bring their families into town. Sort of like a grandmother."

She stirred something on the stove, then hesitated and glanced over at him, her smile less sure. "I thought it would be best if Kate wasn't here when we talk."

Talk? Jack sighed. Of course she would want to talk. Women always wanted to talk. Just as well. He had some things to say too. "Let me get dressed first," he said, ducking back into

556

the bedroom. It was hard for a man to be taken seriously in a confrontation when he was wearing nothing but his drawers. Besides, he wanted to wake up a bit more before he called her to accounts.

He took a little longer than he needed to, going over in his head what he wanted to say to her. Like his brothers, Daisy had apparently underestimated him. But having had the long ride from the ranch to think it over, Jack couldn't say he blamed them. He hadn't been the most committed fellow. But then, he hadn't had anything worth committing to.

Until now.

Daisy had a feast waiting when he returned to the kitchen. Moving past the bench, he took a chair at the end of the table, all but smacking his lips as he watched her load a plate with beefsteak, collards with bacon, potatoes, carrots, green beans, and thick slices of black bread. As she set it before him, he picked up his fork, then saw that she hadn't served herself, and set it back down. Resting his hands beside his plate, he tried to be patient and ignore the growling of his stomach.

"How did you know where to find us?" Daisy asked, going back to the stove.

"Brady."

"Typical." She lifted a clay mug from a peg, filled it with coffee, and carried it to the table. "Did you read my letter?" she asked, setting

557

it beside his plate.

"I did."

"So you know why I had to leave."

"I know why you *thought* you had to leave."

"But you came after us anyway."

"Did you doubt I would?"

"I wasn't sure." With a sigh, she sat on the bench at his right and folded her arms on top of the table. "I should have told you, rather than leave it in a letter."

"You should have. Could have saved us both the trip. You're not eating?" he asked when he saw she wasn't filling a plate for herself.

She explained she'd just finished lunch a while back and for him to go ahead and eat while she talked.

Which he did. Most of the time, he listened too.

It didn't much matter what Daisy said. He'd read her letter and knew what was in her mind. Again like Brady, she'd made some assumptions about him that had no basis. Did she really think the wandering life would appeal to him more than being with her and Kate? And *"fondly"*? What man wanted to be remembered "fondly" by the woman he intended to take as a wife? *Hell.*

But he'd let her say her piece. Then he'd tell her she was wrong, and explain how it was going to be, and then they could escape this ghost town and get on with their lives.

So while she talked, and he ate and mostly listened, he studied her across the table.

She was looking especially pretty today. The sun had put gold in her light brown hair and with all their walks, her skin had lost that San Francisco pallor and had taken on a rosy blush. She was a fine-looking woman. And all his.

His gaze drifted over her as warm memories filled his mind.

He liked that yellow dress. It brought out the yellow-green in her hazel eyes and it fitted her much better than the dresses she usually wore. In fact, the soft cotton of her shirt molded around those round, perfect breasts like . . . well, his hand. He smiled, thinking about how she squirmed under his fingers when he —

"Stop staring at my breasts," she said with a note of exasperation in her voice.

Yet when he looked up, he saw laughter in her eyes. He grinned. "But they're so noticeable."

"They're just breasts."

"*Perfect* breasts," he amended. "So round and soft and . . . happy."

"Happy?" She laughed. "Breasts don't have feelings."

"Sure they do. Come over here and I'll show you."

"Honestly." She sent him that smirky smile he loved. Then waving all that aside, her expression sobered. "So you agree?"

"With what?"

"Jack!" She slapped her hand on the table. "Haven't you heard a word I said?"

Caught off guard, he tried to remember what she had been talking about before her breasts demanded his attention. Something about singing. And not caging him. And doing what was best for Kate. Whatever. She could offer all the excuses in the world, but there was only one truth that signified.

Downing his last bite, he pushed aside his empty plate and slouched back, his left elbow hooked over the top slat of the wooden chair, his right hand gripping his coffee mug. He smiled friendly-like. "You said your piece?"

She nodded.

"Then I'll say mine." He decided to get the inconsequential matters out of the way first. "I had the sheriff check on that poster Ashford brought."

A stricken look came over her face.

"Sheriff Foley found out some drunk lady shot Johnson then fell down the stairs and broke her neck. Case closed. So you don't have to worry about that anymore."

Oddly, she didn't show the relief he'd expected. Instead, she turned to look toward the window and said in a flat, emotionless voice, "Johnson was going to steal Kate."

For a moment Jack just looked at her,

wondering if he'd heard right. "Steal Kate? Why?"

"To sell her to a brothel."

Katie? His Katie? In a whorehouse? Disbelief exploded in rage that boiled up inside him, and kept boiling until his chest and throat and head felt like they were on fire. A sharp cracking sound, and he looked down to see the broken mug in his hand and coffee spreading across the tabletop. "Goddamn."

He watched in silence as Daisy wiped up the mess, a part of him amazed at how removed he felt, as if he were watching the whole thing through a glass window and the terrible images Daisy's words had conjured had no meaning for him at all.

Daisy's hand cupped his cheek. "Jack. Jack!"

And suddenly that window shattered and all that fury and terror flooded back in. He slammed his fist on the table and started up out of his chair. "That sonofabitch! I'll kill him!"

Daisy put a hand on his arm to stop him. "I already did."

He froze, not sure he'd heard right. "You what?"

"Edna Tidwell didn't kill Johnson. I did."

His legs seemed to give way. He fell back to the seat. "Christ, Daisy. How? What happened?"

"Remember that little double derringer you

561

won in a card game and gave to me?"

Jack nodded.

"I shot him with that. Once in the belly and once in the mouth." He saw a shudder run through her despite the defiant set of her jaw and the flash of anger and pain in her eyes. "And I'm not sorry for it."

"Sweet Jesus." Elbows braced on the table, Jack clasped both hands to his temples as if that might slow the thoughts swirling in his mind. His gentle Daisy a killer? Forced to shoot a man to protect their daughter? *Sweet Jesus.* Another thing Jack would carry on his conscience. How many times and ways had he failed this woman? "I should have been there to protect you, Daisy. I should have been the one to kill him. I'm sorry."

Her hand stroked the hair at the crown of his head. "I'm sorry too."

He had a lot to make up for. And a lot more apologies to make. Straightening in the chair, he took her hand in his and tried to find the words. "And I'm sorry I left you, Daisy. I made a terrible mistake. And not just because I wasn't there to protect you and Kate. I was drunk and confused and stupid. I wasn't ready for what you offered. Or for you. But I'm ready now." He looked directly into her beautiful eyes to show her the truth of his words. "I promise from now on I'll always be there to protect you. I'm not going anywhere without you and Kate. And you're not going anywhere without me. We belong together, the three of us. You need to understand that."

Her chin wobbled on a tremulous smile. "I agree."

He blinked. "You do?" *That's it? No argument? No demands?* He felt like he was on goddamn teeter-totter.

"You're too important to Kate — to both of us, Jack. We need you in our lives. I realize that now." She pulled out of his grip and sat back, her eyes going wet again. "I've been so selfish. Thinking only of myself and my own ambitions. What kind of life would that have been for Kate — stuck backstage, practically being raised by a nanny? No, we're a family and families should stay together." She smiled — a bit weakly, he thought. "So it's settled. When do we leave?"

"Leave?"

"When do we go home?"

And finally he understood. He wanted to shake her. It was an effort to keep his voice even. "And where is home, Daisy? San Francisco? Rome? Here?"

She frowned. "It's with you, Jack."

"Exactly." He leaned over and gave her a quick kiss, then rose. "We'll leave tomorrow. Assuming Hank's contraption is ready and can get us up to the transcontinental line."

"The transcontinental line? Why would we go there?"

"So we can get you to Rome for the singing thing."

She studied him for a moment, her expression both confused and hopeful. "But, Jack, you know you'll hate that, being penned down and —"

"Don't!" Bending down, he planted his palms on the tabletop. "Don't tell me what I'll hate and what I won't, Daisy. And don't make my decisions for me. I get enough of that from Brady." He straightened. "You're not giving up your singing because of me. That's that."

"And you're not giving up your freedom because of us," she countered.

Lest he give in to the urge to shake her, he crossed his arms over his chest and wondered how to make her understand that he'd changed. He was no longer the carefree wanderer he had once been. He had a family now. He was ready to be taken seriously.

"I know you, Jack," she went on before he could speak. "I've seen your ocean in the mountains and I know why it draws you. You need to be out there somewhere, chasing the sun across the sky. You need to be free."

I need you. It was a wonder to him that she could know him so well and still be willing to give up her dreams for his. It was wrong. Plain wrong. "Being free is just a dressed-up notion for being alone," he said. "And I'm tired of being alone, Daisy. Brady told me to commit to something bigger than myself, and that's what I'm trying to do here — commit the rest of my life to you and Kate."

"But what about your family? And the ranch?"

"You're my family. And my brothers and the ranch will always be here if we decide to come back." *No. When we come back,* he amended silently. But only for a visit, of course. Although, now that he was no longer choking on resentment, he didn't feel such a driving need to escape as he once had. Strange.

"It's our ranch, too, Daisy. And Kate's. She'll need to know that."

When he saw more tears spill from her beautiful eyes, he sank down on the bench beside her and brushed them from her cheek. "There's no need to cry, Daisy. It's good. All good. We'll have a grand life, the three of us. You'll see."

"But, Jack," she said in a shaky voice. "What about traveling and seeing the world and —"

He bent and pressed his mouth to hers to shut her up. When he drew back, he tasted the salt of her tears on his lips and tongue. "It doesn't have to be one or the other, you know. I want to see Rome too. Now I'll be able to explore it with my pretty ladies when you're not practicing or training. We'll see the *Pietà* together."

She started to say something, but he saw the doubt in her eyes and cut her off. "How about a compromise?" he offered. "After you finish your training, for every three months you tour, we'll take a month off to go exploring. Anywhere we want. Just the three of us. Europe, Africa, India, the islands of the Mediterranean Sea. We can see it all, Daisy. We can do it all. Together."

"Together." He watched hope fill her eyes until a smile spread across her beautiful face. It was like watching the sun rise after a long, dark night. "I can have you?" she asked, crying and smiling at the same time. "And still sing?"

Watching her tears fall made his own eyes sting. *Christ. I'm turning into a woman.* Next thing, he'd be hugging his brothers and trading recipes.

To cover that weakness, he forced a laugh. "Oh, you can definitely have me. Anytime you want. And" — unable to help himself, he leaned over, kissed her again, then sat back with another shaky laugh — "you can still sing."

But tonight, he promised silently, *you'll sing only for me.*

Or maybe right now, he amended in happy surprise when she threw herself against his chest.

"Oh, Jack," she cried, wrapping her arms so tight around his neck he could hardly draw in a breath. "Do you mean it? We can do this? Truly?"

"Truly." Looking hopefully past her shoulder toward the bedroom, he wondered if his leg would mind if he picked her up and carried her in there right now. It didn't look that far. "How long before Kate comes back?"

Her soft laugh tickled his ear. "Long enough."

Twenty-Eight

Jack noticed right away the change in Daisy. And it wasn't just that her high notes were higher. And longer.

That barrier he'd felt before when he took her to bed — was it only two nights ago? — was gone now. This time, she held nothing back. Her hands were everywhere, gentle touches on his arms, his face, his chest — almost as if assuring herself that he was real and right there within reach. Hers.

He understood. He felt the same way. But then, given the opportunity, he had never been able to keep his hands off this woman, even when he'd thought he'd been in love with Elena.

"When do we sail for Rome?" he asked.

They had just finished making love, and were lying side by side on top of the rumpled quilts, their bodies sheened with sweat. Daisy was smiling at him in a way she never had before — it was at once possessive and wondering and sated — her eyes softened by

568

laughter and love, her light brown hair clinging damply around her flushed face, her beautiful body open to his gaze and his touch.

She'd never looked more beautiful to him.

"I have to be in New Orleans in two weeks."

Plenty of time. And speaking of time . . . His eyes drifted over her. He smiled. "When exactly is Anna Strobel bringing Kate?"

She smiled back. "Soon."

"But not that soon." He rolled on top of her, his weight braced on his elbows.

She laughed softly, which did wondrous things to the rosy breasts brushing against his chest. "No, not that soon."

"Did I tell you how much I love you?" he whispered as he kissed her.

He felt her answering smile beneath his lips. "I'd rather you show me."

He was settling in to do just that when a distant sound intruded. He tried to shut it out, but it didn't go away, and instead got louder.

Voices. The rattle of wagon wheels. Laughter.

Oh, hell. He knew that deep laugh. Quickly he rose and limped to the window. Sure enough, his entire family, kids, keepers and all, were milling at the front gate. Even Kate was there, bouncing on the hip of some elderly lady he didn't recognize. "What the hell?" he muttered, then saw they were all dressed in their Sunday meeting clothes and the buckboard was filled with buckets of flowers and baskets of food and what looked like an entire fully-dressed yearling calf. And suddenly he knew. "Hell and damnation!" he said and laughed out loud.

"What's happening?" Daisy asked, watching him with alarm, the covers clutched to her wondrous chest.

Returning quickly to the bed, he captured her face in his hands. He had a feeling things were about to start happening fast and he had to settle some issues first. "Will you marry me, Daisy?"

Confusion wrinkled her brow over her pert little nose. She nodded.

"Say it."

The approaching noises grew louder. She tried to turn her head toward the window, but he held her fast. "Say you'll marry me, Daisy."

Her gaze flew back to his. "Yes, all right. I'll marry you. But what's this all about, Jack? Who's that coming?"

"Everybody." He grinned and gave her a hard, quick kiss.

"Everybody? Here? Why?"

"I suspect they've come for a wedding."

Her mouth dropped open. Her eyes went as round as eyes could get. "Wedding? *Our* wedding? *Now?*"

"That'd be the one. Brady said the ladies were planning something. I should have known they wouldn't let us leave without a proper send-off." Laughing at her shocked expression, he hopped out of bed and went back to peer through the window curtain. "Better get dressed," he advised, bending to sort through the clothing they'd left strewn across the floor. "They're heading up the walk right now."

Jack exaggerated, Daisy realized. It wasn't everybody. Dougal and Consuelo had stayed back to keep an eye on the house, and the long, rough buggy ride would have been too hard on the aging Buck and Iantha, the ex-slaves and old friends who had been with the Wilkins family for twenty-five years. But everyone else was there, including the children and the Ortega sisters, as well as Carl Langley and over a dozen ranch hands. And with the addition of the Strobels and Reverend Westerbury and his wife, the little church with the empty steeple was almost full when Daisy walked through the doors on Hank's arm that evening.

Jessica and Molly had performed miracles. Dozens of candles flickered on the window-sills and in tall, footed candelabras scattered throughout. Ribbons with big fluffy bows hung at the ends of the pews, and huge bouquets of mountain daisies graced the altar. And as Enid Westerbury struck the chords of the wedding march on the upright piano beside the altar, and Daisy started up the aisle to where Jack and Kate and Brady waited with Reverend Westerbury, she felt like she had stepped into a fairy tale.

She felt grander than she ever had in her life, wearing Molly's altered wedding dress. And although it was a bit tight across the bust, it was a shimmering confection of lace and tulle and tiny seed pearls that would have been fit for a princess. Jack looked grand too, standing proud and tall in a fine suit that must have been loaned to him by Brady because it hung slightly too long in the cuffs and pulled a bit across the shoulders. But the dark, somber black set off the gold in his hair and brought out the smoky blue-gray in his beautiful eyes.

"Mama," Kate cried, bouncing up and down in Brady's arms and waving her stuffed cat as soon as she saw Daisy. "Titty come too!"

And that was when Daisy's tears started.

It was a simple ceremony, but even so, Jack was nervous as hell, alternately terrified, proud, so happy he wanted to shout, and terrified. But mostly when he looked over at his beautiful bride, he thought what a lucky sonofabitch he was.

Thankfully, Daisy got control of her tears by the time they started the vows, and everything progressed smoothly until the Reverend asked for the ring and Jack realized he had never gotten one when he'd been in Val Rosa.

You stupid bastard.

Staring in stricken dismay at the Reverend, he started to stammer his excuses when he felt a nudge on his arm, and looked over to see Brady holding out his hand. In the middle of his broad, callused palm was a thin gold band.

Jack blinked stupidly at it, then up at his brother.

"It was Ma's," Brady whispered so Daisy wouldn't hear. When Jack still didn't move, he muttered, "Close your mouth, little brother. You're catching flies."

Then a few minutes later he was kissing his wife to seal the deal.

Jack Wilkins, hog-tied at last.

He felt wobbly with relief. Or fear. Or something. He was now a married man, as well as a father, and responsible for lives other than his own. A strange, overwhelming, wondrous thing. And as he walked out of the church with Daisy on one arm and Kate bouncing in the other, he felt important and proud and worthy — no longer a tagalong in the shadow of his big brothers — but finally, his own man.

They led the way to the hotel, where Jessica had hired the few remaining townswomen to cook up a feast. It was the usual lively gathering of Wilkins children and their parents, everybody talking at once, with lots of laughter and gentle jibes at the bride and groom.

When the meal was over, Hank rose to offer a toast to the newlyweds. As he raised a coffee mug full of Jessica's fine Scotch sipping whiskey, a distant sound caught his attention. He tilted his head and listened for a moment, then slowly turned to Brady. He didn't look happy. "Is that what I think it is?"

"What do you think it is?"

"A train whistle."

"Hellfire," Ben shouted. "The train!"

Penny and Charlie giggled. Jessica pressed a hand to her forehead.

Brady sent a sharp, questioning look at his wife, then glanced back at his towering brother. "By God, I think you're right. It's definitely a train whistle."

Hank's mug slapped onto the table, sloshing whiskey over the rim. "And what the hell is a locomotive doing here?"

Jessica cleared her throat. "I sent for it."

Both Hank and Brady turned to stare at her.

She made a dismissive gesture and straightened the napkin in her lap. "Cusack owed me a favor."

Brady's eyes narrowed. "For what?"

"Actually it was his wife who owed me. Her daughter wanted a title, so I sent her to Annie for her come out. I think she snagged a baron. Isn't that lovely?"

The brothers continued to stare at her.

"Well, really, you two," she scolded. "Did you honestly intend to send your brother and his family off in a handcar? It's too dangerous by half."

"It had a sail," Hank defended.

"Did you even try it out?" Jessica demanded.

"Brady said he would once I got it together."

Brady's head whipped from his wife to his brother. "No, I didn't."

Jack slipped his hand over Daisy's. Leaning down, he whispered in her ear. "You see now why I want to leave? They're idiots, both of them."

"Hush. They're your brothers."

"My idiot brothers."

Abruptly Jessica rose. "Molly, if you don't mind, could you please take Daisy to change into her traveling attire?" She glanced at her husband's set face, then sighed and added as an afterthought, "Perhaps you'd best take the children with you."

Signaling the Ortega girls to assist, Molly rose and herded the children from the table. "We'll meet you at the depot," she said, snagging Daisy's arm as she went by. "One hour."

Jack watched his bride leave then settled back to enjoy seeing his brothers dressed down English-style.

Instead, he got the first salvo. "If you had done the correct thing back three years ago,

Jack, none of this would have been necessary."

Jack grinned. "And have you miss planning this fine wedding?"

That set her back, but she quickly recovered and aimed her next volley at his brothers. "And you two," she snapped in her haughty Her Ladyship voice. "You cannot put a child in a dangerous contraption that has never even been tested. I simply will not allow it. Besides, the wind would make a shambles of Daisy's hair and dress, and — well, it's simply not going to happen, and that's the end of it."

"It's not that dangerous," Hank protested, but without much conviction, Jack thought.

"How many other men owe you favors?" Brady asked.

"Oh, botheration!"

"It's a righteous question."

"It would have worked," Hank muttered.

"Where's the whiskey?" Jack asked, feeling a headache form.

A while later, the three brothers were sitting on the edge of the depot platform beside the idling locomotive, waiting for the women and doing serious damage to a bottle of Jessica's finest.

"It would have worked," Hank insisted, staring morosely into his mug.

"I never said it wouldn't," Brady said for probably the fifth time. "It's a fine idea. But I

576

do wonder how safe it is. What if a big gust came along? Hell, it would probably blow the thing right off the track. Or what if the wind died before they made it to the pass and they came screaming back down, arms and legs flapping like crazed chickens?" Brady grinned. "That'd be something to see though, wouldn't it?"

Jack gave him a look of offense. "That's my wife and daughter you're talking about."

Just saying those words aloud sent a jolt through Jack.

Wife and daughter. Jesus.

He was all grown up now. Pretty soon he'd be sprouting hair out his ears and complaining about his rheumatism. But it didn't sound so bad, knowing he wouldn't be alone.

"So this is it, then?"

Realizing the question was directed at him, Jack looked over to find Brady studying him, a thoughtful look in his blue eyes. "This is what?"

"You're leaving the ranch for good this time, aren't you?"

Jack stared into his mug, his throat suddenly tight. "I'll always love the ranch, Brady. But I can't live here. Not for the rest of my life."

"No, I don't expect you can."

Hank said nothing, just looked at him with that probing gaze.

Jack thought about the years ahead — him

and Daisy and Kate seeing sights barely imagined, while his brothers stayed here in this valley, following the cycles of RosaRoja. It struck him that no matter how far he traveled, or what lay ahead, the ranch would go on — with or without him or his brothers. It was the one constant around which all their lives revolved. RosaRoja would always be a place to come back to. No matter how far he roamed, it would always be home.

Odd, that now he had the chance to leave it, he wasn't that anxious to go.

"I won't be gone forever." Jack looked at his brothers, realizing how much he admired them, and cared about them, and needed them in his life. A hardheaded, contentious pair, to be sure. But they were part of the history that made him who he was. And they were, and always would be, his big brothers.

Fearing another unmanly bout of emotionalism, he laughed and said, "Hell, I'm like that throwing stick I gave you. No matter how far you throw it, or how many times it leaves your hand, it always comes back."

"That damn thing doesn't work," Brady muttered.

"In other words, we'll never be rid of you," Hank said.

"Exactly. I'm the boomerang man." Jack laughed and made a tossing motion with his mug, nearly slinging whiskey on Brady's boots. "I may sail off now and then, but I'll always come back. And that's a promise, girls."

"Careful," Hank warned. "You'll make Brady cry."

Brady made a rude gesture to his second brother, then quickly dropped his hand when he caught sight of the ladies coming back, trailing kids behind them like goslings on parade.

All three brothers fell silent as they watched their wives walk toward them.

"They're a fine-looking bunch," Hank said.

"That they are," Jack agreed.

"Hell," Brady muttered. "They've been crying. I hate when they cry."

"That yellow dress sure fits Daisy well," Hank observed.

"Stop looking at her chest. That's my wife, for Crissakes." Yet Jack couldn't help but appreciate how the bounce in Daisy's step brought a corresponding bounce to other bouncy parts.

Brady smiled, his gaze pinned on his wife. "We got lucky, boys."

"We surely did." And setting his mug aside, Jack rose and went to meet his bride.

EPILOGUE

It was the last day of the last May, of the last year of the century, and as another summer blossomed across the hills cradling RosaRoja, Jessica and Brady sat in their rocker on the porch of their sprawling log home, contemplating the glorious sunset and enjoying the solitude.

The house was silent now, as it was more often of late, but summer roundup would start in a week, then the hordes would descend and the halls would once again echo with the sounds of laughter and love and family.

Jessica was in a dither of excitement.

Reaching over, Brady took his wife's hand. Twining his fingers through hers, he bound them palm to palm, their arms resting on the wide center armrest. They had given up their separate rockers years ago when he had commissioned a single double-seated rocker to be made, so they could rock at the same speed without her fussing that he was going too fast.

The woman had a lot of rules. He'd also made sure the armrest was detachable in case . . . well, just in case. Maybe later.

"Harvey sent word," he said.

Jessica looked over, her whiskey brown eyes alight with excitement. "Did he say anything about Ben?"

"He did." Harvey was Penny's husband and the newly elected sheriff in Val Rosa. A good man, with high ideals and a gentle heart, who dearly loved his family. And Penny, well, Penny was still Penny. Everything had to be right and proper with her, and she managed her five kids with fierce determination. A lot like Jessica, in that respect. God bless them both.

"Well?" Jessica prompted, her grip tightening on his hand. "Tell me."

"Says Ben's on his way."

"Oh, thank goodness. I was so worried he wouldn't be able to come."

Knowing where she was going, Brady tried to head her off. "You know he has those meetings in Arizona, Jessica. He won't be able to stay long."

She hiked her chin and rocked harder.

"It's important work he's doing," he added. "We need statehood."

"I know that." She gave an impatient wave with her free hand. "But this is a special time for us, as well. We need him here."

He bit back a smile. "It's just roundup," he

reminded her gently. "And I think working on a statehood proposal might be more important that herding cows."

"Don't be pert. Besides, this is the last time the family will be together until Christmas."

Recognizing a losing fight when he saw one, Brady said nothing more. When his wife got a notion in her head, she could be as stubborn as a rented mule. A really pretty rented mule.

They rocked in silence, the heels of Jessica's shoes gently thumping against the plank floor. A deep feeling of contentment filled Brady as the evening breeze drifted in, bringing with it the scent of early summer roses and the music of RosaRoja — crickets, cattle, the nicker of horses in the paddocks, male laughter, and the idle plinking of a guitar from the bunkhouse. Comfortable sounds that were as familiar to him as the beat of his own heart.

"I shall miss Abigail, though," his wife said, breaking into his thoughts. "I worry about her being all alone so far from home."

He turned his head and looked at the strong profile that had softened a bit with age, but was still proud and sure, that little chin ever the signpost to her emotions. And the tremble he saw in it now told him she was getting herself worked up. "She's not alone. She's got aunts and uncles and cousins all around her, and a wealth of new friends to keep her from getting too lonesome."

"That's what I'm afraid of," Jessica admitted. "You've read her letters. What if she falls in love and decides to stay over there? What if she never comes home?"

Brady gently squeezed her hand. "She is home, Jessica. Bickersham Hall is her home. That's the way it was set up almost four hundred years ago — the eldest daughter of the eldest daughter inherits. You sent her there."

Turning her head away from him, she swiped at her cheek with her free hand. "It seems a silly tradition," she said in a voice that told him she was starting to tear up.

"Jessica." Even after spending almost half his life with this woman, her tears still got to him.

"Well, it's extremely vexing! And the twins — what kind of foolishness is that? I thought once the war was over they would give up the military life, but oh, no. Three days is all we get, then they're off to some reunion with Roosevelt and the other Rough Riders, and then where? Back to Cuba? South America? It's absurd. They're needed here. At the ranch."

Brady knew how hard it was on his wife to have the children so scattered and he knew how much she missed them. But as she had taught him long ago, if you want to bind your family close, you have to let them go. So while she battled her tears, he rocked in silence and battled his feelings of helplessness in the face of her tears by making lists in his head of all the chores he would need to tend to before roundup started.

RosaRoja was a greedy, demanding mistress.

But he loved her still.

The sun sank, slipping coyly behind the mountaintops like an aging saloon dancer, trailing wispy clouds in her wake like tattered scarves of red and orange. Then too soon all that remained of the day were purple and gold bands that lingered in the fading sky like trailing puffs of smoke. Even after fifty years of RosaRoja sunsets, each one was a wonderment to him.

"Hank and Molly will stay the full week," he said after a while when the sniffling stopped. "And they'll bring enough children to fill the nursery *and* Jack's wing."

Even though they had never been blessed with offspring of their own, Hank and Molly always had a houseful of children — many straight off the Orphan Train — and others from the children's hospital and foundling home they had built years ago in Santa Fe. "Hopefully Charlie can come with them." As the resident doctor at the home, his duties to his patients always came first.

Brady didn't mention the lost ones — Elena, who was continuing the late Father

Damien's work in Hawaii, and who was still healthy, thank God. And George, Jessica's brother, who had set off for Alaska back in sixty-eight and had never been seen again. Nor did he mention Jack and Daisy. Daisy's final concert tour through southern Europe wouldn't end for another month. But they would be back for the Christmas gathering, and he knew Jessica was pleased about that. Their daughter, Kate, would be delighted to have them home for a while too. She was anxious to show off her new foals.

"Isn't it odd about Kate," Jessica said, as if she had read his thoughts, which she did with alarming frequency, "that the child with the strongest tie to RosaRoja is the daughter of the brother with the weakest. I had always hoped the twins —"

"The ranch was never their dream, Jessica. Nor Jack's."

"But it *is* his daughter's dream. Don't you find that ironic? Now Kate is the new heart of RosaRoja and is as devoted to the ranch as you ever were. Now it's her vision that will protect it and hold it together for the generation to come."

"Hell, I'm not dead yet," he complained, then shot her a rakish grin. "Want me to prove it?"

Jessica laughed, seeing in her husband the same teasing rascal she had fallen in love with over thirty years ago. There might be more gray than black in his hair now and a bit of a hitch in his fluid, rolling gait, but he was still a strong, vital man. And her feelings for him were as lasting as the land he loved.

The land they both loved.

Turning her gaze to the hilltop cemetery, she watched the gentle breeze send the thin, drooping branches of the mesquite tree swaying like one of those grass skirts Jack had brought back from some island in the Pacific. A lonely sentinel, it still stood guard over the living and the dead. Like this land, it endured. Over the years, other markers had sprouted beneath it; Dougal and Consuelo — what must Saint Peter have thought when that pair showed up? — Buck and Iantha, and Carl Langley, as well as several other retired ranch workers. It was getting crowded up there in the little graveyard, but even in the fading light, Jessica unerringly found Victoria's marker and the rosebush Brady had transplanted beside it.

The last red rose.

How far this family had come since those turbulent days, she thought, tipping back her head and closing her eyes. So many changes. And yet, as she rocked on the porch with her hand securely anchored to the man she loved, and memories of their life together floated through her mind like a gently remembered tune, she realized the important things remained the same.

"I love you, Brady."

"I know."

Opening her eyes, she turned her head and looked at him. "You *know?*" She tried to sound indignant, but he knew her too well.

And even after thirty years, that dimpled smile stole her breath away.

"You'd be a fool not to," he said, his vibrant, sky blue eyes dancing with merriment. "And you're not a fool."

Finally the laughter broke through. "You're such a dolt."

"I know that too," he said. And leaning over the armrest, he gave her a thorough, heart-stuttering kiss, reminding her again that the very best things in this life never changed at all.